STEEP CLIMB TO ELSEWHERE

THE RETURN

L. P. FAIRLEY

Published by Katchphrase International SL
Barcelona, Spain
www.katchphrase.com

1945-1956

CHAPTER ONE

WHEN JOSEP BALAGUER approached the outskirts of Pujaforta almost seven years since his departure, he felt as if the weight of the hidden weapons was still on his shoulders. Instead, he carried the burden of some unfortunate events during his years away, the deadweight of his conscience and, above all, the defeat of returning home alone. He had left Montreal without being able to say goodbye to anyone, and worse, he had abandoned a young boy. Luckily he had managed to shake the police, who always seemed to be lurking behind him. Now he was heading straight for Pujaforta and the Guardia Civil.

His tired feet carried him back along the same road he had used when he left, trekking through the woods from France. Climbing through the trees and into low-lying clouds, he stopped for a break, lit a cigarette, and watched the buildings of Pujaforta appear on the mountain tip as if the town was melting the layer of fog. It was a mid-November day and everything, even the pine trees, looked gray in the pre-dawn light. As he inhaled smoke mixed with his first Pujaforta air and heard the frozen dew crunching under his feet, Josep also felt gray from head to toe. He had imagined this moment for so long, so often, that to him it had only meant joyful colors; the yellow and red leaves on the trees, now bare, the blue of the sky so close overhead.

Slowly he sneaked into the town, skirting the church square and the bell tower that had been the last place to shelter Eduard. He thought how time had not brought them any closer. Yet Josep was determined not to care. As far as he was concerned, he had done everything he could for his brother: he rescued him from Franco's prison, he saved him from the camp in Argelès, and he even traveled to France to meet him, despite his gut telling him not to. He should have listened, since once at Eduard's house, he did nothing but wait in vain for his return.

1

When he had been off the Canadian coast of Labrador, nuclear clouds had descended on two Japanese cities, and, mid-Atlantic, Japan surrendered and the war was finally over. After landing in Bordeaux, Josep had boarded a train to the rose city of Toulouse, where he found a bus to Fontsec, and to the address Eduard had sent in his letter. But after such a long, meandering journey, when he arrived, Eduard was gone. Despite his nearly tangible proximity to Pujaforta, Josep waited for weeks with Francine and Gaspard, Eduard's new family. At first he was shocked by Francine's towering height and the enormous strength of her character. After weeks of waiting, he realized that her size was a convenient disguise for any weakness. She was alone with a child and fretting about Eduard. Yet one morning, when Josep was staring into the mountains nearby, hoping for another letter from Àngels, Francine put a hand on his shoulder and urged him to forget Eduard for now and to return to his family in Pujaforta. Since his hope of rejoining his brother had faded, he took her advice and headed homeward.

Now, wearing a shirt borrowed from Eduard, Josep stood in front of his childhood house. The stone façade appeared slightly more weathered than in his memory, but his gray mood brightened. He felt a rush of excitement and a throb in his chest as he approached the wooden door. Faint light glowed in the windows and he saw a shadow pass in front of the lace curtains. It would be Àngels, or maybe even his mother. Josep knocked when really he just wanted to burst inside. But he was arriving practically unannounced and he almost giggled in anticipation of Àngels' reaction. He knocked again and heard movement inside and footsteps approaching the door. As it opened, he whispered, "Àngels, it's me." When the door flew open, it was not Àngels in her nightdress. It was Carme.

"Josep!" Carme staggered and steadied herself using his shoulders. Before he could express his surprise and delight at the sight of her, she had dragged him inside, calling, "Àngels, hurry, wake up."

Josep heard stirring in the loft. Àngels came down the stairs and stopped fast the moment she saw him. She blinked and clutched her nightgown to her chest. As she dashed down the stairs toward him, her dark curls shone amber in the light and her face glowed. Josep gripped her slight shoulders in his dirty hands and she held him gently at the waist before putting her fingers in his thinning hair. He wrapped his arms around her.

"It's been so long," she said and pushed him back, her gray eyes searching his. "I don't believe it's you. You look so strong, so well fed. Why didn't you tell us you were coming now?"

"And miss this reaction?" Josep squeezed her hands and the curls of her hair as if they hid the secret to all the years past. "It's grown back."

Àngels raised a hand to her head. "Fortunately it does that after so long." She looked behind him and shut the door. "Did anyone see you coming?"

"No, I was careful."

"You'll have to check in with the Guardia Civil before they think to arrest you. First we'll let Dolors and Sr. Palau talk to them. Until then you are a mouse." She steered him into a chair.

"Trying to avoid a trap." Josep sat and looked from Àngels to the room around them. It was almost the same as before he left: the large table, the bed in the corner, the fireplace. The only differences were some rudimentary toys on the floor and his mother's chair was in a new place. He took a better look at Àngels. Sleep had teased her curls into a cloud of tangles, and her face was gaunt, thinner, as if the flesh had been sculpted out of it.

"So tell me about Canada," she said.

"That can wait." He waved it away. "And *Mare?*" Josep took her hand across the table.

"She is the mistress of the Palau residence." Àngels pointed up the hill.

"You mentioned that in your letter, but I can't get my head around it." Josep frowned. "The landowner Palau, who has influence with the Guardia Civil. How can *Mare* live with someone like that?"

"You'll be thankful she does." Àngels shifted in her seat. "And Albert is good for her. It's true, at first he was inflexible, but now he knows who's boss. And since he broke his hip she runs circles around him."

Josep smiled at the image. "And how is our crafty Dolors? Last time I was here I was staying at her house, with all the added benefits of her baking. What's she got to do with the Guardia Civil?"

"Not much anymore. She has hardly baked or left her house in about a year and a half, since Baltasar did a runner."

Josep clicked his tongue and imagined his friend in panicked flight. He looked around the room again. "Where did Carme go? We have so much to get caught up on."

Àngels looked past his shoulder as Carme emerged from the shadow. Josep kissed her flushed cheeks, holding one of them against his and breathing in deeply. "It's so good to see you." She had also grown much thinner, but her eyes still wore a lively expression.

"You might see her a lot since Carme also lives here," Àngels said. "Carme and her son."

Carme smoothed her hair. "I should look better than I did last time you saw me. I should smell better, too."

"Argelès," Josep said and shook his head, the dugout in the sand seeming so far away. "I certainly do not miss that beach."

"We made the most of it." Carme looked him square in the eye.

"We did, didn't we?" Josep held her gaze and actually felt as if no time had passed between them. "So you have a son."

"Yes, he's already six."

"Six?" Josep said while silently counting backwards and feeling a rising lack of oxygen.

"Yes, it was from that time." Carme stood and walked to the back of the room. After a few moments she returned. "But you don't have anything to worry about." Standing beside her was a thin boy with skin as dark as aged tobacco leaves. "This is Víctor."

"Hello, Víctor. It's a pleasure to meet you," Josep said, breathing deeply as the boy waved.

"Josep, you can sleep in my bed, if you're staying," Carme said.

"Do you think that's a good idea?"

"We'll sleep in the loft with Àngels, won't we Víctor?" Carme said, and led her son upstairs.

Josep watched them go and shook his head. It was strange to see his years away reflected in the size of a boy. "Eduard's little Gaspard is getting bigger. He looks just like his mother but he has Eduard's eyes."

"I'm sorry that you waited so long for Eduard," Àngels said. "And it kept you away from us for even longer."

"He must think I'm an imbecile, always believing in him, when he didn't even have the courtesy to send a message. Francine is beside herself."

"I don't think he had a choice. They told me he was in hiding after what happened to the border guard. I wrote to you about that."

"Yes, but he'd come out of hiding a few months ago when some of those German camps were liberated. Francine said he went to find Artur, who had been sent to a place in Austria. Machusen or something like that."

"Mauthausen," Carme said from the stairs. "Many of ours were sent there, but I didn't know about Artur. I'm sure Manel doesn't even know." Her brow creased. "I heard that when it was liberated, the Spanish prisoners hung a banner across the building and executed most of the remaining SS officers."

"Knowing Artur, he was probably the head of it," Josep said, thinking of Artur's boyish face that was far from innocent. "In any case, no one has any news of Eduard since he left. Francine was distraught and, despite everything with Eduard, I even offered to go find him in Austria myself. He has left Francine all alone with Gaspard. There's little food and everything is a mess."

"We know what that's like," Àngels said. "What on earth happened between the two of you anyway?"

"You'll have to ask Eduard." Josep pulled a small *caganer* out of his pocket. The trousers of the squatting figurine were wearing away. "I myself would like to ask him why he left me this in Montreal without even saying goodbye." He watched Àngels pick it up with two fingers and examine it, wrinkling her nose. "Something happened in that camp in Barcelona," he said. "And then Artur happened to him. He hasn't been himself since I left him in the church square."

"He seemed more or less himself when we saw him, didn't he, Carme? He was thrilled about his son," Àngels said and Carme shrugged and nodded. "In fact, he gave me something," Àngels said, but as she stood to go fetch the key, the door opened.

"Is everything all right? You're up very early."

Josep heard the man's voice behind him and turned. His mind scanned his memories for this familiar face. Then he found it. It was the *Franquista* that they had arrested in the woods, the one he had taken prisoner in this very house. Josep rushed forward ready to defend them all. The shouts from Carme, Àngels, and Manel himself stopped him.

"What is he doing in this house?" Josep demanded.

"Manel also lives here, in the garden," Àngels said. "Seven years make for a very long story."

"I've changed," Manel said. "I did many things I'm not proud of, but I'm on your side now. I've had a good teacher." He reached for Carme's hand, but she did not offer it.

Carme touched his shoulder instead. "Manel, Josep says that Eduard is searching for your brother, Artur."

Josep stepped forward, nodding. "So you're Artur's *Franquista* brother. Do you have news from him?" he asked, thinking that while unlikely, he might have a clue as to Eduard's whereabouts.

"None recently." Manel shook his head. "It was hard to get word through during the war."

Àngels reached toward Josep. "But you did get my letters in Canada, didn't you?"

"Not even a handful," Josep said. "After the bushels of letters I wrote to you."

"Then, you see," Manel said. "Artur might have written and I just haven't received it."

Josep looked at Àngels and decided to let her tell Manel the real reason he hadn't heard from him.

Josep followed the others up the hill to the Palau residence, where they found the mistress of the house still in her nightdress and Sr. Palau hopping along on short crutches. Josep had only seen this looming house from the outside, its ruinous façade with the shutters hanging on their hinges; he was overcome by its dazzling interior. He assumed that the taste was Albert Palau's, since he doubted his mother would mirror a foyer and spray it in gold. Nonetheless, the meticulously polished mirrors augmented the effect of Josep's arrival hundreds-fold. As he stood inside the doorway, his multiplied reflection caused his mother to swoon. She would have fallen had he not caught her. Then she went hysterical. "My son from the Americas!" Núria shouted. She was so ecstatic to see her long lost son that her tongue didn't rest all morning. She led them straight into the kitchen and started piling plates full of food. While times were still tough and food was scarce, she insisted that such an occasion should be celebrated. With Núria's enthusiasm Josep felt the color of joy he had been so expecting. He looked around at the lively decor and out the great windows, and rather than gray he saw stunning brightness. He felt thrilled to be home. Núria declared that they would not go to work at the co-op. They would spend the day together as a family. When they had emptied the plates and were digesting in the red room, a head poked in the door followed by a female voice.

"Dolors," Josep said as Carme nudged Dolors into the room. His cousin was shyly smoothing her hair, which had grown rather long and unruly. Her face was as pale as refined flour, but smiling, showing her small white teeth.

"Josep, I'm glad you're back," she said and kissed him on either cheek. "Are you staying for good?"

"You're darn right he is," Núria said, grasping Dolors by the elbow and sitting her on the settee. "And so are you. No more hiding away. You're too young and lively to waste your life like that."

Josep sat beside them. "I'll stay as long as they don't arrest me, in which case I would have to stay, wouldn't I?"

Núria grasped her temples. "Arrest you. Don't even say it. Darling," she looked at Albert, "you'll have to talk to some people. And you too, Dolors."

"I've let my contacts slide. After everything I did to make them," Dolors said. "But I do know that the Vidals, especially Mayor Vidal, like my bread, which means I would have to bake some."

"Yes," they all said at once.

Núria clasped her hands together. "I have an even better idea to get you baking again and to make some ins with the powers that be. Let's have a party for Josep's return. We can invite the whole town. We'll have to invite the authorities anyway and they'll see we mean no harm." She kissed Josep loudly on the cheek. "We can also celebrate the birthday of my two sons, now that we finally have one of them with us."

In the days following his arrival, Josep kept a low profile when Carme told him what had become of their old friends and comrades, the lucky ones in exile in Mexico and Chile, and the unlucky ones locked in prison, forced to build mausoleums or shot. Discreetly he observed the church square with its guarded town hall, before ducking into the safe ground of

Núria's co-op, where the women treated him as if he were dusted in gold. He watched as they slowly sewed, stitched, wrapped, packed, boxed, and shipped the results of their labors. It was vastly different from the Melchior knitting mill in Ontario and Josep couldn't help but feel slightly nostalgic about his patron's knitting operation. Josep had been his window into the minds of Melchior's employees, who had been set to strike despite the demand for goods for the war. He had managed to avert the strike, thus winning a ticket back to Europe, where he would have to rediscover his unionist roots. In comparison, the co-op was like a ladies' club with a handful of members volunteering their time. When he questioned their speed and dedication, the protests were as rapid and injurious as rifle fire. "Listen to the *Rei del Mambo*," they said, Mr. Hotshot. Ever since the end of the war in France, their orders had been abysmal. The women said they suspected that people must be going barefoot, so few were their orders.

Also since the war, all hopes for outside help in restoring democracy in Spain gradually faded. Even the protests from the exiled King went unheard. As the countries in which they had placed their hope instead turned their backs on Spain, Catalonia, and other provinces that had so vehemently opposed Franco found themselves isolated within their own nation. The Iron Curtain had dropped and Spain was locked away as if in its own bubble. The regime was as strong as ever and was still making people disappear. Carme insisted that it was not over: a large group over the border was planning an attack on the regime. This made Josep very nervous when he was summoned to the town hall, although his family assured him it was all part of the plan. Manel accompanied Josep at the appointed time and waited on the bench with him for hours, during which they had time to clear the air.

"You should try to convince them you've changed," Manel whispered. "It's not easy. I know." He raised his eyebrows. "For now, The Caudillo must be your mentor."

Josep felt all the more nauseous. "I think I will just try keeping silent. Dolors assured me that they won't lock me up."

"Speaking of which, Carme told me that Artur was taken to that camp Mauthausen," Manel whispered. "She also showed me some newspapers with horrific pictures of those camps. He's the only family I have left."

"Eduard will find him." Josep tried to sound reassuring. "As much as it hurts me to say it, Artur means everything to him."

"Yes, and Carme and even Àngels mean everything to me." Manel wiggled closer. "Can I ask you something?" Josep nodded and Manel asked, "What are your intentions with Carme?"

Josep jumped in his seat. He thought of the determined girl he had known as a child and the driven woman she had become, one whose sad eyes awakened when she looked at him. "I don't know really. Carme and I have always been together. It's a tradition, but I need a little time."

"Don't take too long. I suspect she'd wait around for you forever. But I won't."

"*T'entenc*," Josep whispered, though he had had recurring thoughts of Carme and was looking forward to getting reacquainted. "I understand, but give me a little time to adjust to being back. I have to survive this interrogation first."

When their buttocks were numb from waiting, they finally called Josep's name and led him alone into an office where he was submitted to a battery of questions, mostly related to blood. Where had he been? Who had he killed? How had he killed? Who did he have contact with? Where was his brother? When would he be back? Who had *he* killed? As instructed, Josep provided the most minimal, uncompromising answers he could while also maintaining some semblance of cooperation. Just when he thought he would explode with the next question, they made him stand and told him he was lucky that his friends were on their side. They also said they would see him at the party at the Palau's. At that point, Josep was tempted to ask them some questions, but instead left and asked his sister.

"Who exactly is protecting us against the regime? It can't just be Palau, and Dolors' bread can't be that good."

Àngels was at her table sewing some fabric remnants together in some form of decoration. The table was piled high with multicolored fabric and bits and pieces circled the foot of her chair. "It could be no one and everyone. And Dolors' bread was always excellent."

"Seriously, those guards told me clearly that I am being protected by a *Franquista*. Don't you think we deserve to know who it is? Maybe I don't want their protection."

"I don't know what they are talking about and, yes, you do." Àngels looked at him over her sewing. "Josep, you've just returned. I beg you not to do anything to get yourself arrested. You weren't here when we lost Pau. *Mare* couldn't go through that again. And neither could I."

"I know, but is this what all our fighting has come to? *Mare* marries our enemy. We just give in."

Àngels threw the decoration on the table and stood. "You have no idea what we have been through all these years. You can't judge us. We were forced into this situation, and we have learned to accept it. And so will you." She pointed at him. "As for Albert Palau, he was a horrible bastard, but he has done more than you can know for this family. Now he is family."

Carme came in carrying more decorations and was hit by Àngels' angry tone. "What's going on?" She gave Josep a worried look.

"I've been trying to convince Josep that we haven't just rolled over and let them occupy us."

"We certainly haven't. Though this family is awfully business minded for socialists. Between Palau, your mother, and Dolors."

"We're all fed and housed thanks to it," Àngels said.

Carme put a hand on Josep's shoulder. "We still have much in common, I think. We just can't let them win."

"But we have to," Àngels said. "For now."

"Which means I have to check in with the Guardia Civil two weeks from now," Josep said.

"Every two weeks?" Carme asked. "For most it's monthly. They do want to keep an eye on you." She ran the back of her fingers down Josep's sideburn. "I shouldn't be saying this yet but I'm about to receive some information you could find interesting. I should have it for you tomorrow at the party. It will be the perfect birthday present."

Early the following afternoon, Àngels blindfolded Josep, sat him atop the donkey, and led him up the hill to the Palau mansion. He tried to focus on the excitement of the party rather than the disappointment that he would be celebrating his first birthday back in Europe without his brother. In the front garden, Àngels uncovered Josep's eyes and he was blinded, tantalized by the decorations. The front garden was speckled with hand-made adornments. They appeared particularly new and bright in contrast to the decaying façade. Josep recognized the fabric flowers and birds Àngels had been sewing lining the walk up to the front door. They were vibrant reds, violets, and yellows, such bursts of contrasting colors that Josep felt their life run through him. As Àngels went in, Dolors flitted out and when Josep waved at her, she ran toward him. She still appeared drawn and pale, though her lips were bright with lipstick. Her hair was tamed into a knot at the crown of her head.

"*Felicitats*, Josep," Dolors said. "I'm so glad you came and dragged me back to the living."

"I'm happy to see you out and about and I am proud if I am the reason for it. I hope I didn't make too much work for you."

Dolors took his hand and pulled him inside. "I must admit that I was reluctant at first. Except for one occasion, I haven't baked in," she hesitated, "at least a year and a half. I wasn't sure if I remembered how. Come, have a taste." Dolors first gave Josep some of her homemade bread with tomato. It was crunchy on the outside and soft and chewy on the inside, with the tomato pink and glistening on top. He took a bite and the tomato and olive oil clung to the roof of his mouth. The taste awoke his dormant Catalan taste buds. He chewed and nodded his approval.

"It's delicious. Are you still getting flour from over the border?"

Dolors covered his lips with her finger. "There are the official suppliers and I have my own, although they were surprised to hear from me after all this time. It's not good flour, but it's better than most." Dolors gave him another piece of tomato bread. "You will have to wait to taste my most special item, pine nut *coca*. It was too short notice to collect the pine nuts."

Josep took her hand and examined the back of it for the burn he had dressed all those years ago. "They still look nice to me. You said they would be covered in scars."

Dolors smiled and drew her hand away, examining it herself. "I've managed not to do too much damage. Like I said, I haven't been doing much baking anyway, but I did have a proper bakery going. You know how much I wanted that."

"The whole town will be thrilled that you're back. They must really adore you."

"Some did. Some definitely did not." Dolors sighed. "Being humiliated on your wedding day doesn't help. Let's just say I made some inappropriate contacts during the war and some people in town are holding a grudge." She leaned in. "What they fail to know are the appropriate contacts that I made. Somehow I have to convince them and make some ins with the new mayor, although we used to be like this." She crossed her fingers. "He and his cronies are already inside." She pointed to the house as Núria, in a burgundy knit outfit, burst between them. At her side, Sr. Palau's tall frame bent over his crutches as he favored his bad hip.

Núria hugged Josep and kissed him on the cheek. "Happy birthday, my son. This is the best present ever to all of us, except of course having your brother here as well. We are so happy to have you back. Sometime you'll have to tell us all about Canada. You know how your father had always wanted us to travel. What season is it there now?" She pulled Josep into the red room.

***

Meanwhile, Àngels stood in the walkway outside, greeting their friends and townspeople as they arrived and leading them towards the house. There was Salvador the *Maquis*, Antoni the barber, as well as the electrician, the plumber, the entire Vidal family, all the women from the co-op and their families, and finally Manel. He arrived red-faced and wheezing from an obvious run up the hill, dragging the boy Víctor by the hand. "I can't find Carme," he said, looking desperately around him. "Is she here?"

"Not yet. But it's still early. She has a habit of disappearing before grand occasions." Àngels gaped toward the entrance to the path. "Well, look who's here." A thin form with bushy hair had appeared on the crest. "Baltasar!" she shouted and left Manel standing alone. "You made it." She kissed him on either cheek and stood back to take a look at him. He was as slim as ever, but in the year and a half since his cancelled wedding, the hair on the top of his head had thinned to wisps while the tufts above his ears were as plentiful as ever.

"Hello, Àngels, my sweet. Is Josep here?" He asked looking anxiously over her shoulder.

"Yes," Àngels said. "And so is Dolors."

Baltasar nodded. "So I imagined."

"It's the first she's left the house since that day. Let's try to keep her spirits up, so she doesn't lock herself away for good."

"Yes, I wouldn't want to be responsible for that." Baltasar held Àngels' arm. "You are looking fabulous."

"Really?" Àngels touched her hair. "How long it's been since I heard that."

***

Inside, everyone gathered in the red room, after first having their shock at the décor reflected back at them in the foyer mirrors. For a majority it was the first time they had ever even climbed this high above the town, let alone entered the infamous Palau mansion and its enormous salon. The townsfolk stood in stiff groups looking at the fading red walls around them, some clearly surprised to have been invited, while Dolors offered them platters of baked goods that quickly captured their full attention. They would scowl at her and then pop a pastry in their mouths. The offerings, though sparse, clearly tempted their deprived palates while testing their convictions; for many, Dolors was still a traitor.

While Josep mingled he was shocked to see some families, like the Vidals, who he had fought against at the front now standing in his mother's living room wishing him many happy returns. Things had changed, though he was sure that like two opposing wires of electrical current, they would clash and spark if crossed. Yet most appeared calm as they chatted somewhat stiffly in clusters reflecting their political color. He looked up from his thoughts into the grinning face of Baltasar Sort.

"Well, isn't it the doctor himself," Josep said and hugged his friend while slapping him on the back.

"And how is our lumberjack, or were you an ice man?" Baltasar said and gave Josep a good look. "I think they were treating you well. You're certainly fatter than anybody here."

"I'll take that as a compliment. Lord, it's good to see you and a friendly face," Josep said and offered Baltasar a cigarette, which he accepted with a smile. "I also became very familiar with this stuff. I counted more tobacco leaves than you can shake a stick at, as my workmates would have said. Now I like to keep them in their jobs." He lit both of their cigarettes and rubbed his belly. "I suppose I can't complain."

"Good food and good women too, I bet." Baltasar nudged him.

"I suppose I had my share. Of both."

"You'll find things here much different. Slim pickings all around, except for Carme, of course." Baltasar nodded, then looked like he'd seen a ghost.

"Baltasar," Dolors said in a voice sweet as dripping honey. "Would you like one of my buns?"

"Hello, Dolors." He nodded shyly and took a pastry off the platter she had propped under his nose. Dolors whirled away.

"I hope it's not poisoned," Baltasar said to Josep, then took a bite.

"You'll have to tell me what happened there. Cold feet?"

"Bone-numbing frozen feet." He popped the rest in his mouth.

"Scared you away to the city. I had my fill of big cities. It's not for me." Josep looked out the window with his thoughts momentarily far away in a city on a river almost as wide as a sea.

"The city is not really for me either," Baltasar said brushing the crumbs from the tips of his fingers. "In fact, I'm considering coming back."

Josep jumped toward him. "You must. Come, it will be like the old days."

"I hope not. Surely they won't arrest the two of us."

"Then again, why don't you wait it out a bit? I have to check in fortnightly with the *fills de puta*. I'll put my feelers out. Then you can come," Josep said. "Besides, from what I hear the town needs a doctor. Surely they won't arrest him."

"My house is all set up for consultations, thanks to Dolors," Baltasar said and glanced at the Guardia Civil standing in the corner. "I will mull it over."

As Josep chatted with the guests, he found that his morale, rather than climbing, plummeted. His usual feeling of guilt overwhelmed him and brought back the thoughts he had tried to throw overboard into the Atlantic. A number of people in Canada would be wondering what had happened to him. He only wished that his brother would do the same. Again he looked toward the window and for an instant thought he saw Eduard's face through it, one with fatter cheeks but the same smoky eyes. When he stepped toward it, it moved: he was reaching out towards his own reflection.

"You're too quiet and pensive for such an occasion."

Josep looked up and saw Àngels standing beside him. He shook the image of Eduard from his mind.

"Want to lighten the load?" she asked.

"I will tell you if you'll tell me something." Josep took a deep breath. "I want you to know that I tried to come back here after I received that letter about your daughter." He squeezed her hand. "I'm so sorry."

"It's all been hard but that was the hardest." Àngels stared out the same window. "I can still feel her, still smell her skin. But some might say I didn't deserve her."

"That's ridiculous," Josep said. "What could you possibly have done?"

"Let's just say I was not accepting of her arrival."

Josep put a hand on her shoulder. "It's something I've been wondering for a long time. I need to know. How did you get pregnant? Or more importantly, who?"

Àngels looked around the room. Josep followed her look and saw the joyful faces around them. She looked back at him and the weight of everything that had happened to her appeared to be released. "In prison." She stopped. "But it doesn't matter. Carles has left town. Frankly, Josep, I can't talk about it."

"Carles? Carles Puig?" Josep slapped the red wall with a crack. Now his cheeks were burning. "I knew it. Those bastards couldn't wait to lock you up. Ivan Puig promised me you would be protected." Everyone was looking and Àngels waved them away.

She cupped Josep's red hand. "The Puigs are all gone. They can't hurt us now."

"You said Ivan is dead, crushed inside his own car, the bastard," Josep said. "Carles was mayor before this Vidal fellow."

"Carles was called away. Being Ivan's brother was his only protection, even if they didn't get along."

"If he left, he could come back."

"Maybe someday. Believe me, I have never felt such hatred for a family," Àngels said. "But I really think they can't hurt us anymore." She squeezed Josep's hand. "Now you have to tell me what had you so pensive. Were you thinking about Marie-Claude? You almost brought her back here with you."

Josep looked at the wall he had slapped. "Yes, I was thinking about her, in fact, and about everyone over there, really. I hurt her a lot, and myself in the process. But I had no choice."

"She lived in the house where you were staying?"

"Yes, one of the first houses. She was one of five daughters of Henri Bouchon, who hired me, and she was the cousin of Jean-Pierre, the fellow from the International Brigades. Marie-Claude was a staunch communist and she used to take me to secret meetings. After it all went wrong, I realized that she was a lot like Carme. In the end I wasn't sure if I had really loved Marie-Claude. I was about to get a passport and a ticket back here to Europe. Two tickets really, one for Marie-Claude and the other for me. It is probably a good thing that I didn't bring her back here."

"So what went wrong?"

Josep felt his face redden. "An accident, but I'd rather not talk about it."

"Are you in touch with her at all?"

"I was just before I left. I dared ask her for a huge favor, and strangely enough she accepted. She responded and didn't ask me anything about myself or tell me anything about her life, but she accepted to take the boy Luc from me." Josep swallowed and leaned against the wall. "I'm sorry I can't talk about this. Not here. Not now. It's like I'm talking about another life."

"While you had another life, we were living the same old one here." Àngels sighed. "Sorry, I don't mean to accuse you. I know it wasn't easy for you either. I'm so glad you're back but I wish you would try to contact Eduard again. We have to find him." She paused and her eyes brightened. "When we're back at the house remind me to give you something that Eduard gave me." She took his hand. "I just wish you would forget your grudges. If you can't do it for him or yourself, do it for me."

"I would love to do it for you, but I can't keep getting sucked back in. He's done some unforgiveable things. I had even stupidly begun to feel that I had done something wrong." Josep remained silent, lost in the loneliness he had felt. The abandon. Then he nodded. "Francine said that ever since he came to Pujaforta, he's been acting strangely, paranoid. He hardly sleeps." Josep sighed. "Do you think he's celebrating his birthday today? I keep thinking he'll walk through that door and surprise us."

"I had that same feeling." Àngels leaned her shoulder against Josep's. "But I'm sure he won't." She lowered her voice. "I suspect that Carme is about to receive some news."

"She said she would give me a birthday surprise." Josep scanned the room. "I've been looking for her."

"She's always late for parties." Àngels searched the room as well. "But I thought she would be here by now. Manel has been trying to find her everywhere."

"He does seem quite attached to her. He even asked me what my intentions were."

"And what are they? I for one would be happy to see you and Carme together. Carme and I could be sisters-in-law."

Josep shrugged. "We've both been through a lot. She has a son now and by the looks of him, I suspect I know how that came to be. We will just need to get to know each other again."

At that moment, the dusty chandeliers overhead dimmed, the crowd parted, and a glowing cake came in their direction. Dolors was carrying the whole-wheat vanilla cake with a thick whipped cream filling and a sprinkling of toasted almonds pierced by one fat candle. Given the police presence, the guests sang "*cumpleaños feliz*" in Spanish rather than Catalan. Dolors put her creation on the table and with a brilliant smile beckoned Josep to make a wish. He made the one wish that he would continue to make for many years to come. While he was enjoying his piece, Dolors came smiling up beside him.

"Do you like it? Are you enjoying the party?"

She was smiling with such an expectant look in her eyes that Josep could only respond, "Yes, I do. Of course I am. You've done a fabulous job."

"I'm so glad," she said, looking very relieved. Then she pulled Josep in close, so close that even Josep thought it was awfully close. "I need to ask you a favor."

Josep pulled back in surprise. "A favor?" He shrugged. "Well, ask."

"I need you to talk to Baltasar. He'll listen to you." She nodded her head in Baltasar's direction.

"What can I possibly say to him?"

"That he's made the mistake of his life. So the ceremony was religious. He knows that the priest was embellishing it on purpose. And he let him win. You must see that, that he can't let those people win?"

"Don't you think too much time has passed now? I don't think you've even spoken to him since."

"But Josep, he left." Dolors' bright eyes were now large and sad. "I can't talk to him if he's not here."

"He's here now. You could talk to him now."

"I know. I thought he might come. In fact, I knew he would come, for you. That's why I think he'll listen to you." Dolors was gripping him so tightly he feared she would strip the hair from his forearm. At the same time he got a whiff of the familiar vanilla smell of Dolors' skin.

He released his breath. "If you don't mind my asking, do you really want him back after what he did to you?"

"I hated him for the first year afterwards, but for the last six months I've missed him. It's always been Baltasar and me. Without him, who else will have me? Everybody hates me."

"You would probably be surprised that there would be many happy to have you."

"But I don't want many, I just want Baltasar and the life I planned for us."

"Fine, I'll talk to him. But no guarantees," he said, regretting it the instant the words were in the air. He didn't want to get in the middle of Dolors and Baltasar, especially when her vanilla scent was still fresh in his nose.

Dolors jumped up and down and as she did so someone whispered in her ear and she ran out the back door. The party guests were now devouring second helpings of cake. Josep stood silently and watched. His mother was laughing beside her new husband, who was looking down at her with a doting expression. Josep felt more guilt for judging this man so harshly. Àngels was talking to Manel, and they both wore looks of serious concern.

Dolors ran back into the room. She was holding a piece of paper in her hand and glanced at the Guardia Civil before waving the family into the kitchen. Once there, they all gathered around her in expectation. The new electric refrigerator hummed in the background.

"Pep, my supplier, has just brought some news. Good and bad. He received it and ran here immediately."

"What is it, Dolors?" Àngels demanded.

"Eduard is safe at home. He's returned from Austria or wherever he was."

They all sighed and laughed in relief, gripping each other's hands.

"How did Pep know this, Dolors?" Manel asked.

"That's the bad news." Dolors held the letter to her chest and met the worried eyes of each of them. "Carme gave Pep the note about Eduard just before they arrested her."

"Arrested?" Àngels face whitened and Manel and Baltasar held her as she slumped to the floor.

"She was captured in the woods. We don't know where they've taken her."

CHAPTER TWO

IN THE AFTERMATH of the party, Àngels attempted to distract herself from the harrowing news of Carme by tidying the red room and focusing on the reassuring message that Eduard was well. But it was no use. Her dread eventually spread throughout her body to her fingertips until a *xampany* glass smashed on the floor. As Àngels stared at the puddle of bits, she could only think of Carme suffering in a prison somewhere. She swept away the glass and felt her despair and anger rising. After everything she had done to have Carme released the last time, they had locked her up again. This time it could be even worse. Now, right when the screws of control appeared to be loosening, there had been a crackdown across the country. There was a short wave of arrests, almost as if to shake reality into the people, so they wouldn't expect a change of regime now that the fascists in Germany and Italy were defeated and the communists were as near as Eastern Europe. While Àngels was well aware that Carme's activities had been daring, she was unaware why, after Carme's years of people smuggling through the forest, they had arrested her like baited prey now that the war next door was finally over.

Just as Àngels wiped the last crumbs off the table and put away the party dishes, Manel arrived with the news of Carme's whereabouts. She followed the family to the kitchen, where Manel revealed what he knew: She was in prison in Adiol, Manel's childhood home down the mountain.

"They say she's well. Feisty as ever, which should be a good sign," Manel said.

"Or a bad sign. We all know that Carme's insolence could get her in trouble," Àngels said. "Will they let us see her? Can we bring her some of her things? Víctor will want to see his mother."

"We need to find out about the conditions first."

17

Àngels nodded. "And we have to get her out of there." She looked straight at Manel. "I'd like to know who your 'they' are and just how you get this information. It's a little suspicious, don't you think?"

"You know I would never hurt Carme," Manel said, looking hurt himself.

"No, actually, we don't." Núria stepped between them. "You know I've always spoken in your favor, even when the others warned me against it. But still, there is much we don't know."

Àngels put a hand on her mother's shoulder and pointed at Manel. "Now you have a chance to finally prove yourself to us. You can see that 'they' get her out of that prison."

"I will, because I can't lose her, too." Manel's dark eyes actually filled with tears. "I'll remind you, Àngels, that at least you know where your brothers are. Eduard is now somewhere safe in France, whereas my one remaining brother is nowhere to be found."

Àngels looked from Manel's watery eyes to the floor. She thought that he did seem genuine, and he had lost almost his entire family. She looked at him. "Yes, I'm sorry that Eduard wasn't able to find your brother. But I refuse to feel guilty for knowing that Eduard is safe."

***

When Josep heard the news about Eduard, he felt such relief, like his brother was tangible, no longer just an idea, and he even began to miss him. Then he began to resent him again for putting Artur ahead of him and their arrangement. With Carme's detention, he missed her all the more, and he was reminded exactly what this regime was capable of. The fact that he couldn't see her gave him an almost physical need to do so. Perhaps the talk of imprisonment made him think of his own confinement, and the nights he had spent with Carme. He always had this underlying feeling that Carme would be there to fall back on. It was a pattern they had followed since childhood. Plus, after just weeks in town, Josep could tell that Baltasar was right: There were slim pickings to be had in Pujaforta. Other than Carme's provocative stare, or a slight brush of her fingers, he had no hints of womanly companionship. The only other woman of interest was Dolors, but not only was she family, she would not settle for anyone less than Baltasar, the doctor and Josep's best friend. Regardless, the more he thought about it, the more he was sure that only one woman would do. But the regime had got to her first. When he tried to do something about it, he realized that seven years away had not only distanced him from the current realities, it had effaced any power that he had once had, however remote. Yet somehow others still seemed to think that he had some pull.

Since his return, Àngels' house had become a confession booth of sorts. Everyone was coming to Josep for advice, and he learned that on top of everyone's concern about Carme, his mother and Sr. Palau were on the brink of financial ruin. The co-op had almost no orders since the war had ended, and Palau's assets were heavy on property and very light on cash. The people were too poor to pay their rent, let alone buy the land even if he was willing to sell it. Although Josep had given them most of his remaining savings from Canada, maintaining the Palau mansion was a costly endeavor, and Palau had lent the rest of the savings to Dolors for her bakery.

Núria and Albert thought if they could convince Dolors to restart her bakery, then she could repay some of the loan. People couldn't buy property, but they could buy a loaf of bread. Besides, as a rationed item, all the bread Dolors sold above board would be reimbursed. When Josep approached Dolors about her bakery, she treated him like her ticket to Baltasar. She gave him only unending demands to talk to Baltasar about marriage on her behalf, a task which he had been avoiding. Dolors would not discuss the subject of baking until she had her answer.

Josep saw his opportunity one afternoon in the bar, just a day before Baltasar was scheduled to return to Barcelona. Baltasar was seated across the marble table, slowly sipping a glass of *ratafia*. There was a chill inside, but nothing resembling the cold outdoors. The alcohol warmed their cheeks. They had been discussing Josep's fortnightly visits to the Guardia Civil, which consisted primarily of humiliation through waiting. Baltasar warned Josep never to let down his guard, since every time Baltasar returned he had the regime to deal with.

"The bastards love to arrest me just as I am about to leave town," Baltasar said. "They should be getting ready to arrest me now."

"They wouldn't dare," Josep said and winced, thinking of where Carme might be at that moment. "Maybe if you didn't leave you wouldn't have the problem."

"Perhaps. I am feeling quite settled here, you know. My town, my house, my friends." He raised his glass towards Josep. "All those renovations that Dolors had Manel make to my father's clinic, I might be able to live with them, perhaps even work with them."

"Why don't you stay and get back together with Dolors? The town needs a doctor. You don't have to get married now. You could just move back and you could spend some time together."

Baltasar sipped and licked his lips. "I don't know. I suppose I could. Perhaps."

"You were about to marry her. Didn't you, you know, love her?" Josep was hesitant to ask, but also very curious.

"It was expected of us, of me, for such a long time, I felt I was almost without a choice. But, yes, I did love her. There's no one like Dolors. She's lively, energetic, creative, stubborn, selfish, snobby, and irresistible," Baltasar said. "She's unique and no one has her character."

"Except for Carme, perhaps," Josep said and looked into his almost empty glass.

"Yes, poor Carme. That woman is persistent and she had been very lucky, until now." He leaned across the table. "I hear they're pulling all the strings they can to get her out."

"I wish I could pull some, but I'm a nobody around here now. I'm really starting to miss her," Josep said.

"Yes, you and Carme are a bit like me and Dolors. The story goes back so far you don't know how it started and you don't know how you got to where you are now."

"Maybe romances begun in childhood are best left that way."

"Or they create a good base for an adult relationship," Baltasar said. "I really don't know anybody like I know Dolors and surely no one knows me as well. I suppose that is a good thing." He drank the final drop from his glass. "I am enjoying staying in my house. Maybe I should come back and try again. But don't tell Dolors. I'm going to mull this one over."

Josep emptied his glass. "Next to knowing that Eduard is safe, that's the best news I've heard since I got here."

***

Early the next morning, the whole family left for Adiol. Sr. Palau, Núria, Àngels, Josep, and Manel all rode in Sr. Palau's car across the uneven roads to the jail in the neighboring town. The car lurched up the crest and began to careen down the other side into the valley. From the height of the peak they could see the few dozen roofs forming a circle around the church, whose steeple rose out of the center like a sundial. The town was surrounded by house-lined cliffs and the snow-covered mountain face. The car traveled down the road as if descending into a gigantic drain. Why the regime had chosen this faraway town to imprison any captured *Maquis* or smugglers of people and goods, was a mystery, Àngels thought. As they descended, she soon suspected that it was due to the rampart of a mountain around it. Anyone able to escape from the jail or town would never make it up the mountainside.

On her lap Àngels held a bag of clothing for Carme: a sweater, some old boots, a heavy dress, and some gloves. She remembered the cold of prison, and her experience had been in the late spring, whereas now winter was fast approaching. The very thought chilled her to the marrow. Ever since she had learned of Carme's arrest, she felt guilt and regret. A distance had been growing between them, due partly to Carme's frequent absences and partly to Manel's constant presence. As she slowly let go of the bitterness, recent joyful memories reappeared. Just a few days ago they had been making the decorations together for Josep's party, sewing flowers and birds out of strips of old fabric. Carme, daring activities being more her style than

20

sewing, had been creating a warped bird on her lap. She took hold of it to show Àngels and exclaimed, "This thing would never fly." As she yanked it there was a ripping noise. Sewn to the bird's faulty wing was a section of Carme's skirt. When Carme stood, the hole in her lap was strategically placed signaling her crotch like a target. They had both laughed till they fell to the floor.

"What could possibly be so funny?" Núria asked. She was looking at Àngels, whose smile quickly faded from her mouth.

"It's nothing." Àngels felt the reality engulf them like a cloud of poisoned air. The car was entering the narrow streets of the town, which appeared to be deserted but for one man with a donkey cart wobbling ever so slowly over the cobblestones in front of them. As the car followed behind him, the man did not glance back, even given the rarity of a private automobile in these parts. Once they were parked near the main square, they all piled out of the car and Josep started walking toward the police station.

"Wait," Àngels said. "I'll go alone first. I'm not taking any chances that they arrest you, too."

"What about you?" Núria said.

"I haven't done anything wrong." She shifted the bag of clothing on to her hip. "Lately."

"You're all staying here," Sr. Palau said. He began to limp toward the station. "They wouldn't dare arrest me."

"After all these years, I've come back to be useless," Josep said before climbing back into the car. They all sat and waited. And waited. Snow flurries began to dance on the rising wind and formed a thin blanket on the windshield.

"If he doesn't hurry, we won't make it back across the mountain," Núria said, knitting her hands with worry. Beside her was a basket of dried sausages, stewed beans, and some bread Dolors had made for the occasion.

"It's Carme in there. I've got to do something," Josep said. As he opened the car door, Sr. Palau hobbled towards them. He waved for them to join him.

"I'll explain later, but I've had to do some string pulling."

They all entered the bleak room that was assigned to visitors. It had no windows. Its walls were of dank stone. Dissecting it across the middle was a double row of wire fence, with a space down the middle. A guard in green uniform, with a rifle almost to his height and a pistol on his hip, stood in the space. He put his hand on the pistol as a door beyond the two fences opened. Two guards came through and Àngels saw Carme emerge between them. She was limping heavily. Àngels thought she looked drained, and although it had just been a few days since her arrest, her clothes seemed to hang from her shoulders. Her hair lay flat against her head and fell in strings about her face. Àngels was searching her eyes for her strong Carme, but she hardly recognized her. When Carme reached the fence on her side she linked her dirty fingers through it and leaned towards them, Àngels grasped their side of the fence, while the entire Balaguer-Palau family plus Manel did the same and the guard with the guns paced back and forth in the space between them ordering them to speak *cristiano*, not Catalan.

"Carme," Àngels said. She felt a sob catch in her throat. "What have you done to your leg?"

"It's my ankle. I twisted it in the woods." Carme's eyes widened in desperation. "Tripped over a tree root, then I couldn't get away when they spotted me."

"Carme, don't worry. We'll get you out," Manel called through the two fences.

Carme looked at them. Her eyes were no longer bright and strong but frightened and pleading.

"We will get you out of here," Àngels said forcefully.

"Yes, we will," Josep said.

"Look," Núria said holding up her bag of food. "We've brought you some *fuet*, some bread and some of your clothes." She was smiling and clearly trying to sound cheerful.

"Thank you," Carme said, though her expression hadn't changed. "But I don't think there's much you can do. This time I really think I'm done for."

"Don't even say that," Manel said. "The last thing you can do is lose hope. I still have some old contacts."

Carme looked at the floor between them and shook her head. "But you don't, not any more. We both know that. Carles is gone."

"Carles?" Àngels said. "Puig?" She loosened her grip on the fence and her hands fell to her sides. She was looking at the cold stone floor and didn't see Carme nod. Grasping the fence again until her knuckles whitened, she put all her weight towards Carme. "Carme, he's the one who's been protecting us? You knew this and didn't tell me?" Àngels turned to Manel.

Carme's voice was weak. "I'd just figured it out and was about to tell you, but they got to me first."

"Because Carles is gone," Àngels said more to herself than to anyone.

Sr. Palau said in a firm voice, "Let's not lose hope now. I have contacts. Dolors also has contacts. We will all have to have a little patience."

"Especially you, Carme," Josep added. "It may be presumptuous of me to say, but I miss you terribly."

Carme met his gaze and her eyes seemed less frightened. "Really?"

Manel cleared his throat. "We all miss you. Especially Víctor. You must keep your hope, at least for your son."

Carme nodded slowly.

The guard who had been pacing between their entire exchange stopped right between them. "Your time is up."

"But," Àngels started.

"Consider yourself lucky. It is not visiting day," the guard said.

"These are for her." Àngels passed the bags through a window to the guard, who rifled through the contents, took a piece of bread, and tossed them on the floor at Carme's feet.

Carme and Àngels each clung to their fence until the guards pulled Carme away by the elbows. Àngels held her frightened gaze until they pushed Carme from the room.

Back in the car no one spoke. The snow flurries had stopped but had left a dusting of snow which the tires cut through as they returned up the mountain road. Àngels looked out the back window, down the hill toward the town. Their tire tracks left two black lines in the snow, as if connecting them to Carme.

"So it was you, indirectly," Àngels said to Manel, who was sitting beside her in the backseat. Núria was on her other side.

"You wouldn't have believed me anyway," Manel said.

"Why didn't you tell me? All this time I've been accusing you and not trusting you when you knew we were being protected, that Carme was protected."

"I was under strict orders not to."

"From Carme."

"She didn't know. Carles wanted it kept secret."

"But he was horrible to us until the very day he left. Why would I believe this?"

"Carles only told me, 'Àngels will know why.'"

Josep looked at them from the front seat. "*Em cago en la puta.*"

"I didn't want his protection." She shuddered visibly. "But now that we don't have any, what will we do for Carme? We can't leave her in prison."

"I still know some people. I used to be on duty with the new mayor, Abel Vidal," Manel said.

"And I know some, too," Sr. Palau spoke up from the driver's seat. "In fact, I still appear to have quite some pull."

Núria stroked the back of his bald head. "I'm sure you do, dear. What can you do for Carme?"

"I managed to get us in to visit her, didn't I? That was like pulling teeth on a wild boar. And it was quite costly." He turned to Josep. "That matter that we discussed earlier. We will need Dolors to sell lots of bread if these visits to Carme continue."

"I don't mean to seem unfeeling, *filla*," Núria said. "But Carme brings us news of our Eduard. What if something happens to her?"

23

"Nothing is going to happen to her," Àngels said sharply, slamming a door on the conversation.

***

The following day in Pujaforta, Josep, desperate for money that might help to free Carme, finally broached the dreaded subject of baking with Dolors. As he approached her door, it triggered an old memory of Carme. They had been standing on this very spot, well before either war, when Eusebi Hereu was still using his house as a base from which to taunt Josep's family. It was dark and Carme and Josep's adolescence was fresh, like the spring air. Carme had grabbed Josep by the hand and pulled him to the hen house.

"*Li ensenyarem qui té ous*," she had said, giving Josep's testicles a light squeeze.

"Yes, let's show him who's got the balls, or the eggs," Josep had said, returning the squeeze to Carme's newly budded breasts. Josep's excitement fogged his head and filled it with one thought. Then Carme placed two perfectly formed eggs in his palms. They were so smooth and warm from the hens' under feathers that it was all he could bear. He wrapped his arms around Carme and the pressure of her body along his front provoked the release of his excitement and the simultaneous squeezing of the two perfectly formed eggs down the back of Carme's neck. When pleasure left his head, embarrassment replaced it. He promised Carme that it would be much better the next time.

"It had better bloody well be, because that didn't count," Carme had responded. She wiped the running egg with some hay, grabbed a handful of fresh eggs, and ran out of the hen house. Before Josep had time to recover from his first accompanied sexual experience, he heard the splattering of egg on glass, Carme's scream of "*Fill de puta*" and his uncle's hollers from inside. By the time Josep walked empty-handed out of the hen house, all the lamps were lit and his uncle was fuming on the doorstep.

Josep looked down before him to that very step and remembered the burning of his uncle's belt on his spine. He also felt the scar on the bottom of his foot throbbing, a reminder of the thorns he had put there long ago. He tapped the door lightly and entered her kitchen, which now only vaguely resembled the room he and Dolors had baked in at the end of the war. It had a long counter with shelves to display pastries, large baskets for bread lining the wall behind the counter, and even a small sitting area for customers. Josep looked at the setup approvingly. It looked like a proper bakery. All it needed was some bread, cakes, and customers. Dolors head slowly appeared over the edge of the counter.

"Oh, it's you," she said, and rose to her full, short height before him. "How's Carme?"

24

Josep bit his lip. "It's not looking good. It's not just the situation, but her attitude. It's like she's already given up. I feel so powerless. Do you think you can do anything?"

Dolors sighed. "If only Carme were in Pujaforta instead of Adiol. I have no influence there. Here I'm just getting my contacts warmed up again and it's going to require a lot of kindling."

Josep pointed to the counter. "Who were you hiding from just now?"

Dolors' eyes grew wide and she pushed him into one of the chairs. "I'm being harassed."

"Harassed? What do you mean? By whom?"

"A number of people from this town. I won't tell you who. They are abusing me verbally. Insulting me. They come here just to insult me, then they leave. Every day."

"What the heck for?"

"Ai, Josep," she sobbed. "You weren't here, but we have to do what has to be done, don't we? Certainly you've done things you're not proud of."

"Yes, a number of them."

"You see, during the war, I did a little double-dealing so to speak," Dolors whispered as if someone might overhear them. "These people in town only saw one side of it. They saw the *Franquistes* leaving with their bread. They heard about my orders for the Germans. But they didn't see all of Carme's Resistance people that I had hidden up there." She pointed to the living area. "They didn't see the *Maquis* coming out of the hills for their bread. I made such a good cover that I made new enemies in the process. The only good thing to happen is that Mayor Vidal is one of my old contacts, so he shouldn't stop me from getting my flour, if I feel up to it." Dolors stepped closer. "So tell me, have you asked him? What did he say?"

"The mayor?" Josep said.

"No, Baltasar." She tapped her foot.

He still hadn't decided what to tell her. "There are plenty of others out there who would be happy to have you. But since you're stuck on Baltasar, we did talk about the two of you, though I'm not supposed to say. I will tell you that he's not sure."

"Not sure?" Dolors looked like he'd told her she had a fatal disease.

"But that's not bad news," Josep said. "He didn't say yes, but he didn't say no either."

Dolors' face suddenly brightened. "You're right. Maybe there's still some hope." She embraced Josep. "Thank you."

Josep sat in the chair with his cousin's arms around him and wondered if he'd said the right thing. She might interpret his response as a yes, and if Baltasar were to find out he would feel deceived. The crown of Dolors' head was crushed up against his nose. He could smell that her hair had been recently washed and the rest of her had that sweet odor of vanilla. Perhaps it was the jarring of memories of his sexual awakening that now made him notice the warmth of her skin against his. He grabbed her by the forearms and gently pushed her away. "You mustn't lose hope," he said, and patted the top of her shiny hair. "In the meantime I do have a proposal to keep you busy."

"A proposal, for me?" Dolors looked at him in surprise.

"A business proposal," Josep said, enunciating clearly. "I want to help you get this place running again."

"But what about my potential customers? They all hate me."

"You make good bread, right?"

Dolors nodded enthusiastically. "Good bread. Good *flam*. Good *coca*. Everybody loves it." She wrinkled her nose. "I know it's not legal, but you know I bring in flour for the extras from France."

"What about the Guardia Civil?"

"I thought I might have problems when Carles Puig left, but I'm safe with some extra deliveries to certain addresses." She looked at him flatly. "But that will make things worse with all the people who hate me. And after everything I did to impress them."

"Everybody is starving, right?" Josep stood, his thoughts turning to Carme, who was clearly suffering, and to Àngels, who was a wreck from worrying. "Let me worry about the people who hate you. And you say you're in with Abel Vidal and his people?"

Dolors shrugged. "Once I'm baking again, they should be as smooth as the dough in my hands."

"Good," Josep moved toward the door. "Because you'll need them for the bakery, and Carme also needs them."

***

The Balaguer family marked the weeks to come with their one weekly morning trip to Adiol to visit Carme and bring her much needed food and supplies. Since their second trip, which took place during the set visiting time, Àngels had gradually begun to accept that their contact with Carme had been purposefully severed. While they could see her shrinking form from a distance, and see the hope retreat from her eyes, any words were lost in the cacophony of visitors, family members, and friends who all gathered on one side of the fence and shouted at their imprisoned loved one, lost in the throng on the other side. On the rare occasion when both Carme and Àngels would manage to secure a front-line position against their respective fences, they were lucky to exchange just a few words. Carme rarely said anything anyway. Àngels shouted encouragement and heard it echo around her as other mothers, fathers, brothers, and sisters shouted the same to their own.

When they were not at the prison, Àngels spent her free time with Víctor, just as she had during his mother's past departures. Now it was a more steady absence, but Àngels would not let Víctor see his mother under those conditions. He could see her when she was released, a status that everyone was working so diligently to achieve. Sr. Palau had made some calls. Manel was in touch with old family contacts in Adiol, all the Vidals who would see him, and with others he had made during his days with the regime. He didn't appear to sleep. Àngels would see the lamp in his shack glowing at all hours. She knew that Josep was beside himself trying to find a solution, but was only finding that the power he'd once enjoyed in Pujaforta had dimmed. She knew that instead he was trying to channel his influence through Dolors, who had grudgingly also rekindled some old contacts. Dolors said it could ruin all her chances of unsoiling her reputation and reviving her bakery. Instead, Àngels observed how Dolors had resumed baking bribes for all concerned.

**

In the meantime, Josep was fighting his own internal struggle. With the general worries about Carme, he found that while awake, he had persistent flashes to moments in their youth, their sexually experimental days, as well as their more experienced forays in the sandpits of Argelès. Yet at night, he had vivid disturbing dreams about his cousin. Dolors would enter his sleep in provocative positions, wearing nothing but a strategic dusting of whole-wheat flour. On waking he realized that his boyhood yearnings for Dolors had also been reawakened. Deep down he knew that the culprit was not his libido alone. All of Dolors' talk of marriage had stirred something else inside him. Now that Josep was finally back in Pujaforta, he wanted to stay, he wanted stability, and he wanted his family. He had already broken a heart or two in Canada, not counting his own. He couldn't go through that again. Instead he wanted tenderness, love, and security. It would make his precarious life somehow more permanently rooted. Dolors, who had been alone most of her life, evidently also wanted the same. The only problem was that she was barking up the wrong tree. Every morning Josep would bury his dreams in his pillow. Baltasar and Carme would never forgive him. He was convinced nonetheless that these inklings for his cousin would disappear the day that Carme was standing free before him. For that they would need money, Dolors' money.

As he helped his cousin every day, lifting flour, cleaning ovens, stacking bread, running deliveries, and ensuring the smooth running of the bakery, he found himself attempting to put up a wall between them. Soon he saw that others were trying to do the same to the bakery and in so doing were undermining all his attempts to make it profitable. One morning when Josep was in the kitchen he heard the ring of the bell over the bakery door and soon after, Dolors' scream. When he ran out she was pale, trembling, and covering her nose and mouth. In the middle of the counter was one of Dolors' *flam* plates and in its center a perfect spiral of fresh dung, its origins uncertain. Josep grabbed the edge of the plate and whisked it off the counter.

"How did that get in here?" he asked, looking out the door. "If word gets out no one will buy anything from us."

"I know," Dolors said and hid her nose in his chest. "They hate me."

Josep stroked her back. "How did it get here? Obviously it didn't walk in alone."

"No, it had feet. And a mouth. He said, "*Ets una merda.* You get what you dish out." Then he wafted it under my nose and put it on the counter." She hid her nose again in his chest. "Maybe I am a shit."

"*Em cago en Déu.* Who was it?" Josep demanded.

"I can't say," she hesitated, not meeting Josep's eyes. "Guillem Sabater," she sighed, looking up at Josep.

"Of the grocery Sabaters? His brother fought with me and hid up in the woods with us. He's one of the disappeared. What's Guillem got against you?"

Dolors shrugged. "The same as everybody."

"Who else has been harassing you?"

Dolors frowned and looked at the plate on the floor. "Just his whole family."

"This might not be so hard to fix. I can find Salvador from the *Maquis*, and have him have a word with them. They'll understand where your bread was really going."

"Do you think that would work?" She grabbed his hand. "But I think it's more than that. They don't want the competition."

"Why? Do they sell bread?"

"Some, if you can call it that." Dolors picked up the plate and took it toward the back door.

"If that's the root of the problem, I'll think of something." Josep hesitated. "And I've been thinking, this place needs a name. A welcoming name."

"*Fleca.* It has a name."

"Bakery." Josep shook his head, waving a finger, then he smiled. "Fleca Lola."

"Lola? You know that I'm no 'Lola'. That's a fun, flirty name. How about just 'Fleca Dolors'?"

Josep shuddered. "Fleca 'Aches and Pains'. Not a good name for a food business. No matter what you say, there is a Lola in you. I've met her."

"Really? Do you think?" Dolors looked at him teasingly over her shoulder. "I'm so happy to have someone to help me. And I'm glad it's you, Josep. But frankly, I'm not quite sure why you're doing it."

"Because I like you, whether you're called Lola or Dolors," he said, but she was already out the door. He spoke the truth, and in fact he was finding that he liked her too much, which led him to lie about the main reason for helping her. It was for his mother, it was for Àngels and Carme, and it was for himself. Josep couldn't stand to see Àngels' permanently long face. Núria was equally distraught since without Carme, they had failed to receive any other news from Eduard. And in Josep's internal tug of war, Carme had to win.

In the weeks to come, Dolors' bakery started running and Josep set into motion his plan to woo the townsfolk. Dolors was now receiving a regular, though unreliable, delivery of clandestine flour and supplies from Pep. Now that the war and occupation of France was over, there were fewer obstacles to the delivery on the other side of the border, except for a general lack of goods. Dolors had reestablished her kickbacks to the new mayor, the local police, and border guards, and she had them by the taste buds. She swore that the secret lay in her sourdough base, made with the finest flour and fresh mountain rain water. Josep didn't care how she did it, but vowed that the result was sumptuous. Meanwhile, he and Salvador had a very discreet, comradely chat with the Sabater family, who they managed to load with guilt for bullying a person whose contributions had been vital to years of survival for the *Maquis*. They encouraged them to undo the damage by turning their bad-mouthing to praise. As Josep discussed these tactics with Dolors, he thought of a more direct way to convince the townspeople. First Dolors made a batch of the sweetest smelling bread she could and ensured the ovens were bursting with their essence just before lunchtime. Josep stood by the door with his face in the window. As he saw a group of neighbors scurrying by with baskets of produce in hand, he gave the word to Dolors. She opened the oven as Josep opened the door and fanned the aroma outward. The people stopped in their tracks, their noses in the air as if detecting the finest perfume. When Dolors saw this reaction, she embraced Josep and he embraced her back and felt her soft body against his. He then let go with the excuse of fanning. As soon as the people had moved on, he shut the door and shivered.

"It's a shame," Josep said. "This could be much more effective in summer."

"But did you see their faces?" Dolors said.

"Just wait till they try some," Josep said and bit into a slice.

"Here come some more." Dolors ran to the oven. "Get ready."

Josep opened the door and the wafting bread appeared to halt the people like an invisible wall. Every day for a week they continued this strategy and with each day the people chancing by at that hour escalated. Phase one of Josep's plan had been executed.

The second phase took place just before lunch a week later. While the Sabaters had been reasonably cooperative and even persuasive in convincing skeptics about Dolors' good intentions, they had simultaneously expanded their small section for bread, which the townsfolk bought out of convenience while trading in their ration tickets for other staples. And so, starting at one o'clock, Josep stood along the side of the grocers with a large bag of Dolors' freshly baked loaves and as each bread-bearing customer came out of the shop he offered them two loaves for their one. He reminded them where the best baking was done and pointed up the road, where Dolors was fanning the bakery air out the open door. And with that, their chips were in place.

When Josep returned to Dolors' carrying a sack half full of the Sabater bread, Dolors ran out the door to greet him.

"How did it go? Did they like it?"

"I'm sure they did. I don't think the Sabaters will, though. You'll have to make an extra bag for them. And a really big one for Mayor Vidal in case he gets wind of this." He grinned at her. "You should have seen their faces. It was as if I was offering them a lump of gold."

Dolors jumped up and down and giggled like a girl. "I haven't had this much fun in ages." She hugged him.

"Neither have I." Josep looked at her flushed cheeks and felt his own redden. "Tomorrow we'll know if our plan has worked."

Dolors pulled away and peered at the loaves of Sabater bread in the bag and wrinkled her nose. "It has to. Otherwise the townsfolk's palates died with the Republic." She ran and grabbed a plate. "Here, I've made some of my pine nut *coca* to celebrate, since you haven't had the chance to try it."

Josep took a bite of the thin pastry sprinkled in sugar and let it dissolve on his tongue. He immediately felt parched, breathed in, and began to cough uncontrollably. Once he'd recovered, with a glass of water in hand, he said, "I told you sweets weren't my fancy. Maybe you should stick to bread."

"I'd say the townsfolk might not be the only ones with no taste," Dolors said as she protectively hid her plate of her most valued creation.

The following morning, both Josep and Dolors awoke even earlier than the usual three o'clock and baked dozens of big round loaves of *pa de pagès* in preparation for the flood of customers, which began to arrive at eight on the dot. When all the bread was sold, all the ration tickets were collected, and some pine nut *coca, flam* and *crema catalana* were purchased discreetly on the side, Josep felt an uncanny rush, whose origins he was unable to decipher. He was unclear if it was the thrill of the reconquest of Dolors' customers or of the proximity of Dolors herself. As he looked down at her, her cheeks were flushed with the joy of financial prospects and streaked with crusted flour. He rubbed the flour paste with his thumb.

"Oh, Josep," Dolors cried. "I'm so grateful. I'd almost say you love my bakery as much as I do. And the sign was a fabulous idea." She reached up pointing to her nickname in bold letters above their heads and kissed him hard on the lips. He didn't pull away at first. But when he did he had that guilty feeling again. There was poor Carme stuck in prison, and his best friend Baltasar on the point of returning. He patted Dolors on the head again and said, "Yes, *cosina*, let's see if we can conquer them again tomorrow."

The next few days proved to be a success. Dolors had such a steady flow of customers coming for their rations as well as extra treats from Christmas through to Kings' Day that her coffers grew considerably. Josep watched Dolors' thrill and the growing stash of pesetas silently, not daring to mention her debt to Sr. Palau or their possible need for bribe money for the jail in Adiol. Over these same days and weeks, the heat of the kitchen had brought them closer, though the kiss had been repeated just once when Josep bent down to pick up a box and Dolors mistook his direction. Nonetheless, the sparks were in the air and Josep was sure that the bread was especially leavened because of them.

Over the weeks he had also come to know Dolors' supplier, Pep, though his visits were intense and fleeting. It was during one of their very early morning meetings, when the rest of the town was in its first cycle of sleep, that Dolors made a ridiculous suggestion: Pep should take Josep to France so that he could meet with his exiled brother. She said that Àngels had been the one to suggest it. When Pep nodded saying he would be happy for the company, Josep sputtered and shook his head. He was finally feeling settled here and was not about to make a dangerous climb across the mountaintop to a brother who took not one step in his direction. Besides, he couldn't go to France now, when Carme could be released any day.

After Pep had left, Dolors and Josep sat in the dim light of the kitchen chatting about how to improve the bakery, about their years apart, and the early days of their childhood. Josep even confessed that he had followed his brothers and sister into her family home all those years ago.

"It was the day my father died," Josep said, though the years had not faded his father's last accusing look before he fell. "I used to blame your father for cutting those rose bushes, but now I only blame myself."

"Josep." She clutched his hands. "But it's not your fault at all." She glanced at the floor and he could see that her hair still had a perfect part.

"I think I only disappoint people, or worse. Carme and I were always close and look where she is now. Plus I left a whole slew of them in Canada."

"You're being silly," Dolors said and tilted her head. "So how many hearts did you break over there?"

Josep swallowed. "A few. I broke a few lives too."

"Don't be so melodramatic." Dolors threw back her head and laughed, then put her forehead just inches from his. "You are wonderful, you are charming, but I think you give too much credit to the power of that spell you cast on everyone."

"You don't know the half of it." Josep pushed back his chair and went to the kitchen, intent on rubbing out some frustration in the dough.

As it would turn out, Josep didn't have the chance to explain any of the other half of the story, since Núria beat him to it. One late afternoon, when he entered the bakery, Dolors was fuming in the kitchen. She stood with her hands on her round hips and her small nose in the air. Her cheeks were red, but clearly not from the rush of counting her earnings.

"Now I know what this is all about," she said and stomped her foot. A cloud of flour rose around her shoe.

"What?" Josep said.

"It's all about the money, isn't it?"

"What money?" Josep instantly sounded less certain.

"Palau wants his money back. Your mother told me." Dolors roared and shook her fists. "I should have known I couldn't trust that man. After everything he did to my father. I only gave in to please your mother." She pointed a finger at Josep. "And now look at me."

"But Dolors, you wouldn't have any of this if it weren't for Sr. Palau." Josep gestured to the shop around them.

"I would have found the money somewhere, just not from him," she shouted again and dropped into one of the chairs. "But what really goads me in all of this," she said and looked straight into him, "is you. You've been pretending to help me all this time. And you were after the money. You were even pretending to like me. And you were after the money." She held her head in her hands.

Josep sat down softly in the chair beside her. "But I do like you. Very much. I've only just realized how much."

Her hands dropped to her lap revealing her straight face. "Don't expect me to believe you." She stood up, walked to the counter and returned carrying her locked box of money. "Here, take it." She handed him the box and the key.

"No, I can't take it now." He stepped toward her. "Lola."

'It's Dolors, and take it," she said. "They need it for Carme. I wish you had just asked me sooner. Palau thinks that for the right price they can get her out."

***

The next day was visitors' day at the prison. Àngels sat in the backseat of Sr. Palau's car feeling relief that this would be the last time they would have to perform this ritual. They had left extra early in order to be right at the fence and be able to speak to Carme. They had news for her. Good news. Sr. Palau had arranged to hand over Dolors' box of money to the necessary people before the end of the week, so their next trip to Adiol would be to take Carme home.

However, when the entire family plus Manel piled out of the car carrying their bags stuffed with sausages, bread, sardines, shoes, and sundry other items, they found the prison door locked. They took turns first knocking and then banging on the door, but the old wood may as well have been lead. Àngels looked around the empty square, full only of crusted, gray snow. The few bare trees hulked over them and the stone façades appeared to watch her family in stoic silence. Where were all the guards? Where were all the visitors? Where were all the prisoners? A chill ran from the snow underfoot straight into her gut. Then she saw a face in an upper floor window of a house before a curtain was quickly drawn in front of it. Keeping her eye on that window, Àngels scrambled through the snow banks until she was at the house's main door. She knocked the enormous door-knocker, an iron fist. Her knocks and those of her family on the prison door echoed off the dull façades and spiraled up the mountainside. There was a slight creaking behind the door.

"*Bon dia*, hello," Àngels said to the one eye that appeared in the crack. "Can you tell us where everyone is?"

"They're all gone." It was the ragged voice of an old woman.

"Yes, but where?"

"Gone. In the middle of the night."

Àngels felt her earlier chill trace her spine. "Are you saying what I think you're saying?"

There was no answer. She felt her empty stomach seize.

The door clicked shut.

Àngels ran blindly through the dirty snow, through the gray square, her panic swollen in her throat. When she was standing beside her family, she was breathless.

"What is it, dear?" Núria asked. "You look frightful." All the others turned toward her.

"They've taken her away." The sentence came out in a whisper.

"What do you mean they've taken her away?" Josep demanded.

"Who told you? Where have they taken her?" Manel demanded.

Àngels pointed toward the door and the old woman's voice. "A neighbor. It was in the night." She sobbed and threw her arms around Josep, who held her tightly and stroked her hair. Then he gently pushed her away.

"Let's not rush to any conclusions," Josep said, though clearly everyone's imagination had already leaped to the worst.

Àngels shook her head and began to tremble. "You don't know what they're capable of. You weren't here to see it."

"I was," Manel said. "First, we need more information. This can't be. Albert, you had it all arranged, didn't you?"

"Yes, it was just a matter of paying," Sr. Palau said. "Let's get back in the car. We'll go home and I'll make some urgent calls."

They all piled back into the car, and Àngels rested her head on Josep's shoulder. As the car pulled out of the town, other families were just starting to arrive at the prison door.

***

On returning to Pujaforta, Josep could not stop the images in his mind of Carme being defeated one final time. His Carme taken from him yet again. He saw her with a flimsy blanket around her shoulders and a metal dish in her hand walking toward the door of the camp in the sand. He saw her face turn to him and her eyes saying goodbye. The thought made him ill and began to churn all those sentiments that he had buried in all his years of exile and since his return. Visceral hatred for the injustice. He asked everyone he knew who might help them and realized he knew only one. While Albert Palau and Manel were searching for news of Carme, Josep went to see Dolors. In addition to Carme's frightened face, he kept seeing Dolors' hurt and anger. She had to help him. They needed her and her contacts with the new mayor, but he feared she would not open the door. He knocked and when she opened it his fears were realized. He hardly had a chance to see the scowl on her face before she slammed the door.

"Dolors, I need to see you," Josep said pushing it open before she could secure the lock.

"I, on the other hand, do not need to see you," she said.

Josep instantly felt all his previous anger take a different tack. "You might get all your money back, if that's all that matters to you, Dolors." Even he was surprised by the nastiness of his tone.

Dolors looked at him, clearly shocked by his mood swing. Then she spoke. "My anger is not because the money matters to me, it's because it mattered so much to you that you hid the real reasons for helping me."

"Carme may be dead."

"What?" Dolors cried. She sat in the chair. "Don't say that."

Josep collapsed into the chair beside her. "I don't know what to do." He looked at Dolors and felt his eyes sting. "The others are trying to find out, but I don't know what to do." He looked at his fists. "I was always the one with all the answers. People came to me. Ever since I've been back I've felt like an outsider. A lot happens in seven years, I know, and life here went on while I was away, but I just want it to be how it used to be. With everyone safe. With Carme. With Eduard."

"I'm sorry I've been so hard on you. I know you've just been trying to help. And my kitchen is lonely without you." Dolors pulled Josep's head to her chest and stroked his hair. He began to relax, so at home with his cheek on the soft pillow of Dolors' breasts. "I also wish we could just go back in time." Then she lifted his chin. "But there is one thing I wouldn't want to go back to. At least at this very moment I don't think I would."

Josep gave her a questioning look.

"The loneliness," she said. "And now I'm not so sure about Baltasar."

Before Josep could provide the appropriate protest on behalf of his best friend, there was a pounding on the door. When Dolors opened it, Manel was standing there with an urgent look in his eye. "Come. We have news."

***

The whole family gathered silently in Àngels' living room and waited for Albert Palau, who had just received news by telephone. He arrived wearing a flat expression and handed Manel an envelope before telling everyone to have a seat.

"I won't pretend," he said running a hand across his bald head but without dropping his eyes from theirs. "The news is bad. She was taken away with some others in the middle of the night."

"We know that," Àngels said, digging her hands into the knot in her stomach.

"I'm told that they walked them out to the woods." He still did not look down. His voice turned ever so quiet. "Then they shot them."

Àngels moaned and covered her face. The room spiraled around her.

"On what grounds?" Josep looked incredulous. "They can't just shoot people."

"But they do," Dolors said.

"They say Carme tried to escape," Albert said.

Àngels hands fell to her lap revealing her red, wet face. "We know that's a lie. She could hardly walk. She was surrounded by walls and locked doors. Mountains all around. Carme would never have tried to escape. She knew we would get her out." Her body was trembling. She couldn't stop seeing it in her head. She kept hearing rifle fire echoing in the darkness and covered her ears with her hands. They may as well have put the bullet through her own chest. She saw a sudden flash of her twin Pau, the bullet hole through

35

his heart. She shook her head. "Where is she now?" she whispered. "What have they done with my Carme?"

"They don't know, or so they say." Sr. Palau bowed his head then looked up as if searching for a sign. "But I did hear that she stayed our feisty Carme until the very end. They say she was the bravest of all." Slowly he looked down at them one by one. "There were guards everywhere and she knew there was no escape. So instead she rebelled. She raised her fist and started to sing. The others following behind looked up from their footsteps, raised their fists and joined in. They were singing *La Internacional* so loudly that it echoed in the mountains and trees around them and when the gun shots fired, they couldn't even hear them."

They all sat silently with the scene unrolling in their minds, until Àngels sniffled and spoke, "Thanks for trying, but she's in a mass grave somewhere, isn't she?"

Albert gave a hardly visible nod. "Probably."

They all moaned. Àngels sobbed. Núria shook her head. Josep kicked the table leg. Manel slumped further into his chair.

Sr. Palau walked behind Manel and put a hand on his shoulder. "Maybe that envelope contains some more news. Some good news. I hope so."

Manel looked at the slightly crushed envelope in his lap and turned it over to examine the French post mark. He carefully opened it. Silently he read the contents, then his face turned whiter. He hid his eyes in the crook of his arm. Josep rubbed his own eyes before gently taking the letter from his hand. He skimmed it before dropping it like a falling leaf onto the table. "As if Carme wasn't enough. It's about his brother, Artur," Josep said softly. "It's not good news. Manel, can I tell them?" Manel nodded without uncovering his face. Josep looked down into the eyes of his family. "It seems that there were clashes right before the Americans liberated the camp where Artur was held. It says he was killed." Josep gently patted Manel's shoulder which had begun to tremble. The others gathered around and stroked his back and hugged him. "That would be why Eduard was unable to find him," Josep whispered.

Àngels uncovered her face when really she wanted the earth to swallow her, just like it had done with Carme. She had already lost a brother and could not imagine receiving such news on the same day. "I'm so sorry, Manel." She stroked his hair. "I'm so sorry about your brother. I'm so sorry about our Carme. I'm so sorry for not trusting you. You don't deserve this."

Manel looked into Àngels' eyes and a tear from his cheek landed on her hand.

"I'm the only one left," he muttered. They hugged and cried and rocked each other. "What will we do without her?"

At that moment there was a knock on the door, causing them to jump as if it had been a gunshot. Àngels pulled away and rose from her chair.

"Maybe they were wrong. Maybe it's Carme," she said. When the door opened, Baltasar was standing on their stoop wearing a wide grin.

"I'm here. I'm moving back," he said, his outstretched arms falling to his sides. "I came to celebrate, but you look like you've been to a funeral." He sucked in his breath, his eyes wide with comprehension.

Àngels didn't raise her head. "We won't even be able to bury her. They've even robbed us of that. They haven't let us say goodbye."

CHAPTER THREE

ÀNGELS STAYED INSIDE her house with all the lamps out and the lock bolted, opening it just once to put Víctor into Núria's pounding hands. Shutting the door to her mother's cries, she sat in the armchair and stared at the unlit fireplace. Tears flowed down her cheeks and into her mouth, which was warped with pain. Hugging her knees to her chest, she rocked and shivered from the chill of the room, imagining Carme's fear as she walked her last steps through the snow with the other prisoners, yet entirely alone. If Àngels had been with her, neither of them would have been alone, not then and not now. At first she blamed herself, then she blamed Carles Puig for leaving, although she was indeed thankful that he had left. There was more banging on the door and loud voices—Núria, Sr. Palau, Dolors, Josep—but she heard none of them.

"You must do something," Núria said to Josep on Àngels' doorstep. "She's catatonic. You didn't see her when her little Joana died. She hit bottom and now she's fallen even lower. She's even ignoring Víctor. We must do something."

"What can I do? All the doors and shutters are locked. There's no way in." Josep held his mother's shoulders. "Go home. I may have to join you there. Try to stop worrying. I'm working on something and if it's successful it will cure her. I promise you."

"Is it safe?"

"Not entirely, but don't you worry. It will also make you happy, but I can't tell you about it now. So go home or go to the co-op. Keep busy. Dolors and I will check on Àngels."

"I can't go to an empty co-op or a house in darkness. Remember, you must have a word with Dolors," Núria said. "Maybe she can help us out of this mess." Although Dolors had slowly and quite reluctantly begun to repay part of her loan, and she had agreed to let them keep most of the unused bribe money for Carme's release, they were still in a dark state, literally. Núria and Albert could no longer afford to light the chandeliers at the Palau mansion. Instead they resorted to oil lamps. While they had located a fuel supply for the car, they could not pay for the petrol. Instead they used the donkey. Business at the co-op had slowed to a near stand-still and no one was able to contribute their share. The women were worried and applying pressure. Núria was the best target: they had not married the richest man in town. "I hate to ask for money from family," Núria continued. "But we either need to convince Dolors to pay us back or we need to boost the co-op's business another way. Or both. Àngels needs it more than anyone. Working at the co-op could be her salvation. It was last time."

***

For his part, Josep had a growing stack of worries on his plate. Some were enormous and difficult to digest, like the regime summarily executing Carme, and Àngels' despondence. Others could be considered more frivolous, and most were the result of his shame for his own selfishness. What would he do without Carme to hold him up? He once again felt his fingers dusting sand off her eyelids and his lips kissing them gently. She had helped him survive so much: that camp and his brother's indifference towards him. Carme's death also meant the cutting of contacts with Eduard, at a time when the thorn by the name of Artur had been definitively removed from between them. Then he thought about Manel, whose mourning was still fresh and debilitating. And there was the guilt about Baltasar. After encouraging him to come home, now he wished he hadn't and even felt some jealous inkling. Of one thing he was sure: any complacency he had begun to feel for this regime died with Carme, along with the ideals and temptations of his youth. As it stirred old feelings and anger about the inequalities, he felt the need to talk about it with his brother. The old one, the pre-camp Eduard. It was Àngels who had planted the seed. He hoped that if he brought her news of Eduard or even Eduard himself, it would pull her out of her house and give her with a reason to go on. It might do the same for him. And it might heal his aching family in the process.

So Josep once again knocked on Dolors' door and offered his assistance with the bakery. He had two reasons for being there: he needed a good dose of Dolors' sense of adventure and he needed to talk to Pep about taking him over the border. Despite the headway he had made in regaining Dolors' trust, ever since Baltasar's return, she wore her misgivings like armor of ice. All he knew was that he yearned for stability, which Carme could probably never have provided. Not for the first time, he began to think that maybe his ambitious cousin could.

"I suppose you're here about the money," Dolors said when she opened the door. "You can tell them to wait till next month. And you can tell *Tieta* Núria that I'm very disappointed in her. I know what I said before, but I'm still disappointed in you, too." She tried to shut the door, but Josep held it open.

"I'm not here about the money. I've come to see you, Lola."

"Me and my earning potential. And don't call me that," Dolors said flatly.

"I see you've been baking." Josep tried to change the subject by pointing to the flour on her nose, accidentally stroking her cheek. It was smooth, like an overripe fig.

Dolors gently touched where his skin had met hers and stepped inside. "I have so much to do. I have a new plan," she said, letting him enter the kitchen. Her voice lightened with excitement. "I'm going to give everyone in town a *flam* or the likes on their birthday and their saint's day. It should help to improve my image even further. Your help has done wonders, by the way. And now Baltasar is going to help me."

"Baltasar? Really?" Josep tried not to sound surprised or disappointed. "So you two are speaking again."

"Yes, thanks to you. He told me that you convinced him to return."

"Yes, I did." Josep felt guilty again. "But with everything that has happened I haven't had much time for my friend."

"He did say that he has something he wanted to see you about," Dolors said as she removed some round loaves from the oven. "Pep will be coming with my flour tomorrow if you want to discuss that matter with him."

"I do. I've decided. I am going to find Eduard and demand an explanation. Hopefully that will settle this rift between us. That should help make Àngels better. I also want to find out if any opposition is planned over the border." He peeked into the empty oven then slammed its door. "I can't put up with this regime any more. Not after what they did to Carme."

Dolors let out her breath. "I wouldn't rock the boat, not now. You should wait for the waters to calm first." She clasped Josep's hand. "If you go with Pep, you must listen to everything he tells you. I don't need to remind you how dangerous it is."

The next day Josep tried to distract himself from Carme's absence by preparing for his meeting with Pep. He was also considering how he could help to improve the situation of the co-op. The most likely local solution was Dolors, until another option unexpectedly presented itself during a conversation with Baltasar. The doctor had only been back in Pujaforta a few days, and the townsfolk already appeared to welcome him. He and Josep met in the town's bar for their usual glass of *ratafia*. Baltasar was looking much more relaxed than at their last meeting, like he was finally at home.

"The doctor is looking very healthy," Josep said and raised his glass.

"I wish I could say the same for you."

"It's been a harrowing time. It's been awful." He rubbed his eye. "Listen, maybe you could try to reach Àngels again. I'm worried and my mother is beside herself. Losing Carme was enough."

Baltasar nodded. "I'll gladly check on Àngels again, if the poor thing opens the door. First Joana and now Carme. She wasn't able to say goodbye to either of them." He shook his head. "Dolors tells me that on top of it your mother also has money worries. That's where I may be able to help." He looked over his shoulder. "I'm told you're in contact with Pep, Dolors' man."

"I'm seeing him later today. Did Dolors tell you?" Josep asked.

Baltasar nodded. "And a few other people mentioned it."

Josep tried to keep his shout a whisper. "What other people? I still have to check in with the Guardia Civil regularly. If this gets around, I've had it."

"Don't worry, my friend. You know I would never do anything to endanger you. They are the right people. I want to help. Once you're over there, if you find out about any resistance, you can count me in. It will be like old times."

"Much has changed since the old times. Look at you, you can't give up everything you've accomplished. You're finally a doctor." Josep reached over and slapped his friend on the arm. "And what about Dolors? You would risk everything now that you're reconciled."

"We're only reconciled. We're not married, nor are we engaged." Baltasar sipped his drink. "Not yet at any rate."

"But you are considering it." Josep attempted not to sound too interested.

"Just as I am considering taking up arms again. They both could be risky. Besides, first Dolors has to forgive me for humiliating her in front of the whole town."

"That could be tough. So you're not convinced yet."

"No, not yet. Why are you insisting so much?" He rested his glass on the table. "She put you up to it, didn't she?"

"No, it's just that other people may be interested. How would you feel about that?" Josep heard the words come out of his mouth as if someone else had spoken them.

"Other suitors? For Dolors? She is a remarkable woman. Who is it? This Pep fellow?"

"No, no. Don't worry. It was hypothetical."

"That would be too ironic, to give Pep business and my girl. That's what I wanted to talk to you about."

"Pep?"

"Yes, the people that I mentioned. The people who know about your contacts with Pep, they're patients."

"This entire town is full of your patients or at least it will be."

"Good point. These are people we can trust." He leaned across the table and whispered. "You see, if you do go across the border, they want you to bring some things back. And they'll pay handsomely."

"Illegal things."

"Not illegal things per se. Surely you're aware that just the act of bringing anything back is illegal. It could be very risky. So think about it. Talk to Pep. I don't want you to be in danger."

"But what kind of things?"

They both stopped talking. Everyone in the bar turned to look outside. There was shouting in the church square. It was a woman's voice. It was high-pitched and high volume and the woman was clearly outside herself. *"Fills de puta. Que se'n vagin al diable, tots. Carles Puig és un fill de puta."* Josep looked at Baltasar, both of them recognizing the voice simultaneously. Josep ran to the door. In the middle of the square right in front of the town hall, Àngels was calling Carles Puig a bastard and sending them all to hell at the top of her lungs. She stood barefoot on the frozen ground, in her nightgown, and her wild curls formed an enormous nest around her head. Josep ran toward her as the townsfolk began to gather around. A Guardia Civil was walking toward her with his club in hand. Josep hugged her to him and swept her away just before he could strike. Putting his jacket around her shoulders, he steered her away from the staring crowd. Behind him, he could hear Baltasar making excuses to the Guardia Civil.

At the house, Josep put a blanket on Àngels. She was twitching and trembling. Her eyes were wide open but she clearly did not see Josep beside her, even when she started shouting his name. "Josep! Eduard!" She shouted again and again with panic that curdled Josep's blood. She wouldn't stop. He shook her. She seemed lifeless, but for her aching scream. Finally he slapped her. Her mouth shut and became silent. She lay on her side shivering under the blanket and staring straight through him.

Josep ran to Manel's shack and pulled him out into the daylight. His squinting eyes looked equally blank. His face was pale and covered in the beginnings of a scraggly beard. Josep sniffed and was sure that he hadn't bathed in many days. When Josep shook his arm, his eyes focused. "Manel, do you hear me? Go get Dolors, and my mother and Palau," Josep ordered him and pushed him out of the garden. Then he went back inside, where Àngels was rocking back and forth and her mouth was speaking silently. She had begun to sweat profusely.

43

Dolors came running in. "What's happened? What's the matter with her?" Dolors dashed to Àngels' side. She gingerly tried to cover her with another blanket but then stepped back. "Carme was so good at these things. I'm not." She looked at Josep shyly.

"She's gone mad all of a sudden."

"Not so sudden, really."

"Well, today she snapped." Josep pointed outside. "She was screaming insults at the Guardia Civil. In her nightgown. In the square. Luckily we were there to stop her."

"Did the guards hear her?"

"Yes, the entire town heard."

"Oh, no. What are we going to do? They'll arrest her."

"I know. That's why I've called everyone together. Baltasar was with the Guardia Civil last I looked. He was trying to explain."

"You left Baltasar alone with the Guardia Civil?" Dolors' face paled.

"I had to get Àngels out of there. He wasn't alone. A whole crowd had gathered."

"I knew it. He's just back in town and they're going to arrest him." Dolors started to cry.

"We don't know that." Josep felt like shaking her but he didn't. "Let's concentrate on Àngels. Baltasar will be here at any moment."

Manel, looking and smelling none the better, entered followed by Núria, Albert, and little Víctor. Núria ran to Àngels' bedside. "I was so afraid this would happen. *Filla*," she said holding Àngels' face. "She's so cold and what's wrong with her eyes?"

Josep told them about the incident in the square and Núria began to sob. "This is it," she kept saying, shaking her head and clutching her fists to her chest.

"We'll have to send her away somewhere," Albert Palau said. "For a time, until they forget about it."

"But where can she go?" Dolors said.

The door opened and Baltasar came in followed by a cold wind and some blowing snow. He held his back against the door and hugged his doctor's bag to his chest. "I think I got away," he said.

Dolors ran to him and hugged his shoulders. "I was so worried about you. Thank heavens you're safe."

"We're safe for now. I think I've managed to appease them for a while."

"What did you tell them?" Josep asked.

"That she's lost her mind. That her insults weren't directed at them but at Carles Puig. I reckon since he's gone, they should be more lenient," Baltasar said as he approached Àngels, who was still trembling on the bed. He gave her a shot and she relaxed instantly. Then he examined her blank eyes, her limp limbs.

"I could take her with me," Josep said to him. "When I go to see Eduard."

"What?" Núria and Albert said at once.

"I've been meaning to tell you, but I didn't want to get your hopes up. It's not fully arranged," Josep said.

Baltasar shook his head. "Regardless, she'd never make it. She's too weak to climb through these hills in this weather."

"We have to find a safe place for her," Núria said, her eyes pleading.

Baltasar put his hands flat on the table. "I'll take her to the city. The women I stayed with in Barcelona will take care of her. If any regime doctors were to see her in her current state, they would put her in an asylum and she'd never get out."

"If they don't just arrest her first."

"Then she'll need something to focus on, something to live for," Baltasar said. "Something to come back here for."

"The co-op," Núria said. "It helped her last time. The co-op and little Víctor."

Josep stood. "And Eduard. I'm going to bring him back."

Very early the following morning Baltasar left for Barcelona with Àngels. He carried her suitcase in one hand and held her hand in the other. As the others watched her go, Àngels did not look back. She only stared at her parting feet. The same day Josep met with Pep and made plans to cross the mountain in a couple of weeks when the snow would have slightly melted. Josep asked Pep about the chances of returning with some extra goods. Baltasar's contacts had requested a few simple items: coffee, chocolate, stockings, a book by Voltaire. Pep told him they could indeed bring back the goods, but such literature would have them excommunicated. It was not that this concerned them so much as the punishment the regime could dish out.

"There may be some hope, you know," Pep told Josep. "There have been protests outside, in France and other countries. We don't hear about them here."

"So you think they might do something about Franco? Could it go that far?" Josep asked. His mind began to flow with ideas of what he, Eduard, and even Baltasar could accomplish together.

"All these recent killings are getting people riled, not just here."

"Really?" Josep said. If Carme's death could help bring down the regime, then even she might think it served a purpose. Even Àngels might come round.

"There are big protests. But they're also being more vigilant at the border."

"So our trip to France could be even more dangerous?"

"Especially with the contraband. If you want to get into this seriously, you'll need some specific training. This is not a trade for everyone. You have to be fit. You have to always be looking over your shoulder. You have to always be away."

"I don't want to do this regularly. We just need the extra money. It's just the one time."

"That's what they all say. This is like alcohol or gambling. It's awfully hard to stop once you've started. I know," Pep said. "If you need money surely Dolors could spare a little." They were standing in her back room amongst the bags of flour and yeast.

"No, I can't," Dolors' voice came through the door. "You keep out of this, Pep."

Pep shook his head. "I'm off. I'll see you next week, Dolors. And I'll see you in two, Josep." Then Pep was gone and Dolors and Josep were alone.

"Here," Dolors said and handed Josep an envelope. "That will cover what I owe this month." She was standing up to her waist in sacks of flour, but her face saddened. "You make me feel so terrible. I will help if you need the money, you know. With Àngels being ill and Carme gone. I will help."

"For now, you can just pay Albert what you owe him, then we can see." Josep let his finger graze hers as she put the money in his hands. He felt how decided she was in that one touch. With everyone lost to him now— Carme, Àngels, Eduard, Pau, even his remarried mother—he had no one strong to guide him, other than himself. "Your offer means a lot. Can I ask you something?" He held the tip of her finger.

"Yes, I suppose." She gently pulled her hand away.

"Do you really want to marry Baltasar?"

Dolors cheeks flushed pink. She hesitated. "The question is whether or not he wants to marry me."

"And if he did?"

"I'd say yes, I think," she said and looked at the ceiling. "But then I would be afraid."

"Of what?" Josep took her hand again.

"That he wouldn't show up. Or that he would leave me."

"I hope you know that I would never do that." He stroked the small scar from years back.

Dolors looked at her hand and looked at Josep. She tilted her face toward his. He kissed her quickly on the cheek. It was as if Baltasar was a pane of glass between them.

When Baltasar returned from Barcelona, Josep was feeling guilty again. While Carme was hardly cold in her common grave and his friend was taking his sister to safety, Josep was moving in on his potential fiancée. The days went by and Josep prepared for his trip to France, borrowing warm clothing and boots, writing a letter to Francine since he feared Eduard might dash before his arrival. As he got ready for the journey he became gradually convinced that he would never return. After all his time away from Pujaforta, he could not stand such a thought. And with all the dread came other thoughts of Dolors. This had only happened to him with Carme, and with Marie-Claude in Quebec, and he had to force himself to live without them. He didn't feel capable of that with Dolors. What if he never saw her again? He didn't think he could live with that either. With each passing day his fears and urges grew stronger, in step with his growing guilt. Finally he went to see Baltasar. Perhaps if he lightened his load, the journey would be easier.

Josep found himself sitting in Baltasar's surgery in the chair meant for patients and family members.

"Dolors made you a good little office here," Josep said, looking at the desk, the cot, and the book-laden shelves. "You almost look like a doctor."

"Appearances can be deceiving. When they call me Dr. Sort I still look around me for my father. Then I realize he's dead and I'm the lucky doctor now."

"Any word of Àngels?"

"The ladies in the city are taking excellent care of her. They say she's started eating and has even slept a little. I think she needed a change of scene to help her get past this. She's been through far too much."

"I know you won't want me to say it, but thank you, my friend," Josep said. "Thank you also for your old Republican boots. Mine were worn through."

"May they lead you safely to your brother." Baltasar pointed at him. "How is that allergy? Dolors said you get wheezy in her kitchen, but who wouldn't?" He winked. "I told her it was due to the *Dermatophagoides farinae*."

Josep raised an eyebrow.

"Flour mites. You'll just have to stay clear of her kitchen."

"I don't think I can." Josep glanced away and then back at Baltasar. "I have something to ask you, something difficult. I'm asking you because of our friendship."

Baltasar raised his unruly eyebrows. "Well, ask."

"Do you love Dolors?"

Baltasar's eyebrows arched. "Love her?" He leaned back in his chair. "Yes, I do."

"Enough to marry her? To go up to the altar and not run away?"

Baltasar laughed nervously. "Are you asking on her behalf?"

"I'm asking on my own."

Baltasar's forehead creased like he was trying to work out a baffling puzzle. He took a drink. "The other day you alluded to someone being interested in Dolors."

Josep nodded and did not take his eyes off Baltasar's.

"You were referring to yourself the whole time?"

Josep nodded again.

"You mean to say the whole time I've been in the city you've been out here falling for my Dolors?"

Josep shrugged and winced. "You could put it that way."

Baltasar rubbed the back of his neck and leaned back. "How does Dolors feel?"

"I'm uncertain right now. But there was a moment there that I was convinced she felt the same. Really, Baltasar, I don't want this to come between us. You're my best and only friend."

Baltasar sipped and licked his lips. "You'd never know it. No wonder Eduard keeps giving you the slip."

"That's different. Besides, you were never convinced about Dolors. You told me yourself. You had your chance and you ran. It's not like any of this happened intentionally, and if I thought that you would really mind, I would have put a stop to it." Josep tapped his chest with the edge of his fist. "For you she's not lodged in here. For me she is. I now realize that she has been for years. I thought I would be doing you a favor."

"This is all a bit of a blow." Baltasar breathed in. "Let me recover and see how much of a favor it is."

"In the meantime we're still friends?"

Baltasar nodded slowly.

"You won't mention this to Dolors will you? I'm leaving tomorrow and I'll talk to her when I get back."

"I'll definitely mention it to her. It will give you something to think about while you're climbing through those mountains." Baltasar finished his glass and leaned in. "When you're there can you get me a bottle of something good, something strong? I think I might need it."

Late the next night, well after sunset, Josep put on his boots and heavy coat and headed into the mountains. He and Pep were to meet at the hideout Josep and his group had used at the end of the war. He hadn't been back since, and as he climbed through the snow, he remembered those days so vividly. The hours of waiting. The limited supplies. The skirmishes and the final defense of Pujaforta, which he had missed. Would it all be different now if he had been there? He relived the moments and he felt tired, not only because of his climbing legs, but because he always seemed to be climbing in one direction. Eduard never met him half way.

As Josep approached the hideout, he began to walk in circles amongst the trees as he was instructed. The intention was to create a confusing pattern of foot prints that no border guard could follow. Afterwards he went beyond the thick of trees and found the boulders that nature and time had used to form the cave they called Turtle Rock. He whistled. He heard only the silent forest around him. The wind skirted the leafless branches and whispered in his ear. He shivered. Taking shelter in the cave, he waited. He thought of how his brave sister had brought them supplies that one day, and how now she had been robbed of her wits. His dear Àngels, again an accessory victim. She had been so daring that day they sneaked into Uncle Eusebi's house, the day that their father disappeared and their childhood ended. Dolors had also been a victim. Now Josep could only imagine Dolors' reaction when Baltasar revealed what Josep had told him. The thought left him embarrassed and exposed since he had yet to reveal such feelings to her himself. As he sat in the dark and the night became very cold, he was even surer that those feelings were real. He heard approaching footsteps in the snow. Then he heard the whistle. Whistling back, he stuck his nose out as Pep collapsed into the cave beside him. He was breathing heavily and sweating despite the cold.

"You're still here," he said. "I was afraid you had left. We have to go now before daylight. They almost stopped me. That's why I'm late."

"But is it still safe to go? Shouldn't we wait?"

"No, it's now or never. There's more talk about closing the border."

"I'll be able to come back, won't I?"

"Probably. Let's go."

Josep reluctantly followed in Pep's footsteps out of the cave and up the mountains through the bare trees. As they approached the highest point of the peaks, they no longer had the cover of pine needles and were forced to hide from tree to tree. This was why Pep had instructed Josep to wear gray. Josep also carried a small pack on his back containing local sausage for Eduard, a letter from Núria, and a large empty bag to fill for this return trip. The last time he had climbed out of Pujaforta to find Eduard he had been carrying sausage and bread from Uncle Eusebi's funeral. Yet as far as he was concerned the man he had found waiting to cross over into France had not been his Eduard. He looked up from his thoughts to see Pep's arm motioning for him to stop.

"The border guards are usually here," Pep whispered and crouched behind a wide tree. Josep hid behind him. They listened. "I think it's clear," Pep said. "Ever since one of them was killed, they're like the plague: silent, numerous, and deadly." Pep stood and looked around them. "Let's go." He began to run like mad, zigzagging between the trees. Josep followed, slightly baffled. A shot echoed around them.

"Did they see us?" Josep whispered when they reached a tiny stone house at the base of the hill. Inside there was one table and a few chairs. It was dark and only the dawn light streamed in through the open door. Josep saw the dirt floor, the dark pools of wax melted long ago on the table top. Pep closed the door, sealing them in darkness.

"We don't use this place much anymore, but it's our only choice right now." Pep was breathing heavily. "*Em cago en l'hòstia.* They were right behind us."

Josep collapsed into one of the chairs. "How are we going to get back?"

"We'll have to find another way," Pep said. "For now, let's keep going. The sun will be up soon." They left the stone house and continued walking until the sun peered over the horizon, as if beckoning them forward. They emerged from the trees into a village where a truck was waiting. Once inside it, they began to drive down the mountain and slightly inland. The distance between them, the border guards, and Pujaforta grew. Josep recognized some of the landscape from his earlier journey to find Eduard, when he had instead spent time with Francine and Gaspard. They should greet him warmly now. As the vehicle moved through small villages of stone houses with brightly painted shutters and plane tree-lined roads, Josep's nerves began to jump. What if Eduard didn't greet him warmly? What if he didn't greet him at all? Finally, when he recognized the town, the truck stopped up a side road and he got out. He put his bag over his shoulder, waved back to Pep, and walked the rest of the way to Eduard's front door.

CHAPTER FOUR

"JOSEP." JOSEP HEARD his brother's voice and saw him grinning in the doorway inviting him to enter his house. Eduard's eyes caught the daylight and were also smiling at him. Strangely, his features looked as prominent as they had been during their starving days in the French camp, but his jowls were puffy. The circles under his eyes offset his dark eyebrows, his skin was abnormally pale, and his hairline was creeping back at the temples. More than anything Josep couldn't get over the unexpected smile. Josep felt opposing charges inside him: he was drawn toward his brother and felt their proximity fill the void inside him; at the same time he felt wary, since it was his brother who had created the void to begin with.

"We've been expecting you. Come in," Eduard said in such a normal, brotherly tone that Josep hesitated, gauging how much of this was real. When finally he crossed the threshold, he gripped his brother by the shoulders and bottled all his questions and frustrations inside, saving them for later. Eduard also had to be on edge, clearly feigning this calm state of mind, acting as if they had seen each other yesterday and the years of distance were no longer hovering between them. Yet he appeared genuine as he put his arm around Josep and steered him into the shadowy foyer. Josep felt his brother's warmth and the heat from the house waft around him as he stepped toward the darkness.

Francine, as tall as she'd always been but now significantly wider, came forward into the light. She wore a welcoming smile, but her dark eyes were drilling into his. Unable to read her message, Josep looked to her side where her son was holding her hand. Now a toddler rather than a baby, little Gaspard had his mother's wide forehead but the Balaguer light gray eyes. Josep felt a surge of longing, realizing that he had missed Eduard's family, the boy's sputtering giggles, and Francine's hidden vulnerability. Josep crouched down in front of the boy and scooped him into his arms. As he raised Gaspard to Francine's height, Josep said, "Hello, Francine." He kissed her on the cheek, and he asked the boy, "*Ça va*, Gaspard? Do you remember me? Your uncle Josep?" At first a startled expression crossed the boy's eyes but then he laughed and Josep reluctantly put him down.

"He likes you," Eduard said, watching the familiarity with astonishment. "That's a rarity."

"Come in, you must be exhausted." Francine led them out of the dark hall into the slightly brighter kitchen with a large wooden table in its center. The smell of burnt toast lingered in the air. It all looked exactly the same as the last time Josep had been there, except that Eduard was standing in it, the soft light from the window turning his eyes a celestial shade of gray.

Despite the long trek and the bouncy ride in the truck, Josep was anything but tired. The sight of this calm Eduard instantly energized him and his mind flowed with questions rather than accusations. "So you did get my letter? I was afraid I might not find you here."

"I was just about to leave, but I didn't want to miss you. Your coming means so much to me. Francine here," Eduard took her hand with his good one, "told me all about your stay here with her. I'm sorry I didn't make it. I got delayed trying to find Artur. You remember the fellow from Argelès and Montreal? After all that time here waiting, it was right for you to go back home. How is *Mare*? How is our dear sister?" He asked putting down some small glasses and filling them with a clear liqueur. "But first, let's toast them all." They clanked glasses and sipped, despite the early hour.

Josep smiled, relaxing and lowering his wall slightly, despite the mention of Artur. "*Mare*'s having some money worries. The co-op hardly has any orders."

"But she married the richest man in town. Don't tell me the grand Sr. Palau is broke. If it weren't for *Mare*, I would say it serves him right."

"He still owns all that land but apparently has little cash coming in, which is no surprise because no one has any. His lumber mill is at a standstill and he says any money he gets goes to paying his workers."

Eduard frowned. "What do you think of him?"

"It's true that when we were younger we only heard the rumors of the man's nastiness and eccentricities, but we didn't know the man himself. He's definitely eccentric, but he's become like a backbone to our family. The important thing is that *Mare* seems happy." Josep sighed. "Àngels, I'm afraid, is another story. You can actually thank her for my being here."

Francine leaned in. "I was very sad to hear the news about Carme. She was so strong and highly respected in our organization. She treated each person she helped escape like one of her own family, which I also heard she was unable to save. I know that she was in Argelès and she told me that she was there with you."

Josep nodded.

"Carme cared about you. She was also concerned about your sister and even introduced me to her once. We were in the safe house in the woods and Àngels was so determined to see Eduard. I thought she would crumble right there when I told her Eduard couldn't come." She touched Eduard's shoulder. "She pretended to be strong for Carme, and probably because of me, by showing a thick skin, but underneath it she was trembling. So how is she handling everything now?" Francine asked, cupping her glass with her hands, her single eyebrow peaking over her eye.

Josep swallowed and sighed. "Yes, our poor Carme. And our poor Àngels. She hasn't handled it at all. I mentioned in my letter that after she cracked in public, Baltasar took her to safety with some friends in Barcelona. We are all relieved to hear that she's improving. They say she is more rested and has begun to hold normal conversations. Hopefully it won't be long before she's home." Josep looked through the window without seeing the outside. "We've all had too much to deal with, but Àngels was younger when the losses started. Father. Pau. Eduard, remember how she used to be so bossy and, well, enterprising? Remember when she didn't want to take the cow to pasture, so she sent Pau to collect grass in a bucket?" Josep laughed and his eyes met Eduard's. "While the two of us were away I think the regime, particularly the Puigs, set out to break her." Josep's jaw tensed. "They are gone now, but for Àngels it has come too late." Josep shook his head. "*Mare* is lost without her. She comes to Àngels' house, which is our family house, every day to clean and arrange things, even though she had cleaned and arranged them just the day before."

"I think about Àngels every day and how I would love to go and see her, help her. But I can't." Eduard took a gulp from his glass. His gaze then paused on Francine. "Some of us have been very lucky. I suppose it's all a matter of timing. Francine was in those woods as much as Carme was, but it wasn't the *Franquistes* it was the Nazis. I'm thankful every day that nothing happened to her and that little Gaspard is also with me."

Francine tapped the table with the point of her index finger. "What I don't understand is why Carme was still running through the woods. The war was over."

Both Josep and Eduard looked at her. "Your war."

"Our war is not over," Eduard said and Josep met his wild look. It was like fire was burning behind his eyes. "They just want us to think it is. I know for a fact that Carme was meeting some Resistance members in Toulouse. Some others were in Paris. And I'm referring to resistance to Franco, how all this started."

Francine stroked the back of his head and he grasped her hand and kissed it. Josep felt comforted to see that while Eduard still had the fight in him, Francine had a calming effect. With Artur no longer a barrier between them Josep envisioned him and Eduard working together, being a family again. But he knew that Eduard could not risk going to Pujaforta. There was only a guarded border stopping Josep from coming to visit him regularly. They just had to put their differences behind them.

Eduard released Francine's hand and rested his good hand on Josep's forearm. "Josep, there's a hideout we used during the war. I'd like you to see it." Eduard stood. "What do you say we go right now?"

Francine touched Eduard's shoulder. "*Chéri*, surely you can wait a while. Josep must be exhausted from his journey."

"If you want to go, we can go."

As they made their way to the door, Francine squeezed Josep's elbow. He gave her a questioning look as she whispered, "Did you get my note?" He frowned and shook his head. As she kissed his cheek she said softly, "Watch what you say."

Beyond the town, the forest was colder than the one beyond Pujaforta, despite the lower altitude. A recent shower had left its traces in the muck through which they trudged, silent as the woods around them. Josep followed his brother anxiously, yet apprehensively. Eduard seemed tenser than he had been back at the house, his dark mood mounting like a wall.

After continuing in silence, each brother guarding his own thoughts through many afternoon hours, they finally emerged from the woods into an overgrown garden. Tucked into the trees on the far side was a small stone house with the faded wooden shutters drawn. Eduard motioned for Josep to stop and stay quiet. He tiptoed to a small unshuttered window and looked through the dirty pane. Putting his ear to the peeling paint on the door, he waited for a number of minutes before finally pushing it open. Josep followed Eduard inside, where there was a bare living room with a cold stone floor, two chairs, a table, and a towering stack of wood beside the walk-in fireplace. Boxes of supplies lined the other wall, which was bare and unadorned like the rest of the house. A layer of dirt coated the ceramic floor. Again Eduard gestured for Josep not to speak. They sat quietly waiting for it to grow dark before lighting a fire. "We can't let them see the chimney smoke," Eduard whispered and when Josep tried to speak he silenced him. The look on Eduard's face as he built the fire was so stern and absorbed that Josep began to doubt that Eduard remembered that he was there. They both watched the flame stroke the edge of a log as if tasting it before devouring it whole.

"So, it should be safe to talk now, shouldn't it?" Josep said quietly.

Eduard jumped slightly and nodded. "Yes, but keep your voice down." He pulled some raw sausages out of his bag and put them on a grill on the fire. Taking out two bottles of Ricard, he poured some of the clear anise liquor into two metal cups.

"Who are you afraid might hear us?" Josep asked, thinking that on the way they had seen nothing but trees.

"The Guardia Civil. I'm wanted everywhere, ever since that *cabrón* of a border guard got in my way."

"Are you sure they even know it was you?" Josep began to think that his earlier impression of his brother's natural, normal mood was mistaken.

"Yes, I am. I was so close to home, just meters from crossing into France and we practically came chest to chest. Scared the shit out of each other. But I was faster. I left him lying bleeding into the pine needles and ran. I've been running ever since really. I've already spent enough of my life in prison. You saw what they did to Carme." He looked at his folded hands. "Sorry about that, by the way."

Josep nodded. "But surely they won't come to your house. They have no jurisdiction here."

"You think I'm paranoid, too. They can talk to the Gendarmes. They'd be glad to get rid of another Spaniard. I have Francine and Gaspard to think of." Eduard poked the fire abruptly. "You can tell you've never run from the law."

"I only wish that were true," Josep said and raised his eyebrows, but he preferred to change the subject. "So you've spent a lot of time here, in this house then?" Josep took a swig of the cloudy drink which was sweet yet burnt his throat.

"We used this house and a few others nearby. There was a group of us, some Catalans, a couple of other Spaniards and French. We did most of our planning here. The path into the house is overgrown, so it's secluded. We couldn't risk being discovered. Plus the train track, the line from Toulouse to the coasts north and south of here, isn't far away, so we didn't have to carry the explosives too far."

"So you were mostly doing sabotage?" Josep asked trying to picture his brother and Artur and the other men as part of this clandestine group, and wondering what kind of a role his brother had played. The Eduard he used to know would have been following the pack. He was less sure what this Eduard before him would have done. "Is that how you lost your fingers?" Josep pointed to Eduard's hand.

Eduard stuck his two fingers inside his coat and continued as if Josep had never raised the subject. "Sabotage and kidnapping. Artur was a genius, though I did teach him how to stash grenades under his arms, like we did with Uncle Eusebi's potatoes when we were kids, remember? Artur had a knack for it and espionage in general. He would gain people's trust and they would give him information without ever suspecting what he would use it for. He managed to get close to a German officer." He pointed to the corner beside the fireplace. "We had him tied up right there, until Artur shot him. The man was pathetic. First he was belligerent, then he curled into a ball in the corner and pleaded for his life for the sake of his newborn son. I thought he might get to me, but I was just relieved when the bullet stopped his crying."

Josep stared at the corner for a moment and wondered where his sensitive brother had gone. "I knew that Artur was into politics in the camp, but I didn't think he had that in him." Josep thought back to the young man's beardless face and naive look.

"That was the advantage with Artur. No one ever suspected him of anything," Eduard said. His voice turned soft and sad. "Many innocent people paid after he killed that SS officer. The Nazis took their revenge on anyone they could find. They went into towns and randomly shot people, or closed women and children in churches and burned them down. That is what we were up against. These years of war really opened my eyes." Eduard sighed and paused, swirling his cup. "It was after that that Artur went into hiding. But then someone found him and sent him to that camp in Austria. When I got there it was chaos. The Americans wouldn't let us near the camps, but people were talking about them everywhere. The atrocious conditions. The stone quarry. The bunks for three people, which given how skinny they were doesn't seem impossible. We thought the camp in Argelès was bad, but this was pure cruelty. There were so many of our people, Republicans, in there. They even helped liberate it." Eduard pointed to the corner and his memory of the SS officer. "My last and only trip to Pujaforta since the battle there was right after we killed that Nazi. That's why there were border guards everywhere. Francine doesn't want me to try to go back again." Eduard turned the sausage on the grill with his two bare fingers and poured more Ricard into their cups. His face brightened. "I imagine that you noticed she's an intriguing woman. I love her so much. She's been my beacon, particularly when they sent Artur away. She outranked me in our movement, but I found it a bit exciting." Eduard grinned. "She used to be tougher and meaner than any of us. Then she had little Gaspard and she's become really cautious."

"That makes some sense, don't you think? You look like you're being quite cautious yourself." Josep looked at the room around them, wondering how he was supposed to bring Eduard home for Àngels' sake. "Perhaps a little too much."

"I am because I have to be. Besides, regardless of how much I love Francine and Gaspard, I need time alone. I think it's something the wars and probably the prisons did to me. There was never any privacy, even for the most intimate matters. I'll tell you a little secret." Eduard filled their cups again and took the sausages off the fire. "At one time I doubted that Gaspard was my son." He held his throat and swallowed as if clearing a lump. He took a swig from his cup. "That was before he was born. When I saw him I had no doubt that I was his father, even though he looks a lot like Francine. It's in his eyes." He pointed to his own. "It was during that time, while I was doubting, that I felt lower than ever—and I've fallen very low. I realized that Francine wasn't just another fighter or just another woman. It was a unique, absorbing feeling. She had been with another man and it drove me mad. I should be ashamed to say that I was relieved that in one of the Nazi raids Francine's other man was killed, but I'm not ashamed at all." He jabbed at the fire. "Never mind, it was at that time that I realized how much I loved every bit of my giant Francine. You've had so many different women, I doubt you know what I'm talking about."

"I do," Josep looked into his cup as if searching for her. "And you know her." Josep felt that now, in exchange for Eduard's opening up, he could do the same.

"Sorry, I didn't want to make you sad about Carme again." Eduard rested a hand on Josep's arm.

"You can't imagine how sick, how helpless we all felt. *Fills de puta.*" Josep put a hand on Eduard's but he gently brushed it away and reached for a sausage. As Eduard handed one to Josep, he shook it in anger and it splattered. They both bit into them, the fatty juice dripping down their chins. Josep chewed and nodded. His arm still felt warm from Eduard's touch.

"When she disappeared I had really only been back in Pujaforta for a short while, but perhaps it was the setting, being back again, that drew me to her again. I was searching for that comfort. It seemed that no matter the distance and what had happened to us in between, we always found each other and it was always like it had always been." He paused. "In fact, I had hoped it would be like that for the two of us, you and me." Josep glanced quickly at Eduard, who was looking at him warmly. "Anyway, then I found that at the same time I was being drawn to another woman, someone who has always been there, right under my nose."

"Dolors. You always fancied her. You never actually told me, but I could tell. Even Baltasar could tell."

"Really? But I hardly realized myself." Josep lowered his glass and leaned back. "I do know one thing that she doesn't. She's going to be with me. I think I've even managed to convince Baltasar."

"He's agreed? I suppose he should after he abandoned her in front of the entire town. I saw Dolors that day. I came to find everyone and instead I found her lying in her wedding dress in the middle of the floor wailing at the ceiling."

Josep pictured his Dolors in such pain and he wanted to run back across the mountain and hug her until she laughed her usual laugh. It also made him feel less guilty where Baltasar was concerned.

While Josep covered his cup with his hand, Eduard refilled his own and said, "So you're serious about you and our cousin Dolors? That seems too boring for you."

"Perhaps, but it is also stabilizing. I just want a home and I want a family. My own. I see little Gaspard and I'd like one just like him. You won't believe it, but in Canada I took care of a boy for a number of years and he even called me Papa."

Eduard pulled back and frowned at him. "No, I don't believe it unless there was some woman involved. You probably had a long line of them. I'm not talking about the ones you paid."

Josep ignored the comment and bit back his urge to ask what had happened between them in Montreal. "I did meet some very special people there, one of whom was a woman who was trapped in that profession you mention. I tried to help her but it backfired so to speak. I did almost bring another woman to Pujaforta with me. Marie-Claude, the communist school teacher," he grinned. "I think you would have liked her."

"So is she the reason why you didn't come back to fight in the Resistance like the rest of us?" Eduard's gray eyes had turned icy.

Josep paused and felt his breath hold in his chest. Here it was in front of him, the moment he had been waiting for and the one he had been dreading. He reached into his pocket and put the *caganer* figurine, with its worn trousers around its knees, on the table between them. Eduard stared at it as if the man himself had spoken.

"Will you explain that to me? Why did you leave that and a note on my bedside table in Montreal?"

"Why did you blow us off? You were supposed to meet me at the ship."

"Why did you steal all my money and my passport?" Josep was trying to still the gushing anger he had kept bottled for so long.

Eduard cut the air with his arm. "I didn't steal your money, *collons*. What are you talking about?"

"You're the only one who knew where it was. Under the floor boards beneath the wardrobe. After all the money I had given to you and you had lost at cards with Artur and his anarchists." Josep leaned in and pointed at him. "You know why I didn't get your note in time? When I got back to the rooming house, the police were there searching the whole building. Other rooms had been robbed as well, but the police were right outside ours. When they finally left, I went into our room and my money was all gone. There I was, penniless, with no identity, whether false or real, I couldn't go to the police because they would arrest me, and my brother had left me a note. Too late. I ran to the docks, even though I could never board a ship, but the boat had already sailed. There was no sign of you, no sign of Artur and the others. I waited for two weeks at the house for you to come back or send word, but neither came. Finally Jean-Pierre's father told me his brother-in-law way up north could help me. And he did. A pure stranger helped me. It took me ages to get back on my feet. And so that is why I did not fight in your Resistance."

"Can I say something now?" Eduard picked up the figurine and put it down as if stopping it from hopping away. "I know I should have given you more notice about leaving. I did tell you that we had the plan and it was imminent. But frankly, that you would think that I stole your money and left you with nothing shows that you don't really know me at all."

"Actually, most of the time I think I don't. If it wasn't you, then who took it? I can't help but think that there was someone who was always trying to separate us, wasn't there?"

Eduard jumped to his feet. "Are you accusing Artur of doing it?"

"You did say he was very sneaky and nobody ever realized it. I would suspect not even you."

Eduard began to pace. "*Em cago en la hòstia, tu.* I can't believe you could outright accuse him like that." His face had turned purple.

"Eduard, Eduard," Josep said holding up his hands in a halting motion in an attempt to calm him. "I've been so angry. It's been ever so slowly eating away at me. But I want to put this behind us. We had to get it out in the open. I hope that we can understand each other and then we can get back what we had."

Josep's eyes met Eduard's, and the sadness and anger of their separate and shared experiences seemed to join in their look. "By the way, I do know what it's like to be wanted by the police," Josep said and put the figure back in his pocket. "I can never go back to Canada, and wherever we go in Pujaforta they're right behind us. Later I'll have to get past them to get home." He finished his drink and Eduard refilled his glass. Josep didn't dare suggest Eduard accompany him home. Not yet. "Can I ask you something?"

"Of course."

"Why were you so calm and friendly at the house?"

"I promised Francine."

"That's the only reason?"

"That and the fact that time and seclusion have helped put things in perspective. I've got to admit that I have had some moments on the edge, on the very edge." Eduard held up his missing fingers. "This was not exactly an accident. It sounds better if I say it was, because no one will understand a man who let his fingers be blown off. I didn't try to save myself. Francine had left me for the Alsatian, Artur had been sent away on a special mission with no warning, and I thought you had abandoned me, first in the church square and then again in Montreal." He tossed a log onto the fire and turned his back toward Josep.

59

"I've been trying to help you all this time. Ever since the battle in Pujaforta, my every last minute has been trying to save you. I even gave up everything and made that deal with Ivan Puig to get you out of prison. I sold us both. That in itself has led to a whole series of circumstances out of my control. Don't you see, after what happened during the battle, I had to get you out of that prison, because it was you and because I felt responsible."

"And so you should have. I still can't understand where the hell you were. But never mind that right now." Eduard turned another sausage with his bare fingers and stepped back. "When I visited Pujaforta I saw Manel, Artur's *Franquista* brother. He seemed close with the family, though I can't imagine why. Did he mention Artur?" Eduard was pacing a crooked line.

"We were there when he received the letter about Artur. Manel's been devastated between that and Carme." Josep was picturing Manel's drawn face as he pulled him out of his shack in the yard the day that Àngels had gone mad.

"But Artur went back to Adiol." Eduard sat down and looked at his hand, which was obviously full of severed nerves.

Josep held his jaw, feeling the words physically. Even without the actual blow his head began to hurt. He could not be the person to tell Eduard the truth about Artur. Josep held his temples and said nothing because he didn't know what to say.

"Francine told me that he went home," Eduard insisted but his voice weakened with every word. "She said that a letter came. But she didn't let me see it." Eduard's eyes flashed. "Tell me what you know."

Josep shook his head, partly in response to Eduard and partly in reaction to his own situation.

"What happened to him?" Eduard was standing over him.

Josep looked at the fire instead. "He never got out of Mauthausen. Not alive anyway."

"*Cony.*" Eduard stumbled backwards. Then he hesitated and pointed a finger at Josep. "You've come here to lie to me again. Why do you want me to be unhappy?" Eduard sank to his knees and grasped the hair at his temples. "First you accuse me of robbing you. Then you accuse Artur, which is very convenient since you knew all along that he could never defend himself. But first you left me alone in Pujaforta." He waved Josep away. "Go. Leave me alone."

Josep tried to put a hand on Eduard's shaking shoulder.

Eduard swatted it away. "You may as well have killed him yourself. That's what you always wanted." Eduard looked at him with eyes the color of solid hatred. "Get out," Eduard shouted. "Don't ever come back."

"You're not being reasonable. I came here to bring you back, for Àngels. And for me. If I leave here now, like this," Josep said pointing to the door, "I won't be back."

"Good. And I'll tell you something." Eduard stood tall. "I did take your money."

Josep collapsed against the doorframe and put his hands on his knees. "You what?" Josep stared, feeling the blood fill his face and seeing Eduard's face redden.

"But I didn't take your passport."

Josep looked at the stone floor and shook his head. "Why did you take it? I would have given it to you."

"I borrowed it. I owed a lot of people. For the cards. And they weren't all anarchists," Eduard said calmly like it was clear justification.

Instead Josep relived the scene in his head, saw the empty hole under the floorboards, felt the loneliness and the desperation of having nowhere to go. Abandoned, robbed, and left to fend for himself by his own brother.

"You are sick." Josep opened the door and left. Even the cold air failed to calm his boiling blood. Slowly he let the night forest absorb him and wished it could swallow him whole.

Before dawn some days later, Josep was almost back in Pujaforta with a heavy bag on his back and a hard lump in his chest. He left Eduard in France, along with all thoughts of Eduard making Àngels well again. There was no use yearning for his brother anymore. He would have to find someone to replace him.

Josep had traveled quickly, determined to make it past the guards no matter what. It was as if his rage at Eduard pushed him up the mountain and the love that he openly felt for Dolors tugged him towards her. He arrived in Pujaforta before the light of dawn, and rather than going straight to his family house, he arrived at Dolors' door. He knew that unlike the rest of the townspeople, she would already be up and baking. His knock sounded more anxious than he intended, and the door sprung open as if under the pressure of Josep's emotions. In the doorway Dolors stood with a lump of dough in her fist and a look of shock on her face.

"Josep, what a fright you gave me," she said, but her face was thrilled to see him and he was relieved to see it. She pulled him inside leaving a floury handprint on his arm. "You're back already?" She looked over his shoulder. "So, how's Eduard?"

Josep's look turned to stone and his jawbone throbbed. "Don't even say his name."

Dolors bit her lips and shrugged. "Well, I for one am very pleased to see you. You can tell me what happened another time."

"Is there any word of Àngels?"

Dolors shook her head. "I hope this will cheer you up." She linked elbows with him and guided him into the kitchen. "Today is Sant Josep. I have to make *flams* for all the Joseps, remember? I would offer you *coca*, but you weren't very keen on it, strange man."

Josep shook his head and let the pack slide from his back to the floor, along with the worries, disappointment, and fear of the last few days. He didn't expect to feel so at home, so comfortable. Reaching into the bag, he pulled out a box that he had carefully packed on the top. He handed it to Dolors. "This is for my Santa Lola."

She took it from him with such a look of delight on her face that it soon spread to Josep's. The pink cardboard box was delicately wrapped with a ribbon, which Dolors gently opened. "I can't believe it. *Éclairs. Pains au chocolat. Mini-bûches.*" She sniffed each pastry as if trying to identify its ingredients. They had melted only slightly and had maintained their shape despite their long journey. After putting them on the table, Dolors wrapped her arms around Josep. "You do know how to conquer my heart." Josep felt her soft body against his and felt even more pleased to be home. This had to be what life was about.

"They weren't that easy to come by and I am no connoisseur of sweet things. When I finally found them I thought you could use them to experiment. If they'll let you, you could try to make something similar here. Just don't ask me to try them."

"You haven't heard." Dolors face fell. "The French have cut us off, or at least the regime. Finally all the protests in France have amounted to something. But we don't know who it's going to smother in the process. I won't be able to get my ingredients." Then she took a step back. "How did you get here? Where's Pep? He told me he couldn't deliver any more, at least for a time."

"I managed," Josep stood proudly, but didn't dare tell her how guards were almost as thick as the trees and that he'd hidden in a burrow for hours waiting for it to be safe. Instead he began to show her all the black-market goods that filled his pack: cigarettes, chocolate, alcohol. "I knew about the border closing and I was terrified every step of the way, but it wasn't so bad really. And once I sell this, my family won't have to worry for a while."

"Josep, how dangerous." Dolors covered her mouth, but then she laughed a low laugh. "You are good. Baltasar will be very pleased."

"Yes, I got everything his people asked for, except for the book. I didn't want to chance it. Maybe next time."

"Next time? I thought it would just be the once. It's too risky." Worry filled her face.

"It is, but it's also very tempting. You said yourself that you need ingredients. I'll see what Baltasar says. Right now I'm still running on the thrill of it all. And of seeing you." He stepped closer to Dolors. "I can't begin to tell you the thrill I feel about that."

"I am so glad to see you, too." She pulled him to the table and told him to sit. "I've been so lonely since you left, even if it's just been a few days." She sat down facing him.

"I have something to tell, or rather to ask you." He pulled his chair up to hers so that their knees were almost touching. "I've been doing some thinking. I spoke to Baltasar before I left. He hasn't talked to you, has he?"

"Baltasar? He's been strangely avoiding me." She pulled in closer. "What did you talk to him about?"

"About getting married."

"He's finally accepted?" Dolors clasped her hands together and her face filled with light. "What wonderful news."

"No." Josep held her clasped hands and tried to ignore the sting in his chest. While he was wondering if he should try to back step, delicately remove himself from the situation, he pictured Àngels, Eduard, and Carme, all gone, and it rushed out. "He more or less accepted if we were to get married. But he'll want to hear it from you first."

Dolors pulled her hands away and stood up. She suddenly looked worried again. "The two of us?"

"That's what kept me walking across the mountain, despite those guards, despite it all." Josep looked at her with wide, expectant eyes.

"The two of us?" She paced around his chair before sitting slowly across from Josep. She edged ever closer until their knees touched firmly. Resting her hands on his thighs, she grinned at him. "That's the best proposition I've heard in ages."

CHAPTER FIVE

THE DAY OF Josep's wedding to Dolors, much to his bride's obvious disappointment, the eyes of the town were elsewhere. After her months of absence, Àngels had returned to Pujaforta. Those who had witnessed her screaming in the town square wearing nothing but a nightdress gathered to watch as Àngels once again crossed the square, this time fully clothed in a blue cotton dress and with her head held high.

A few days earlier, when Baltasar had come to Barcelona and told Àngels that she was wanted as maid of honor at her brother's impending wedding to Dolors, at first she thought it was a doctor's trick to test her grasp on reality. When she later realized that he was speaking the truth, she hugged him.

"To step back and let Josep marry her is certainly one of the kindest things you have ever done, even after everything you have done for me. You are a very strong and giving man." She looked around the small room, not much larger than the single bed against the wall. It was where her mental health and future safety had gradually been restored. She no longer saw Carme's terrified face on all four walls or Carles Puig sneering down at her. Both visions had been equally disturbing. Now she would have to get used to the idea of having her cousin Dolors as a sister-in-law instead of Carme.

"At first I was really surprised and angry at Josep," Baltasar had told her. "But as I thought about it, I realized it was the best for all of us. He's probably doing me a favor. Dolors was always just a little too much for me to handle. Besides, after what I did to her, I couldn't expect for her to wait for me to make up my mind."

"Perhaps it was already made and now you've just shut that door and are walking away. You must feel some relief at being able to move on. I wish I could." Àngels hesitated. "Listen, did Josep tell you what happened on his trip to visit Eduard? I need to know."

Baltasar shook his head. "His lips are sealed, and I'd say that his ears and heart are as well." He sat on her bedside. "Now for my favorite patient, I have just one more prescription for you, besides not worrying about your brothers."

"More medication?" Àngels asked, disappointed. She really felt that she had regained her strength and was ready to confront a Pujaforta without Carme.

"Medication of sorts. You must return home for the wedding. It is my last order as your doctor."

Àngels put her arms around Baltasar and said, "When are we leaving?" Then she drew away. "But what about the Guardia Civil? After all those things I said?"

"Dolors, Sr. Palau, myself, even Manel, we have all done some dealings to ensure that you are safe," he said, but refrained from telling her what they were.

When Àngels had arrived back home she had hugged Víctor and not let him out of her sight. She was shocked to see Manel. He was unshaven, pale, drawn, and generally apathetic. His spark had died and Àngels knew exactly how he felt. Almost exactly. She had had some years, rather than hours, between losing her brother and losing Carme. She decided to share with Manel what she had come to understand during her stay in the city: her struggle to accept Carme's absence was due to her being denied a form of farewell for her. On seeing Manel, Àngels had an idea that he accepted immediately. Inside her house, Àngels gathered items that she most associated with Carme: her cardigan, the boots she had borrowed. She suggested little Víctor do the same. She knew that at age seven, he would also need to bid farewell to his mother, even though she had been away most of his life. They carried the articles into the garden where they met Manel, who had a small bag containing his items and a shovel. They chose a spot beside the tree overlooking the expanse of mountaintops. It was the same tree that Àngels had climbed to spy into her uncle's home so many years earlier. It was a similar time of year and its leaves were fresh and bright. She remembered looking down at Pau, jeering, coaxing him to climb and the urge she had had to release the Puig boy's caterpillars. She wished she had done it now, a sort of preempted revenge for what the Puig's presence had done to her and what their absence had done to Carme. Just beyond the stretch of roots, Manel began to dig a hole in the rich but sandy earth. When its rocky insides gaped at them, Àngels motioned for Víctor to lay his objects inside it. He knelt and spread his mother's woolen scarf in the base and then added his favorite *doudou*, a cloth rabbit that she had brought him from France. Then he leaned down to put in a corduroy jacket. Àngels felt her breath catch and grabbed it, brushing off her brother's jacket.

"Let's keep this here with us." She put an arm around Víctor. "Someone else may need it someday."

"But we're keeping these things safe in here for when she comes back, right?" He looked up at her questioningly, but he already knew the answer. He buried his face in Àngels' side. She stroked the crown of his head and his wet cheek. Manel stepped forward and added Carme's gloves, then he kissed the cover of Carme's copy of Trotsky's *The Revolution Betrayed* and rested it on top. He stepped back and bowed his head. Àngels then stepped to the edge of the hole and knelt beside Víctor. She lifted Carme's cardigan to her nose. It smelled of pine needles, earth, and Carme. She inhaled its scent one last time and rested it on top of the other items. She added the fabric bird that Carme had sewn to her skirt the morning of Josep's party and the day she disappeared. Then she put in the boots that they had shared.

"To Carme," Àngels said. She let the tears flow freely over her cheeks. "May she rest in peace."

"May she rest in peace," Manel and Víctor whispered. Víctor sobbed. Then Manel lifted the shovel and threw dirt on top of the mementos. He stopped suddenly and dropped the shovel.

"Just a minute," he said, and disappeared into his shack. He returned and placed a carefully folded flag of the Second Republic in with the other items. "That was my brother Artur's flag, from before he joined the JCAI. May he also rest in peace," he said before sprinkling more dirt on top. His face was also glistening. Each shovelful gradually erased the contents of the hole. The corner of the book and the bright purple, red, and yellow of the flag gaped through the soil. When only a darker patch of earth was left, Àngels put a large stone on top of it and said to Víctor, "You see, this way your mother is always here with us. If you ever need to talk to her, this is where you can come." She had put a hand on his shoulder and looked into his dark eyes. "Of course, if you really need to talk I hope that you will come to me."

"Or to me." Manel held the boy's other shoulder and together they embraced him. Àngels could feel the slight body in hers and the warm hands of Manel around her shoulders, and she had not felt so safe in ages.

As they walked back towards the house, Àngels turned to Manel. "Where did you get that Republican flag?"

"From my family's home in Adiol. After the expropriation, I could never bring myself to enter it. Now that I know that Artur is gone and I'm the only one left, I went to see it."

Àngels stroked his arm. "How was that?"

"It was actually easier than I thought it would be. I had refused to go there. Too many memories. Now I realize, although there are objects in that house that remind me of my family, I have a new family here. There's nothing left for me in Adiol. So I have decided to sell it. It's time to move on."

"I'm happy for you, that you are now able to take that step." Àngels stopped walking and took Manel's hand. "I know that I have not always been fair with you. I'm going to try to change."

"I would like that very much," Manel said and squeezed her fingers. "In fact, I would be honored if you would accompany me to your brother's wedding."

"Everyone does seem to be moving on, don't they?" She smiled and nodded her agreement.

Now Àngels was back in Pujaforta, walking toward the church on Manel's arm, and the strength that she had gained began to waver. She had thought that by returning for the wedding, the focus would be on the bride and groom, not on her every move. Yet, in such a small town, she felt the weight of every eye upon her. She tried to shake them, but it was the stare of the Guardia Civil that raised the hair on her neck. She pictured each and every one of them pointing a rifle at the ghost of Carme's face, the one she had finally put to rest. She expected to not be able to stand the sight of them. What she had not expected was to feel such comfort with Manel after all these years of resenting him. She looked up at him and he put a hand on hers and squeezed it.

***

As Àngels, Manel, and young Víctor walked through the town square and the gaze of all its people, Josep heard a collective gasp and the crowd parted to make room for him and his bride. Dolors was dressed in black from head to foot, but the June sun reflected off the beads she had so painstakingly sewn on it for her first failed wedding. They were almost as shiny as her smile. She raised her head regally under her black lace *mocador* and with her black-gloved hand grasped Josep's elbow. He was dressed in a simple brown jacket and slacks borrowed from his dead uncle. Holding Dolors close to his side, he nodded at their wedding guests. He had slicked back his hair for the occasion, an effect that, he was told, made his eyes more strikingly gray.

He was surprised to see so many people since they had limited the reception invitation to one couple per family. They were in no position to be hosting a large party, and besides, while they had all been co-existing for the years since the war, it was a new concept to Josep, who found it difficult to exchange his guns for a handshake. After all of Dolors' fussing over her dress, its potential to bring them bad luck, and Núria helping to dye and alter it at the co-op, Josep recognized that for his wife-to-be the celebration was almost as important as the state of marriage itself. Regardless, he was just thrilled to be marrying her and the anchor she would provide for him in Pujaforta. While he was looking forward to the party, what tempted him most was the thought of spending his first night with Dolors under her roof.

Now he walked proudly beside Dolors in the direction of the church. Its steps were not far ahead and the door that many of them had tried so hard to break down long ago was wide open. The townsfolk were streaming inside it. They had likely come to witness a wedding that dared such a breach of protocol. Dolors would not hear of walking separately to the church and meeting him there and had thrown tradition to the wind. Once again, given her history with Baltasar and Sr. Palau, whose money she would otherwise gladly accept, the only candidate for best man was Manel and she vowed she would not hear another poem or walk down the aisle with him again. Instead she gripped Josep's arm and did not let him out of her sight. "I will not be humiliated twice in my life," she had said. Plus she had promised the priest a year's free *flam* not to embellish the standard ceremony.

Josep was surprised at the lack of thunder and lightning bolts as he crossed the threshold of the church with his cousin and fiancée on his arm. Josep and Dolors stood side by side before the altar with the townsfolk filling the pews and chairs behind them, and others who had vowed never to enter the church listening from the square. Dolors stood almost businesslike, but her tight grasp on Josep's arm revealed her nerves. As he watched her, he saw tears well in her eyes, and he felt a twist in his chest. Like a warm cushion around them, their family was close by, with Núria sniffing and dabbing her eyes with her *mocador*, Sr. Palau giving them a wink, Àngels smiling proudly on their right, and on their left even Manel was showing a glint of happiness.

After a traditional preamble the priest said, "We have received the Papal blessing to marry these two cousins. I therefore ask you, Josep Balaguer i Hereu and Dolors Hereu i Nadal, will you take each other as husband and wife under the eyes of our Lord?"

"We will," they said in unison and squeezed each other's hands.

"Have you come of your own free will to give yourselves to each other in matrimony?"

"Yes, Father," they said in unison. Josep looked at Dolors but she was staring intently at the priest.

"Will you love and honor each other for as long as you both shall live?"

"Yes, Father," they said and this time Dolors looked at him and grinned.

"Will you accept children from God lovingly, and bring them up according to the law of Christ and his Church?"

"Yes, Father," Dolors said and Josep looked at the floor.

"Yes, Father," he said when he felt her elbow in his ribs.

After the rings were duly on each of their fingers, Josep poured into Dolors' open hand the thirteen unity coins she had insisted they include in the ceremony and said, "These coins are a symbol that I will provide and ensure that nothing lacks in our home."

Dolors accepted the coins and rubbed them together as if testing their value while she repeated the phrase.

After many more words and prayers the priest declared: "I now pronounce you man and wife."

Dolors leaned toward the priest and whispered, "So, is that it?"

The priest nodded. "You can sign in the corner."

Dolors threw her arms around Josep and kissed him hard on the mouth. She quickly turned to the crowd and gave them an electric smile, while clutching Josep's hand and waving it over her head as if in victory.

The townsfolk clapped, while the priest called for calm and welcomed them all to take communion or otherwise leave his church in the name of the Father, the Son, and the Holy Spirit. Josep smiled down at Dolors, whose cheeks were now glistening with tears. They stood frozen like this, as if wanting to stay always in this moment, while all the people filed out, all talking at once and making a terrible raucous. Oblivious to it, Josep embraced his bride. When the priest cleared his throat, gave them a nudge and a raised eyebrow, Josep took Dolors by the hand and led his jubilant family back down the aisle toward the door. Josep looked as Dolors beamed at him and he felt that energy enter his being and vowed to hold it there forever. In the back corner they bound their vows with their signatures and when they were the last couple remaining inside the church, Josep kissed her forehead and her lips. From the shadow beside the door, a tall, gangly figure emerged. Baltasar was stretching his arms toward them. First he heartily shook Josep's hand and hugged him.

"Congratulations, my friend," he said. Josep beamed. Then Baltasar turned to Dolors and held her hands in his. He kissed her on the cheek. "Dearest Dolors, I wish you a world of happiness."

Dolors smiled and touched where his cheek had met hers. "Thank you, Baltasar. I've finally done it."

"Yes, thank you, Baltasar," Josep added and patted his friend's arm. Then he whispered, "We couldn't have done it without you."

"Nor could you have done it with me," Baltasar said and winked. "Now you take good care of each other." He grasped each of their shoulders before ducking through the door. Josep and Dolors clasped hands and followed him outside into the blinding sunlight, where the cheers of the crowd enveloped them.

"*Bravo! Visquen els nuvis! ¡Vivan los novios!*"

As Josep smiled at his family gathered before them, Núria and Àngels, with equal joy spread on their faces, each launched a fistful of rice onto Josep and Dolors. Although it was a small amount, since good food could not be wasted, Josep found that the grains of rice, a symbol of fertility, hid in his hair throughout their wedding night.

For the party, the whole family, many of the townsfolk, plus a couple of Guardia Civil gathered in the garden outside Dolors' house, which would now be Josep's home. The former corn field was hardly visible for the tables dotted across it. Each one had a white table cloth and was circled by mismatched chairs lent by all the neighbors. Dolors vowed that there was no sense in spending money on a restaurant when she was the owner of a bakery. It was also a way to tempt potential customers, all of whom gathered to toast the bride and groom with a rare glass of *xampany*. Josep and Dolors remained joined at the elbow except when bringing out more trays of tomato bread, sausages, and *coca* from the kitchen.

Josep noticed that Núria, in her green dress, followed Àngels all day like an emerald shadow. She seemed so thrilled to have her daughter back that she didn't dare let her leave her sight. During all of Àngels' months of recovery, Núria had been a wreck. All the years of worrying about her children had clearly tattered her nerves. She seemed always on the edge, ready to snap at anything her husband, Albert, unwillingly said to her. Núria had put any energy that was not consumed by worry into building up the co-op, although with limited success. She had told Josep repeatedly that Àngels had to have something to do now that she was home, and Núria needed an occupation.

Núria pulled Àngels to Josep's side and put her arms around the two of them. "You don't know how happy this makes me, to see you so content, my son, and to see you looking so healthy, my dear. This is more than I could ever have hoped for." She paused and caught her breath as if it had been taken from her. "Except for one thing, of course." She looked up at Josep and her eyes misted. "There's just one person missing now."

Josep frowned at his mother. She had promised not to do this. "We agreed that we wouldn't mention his name," he said.

"Have I said his name?" Núria shook her head dislodging a tear from the corner of her eye. "Oh, my dear, Eduard." She covered her face.

"*Mare*," Josep said. "This is not the time, nor the place."

"I know." Núria uncovered her face. "I'm so sorry, *fill*. I'm sorry, Dolors." She smiled at her new daughter-in-law. "I just need to understand what happened between the two of you. If you would just explain." Her eyes begged him. "Another day you must tell me."

"I've told you again and again that there is nothing to tell and I don't want to hear his name," Josep said. "Particularly not on my wedding day." He turned and went into the kitchen to search for more *xampany*, which he hoped would help calm the rage bubbling within him. Ever since his visit to France, Josep had been hearing Eduard's confession echoing in his ears, in his sleep, in his waking hours. It was unforgiveable. He didn't care if the prison had scrambled his mind. Since Josep swore he would never go back, clearly now he could never go back. Nor did he want to.

Dolors followed him inside. "Darling, please don't let this ruin our day. This is our time. Even though they seemed to pay more attention to Àngels than to me." She stood behind him and encircled his waist with her arms. Josep relaxed slightly and let his body fall into hers. Dolors whispered, "Besides, we have a garden full of people out there. What would they think?"

Josep's back stiffened. "I'm starting to suspect that that's all you're worried about." He turned and looked into her face, which, under its uncharacteristic make-up, looked bewildered. "Please tell me you don't really care what those townspeople think."

Dolors' face brightened. "Don't be silly, darling. You know I only have one reason to care about them."

He gave her a questioning look.

"As customers, *amor meu*. Every little taste of my fare that they have here could lure them back, don't you see? I'm just thinking of our future. Unless," she looked at the floor and then at Josep's squinting eyes, "you've put all that money you earned in Canada away somewhere. Our exchange of vows did include our possessions."

Josep felt a chill despite the heat and took a step backward. He couldn't believe that he was hearing this. "Dolors," he said flatly, "you know that there's no money. You've always known that. I've been risking everything to keep my family afloat."

Dolors grasped his hands and pulled him toward her. "Oh, I know, darling. I'm so sorry to ask. I can't help but wonder what you did with it all."

Josep pushed Dolors away more roughly than he intended. "Maybe we should have had this conversation before we got married. I really didn't expect this from you." Josep grabbed a bottle of *xampany* by the neck and walked out the door. As he approached the guests in the garden he felt the heat slowly dissipate from his face, though his heart was still pounding. He felt slightly relieved after releasing the cork on the *xampany* bottle and letting loose all the pressure built up inside it. As he smiled and passed around the bottle, he felt a hand on his shoulder.

"Josep, *fill*."

Josep looked up to see Albert Palau smiling down at him. He squinted at him. "Hello, Albert. I'm not your son."

"Oh, I know. It's a figure of speech." He shook his head and the late afternoon light reflected off his shiny scalp. He raised a bushy eyebrow and said, "Where's your lovely bride? I have something I would like to share with you both."

"She's in the kitchen," he said and filled Albert's champagne glass.

"Do I detect a spat?" Albert shook his head and smiled. "Don't worry, son, I mean, Josep." He grasped Josep's shoulder. "You know, all your mother and I did was disagree through the whole first year of our marriage. Well, almost," he said, this time fluttering both eyebrows. "Besides, once they realize that they need your signature for them to do anything nowadays, they become putty in your hands."

Feeling revolted by the insinuation of Albert and his mother's sex life and by Albert's apparent acceptance of the shackles of the regime, Josep was relieved to see Dolors exit the kitchen. He called out to her. "Darling, Don Albert has something he wants to tell us."

Dolors approached but hardly glanced at her new husband. She smiled brightly at Albert and took his hand. "I'm so happy that you're here," she said.

"Congratulations, my dear. I know that achieving matrimony has been a bit of a challenge for you," Albert said and Dolors released his grip. They all turned and saw that Núria had joined them.

"Darling," Albert said. "I was just about to tell the newlyweds our news."

Núria smiled and nodded. "Yes, do go ahead, dear."

"As a wedding gift to you, I declare you no longer in debt, to me at least," Albert said. "Now that you're even closer family it's no longer appropriate to demand repayment of that loan, so consider it paid."

Dolors smiled, but Josep stumbled forward. "But what will you do to live?" he asked Albert, but he was looking at his mother.

"We have a few plans up our sleeve," Albert said. "Don't worry, I still have acres of land. One day it will be worth a fortune again."

"Yes, dear," Núria said. "Please don't worry. For now we're going to live in just a couple of rooms of the house. It's really too big for the two of us and it's not necessary to have heat or light in all that space. It's really a waste."

"But," Josep began.

Dolors took Albert and Núria's hands. "Thank you so much. This will take some of the pressure off while we are getting started."

Josep frowned at his bride. He was finding that she was rather too selfishly focused on pesetas.

"But," Dolors continued, "This is not a closed matter. As soon as we start making some profit I will pay you back." She kissed them both on either cheek. "You'll just have to get us some dishes or something, like everyone else."

The anger that Josep had felt had now turned to admiration. He put an arm around Dolors' shoulder and hugged her to him.

When all the food was eaten, the *xampany* drunk, and all the people had returned to their respective homes, Josep joined Dolors in her bedroom, where they spent a night that was beyond what he could ever have imagined. The anger that he had felt toward her that afternoon had transformed to a desire unlike any he had ever previously felt, and he was not a stranger to the feeling. When Dolors greeted him in her bedroom doorway wearing nothing but a white flowing robe and hugged him so tightly, uttering over and over again, "I'm sorry, *amor*," he could hardly breathe but for the feeling of her plump breasts flattened against his stomach reminding him to inhale. He clasped her head to his chest and stroked her hair. "I too am sorry, my Lola. I didn't mean to push you. And I am very proud of what you said to Palau." Dolors looked up into his eyes and he kissed her, softly at first, and then more insistently as her lips parted and he could feel the warm tip of her tongue graze his lips. When he abruptly seized her breasts in the palm of either hand, Dolors gasped and stepped backward.

"Please be gentle. Remember, this is a first for me."

Her words helped him surface from the desire that had begun to blind him and he laid her delicately on the bed, slowly stroking her soft, doughy skin, until she demanded with whispering breaths that he knead it more fervently, and that he cover her body with his own.

At daylight when they awoke in a twist of sheets, they proceeded to twist them some more. Throughout the following days and nights, they explored each other's bodies, the reaches of their passion, in almost every room of the house, until one day Dolors awoke and uttered, "I really should get baking. Somebody's got to make a living around here." When she began to climb from the mattress, Josep tried to pull her back, but she stood and put a housecoat around her shoulders. In his nakedness, Josep slid from the bed and pressed his body against her back, cradling her breast in his hands and gliding one hand lower until it reached the fork in Dolors' parted legs. They fell to the little rug warming the floor beside the bed. A short while later, still out of breath, Dolors pulled herself to her knees. "Now, seriously, we've got to give it a rest. We have to feed ourselves, don't we?" She stood and pulled on her robe and descended to the kitchen, where Josep could hear her beginning to bake. The honeymoon was over and real life had begun.

It was not long after this that Josep made his first trips across the border as a true smuggler of contraband. After receiving instruction from Dolors' former supplier, Pep, and a long list of orders from Baltasar, Josep officially had a new trade. Between the list of regular orders, which if all went well he would bring in on a fortnightly basis, and all the goods they would need for the bakery, he could have enough business to keep Dolors baking and to provide a small cushion for his whole family. With the embargo on, he had to be especially careful, since guards were out to catch him on both sides of the border. His first forays into France and back again went off with perfection. He delivered the goods to his customers and returned home with a pocket full of cash. Yet Dolors begged him to give it up.

"Josep, it's too dangerous. The whole time you were away I was worried sick. With this and your political meetings with Baltasar, I feel constantly uneasy," she told him while she grasped his hands in her own. "Don't you miss me when you're gone?" She raised his hands to her chest.

"Of course I do. But Dolors, you need my goods as much as anybody." He gave her right breast a gentle squeeze.

"I know. That's what makes me sick. I can't bear the thought that you are up there because of me." She sank into a chair at the table and covered her head in her arms. Then she looked out from under her elbow shyly. "We do need the supplies. The bakery will go bust without them. What are we going to do?"

"Pep's been a great help, but we can't rely on him. He's taking a long break because he's sure they're onto him."

"I know. What are we going to do?" Dolors threw her hands in the air.

"Tomorrow, to start with, I'm going to check in with the Guardia Civil. It's time already. I'll just have to get a feeling from them. I have to try to make them like me."

"Oh, no." Dolors jumped from the table holding her head with one hand and her stomach with the other. She ran to the sink and began to retch.

***

Àngels and Josep were sitting side by side on the bench at the Guardia Civil station. Àngels was trying to appear calm, though her nerves were sending waves of fear from her stomach to her head. When Baltasar had finally told her that one of the conditions of her return was a monthly visit with the Guardia Civil, she had almost returned to the city. But in order to do this, she would have needed permission from the Guardia Civil themselves. She was just thankful that Josep was here with her. Nonetheless, given his current business activity, Àngels feared the worst, because she had already seen it all. Though she now felt more in control, every morning she still awoke with thoughts of Carme, and every night she fell asleep thinking the same. She was having disturbing dreams in which Carme and her brother Eduard were waltzing around a bonfire, which in turn was circled by a crowd. In the fore she saw her twin Pau, his adolescent face grinning at them as he bounced a baby Joana in his arms. And standing as tall and as bald as ever was her father, though his face was blurred by time. She looked at Josep sitting beside her, alone for once, and saw her opportunity to get some answers.

"So are you going to tell me what happened with Eduard? I know you went to see him," she whispered.

Josep frowned. "I went for you, and for me as well, but it didn't turn out as I'd hoped. I was going to bring him back here to you."

"So why didn't you?"

"You'll have to ask Eduard about that yourself. I wipe my hands of him."

"Just like that? You bury another brother?"

"No, though it seems that he's ready to bury me. I need some time and an apology. If I decide to forgive him it would be for you, and for *Mare*, of course. Right now I think we have more pressing things to worry about."

Àngels' thoughts faded from Eduard to the closed door in front of them and the Guardia Civil standing beside it.

Josep leaned towards her and whispered, "I know I don't have to tell you this, but try not to give them any full answers. Try to appear like you're cooperating. That's what I've been doing since I got back and so far it seems to be working."

Àngels nodded and looked at the guard who was now talking loudly on the telephone. "Yes, I know." She tried not to think of the past interrogations when that strategy did not pan out.

Josep took her hand. "I'm very pleased to see you looking better. You actually appear to be at peace."

"Not exactly at peace, but I do feel better. I still find it hard to accept this hand we've been dealt."

"So do I," Josep said then he whispered, "A group of us are talking about doing something about it." Then he looked up at the desk and changed the subject. "Manel also seems to be recovering."

Àngels nodded and looked him in the eye. Manel was still living in his shack in the garden and given the proximity and their shared tragedy they saw each other almost daily. "Yes, we are all doing much better." She then leaned close to Josep and whispered. "I've seen Dolors look better though."

He grinned widely at his sister. "That's because she's expecting."

Àngels squeezed his arm. "Really? So soon?" She thought of her own pregnancy, the delicate new baby girl, the precariousness and the responsibility and wondered if Josep was ready. "You're sure?"

Josep nodded. "We figured it out last night. You're the first to know. Just wait till *Mare* hears." He swallowed. "I'm thrilled by the thought of being a father, even though I had been looking forward to spending time alone with my new wife." The guard put the phone down as the door opened.

"Josep Balaguer, get in here." Wearing a full uniform and cape even in the summer heat, the Guardia Civil motioned to the room beyond.

Josep squeezed Àngels' hand and walked toward it.

"You, too," the guard commanded, pointing to Àngels. She never thought she would feel such relief at being called into that room. At least she and Josep would be together. She would not have to be alone with them.

Inside the room there was the desk and the window sill where Ivan Puig had sat and tilted his cocky head at her. Now Mayor Vidal, with a significant paunch for his young age, was standing at that window. She also recognized the two guards who ordered her and Josep to stand in the middle of the room.

Abel Vidal turned towards them showing his bursting jacket buttons and strutted around them in a circle. Then he stopped in front of them and leaned on the desk behind him. He removed his hat to reveal hair cropped close to his head. Pointing his hat at Àngels he said, "We won't have any more outbreaks from you."

"No, *señor*." She looked at the floor and shook her head.

"And, you," he pointed to Josep. "What were you doing in the woods yesterday?"

"In the woods?"

"Yes. One of my men saw you."

"I was collecting pine cones for my wife," Josep said soberly.

"Pine cones. Yes. You're married to Dolors Hereu, the baker."

Josep nodded.

The mayor stood, approached Josep and held out his hand, which Josep took reluctantly. "Dolors is a very fine woman. You're very lucky that you're married to her." He put his hat back on. "Believe me."

Then he was looking once again at Àngels. "What's the story with Carles Puig? Why were you shouting my predecessor's name?"

Àngels caught her breath. She had managed to go for months now without thinking about Carles, or feeling afraid of the Puigs. Now the fear and feeling of constantly being watched all surged back.

Josep stepped forward. "It's a very long story. From what I understand, he's gone. Living in Madrid, I believe."

"Yes, that's correct." The guard looked at his pocket watch. "You can tell me about it on another visit. We will have plenty of those." He strutted towards the door. "Now I'm late for lunch."

***

"You didn't tell the mayor that I'm pregnant, did you?" Dolors accused him from behind her bread-covered counter.

"Of course not. I only told Àngels," Josep said trying to ease her into a chair. "Though I was afraid he wanted to arrest us both."

"They won't arrest you," Dolors said shaking her head.

Now Josep was on his feet staring down at her. "How do you know that?"

"While you were gallivanting half way across the world, I was taking care of my future. And now that you are part of it, you should be quite safe."

"I'll have you know I wasn't gallivanting. I worked very hard over there."

"Yet you have nothing to show for it," Dolors said, but then she jumped to her feet. "I'm sorry, darling." She held her head. "It must be the hormones. They're making me say horrible things."

"Maybe you should go to see Baltasar. We really should have him confirm this, don't you think? I'll see him at the meeting later this week. I can ask him."

"Baltasar? I couldn't." She shook her head fervently.

"He's the only doctor in town. What do you expect to do?"

"I wouldn't go to him if he were the last doctor in the country. Not for this. He gave up his right to see that part of me when he ran out that church door."

"Don't be ridiculous. It's not a romantic visit. The man is a doctor."

"I don't care. Your mother can help me. We women have managed on our own for centuries." She hugged his arm. "But don't think you're escaping. I expect you to be here for every grueling moment. I'm so excited." She kissed him.

CHAPTER SIX

DOLORS' BELLY GREW abnormally large: At just six months the bulk under her breasts threatened to keep her from reaching her work table. Regardless, she was not about to let it stop her from baking. She stood on a footstool to make her tall enough to lean over top of her middle so that she could knead her bread and roll her pastry. When Núria came in and saw Dolors' round figure on tiptoe atop a wobbly footstool, she ran to her side and pulled her feet to the floor.

"What do you think you're doing? You could hurt yourself. You could hurt my grandchild," Núria said. She had been thrilled from the moment she heard the news and had dedicated every spare minute to knitting a secret stock of baby booties, jerseys, shorts, and dresses, for her grandson or granddaughter, whichever it would be.

"What am I supposed to do? I have to bake." Dolors wiped her doughy forehead.

"That's enough. I'm not taking no for an answer. Àngels can take care of the co-op. It hardly has any business anyway. I'm coming here to help you," Núria said and went to wash her hands. "It will be like old times," she called. "When is Josep due back?"

"Yesterday," Dolors said and covered her mouth, realizing her mistake.

"When?" Núria rushed toward Dolors, the worry plain on her face.

"Tomorrow, or the day after."

"But you said yesterday. I may be half blind, but my hearing is fine."

"No, I mixed it up," Dolors said. "It's tomorrow. He'll be back tomorrow." Josep had left over a week ago and should have been back by now. Both of the women knew it.

"Àngels did mention that they have one of their political meetings this week," Núria said, trying to sound more optimistic than she felt. She kept telling them how much she hated the idea of Josep sneaking back and forth over the mountains, and of both he and Àngels taking part in a clandestine political group. The meetings at Baltasar's clinic were held discreetly, but nothing was secret in this town. In an attempt to distract herself from her worry, Núria focused on the co-op and now on her arriving grandchild. It also gave her an excuse to get out of the mansion. While she enjoyed Albert's company, Núria found that with their closer living quarters in just two rooms of the big house, his presence was a little too constant. She knew that Dolors was in need of her help, and she was in equal need of it.

Dolors approached Núria and rubbed her back. "*Tieta*, I'm so glad that you're my mother-in-law." She kissed her on the cheek. "If there's a meeting, Josep will definitely be back." She hugged Núria. "He'd never miss one of those gatherings. And I, for one, would be thrilled to have you helping me again."

***

Unaware of his predictability, Josep returned with his back loaded with an overstuffed bag right before dawn on the day of the meeting. He put his bag on the empty table, rubbed his back and stretched his arms toward Dolors, but she stood watching him without budging, wiping her floury hands on her apron. He stepped closer and pulled her toward him.

"Lola, how I've missed you. You look even bigger than you did when I left, if that's possible." He grasped the great ball of her stomach.

Dolors was limp in his embrace. "Yes, it is possible. Where have you been?"

"It's been fascinating," Josep said urging her to sit. He couldn't wait to tell her everything he'd seen. "I've met some incredible people, people really interested in our cause." He jumped to his feet. "I have to go tell Baltasar and the others."

"Right now my cause is being able to stay on my feet all day and making sure I have enough ingredients to earn a living." She rested her hands where her hips used to be. "Who's Marie-Claude?"

Josep sat back down. "Marie-Claude?" He tried to pretend he didn't know what she was talking about, even though he wondered how Dolors knew that name.

She held up a letter. "Marie-Claude in Quebec, Walamasomething."

"Walamagou. That's a letter from Marie-Claude?" Josep grabbed the envelope from Dolors and immediately saw that the seal was torn. "You opened it."

"Yes, I did. It's not from Marie-Claude herself. It's from her father."

The surprise made him forget the issue of his wife reading his post, and Josep said, "Henri? He was such a wonderful man. He took me in, gave me work."

"Gave you his daughter." Dolors raised an eyebrow.

Josep ignored the comment since he didn't know how much Dolors knew of his early days with Marie-Claude and that if things had gone as planned, the Québécoise would be here having his child instead. He quickly pulled the letter out and opened it. It was dated a number of months ago and it was written in French.

September 5, 1946

Dear Josep,

You will be surprised to hear from me, no doubt. Old Henri comes out of the woodwork. You know that before you came to stay with us, I hardly knew anything about your country and its situation. I always thought you were fighting the Communists, but Marie-Claude set me straight one day, in the heat of an argument. As it turns out her leanings are the same. I forgive you both, if that means anything. She told me that even though the Reds lost in your country, you're still isolated from the rest of us. We're not allowed to do any business with the likes of you. That makes an old man like me feel very sad to know that we have been cut off by a bunch of politicians.

Despite everything that happened, in my memories, you are still like a son to me, though you know I would have been happy to have you as a son-in-law. No worries there. Marie-Claude was quick to replace you. She has Thomas now and that little fellow, the son of that Indian woman, to take care of. I won't even get into that. You know how I resented the Indians infringing on my ice business, which by the way, dwindles day by day. Those electric ice-box contraptions are becoming all the more popular, leaving this old man with little to keep him busy.

My favorite work horse died, I'm sure you remember the one. She fell straight through the ice and into the lake. I wish you had been here to help me get her out. Some of the fellows from the lumberyard tried but the cause was lost. They still remember you and ask if I have news of you. I tell them I do not.

I would like to hear from you and I am sure Marie-Claude would too, though she would never admit it. I should imagine that you would also want news of the young Luc fellow. But that is your business.

Sincerely,
Henri Bouchon and family

"You read this?" Josep waved the letter at Dolors.

"I did. Who is Marie-Claude?" She tapped her very swollen foot.

"She was the daughter of the man I worked for."

"I figured that out. What was she to you?"

"She was very special to me at one point. But some things happened that I won't get into. In the end, all I wanted was to come back here."

"Really. So you're keeping your secrets."

"I think it's better that way. Besides, at that time the two of us were just cousins."

"I know." She shifted her enormous belly. "At least something good has resulted from this regime. Between the embargo and the censors it will be difficult for you to have any contact with them. I wonder how the letter even got through."

Josep shook his head to clear his ears. "How you can say such a thing after all we've been through?"

Dolors thrust her stomach towards him. "I forbid you to contact them."

"You can't forbid me to do anything." Josep glared down at her and backed away.

She pouted. "I don't want you to contact any of those people."

"Amor meu, why are you so jealous? You must know that I don't want anyone but you," Josep said and embraced her. "You and our baby, of course." The biting irritation transformed to a surge of love for Dolors and the life inside her and he realized that all his past was exactly that. "If it makes you feel better, I won't contact them again." He knew that it was minor concession on his part, since contact would only serve to stoke his guilt. He would write a short note, however, asking them to try to write in English next time, which would be incomprehensible to his wife, and thus avoid uncomfortable interceptions.

Dolors leaned into Josep. "I know I'm not myself right now, but that would make me feel better." She squeezed Josep's waist.

"I have something that will make you feel better." Josep ran to his bag and took out a small box. He handed it to Dolors. Inside was a tiny pair of leather shoes. Dolors held them on her palm without speaking.

Josep bent down beside her. "You can't find anything like that around here. Our child will not be shoeless."

"They're very sweet and that's very thoughtful," Dolors said putting the shoes back in their box. "But they are also extremely bad luck. What if something happens to the baby?"

"Nothing is going to happen to the baby." Josep kissed the top of his wife's head. "I have to go deliver some of these things before sun-up. I'll be back right after the meeting." He stacked some items in a box, lifted it under his arm, and went out the door.

***

Later, Àngels gathered with Josep and the other five men in their group. Pretending to have doctor's appointments, they met every two weeks on a different day and at a different time in Baltasar's disorganized office. A tangle of instruments sat on the counter and a stack of charts threatened to tumble off his desk, but his appointment book had been cleared of real patients for the rest of the morning. The group members sat looking serious in a circle around Josep, who was practically jumping up and down, excited to share the information he had gained from his trips across the border.

"Over in France there's some unofficial talk about an American called Marshall. They may be planning to give out money," Josep said. His enthusiasm might have been infectious, but Àngels and the others didn't seem to get the point.

"But, Josep." Àngels gave him a disappointed look. "We've been cut off. They've isolated us. The UN has condemned Franco's regime. So we're stuck." She had been taking part in these meetings for a few months now and found that they helped her focus. She convinced herself that she owed it to Carme and to her exiled brother to stay abreast of events. It gave her a purpose again. They couldn't just roll over and take what the fascists were dishing out.

"Sorry to change the subject, but have you had any news from Eduard?" Baltasar asked Àngels, clearly avoiding Josep's gaze.

Josep sighed loudly. "You can talk about that alone sometime. There are some serious political changes about to take place."

"Yes, I have," Àngels answered without looking at Josep. "Just the other day I received a letter from Francine. She's Eduard's wife," she said to the others. "He's in hospital." She looked at Josep out of the corner of her eye and he stiffened.

"His mental health perhaps?" Baltasar asked.

"No. Just some intestinal trouble. She assured me that he will be fine. She said that it's been going on for some time."

Baltasar slapped his thigh. "I wish I could see him. Maybe I could do something. All those camps, the precarious way he's been living, he has certainly been exposed to infection."

"I wish I could see him, too," Àngels said lowering her head.

Josep turned toward them. "I saw him and I confirm he is mad. I don't want to hear another thing about him." Josep began to pace behind them. "We are all risking a lot meeting like this. I don't think we should waste valuable time. What I learned over the border is that the United States might be starting to show some interest in us." Josep sat again in his chair.

"Some interest in Franco, perhaps," Salvador, the former *Maquis* said. "And their fear of the communists," he sniggered. "So they won't send any of that money our way."

Baltasar pointed a tongue suppressor at them. "Why would you think that the US warming to Spain would be a good thing? We need the international community to reject this regime, which is what they have done."

"Yes, that's one way of looking at it," Josep said. "The other way is, if they give us money and it filters down to the people, people like us, and they have enough to live on that their every thought is not only how they will get by today, then, maybe then, we will be strong enough to oppose this regime. If money comes in here, maybe some foreign journalists will follow it. If we can start some protests, the rest of the world might hear about it. That along with all the other protests around Europe might get a response."

"Right now it would seem that Franco is blaming the bad economy, to put it lightly, on our isolation," Salvador said.

"The people are still starving," Àngels said. "The time I spent in Barcelona showed me that life there is different."

"Then there's still the censorship and they are still killing our people."

"Yes, and just try being a woman," Àngels said. "We only exist if we are married, or if we become married to the church. We have to have our husband's approval to travel, to have any money." Her face had turned crimson and the men were staring at her as she continued. "Before we had divorce, abortion, we didn't have to get married, wear long sleeves, cover our heads." Then she shook her finger at the men. "When you think about this regime, try putting yourself in our shoes."

Baltasar approached Àngels and stroked her trembling shoulder. "Àngels." He almost sang her name. "It's all right. We're on your side. We know how bad this is for everyone, especially for our women." He sat down beside her and rubbed her back. As Àngels' nerves calmed, she could feel the comfort of the warmth of his hand even through her pullover. When she looked at Baltasar he was smiling down at her. "Everything will be all right," he said. "Eventually."

"Eventually is right," Salvador said. "If we have to wait for the Americans, or for any outside governments to come to our rescue, or for Franco to distribute any money he receives to us, we'll be living with this regime for decades. We already put our hope in our neighbors and look where we are now."

They all nodded in agreement, except for Àngels. Her thoughts had moved from their political predicament to Eduard living and potentially ill in their neighboring country. She was determined to find out about Eduard's so-called confession to Josep and to bring them all together again. She was convinced that Eduard's reaction was like a flare calling for help but that Josep was too stubborn to recognize the signal.

***

It was a few months later when Àngels and the others found out that Josep's inside information was correct. Franco and the Americans had entered into deliberations. All they could do was wait. As for Dolors, she couldn't wait any longer. She could hardly walk. Núria tried to take over the bakery, but Dolors wouldn't allow it, nor would she believe Núria when she assured her that she did not look like an elephant. Luckily Dolors could not see beyond her stomach to her ankles, which had swelled to almost the same width as her calves. Her foul mood had grown in step with her body. Then, one morning when they were waiting for Josep to return from an emergency trip, Àngels and Núria came face to face with Dolors on her doorstep. She was holding her belly and looking even more uncomfortable than usual. Núria ran to Dolors and held her shoulders.

"Dolors, *maca*, what are you doing out here?" Núria slowly turned Dolors back toward the house but didn't wait for a response. "Sorry I'm late. I had to go find Àngels because I have some wonderful news. Albert has managed to sell a portion of his land, just a small part, but the money will help us live. We'll be able to invest more in the co-op." Núria steered Dolors inside and sat her in a chair. "And you'll never guess who's bought it."

"I certainly didn't," Àngels said, frowning. "In fact, I didn't know anything about it."

Dolors was holding her breath and shaking her head.

"Manel," Núria said. "Yes, our Manel. Apparently he managed to sell his family house in Adiol to some high ranking official in the regime. He's lucky they didn't just expropriate it again. So, he had some money. And we know he has a lot of time. This is perfect for everybody." Núria was so concentrated on her joy that she didn't notice Dolors' growing discomfort until finally Dolors released an exasperated scream.

"What is it, dear?" Núria grasped Dolors' flushed cheeks. She was holding her breath and panting at the same time.

"Let's stand her up," Àngels said. "The baby is on its way."

Dolors nodded and tried to push herself to her feet. "I've been trying to find you," she managed to say.

"Is Josep on his way? Where is he?" Núria said.

Dolors shook her head and bit her lip. Àngels and Núria supported Dolors on either side and walked her in circles around the table. "I know your legs are bursting, but we have to let gravity help. Whoever is in there is enormous," Núria said. Dolors uttered no words, and emitted only screams each time a contraction seized her.

"Let's get her upstairs," Àngels said and they proceeded to push and pull her up the narrow staircase from the bakery toward her bedroom. Once Dolors was lying on the bed she began to yell, "That bastard said he'd be back." She gritted her teeth. "He promised he wouldn't leave me alone for this."

Núria nodded at Àngels, who disappeared out the door.

With every contraction Dolors braced herself against the headboard. Núria helped her out of her underclothes and covered her in a sheet. With all the contractions, the enormous bulge did not appear to budge.

"You're going to have to start pushing," Núria coaxed her.

At the next contraction, Dolors pushed and screamed. And at the next again. When the door opened and Àngels entered with Baltasar Sort behind her, Dolors screamed even more loudly.

"No." She shook her head back and forth on the pillow. "He can't be here. We were doing this alone."

Núria grasped Dolors' hand and leaned down to her. "The baby is too dangerously big. I can't let anything happen to you or to the baby. Josep would never forgive me. And I would never forgive myself."

"Dolors," Baltasar said as he put his doctor's bag down. "Please don't feel embarrassed. I see this all the time. I'm a professional. Besides, Josep asked me to take the best care of you, which I would do anyway." He took out his stethoscope and rested it on Dolors' enormous middle. "Is he not back yet?"

They all shook their heads.

"He spoke to you about helping me?" Dolors demanded.

"Yes, it was all arranged. Don't worry," Baltasar said.

"Bastard," Dolors screamed. Then the door opened and Josep stood with a shocked look on his face.

"Where have you been?" they all shouted at once. Josep stood in the doorway looking at the angry eyes of his wife, mother, sister, and his best friend, but he couldn't tell them where he'd really been, that he had spent the last three days hiding in a cave waiting for a safe moment to escape.

"I'm sorry, I got held up," he said.

They all turned their backs on him, except for Dolors, who couldn't because her legs were spread before him and she was anchored by her mountainous belly.

"Held up?" Dolors shouted. "I'll tell you a little about being held up."

Baltasar looked up from the stethoscope on Dolors' middle and said, "Perhaps, now that you're here you could wait outside. It might be better for everyone."

***

Josep stepped out into the hall and shut the door behind him. He got a chair and placed it right outside the door, where he sat and listened to Dolors' screams, the encouragement of his mother and sister, the mumbling of his best friend, and then the piercing cries of his first born baby. Àngels came out and walked straight past him down the stairs.

"How is she? How are they?" he asked, but she didn't answer. When she returned with a basin of water she didn't even look at him.

Josep jumped to his feet, "What's going on in there?" he demanded, the desperation clear in his voice. If anything happened to Dolors, he didn't know what he would do. The baby continued to cry, and with each of its wails and each moment of silence otherwise, Josep began to panic. He was about to open the door, when it opened itself. Baltasar came out. His normally wayward hair was pasted to his head with sweat. He patted his forehead with his handkerchief and eased Josep back into his chair.

"Josep," he said.

Josep almost jumped from his chair. "Baltasar, what is it, man? How are they?"

"You have a lovely, healthy, very large daughter."

"A daughter? And Dolors?"

"She's resting. It's been an ordeal for her, for her entire body. I have never seen or heard of a baby that size. Your daughter is the size of a six-month old."

"How is Dolors? Will she be all right?"

"She's resting. She's a strong woman; we both know that. But we will need a few days to see exactly how strong she is." Baltasar looked at Josep as if he was trying to gauge his understanding of this message.

"Are you saying that she could die?"

"I am also saying that she could live. We're all going to take excellent care of her. We just can't have any infection. It's essential," Baltasar said and he grasped Josep's arm. "When she does make it, you should know that she probably won't be able to do this again."

"No more children," Josep said, taking stock.

Baltasar shook his head.

"I don't care about that. Just make sure she gets better." He felt so suddenly alone and it terrified him. Baltasar nodded and slapped Josep's arm.

"Can I see them?" Josep asked.

Baltasar motioned for Josep to follow him. Inside the room, Dolors was lying face up on the bed, with a sheet up to her chin. She appeared to be fast asleep. Josep went straight to the bed and stroked Dolors' clammy forehead and kissed her cheek. She was breathing softly and her closed eyes were jerking with the movement of her eyeballs underneath. Her body was quiet but her brain was very active. He kissed each eyelid ever so gently. He then looked toward the baby that was wrapped in a blanket held in the crook of Núria's arm. Àngels was bending over her. Josep put an arm around his sister and looked at his daughter. Her red cheeks were full and she had a shock of black hair.

"Isn't she the sweetest?" Núria said.

"She's enormous," Josep said.

"Dolors is a very strong woman," Àngels said and they all looked toward the sleeping form in the bed. Her chest was rising in shallow breaths, but otherwise she was unmoving.

Josep leaned down until his cheek touched his wife's. It was slightly sticky and rather cool. He put his lips beside her ear and whispered, "Lola, don't abandon me now. Your daughter and I need you."

CHAPTER SEVEN

DOLORS COULD NOT be woken. The family took turns at her bedside, sponging her forehead and arranging her covers, while Josep almost wore the floor away with his pacing. He refused to believe that Dolors would abandon him right when their first child had arrived. Each time he stopped to look at her sleeping form, something inside him withered. "Dolors, Lola, don't leave us now," he would chant in her ear. Still she slept. The peace on her face gave him hope. Surely a dying woman did not look like she was already in heaven. However, when she had still not woken by the second day, they set out in search of a wet nurse. The baby couldn't wait for her mother any longer. Her mouth was searching for food like an airborne fish. When a neighbor who had just given birth to her eighth daughter sat down and put the baby's searching mouth to her nipple, Dolors awoke with a start. With no regard for the trauma to her nether regions, she demanded to see her baby and put her lips to her swollen breast. The creature sucked ravenously until Dolors' milk was gushing as much as her happiness. As Dolors' breasts emptied Josep felt utter relief and pride. He sat on the bed at their side and did not remove his arm from Dolors' shoulders. He kissed her cheek, her ear, her head, her lips. Núria and Àngels took turns holding her hand. Josep was sure that if he had believed in God, it was at that moment he would be kneeling down to thank him.

"What a fright you gave us all," Núria said stroking Dolors' forehead.

"The entire town," Àngels added. "The kitchen is full of baskets of squash, potatoes, bottles of wine, anything that people could spare. They were all afraid to lose you."

"Me or my bread," Dolors said and switched the baby to her other breast. "I'd rather not know the answer."

"Yes, you would. Remember, they used to resent you," Àngels said. "It shows that all those *flams* for birthdays and saint's days may be earning the respect that you wanted."

Baltasar examined Dolors one last time and said, "You're going to be fine. You just need some rest. You'll be able to bake lots of bread, but you shouldn't be doing that again." He patted her still very swollen belly.

Josep expected Dolors to crumble there on the bed, but instead she shook her head in emphatic agreement. "Not on your life," she said and stretched her hand toward Baltasar. "Thanks to you, Baltasar, my daughter and I are well." She grasped his fingers. "I'm sorry I yelled at you. In the end, I think we made a good team."

"You are a brave woman." Baltasar squeezed her hand. He looked at Josep and the baby. "What are you going to call her?"

"Montserrat," Dolors said looking at the suckling baby in her arms.

"After the mountain?" Baltasar asked.

"Yes, for her sheer size," Josep said. "It's fitting, don't you think?"

"I was thinking after the Virgin Montserrat," Dolors said.

Both men shook their heads, "No, definitely the mountain." The baby tried to suck Dolors' emptied breast and wailed.

As Montse grew, her body always appeared six months older than her real age. With Dolors' steady flow of milk and the odd piece of pastry, the baby filled out even more, much to Dolors' delight. Her child was not going to be a malnourished post-war baby. As Dolors became more familiar with her daughter, her mumbles, her screams, and her smells, she appeared to forgive her for almost killing her. She learned to whirl around her kitchen with Montse on a hip and to knead her bread with her free hand. When Núria came to help, they would juggle the baby, the loaves, the *flams*, the *cremes*, and the *coques* between them. Núria was so absolutely thrilled with her granddaughter that Dolors and Josep often had to persuade her to go home. At first Josep was concerned that life in the Palau mansion was not all roses, but then he realized just how consumed Núria was with Montse, and then how concerned she was for him. Every time he was about to take a trip across the border, Núria would start to fuss about Montse, her gas, her diaper rash, and she would delay going home. Finally, one day when he was about to step out the door, Núria grabbed his sleeve and insisted he stay.

"Surely you can find some other type of work here. You can help us with the co-op. I hear they may need our goods in Adiol. Something about a ski resort. Plus there may be orders from other towns." She grabbed his sleeve. "Stop going into the woods. One day they'll kill you and I won't be able to stand it." She sniffled loudly. "You would kill me. Is that what you want? Dolors, tell him."

Dolors slowly eased Núria's grip from Josep's sleeve. "I don't like it any more than you do. But what else can we do? With the rationing I need any extra sales I can get. Besides, I think I have it all covered."

"What do you mean all covered?" Josep asked. His contact with the border guards had been too close for comfort of late, but he had refrained from mentioning it to anyone. He thought it wiser not to compound their fears. Now it seemed that his wife once again had the inside track.

"You know that I supply them," Dolors said. "The Guardia Civil. They know I'm getting my goods somewhere. They also know that if I stop getting them, so will they. I have been laying the foundation of this for years. Neither of you has to worry." She shifted Montse to her other hip with her now very solid arms. "Besides, could it be possible that they're not as bad as we think? I mean, if Eva Perón will meet with Franco."

"I don't want to hear any more about Eva Perón, Argentina, or any of that nonsense. You sound more infatuated with her than The Caudillo is," Josep said.

"That would be difficult," Núria said.

"She is very elegant." Dolors smoothed her hair with the hand that wasn't holding Montse. "I'm just saying that maybe we're taking their harshness too seriously."

"I'll ask them that next time they're interrogating me. In fact, maybe I'll ask Carme," Josep said and turned for the door.

Dolors grabbed Josep's arm. "If there were reason to worry, wouldn't I be the most worried of anybody? What would Montse and I do without you?"

"What would we do?" Núria said and covered her face with her hands. "I've already lost one young son and I feel like I've lost Eduard as well. If you insist on going over there, why don't you try to see him?"

Josep felt the same boiling of anger and frustration. "I've told you again and again, don't mention his name. I've always made all the effort. I had him released from prison. I spent years away because of him. If he wants to try to make it up to me, he knows exactly where I am."

Núria uncovered her teary eyes. "You are both too proud for your own good. Just like your father. If you must go, please be careful out there."

"For us," Dolors added.

"I need to go now. I need every moment of darkness." He hugged Núria, kissed Montse, and rested a hand on Dolors' shoulder. He looked at her as if she were a code he was trying to decipher. Looking away, he tried to blink repeatedly so that she would not see the damp in his eyes. He knew that he would never really feel at ease, and that there was indeed plenty of reason for worry. Despite what Dolors said, these were not people to be trusted to keep their word for a loaf of bread.

***

Over the months, Àngels eventually forgave Manel for not consulting her about his decision to buy part of Sr. Palau's forest. He said that she would have tried to talk him out of it, so he hadn't given her the chance. After revealing that he'd always had an interest in carpentry and using his little shack in her yard as an example, he took Àngels down to a similar shack he had erected as his workshop in the middle of his plot of forest. It was well connected to the roads in and out of the Palau sawmill and Don Albert even lent him some of his men to log a small area and saw the timber. Manel was learning about reforestation, and he would have an endless supply of wood for his work. Àngels at first was very skeptical. Then one day, Manel dragged her down to the forest by the hand and made her cover her eyes outside the door. When he opened the door and she uncovered her eyes, she realized he was an artist; before her was the most intricately carved bed she had ever seen. Its entire headboard was inset with ornate fruit and flowers, birds in flight, and four giant posts spiraled upward as if the birds were carrying the bed skyward.

"Manel," Àngels gasped. "It is absolutely beautiful."

"It's for you," he said.

"For me?" she said and stepped backward. "Oh no, I couldn't. I have a bed."

"You don't have a bed like this one. I made it especially for you." He beckoned her closer. "See here, this little house." He pointed to a spot on the headboard. "That's your house, see?"

"Yes, I do see," Àngels said thinking it did greatly resemble her little cottage but feeling ill at ease with such an extravagant present. "It's beautiful, but I can't accept it. Manel, you're meant to make a living at this. You'll have to sell it, and I don't have enough to buy it."

"So you do like it then? You're saying that if you had enough money, you would buy it. Even though that, of course, was not my intention. Consider it sold."

Àngels backed away and shook her head, "No, no. I said I can't. Besides I doubt it would fit upstairs."

"You have a little free time from the co-op, right?"

"A little, perhaps," Àngels said thinking that in fact she should be dedicating more time to securing orders and filling them. The women were managing to bring in the materials but they would need more people to sell them to.

"All I ask in exchange for this bed is that you work here with me a couple of afternoons a week."

Àngels held up her hands. "Wait a minute. How did this happen? You've managed to sell me a bed I don't need and to make me work for you." Then she laughed. "I should get you working at the co-op doing sales. We do have some potential customers in Adiol."

"Who better than a native to sell to them then," Manel said. "We could help each other out."

Despite her usual misgivings about Manel, Àngels found for some reason that she couldn't resist his offer. Spending more time with Manel would be a change from the co-op and she even felt a slight tingle at the newness of it. Manel was quite intriguing, in fact, and the bed was a work of art.

"When you come here, you could bring Víctor, after school. I could teach him about carving," Manel said, stepping closer.

"All right, let's try it. But I will also tell my mother that we have a new salesman for the co-op."

Manel held out a hand. "And I will try to figure out how to have this bed delivered."

Àngels took his hand and they shook in agreement.

The day that a rickety truck brought Àngels' new bed to her door, Àngels wasn't at home. She was on her way to the town hall where she had been summoned. Josep was walking alongside her.

"I don't know what they could want now," Josep said. "I hope it's not because of all the sloppy people getting into this contraband business."

"I hope they're not trying to dispose of their competition," Àngels said trying to joke, but her insides were in a knot. The fact that they were being made to come earlier, and that they had really only demanded to see Àngels, made her particularly uneasy.

Josep had insisted on coming, certain that the meeting must be for the two of them. He stopped walking and turned to look at Àngels. "I can't give it up," he confessed. "There is a thrill in it. Every time I cross the border it's like a little victory against them. I've managed to make so many contacts. They're mushrooming. Remember how it felt when you brought us our supplies that day at the end of the war? It must have been similar. It's like a tingling feeling that keeps me alive. I can't stop. If I stopped and had to just stay here in town, I think I would die of boredom," Josep said and started walking again.

"*T'entenc.*" Àngels stopped this time. "I understand, but don't you think you reach a point where you want life to be simple? Livable? After all your years abroad, do you really want to spend so much time away from your family? I'm just thankful to have Víctor to take care of. It gives me a more human purpose. Our political meetings are important, but there's so much anger."

"When I finally got back here, before I married Dolors all I wanted was stability. Now that I have it, I'm climbing the walls. After all the trials in my life, this small town lacks, well, adventure. Plus the smuggling is going so well that I have more orders than I can handle, many being from my wife." Josep squinted down at his sister. "How old is Víctor now? About nine?"

"He'll soon be eight. Why?" she asked, suspicious.

"I'm going to need some help. No one would suspect a child, and he would blend well with the night."

Àngels pulled hard on Josep's sleeve. "Don't be ridiculous. He's a child. You're not going to pull him into this. His entire existence revolves around suffering. Now that you have your own family, you should understand. Maybe you need to think more about Dolors and Montse before you head out there."

"Dolors supports my trips. At first she was resistant and begging me to stay, but now she seems quite keen to have me go. Most of the goods are for her."

"Does that make you feel happy, that she's glad to see you go?"

"I hadn't thought about it that way," Josep said. "Dolors loves me. I'm not concerned about that. Besides, we more than make up for it when we're together," he said and nudged Àngels. "I do think about my family, all the time. I'm here with you now, aren't I?"

Àngels nodded. "What about Eduard?"

Josep stopped again. "What about him? I need a huge apology and he knows where I am." He took her arm and whispered. "Why? Do you have news?"

"I think he's not well," Àngels said and put a hand to her pocket where she could feel the freshly opened envelope from Francine.

"I can vouch for that. He's not himself and he hasn't been in years," Josep said.

"I think now it's more physical. Why don't you just swallow your stupid pride and go see him?" she asked, although she had a mind to go and see him herself. She was petrified by the thought of crossing those same woods she had trekked with Carme, the same forest that had devoured her friend.

Josep looked at her and appeared to be bursting. "Listen. Remember all that time I was stranded in Canada? It was because of him. He stole all my money and deserted me there. He confessed to it."

Àngels looked as if he had slapped her. "He stole your money?" She frowned and shook her head. Now she felt more worried than ever. She needed to find out more, since something more than his health must be wrong with him. "Eduard would never do that. And if he did, he had to have a good reason. Maybe it's because he needs our help."

Josep threw his hands in the air. "I gave up enough of my life trying to save him. You can try if you want. Now I need to save myself." Josep took Àngels' hand as they arrived at the door to the town hall. "And my other family."

"Yes, well, one day you may find that you really miss him. I do. And I do appreciate you coming with me today." She watched as the door opened before them.

No one else was there, yet they waited endlessly on the usual bench, with the giant portrait of Franco staring down at them, the only thing to look at. Finally they were called into the meeting room where Mayor Vidal, with the same bursting buttons on his jacket, was sitting on the desk and twirling his hat on his index finger.

"What have you been doing in the woods," he said and slammed his hat onto the desk.

"I've," Josep began.

"I'm talking to you," he said pointing his boot at Àngels and running a hand through his hair as dark as petrol.

Àngels stood up straight and looked clearly surprised by the question. "Me?"

"Yes, you," the mayor said. "We've seen you down there twice now. What's your explanation?"

"It is a simple one. I've been helping our friend, Manel Masplà, with his carpentry. I am sure that you are aware that he now owns part of that land."

"Yes, of course we are aware of that." He scanned them both with narrowed dark eyes. "We are aware of everything. What exactly does this help consist of? Will he corroborate this?"

"Yes, Manel will speak for me. I help him with his orders, the wood, the deliveries, that sort of thing."

"Really? No illegal publications or other illegal activity?" He stared at her. "No contraband?" He looked at Josep.

"No, he's just making furniture, though not many people can afford to buy it right now," Àngels said.

"What are you insinuating?"

Josep stepped forward. "I think we all recognize that there is not excess money for spending. Perhaps you need some furniture or some socks? The knitting co-op is barely running. It would help."

"My wife buys bread every day. Your wife has guaranteed income as a supplier of rations." Mayor Vidal looked from Josep to his boots. "It's not our fault. Those Americans and their Mr. Marshall have passed us by, even after The Caudillo made such an impressive proposal for them." He stood to attention. "It's just a matter of time. Franco will win them over. He always wins."

Josep and Àngels nodded and backed toward the door.

"Before you go, you still haven't told me about Carles Puig."

Àngels stopped and stiffened.

"What about him?" Josep asked.

The mayor ignored Josep and turned to Àngels. "I've asked you again and again: What have you got against him that you were shouting his name out there?" He motioned toward the square.

"Nothing more than anyone else," she said. "I am not the only one pleased to see him transferred to Madrid. Some people have even gained new positions."

The mayor looked at her and inhaled loudly through his nose. "You should be careful with your accusations." He took a slow step forward. Then he took another. "Carles did have few friends in the end." He raised his club toward her. "But he did have a liking for you. He told me all about it."

Àngels' back was against the door but she didn't remember moving toward it. She had her hand on the doorknob because she feared she would collapse. At that moment, all she wanted was to escape.

"I have to meet my boy at school," she said and pushed the door.

"You do that. And tell Manel Masplà that I want to speak to him," Mayor Vidal said.

Outside, Josep hugged Àngels. She felt her entire body shaking. Josep stroked her hair.

"You have to put up a strong front," Josep said. "They find your weakness and scratch at it until it festers." He rocked her back and forth and then steered her out of the square, past the great tree, out of sight of the nosy patrons in the bar.

"I was strong, Josep," Àngels said, her lower lip trembling. "You would have been proud of me. I was really strong when all this began."

"I know you were," he said and embraced her again. "I've always been proud of you."

Josep kept his arm around Àngels the whole way home. When they opened the door to her house she called Víctor's name and when he answered, she saw him sitting comfortably on Manel's giant bed, which filled the corner next to the fireplace. Both she and Josep stood with their mouths gaping.

"What do you think?" Manel's voice said from behind them. "You weren't here, so we set it up. We couldn't get it up the stairs, but it fits perfectly there, doesn't it?" It was tucked nicely into the corner and the birds carved into the bed posts appeared to be flying into the rafters.

"It's really comfortable." Víctor bounced up and down.

"It is absolutely beautiful," Àngels said beaming. All traces of her fear and sadness had gone. She kissed Manel on either cheek. They both turned to look at the bed. It was a far cry from the straw mattress that had been there since her childhood.

"*Mare* Àngels, come and try it," Víctor said and reached for her. Àngels felt the force of his pull from far across the room. She headed straight for the bed and gently sat beside Víctor and put an arm around his growing shoulders.

"It's wonderful," she said and stroked the mattress and the smoothness of the wood with her other hand before extending it towards Manel. He came towards them and sat carefully on Víctor's other side.

From the doorway, Josep watched and felt such relief to see Àngels happy again, even if it was Manel and not him who had managed to achieve it.

Throughout the many months to come, Josep found himself forced to expand his customer base to larger territory due to the growing competition in smuggling. Then came what appeared to be good news for his business and bad news for their plight against Franco. The French had reopened the border, thereby eliminating the risk of Josep being caught by patrols on their side, while also lifting the country's censure of the regime. Àngels was devastated and Dolors was ecstatic. The only aspect that they hadn't contemplated was the increased watch by the Guardia Civil, since the job of patrolling the border had become theirs alone. Meanwhile, Josep still found that the smuggling competition was becoming fierce and, in his opinion, very amateur, thus the risks were even riskier.

Then, not long before Montse's second birthday, two cells collided and danger appeared in its most human form. Dolors was pregnant again. Josep feared that she would be upset, but she took the news remarkably in stride. Although Dolors seemed to hang on to Baltasar's every word, she had gradually refused to accept his warning that Montse's birth would be her last. Yet, the idea of another pregnancy and the ordeal of delivery did not thrill her. Plus she said she feared that her body would again swell to extremes that would keep her from baking. For Josep, the thought of Dolors carrying and delivering another baby seemed even riskier than his trips over the border. Although he didn't believe in it, he feared they were tempting fate. They had been blessed by Dolors' full, swift recovery the last time and asking her body to withstand that trauma once again was just too cheeky. He didn't want to risk it, but it was out of their hands now. Abortion was no longer an option under the current regime. Regardless, Josep knew that it was not an option that Dolors would consider, even to save her life. So as her belly grew, they kept a careful eye on its bulk and were relieved to find that a baby of normal size seemed to be growing within.

As she had all the days beforehand and each day of her pregnancy, Dolors awoke well before dawn to start baking. With the flour, salt, and yeast that Josep delivered, Dolors made the finest bread in the area, which was not a great undertaking, given the general lack of everything but hunger. She sold it on the sly for a reasonable price, since unlike others in the business, Josep refused to let her take advantage of her position. Dolors clearly took pains to see that every customer who entered her shop appeared special. Everyone was greeted with an "*Hola, maca*," or "*Hola, maco*" in Catalan, or a *guapa* or *guapo* in Spanish, depending not on whether they were nice, handsome, or pretty, but on their closeness to the powers that be. When Mayor Vidal's wife or any of the Guardia Civil entered the bakery, Dolors always seemed to know before she turned to face them. She swore the bell above the door rang more shrilly. She said she could feel it in her entrails, and as the months went on, the baby inside her seemed to have the same instinct: whenever the Guardia Civil entered it gave her a whopping kick. In her worry for Josep, and for Àngels as well, she gradually gave the officers more bread each week, which in turn brought them more frequently to her shop. Àngels and the rest of the family warned her that being associated with the Guardia Civil would not only look bad for the family, it could alienate other customers and undermine her business. Already many of the townsfolk resented her for making a living from their need for bread. While Dolors insisted that her coziness with the authorities was for Josep's protection, he and many others began to suspect that she was beginning to enjoy their company.

"What is it with your wife and the *Feixistes*?" Salvador the *Maquis* asked Josep at one of their political meetings. "My wife says that every time she lines up for bread rations, the Guardia Civil strut to the front."

"Yes, I know." Josep shook his head. His face flushed.

"I realize Dolors is doing it because she thinks it will protect you, but don't you think it's a little too close for comfort?" Baltasar said. He looked very concerned. "Distance may be better given your line of work."

"Yes, I know." Josep continued to shake his head. "I've discussed it with her, but she still feels it's the best strategy. She claims that she has no political feelings either way."

"Dolors' political feelings are personal," Baltasar said. "She always has been most interested in what's best for Dolors, sweet thing that she is."

Àngels cleared her throat. "Baltasar, I'll remind you that while you're accusing her of one thing, she might just surprise you by doing another in secret."

Baltasar sat in his seat and looked at his lap. "Yes, Àngels, you're so right. You don't need to remind me of that." He raised his head and looked at her with apologetic eyes. "So are you enjoying working with Manel? I heard he's even made you some furniture."

Àngels looked away. "Yes, the bed and the cupboards and shelves. They're lovely," she said, though she didn't know why she felt so embarrassed. It was only Baltasar. "I'm helping him organize his workshop for now. Then he's going to help get orders for the co-op."

"So you feel you can really trust him then?" Baltasar asked. "I'm concerned about you."

"I do," Àngels said and shrugged. "Please don't worry. I'm so much better than I was."

"I truly hope so," Baltasar said and turned to Josep. "How is Dolors anyway? She is almost there now and luckily everything appears normal."

"I get more nervous the bigger she gets," Josep said.

"I did warn you, but I'm sure everything will be fine. There's only one way out now." Baltasar raised a splayed eyebrow.

"Shall we get to grander matters?" Salvador said. "Chairman Mao has declared The People's Republic of China. I hope Franco is trembling."

"I certainly am," Josep said.

***

When Josep and Àngels arrived at the bakery after the meeting, Dolors was in labor. This time, although the baby appeared to be of normal size, Dolors insisted that Baltasar should be present for the birth, just in case. They all agreed on the wisdom of this given the risks and so Josep ran to fetch him. It was a fortunate choice. When it appeared that the labor would be as easy as baking a loaf of bread, particularly given the elasticity after the last birth, complications arose when a foot protruded rather than a head. Baltasar was forced to do some very skilled maneuvering in a very delicate area until another baby girl shot out, bottom first.

"You are so lucky to be malleable down there," Baltasar said, congratulating Dolors and Josep on the arrival of their second daughter. Josep had entered the room looking equally exhausted by the short wait, but the sight of Dolors' flushed face and the red baby in her arms quickly revived him. They both nodded when Baltasar added, "You probably shouldn't try that again."

"I agree, but at least it all turned out fine this time." Josep kissed Dolors' cheek. "You are conscious." Then he kissed the purple cheek of his new daughter. "And you are precious." Josep was mesmerized by the sight of such a tiny, delicate creature, with her eyes hardly open. "Let's hope she doesn't go about doing everything backwards." He really was truly ecstatic and wished for all of them to know it, for he knew that Dolors feared that he was disappointed not to have a son.

"She's adorable. She looks just like her mother," Josep said glowing over the two of them. "I think I have an idea for a name."

"Really? What is it?" Dolors asked looking more apprehensive than she had during her whole pregnancy.

"Rosa. Don't you think it would make a wonderful tribute to my father?" Josep asked, though he also secretly hoped the gesture would both appease his father and erase his falling face from his memory.

"Yes, his rose bushes." Dolors winced. "I suppose it's a good sturdy name for a flower. I like it. Rosa." She listened to the sound of the name and kissed her daughter on the forehead. "Welcome to our family, Rosa Balaguer i Hereu."

Núria came in the open bedroom door, with young Montse tottering at her side. While his elder daughter hadn't been walking for long, Josep already recognized her determined footsteps. She released her *iaia*'s hand and bounded towards the bed. A smile wedged into her cheeks and she flung her arms around Josep. Looking at Rosa, she kissed her on the forehead and while smiling at Josep, she slapped Rosa's newly breathing nose. It was then that Montse heard her sister's first cry.

"That's enough." Josep lifted Montse from his lap and handed her to Núria.

"The poor thing didn't mean it." Dolors pulled Montse to her side.

Josep kept his arm around Dolors while he admired the wrinkled face of his new daughter, thinking it was the sweetest face he had ever seen.

"What a harmonious family you make," Baltasar said before lifting his hat and ducking out the door.

The harmony continued for quite a number of years, during which time Josep noticed the little hair he had left at his temples was specked with gray and despite all his exercise climbing through the mountain, his love handles were swelling. He figured it must have been from sampling the savory fruits of all his efforts. For her part, Dolors squeezed them proudly. Josep was away for many days on end and Dolors always seemed elated to see him come through the door. At times he wondered if she was more pleased to see him or the goods that he brought her. For now he limited most of his shipments to necessities for the bakery since so many others from near and far had joined in the trade. Most, however, were using the roads and public buses, while the more daring had acquired cars and trucks. Since Josep couldn't compete with their speed or quantity, he was thankful that Pujaforta was closer to France on foot than by road. He made more frequent trips and brought goods in a little at a time. It all went smoothly until the first time he was caught. He had climbed all the way across the mountain and back and was just exiting the woods carrying a small pack containing almonds and flour for All Saints Day *panellets*. When he came face-to-face with a Guardia Civil, he feared the worst and expected to be arrested on the spot. Fortunately for him they only confiscated his goods. Yet in the short walk home, Josep dragged his heels, unsure how he would explain his empty pack to Dolors. She would be livid. But when he opened the door he found both Dolors and Núria in celebration.

"They're ending the rationing," Dolors said. "I'll be able to bake whatever I want right out in the open."

Núria helped Josep off with his coat. "And this means you can stay here. There's no need for you to risk your neck with all this illegal business."

Dolors pulled out a chair for him. "See, maybe they were right about The Caudillo getting this country back on track. So, where are the ingredients for the *panellets*?"

"With the Guardia Civil," Josep said and took off his shoes.

"You were caught?" Núria covered her mouth.

"So there are no almonds, no flour?" Dolors held her temples.

"No, there aren't, but I'm here. They didn't arrest me."

"Thank the Lord," Núria said.

"Thank The Caudillo, or thank me," Dolors said. "It shows that my strategy has worked." She put her arms around Josep's shoulders and squeezed.

Núria brushed off his jacket. "At least now with no more rationing you won't have to leave again. You can stay in Pujaforta and help with the co-op. Àngels and Manel have just brought in a good order from Adiol. Someone Manel knows. They said something about a new ski hill. They want to attract French people because that's what the other hills do. Putting boards on your feet to fly down a hill is something I'll never understand, though your father was always keen to try it. Regardless, things are looking up," Núria continued. "Between the end to the rationing and the opening of the border, both the bakery and the co-op should be back on their feet."

"My bakery always had firm footing," Dolors said. "I have a thought. Maybe Manel and Àngels can ask the ski resort if they want to buy some of my bread or *coca* as well."

"What a wonderful idea, now that it's all out in the open," Núria said. "Josep, why do you look so crushed? You should be thrilled that you can stay around here with us."

"Of course, I'm pleased," Josep said, though he couldn't imagine himself spending all day every day in either the bakery or the co-op. He feared that life in Pujaforta would be too small for him. At some point he knew he would need a dose of adrenaline. "Perhaps I could make some trips to Adiol then, or to some of the other resorts."

"That's a perfect idea," Dolors said. "You and Albert can go together. It will get both of you out of our hair."

The entire family worked for months to fill the special order of knit wear and baked goods for Adiol and other towns in the area. Everyone applauded Manel and Àngels for their work as sales partners, though they seemed to forget the small capacity of the co-op. Dolors, however, was convinced her bakery could meet the demand. She was always elbow-deep in flour, and her smile was dazzling. Josep and Sr. Palau made weekly deliveries of socks, sweaters, scarves, gloves, and mittens, as well as bread and *coca* to Adiol and other towns using Sr. Palau's car. During the trips, Josep was glad to see the mountain from the perspective of the roads and was also happy to breathe some non-Pujaforta air. While Albert seemed glad of the same, he did continuously sing the benefits of staying in town with Dolors and their two daughters, the main one being the physical attentions of his wife. Josep received too much nudging from his mother's husband and tried to keep any other unsettling images of the man and his mother from his head.

On one trip down into the valley that housed Adiol at the base of a giant tree-covered basin, they heard the news of The Caudillo's latest plan. Rather than one of the biggest ski resorts in the Pyrenees, the Adiol valley was to become one of the deepest reservoirs in the country and would supply endless liters of water to a parched nation. All that was needed was a dam.

When Josep returned home with the news, both Àngels and Manel were devastated, but not due to the cancellation of their orders.

Manel looked like Josep had personally drowned his town. "They're flooding Adiol? Just like that?"

"They'll rebuild on the high land. Everyone will be relocated," Sr. Palau said. "Just think how lucky you are that you sold the house when you did. Poor sod who bought it."

Manel held his head. "They'll bury it under water."

Àngels sat beside him and withdrew into herself. "What about Carme?" she whispered and looked as if her mind might scramble all over again. "She could be buried near there. It's the last place I saw her alive." A tear ran from the corner of her eye as she looked at Manel. She was clearly worried that this would be too much for him.

"My parents are buried there," Manel said. "My brothers are lost to me and now they're flooding the only family I know how to find."

"They'll have to move the cemetery," Josep said, trying to help. He feared that if Manel cracked again, Àngels could be quick to follow.

Àngels put an arm around Manel. "Whose side are you on?" she said to Josep.

"Ours obviously," Josep said and tried to change the subject. "That's why I am attempting to find out what will happen with our orders. Dolors will be particularly upset. Luckily we've already delivered most of them and there are other towns nearby that need them."

"It would be best if you took care of that," Àngels said and looked at Manel who failed to react at all.

***

While Josep managed to take care of customer relations, the news had sent Manel into another downward spiral. Àngels worked by his side in the carpentry shop but she noticed that his workmanship was failing. It was as if they were capsizing their neighboring town with his whole family in it. As Àngels tried unsuccessfully to cheer Manel, she also tried keep at bay the images of Carme that seeped into her thoughts. Carme struggling for air, a wave of water in her face, the grit from the common grave in her screaming mouth. They needed to close their reopened wounds. Àngels attempted to stay balanced as she had in the past by focusing on the most important man in her life: Víctor. Finally, she suggested they join together as they had done years earlier. As the flooding began in the town down the mountainside, Àngels, Manel, and Víctor gathered at the garden shrine to Carme and Artur. First they stood holding hands and then they planted perennials so that every year they would bloom in their memory.

***

Once the new Adiol was built and water covered the old town except for the tip of the church steeple, Josep had no place of escape and began itching for a trip to France. Adiol la Nova was just up the road, too close by and he felt the need for a true getaway. Yet at the same time, he knew that during any time away he would miss his wife and seeing his growing girls before adolescence abducted them and their interest in their father. But before he could suggest a trip to Dolors she suggested it herself. She was sifting the new whole wheat flour she'd just had delivered and was wrinkling her nose. "This is not good enough," she said. "Look, it's coarse, not fine and smooth. The bread just doesn't taste the same as it used to."

Josep pinched some flour between his fingers and rubbed, feeling his opportunity. "It is awfully rough. Do you want me to fetch some of the old flour? I could make a quick run over the border. You could mix it with this flour, smooth it out and stretch it further."

Dolors looked as if he had read her mind. She clasped her hands together. "Would you do that? Do you still have the contacts?"

"Contacts for what?" Núria had just entered with Montse and Rosa grasped by the hand. The girls now reached her above her waist, and Montse was considerably wide.

Josep cleared his throat. "For some goods."

"What? Not that again." Núria covered the girls' ears.

"For some flour," Dolors said. "And maybe some of that super fine sugar you used to get, and some almond extract, and some of that butter."

"Are you out of your mind?" Núria said.

"You know that my bread and *coca* haven't been as good as they used to be," Dolors said. "Besides, it's not so dangerously illegal without the rationing."

"The flour we have here is absolutely fine," Núria said. "These are your own little obsessions, Dolors. And for that you would send my son, your husband, trekking through the woods all over again."

"*Mare*," Josep said. "I suggested it. I want to go." He couldn't let his mother talk them out of it now. While he was sure that the local flour was more than edible, he imagined that for Dolors the thrill of the risk accounted for the French flour's better taste. They had a definite point in common.

"You should stay here and take care of your family, your sister. But if you're so keen on going to France, go and see your brother while you're there," Núria said.

Josep held up his hands and felt his previous excitement disappear. He didn't give her the satisfaction of an answer.

Dolors appeared so ecstatic to have her flour back again after so many years that every time Josep returned with a bag, she sank her fingers into the flour and sighed. Then she would run her fingers through his disappearing hair. The return of her quality goods brought back the passion to their marriage, which continued for years to come. Josep was sure that his regular short escapes from the house were the recipe for a loving, enduring marriage. While he was away, his thoughts were on his mission as well as on his wife and their shared excitement on his return. Dolors showed such enthusiasm when he arrived that when she hugged him he had to steady himself and the heavy bag on his back. He felt that the constant backaches were a small price to pay for their mutual happiness. Josep and Dolors lived in the bliss of this arrangement for numerous years, until once again the impossible occurred. When Dolors realized that she was pregnant again, she who had always praised Josep's goods, became enraged about the quality of his imports. The French condoms he brought back were defective. Fearing the end of the volcanic abundance of their sex life, Josep insisted that it wasn't the fault of the merchandise itself.

"These things happen," he said and took her hand.

Dolors shook his hand away. "Then let them happen to you."

"I wouldn't let anything happen to my Lola." Josep once again took her hand and stroked it. Then he ran her palm across the pile of flour on the counter. "Doesn't that feel good?" he whispered with his lips on her ear.

"What was I thinking?" She grasped a handful of flour and rubbed it down his face before kissing him wildly.

The passion lasted for most of the first two trimesters, but as Dolors' girth grew, the flour, the sugar, no matter how smooth or sweet, seemed to turn her stomach. She went for weekly visits to Baltasar's office, but still it did not calm the nerves that were causing it. "What if I die?" she asked Josep one day. "I can't leave Montse and Rosa without a mother."

"You won't die. I won't let you and neither will Baltasar. You see him all the time. He must be reassuring you," Josep said sensing a radical change in his wife.

"Baltasar I trust," she said, her face reddening and her eyes filling with a look that was not her own. "But you. I think this is what you were after all along, bringing me all this flour. You know how it excites me."

"I'm the one who risked my neck and other parts to get those French letters. They're not so easy to come by."

"It's no wonder if they don't work. Who in their right mind would use them?" Dolors' hands were on her very wide waist and she was loudly tapping her foot. "But you knew that, didn't you. You seduced me. Anything to have a son."

All words left Josep's mind. He was too stunned to speak until finally he became angry instead. "Seduce you? A son?" He shook his head. "You're my wife and when did I ever say I wanted a son? I am thrilled with my daughters and until a few moments ago I was thrilled with my wife. Are you really accusing me of getting you pregnant on purpose?"

"No, I'm accusing you of trying to kill me," Dolors said and looked at the bakery around her. "You'll get all of this. Everything I've worked for. Then you can share it with your darlings from Canada. I saw those pictures that Rosa found of your life before me. I wouldn't be surprised if you've been exchanging letters with that woman, what's her name."

Josep tried to clear his ears again because he was certain they were malfunctioning. But Dolors still had an accusing look in her eye. "I don't want Marie-Claude," he said. "I don't want this without you." He gestured to the bakery. Then he stepped towards her. "I just want you. You're not making any sense." He was certain that the pregnancy was sapping any logic from her brain. Holding her hands, he rubbed her back until her mood returned to normal. However, the next day, her sour milk mood returned even worse than before. She made the same unfathomable accusations, but this time took them one point further, which was a point way too far.

"I should never have done it," Dolors said with such confidence she appeared taller.

"Done what?" Josep asked in confused frustration.

"Married you," she said and took a step closer. "I should have waited. I should have married Baltasar."

Josep left without a word since Dolors' final phrase was still stinging his ears and reverberating in his head. He had spent so long trying to recover from the hurtful words from his brother and did not expect this from his wife. For the ensuing months the sting remained as fresh as the day it was delivered and he could not extract the stinger from his heart. He asked everyone in the family and even Baltasar where Dolors would have got the idea that he was unfulfilled without a son to the point that he would go about anything to get one. No one appeared to know. Josep and Dolors exchanged hardly a word during the remainder of her pregnancy, until Josep surprised her and steered her very round body to a chair.

"It's time we talked," he said, holding her hand while trying to ignore the baffled look on her face. "We're going to have another child. Don't you think it would be better if her or his parents were speaking, not to mention the poor example it gives for the daughters we already have?"

Dolors nodded and shifted in her seat. "I hope it hurries up. I'm so uncomfortable. You wouldn't know anything about that, because it's always me that has to suffer."

"That's nature's fault not mine. I want you to know that I will be thrilled if we have another girl. I also know you've been worried about giving birth again. Everything will be fine. Remember how fast it was last time?"

"Thanks to my dear Baltasar. He's saved my life twice now and you've only ever tried to end it. And for what? A Balaguer boy to run the hills with." She looked at Josep and cringed as if afraid he would slap her.

Instead Josep felt the blood drain from his face and placed her hands onto the enormous bulge on her lap. He stood up and as he walked away deflated, he said, "I hope you can count on Baltasar this time around. Don't count on me." He kept the letter that had just arrived from Quebec hidden deep inside his pocket.

1956-1975

CHAPTER EIGHT

ON THE DAY their only son arrived, Dolors was intent on vehemently disowning his father. She was lying on their marital bed, with her legs spread, and with every contraction the passion that had been released over the years seemed to transform into rage.

"I wasn't doing this again. *Fill de puta*," she cried. "No amount of silky flour is worth this." Taking a glass from the table, she launched it at Josep's retreating feet, splattering glass and water everywhere. While he suspected that Dolors was only reacting to the turmoil of her body, each attack drove all of her previous insults deeper, adding poison to the sting and infecting his pride.

Josep shut the door behind him, instantly muffling the endless hours of blasphemy aimed for his ears. Perched on the stairs just outside the door were his two daughters, who at age ten and nine were old enough to understand their mother's threats. They looked up at him with frightened eyes and covered their ears as Dolors shouted again.

Josep patted Rosa on the head. "Everything will be fine." Though he didn't believe it.

The last months had been too dreadful. While he and Dolors had both said some harsh words, Josep only remembered those that were hurtful to him. As he heard another insult screamed from his bedroom, he lowered his head and sought refuge in the room across the hall.

"Where's he going now?" Montse asked as they watched their father retreat. She looked pleased with herself. "*Mare* finally believed my warning that *Pare* would abandon her for not having a son. Sister Amelia says every father wants his own likeness, just like God had Jesus. It's only natural. Luckily *Mare* has Dr. Sort to take care of her." She crossed her arms across her newly sprouted bosom. While Montse's body was maturing faster than her years, Rosa's mind was far beyond hers.

"You're the only one who listens to Sister Amelia. I don't blame him for hiding. *Mare*'s been plain nasty," Rosa said more towards the door than to her sister. She didn't think her mother was being fair, but then again, she didn't know what physical or emotional pain she was in. At that moment Dolors screamed a long stream of foul words aimed at Josep. At the same time, Rosa heard the sound of scraping furniture in the room where Josep had taken refuge. She searched for comfort in the magazine on her lap.

"She's in pain, of course she's nasty," Montse said. "Childbirth is supposed to hurt. *Pare* should understand that. It is woman's punishment for the Original Sin. Sister Amelia says that too. It's in The Bible."

"It's also logical. My books say that it's a mix of hormones and muscles contracting. *Mare* must be suffering," Rosa said, for the first time considering her mother as a real human being. She had always had more affinity with her father. "She can't mean it when she says she'll cut up *Pare*'s parts and bake them in her *coca*."

Montse clicked her tongue. "No, because she wouldn't want to waste good flour." Rosa nudged her and they giggled. Rosa once again glanced at the worn magazine that was folded open at her favorite page. She showed it to Montse, who sighed and said, "You've shown me that camera a thousand times. Besides, I doubt these are moments you want to capture."

Rosa looked longingly at the advertisement. "I know, but just imagine all the pictures I could have taken of our new brother or sister. I tried to convince *Pare*, but instead he brought me more magazines."

"At least he brings you things. He only brings me work. Every time he returns with flour I have to bake." Her cheeks filled with a smile. "Good thing I love it."

"You love eating, as much as baking."

"You love Víctor. He's the one you want to take pictures of," Montse said, teasing.

"I do not." Rosa covered her chest to protect the emotions from escaping. "I just think he's the most fascinating person I've ever seen. His skin looks so rich, like he's coated in creamy Cola-Cao."

"That's just because of the commercial on the radio," Montse said and started singing about the little black African boy in the chocolate ad, "*Yo soy aquel negrito*. Boy, wouldn't I love some hot chocolate right now."

From inside the bedroom Rosa heard a shrill cry more like opera than a jingle and they both fell silent. Adult voices oohed and aahed. Rosa hugged Montse in relief and excitement.

The door opened and their *Tieta* Àngels peered out at them with her hair in a fan of curls around her flushed face. "Would you girls like to meet your brother?" She looked down the empty hallway. "Where's your father?" Rosa pointed to the room across the hall. Montse jumped to her feet and nodded her head of equally uncontrollable curls, while Rosa took her magazine and followed eagerly. When she entered the bedroom, she saw her mother propped up in bed with her hair wet to her forehead. Núria and Dr. Sort were on either side of her and they all looked up from the bundle in Dolors' arms.

"Come," Núria motioned to them. "Give your brother a kiss."

"Perhaps they should just look." Dolors had a wary look on her face. "What do you think, Baltasar? Surely the girls have germs."

Dr. Sort looked at them over his new spectacles that amplified his dark eyes and steered the girls toward their mother. "It's perfectly safe. Exposure is good. You don't want him to be weak, do you?"

"Of course not," Dolors said and displayed the baby enthusiastically. "Where's his father?" she asked as if earlier only praise had been shooting out her mouth.

"Recovering," Àngels said.

Rosa peered in shock at the prune face in the blanket. "Why is he so red? Maybe it's a good thing I don't have a camera."

"He's been through a lot to get out here," Núria said.

Baltasar put a hand on Rosa's shoulders. "You know what it's like when you take a fish out of water? Your brother needs to get used to the air. I have a book on it. Would you like to read it?"

Rosa nodded emphatically, but then she looked at the frail creature in her mother's arms and sobbed. "The fish always dies."

"Yes it does," Baltasar said. "But your brother is not a fish."

"And he is going to live," Dolors said. "Here, give him a kiss." Rosa watched hesitantly as Montse leaned in and then put her own lips to her brother's forehead. It felt like fresh cream and smelled like it too.

"I'm going to check on the proud father," Baltasar said, winking at Àngels.

Dolors cradled the baby in one arm and reached toward Baltasar with the other. "Thank you, my dear Baltasar, for another miracle."

"Not at all, my dear. Let's make this the last one, shall we?"

***

Josep was leaning out the window of the spare room when Baltasar entered. Although he heard the footsteps, he continued looking far into the sky above the clouds. He had pushed the single bed up against the wall and the armchair was next to the open window.

"What are you doing, man?" Baltasar said. "You could catch your death. I've seen more than a few go from pneumonia and the like."

"It's much colder in the other room." Josep brought his head inside and shut the window with a bang.

"She didn't really mean any of those things. You know that. You wouldn't believe the things I have heard women say in the height of pain."

"I would rather hear what they have to say in the height of pleasure, but there hasn't been much of that here." Josep raised his eyebrows.

"Perhaps not for the last nine months." Baltasar put his hands on his hips. "Seriously, Josep, she's your wife. She's just given birth to your son. You can't hold grudges now." He sat slowly on the edge of the bed. "I rather think you already hold too many of those. That's not good for your health either."

Josep's smoky eyes softened, erasing the creases in his forehead. For a moment he thought that Baltasar could be right. He sat down beside him and patted him on the knee. "I'm sorry. I should be thankful to you for keeping her safe again and for bringing me another healthy child. A son. My Josep Jr. He is healthy, isn't he?"

"Indeed he is. And practically as long as Montse was, but not as wide. It's soon to tell, but I think he'll be a strong little fellow, just like his father."

The door squeaked and Àngels came in. Baltasar jumped to his feet and ran to take her hand.

"Is everything all right? Do you need me?"

"Everything is fine. Little Pau is like a suckling pig. He doesn't want to let go," Àngels said and released Baltasar's hand, but he continued to hold her fingers.

"Like father, like son. What did I tell you?" Baltasar looked at Josep. The crease in his forehead had reappeared and Baltasar dropped Àngels' hand. "What is it, man?"

"Little Pau?" Josep was looking at both of them wide eyed, hoping that he was just hard of hearing.

"Yes." Àngels grasped his hands and swung them. "Don't you think that's a wonderful idea, to name your son after our brother Pau? It was Dolors' idea. At first she wanted to name him Eduard. Surely you knew."

"I did not. She did not consult me. But why would she?" Josep sat heavily on the bed and looked at the floor. This was like the final hammer on the nail. "She doesn't seem to need me for any of this."

"She did for one part of it," Baltasar said.

Josep scowled at him. He was feeling purposely excluded from his own family.

"I think I hear them calling me," Baltasar said. "We'll talk later." He smiled at Àngels and left the room.

Àngels took Josep's hand. "Maybe she wanted to surprise you with the name. You have to admit that it's a wonderful idea. It's like my twin, our Pau, has been given another chance. Plus his name means peace. Don't you think Dolors is trying to tell you something? If you can't be happy about it for you, you can be happy about it for me." Àngels squeezed Josep's hand.

Josep nodded and kissed Àngels' knuckles before releasing her hand. As he walked to the armoire in the corner, he felt drawn to the past when he didn't want to go there. Right now he didn't even want to be in the present. The letter from Quebec that he had thought had come from Marie-Claude was actually from her husband. He was asking for Communist Party contacts, something that Josep locally had never had. He had made no mention of Marie-Claude or the other people Josep knew and cared about in Canada. Lost in thought, Josep wiped the dust off the woodwork with the flat of his hand, coughing on the cloud of dust that floated around his head. He opened the window and shook an old blanket outside, freeing the dust into the winter air. When he was finished, Àngels silently took the blanket's two corners and helped him fold it, while Josep finally spoke. "I don't mind the name. In fact, it is a splendid idea. I suppose it's better than Josep Jr., though the regime will make us put Pablo on the certificate." He looked at Àngels and felt the hurt of what he was about to say tighten more strongly in his chest. "It's the fact that she didn't ask me. Did Baltasar know?"

Àngels squeezed his hands. "No, he didn't. She told us after he left. Why is that important?"

"Because not long ago she told me that she wished that she had married Baltasar instead."

"Oh, Josep." The blanket fell to the floor between them as Àngels hugged him. Then she released him. "You are so silly. She can't have meant it. You were probably arguing. Women can say ridiculous things when we're pregnant and uncomfortable. I know I did."

"I can't make excuses for her anymore and you shouldn't either." Josep picked up the crumpled blanket, smoothed it out, and put it carefully at the foot of the bed. "I'll sleep in here for a while. She needs to recover anyway. We need some space to think."

"But how will the girls react?"

"They'll get used to it. And so will Dolors. In fact, she'll probably be delighted."

As the months went by, Montse and Rosa did seem to grow accustomed to the fact that their parents slept in separate bedrooms, but Dolors did not. She tried to hug Josep and apologize for all her cutting words. When that didn't work she tried to heal his wounds through his stomach. She baked his favorite savory fare with the ingredients he silently stored in her kitchen on returning from his trips. She laid out his carefully ironed clothes for him on the little bed in his room. Once she even put herself, wearing nothing but her thinnest apron, on his bed, but when Josep walked in and saw her, he spun on his heel and walked back out. No matter what she did, he was unable to silence her words in his head. If her heart was not truly his, her body couldn't be either. He could not let himself forget it; it was a reminder driven home after succumbing to a moment's temptation.

One evening, while he was carrying some recently acquired goods into the bakery, Dolors was taking some fresh loaves out of the oven and a smear of flour across her rear end stirred some memories and other sensations in him. Without reflection, he approached her from behind and put his arms around her.

"Baltasar," she said before recognizing the sturdier calloused hands of her husband. The scalding tray fell onto Josep's outstretched palms and he felt shooting pain. He jerked back and pulled his hands to his mouth.

"Josep, poor thing," Dolors said and blew on his hands. "You shouldn't sneak up on me like that."

Josep felt the sting in his hands and in the back of his eyes.

Dolors looked at his reddening palms. "It doesn't look too bad. But perhaps Baltasar should take a look. He'll be here any minute."

"Evidently," Josep pulled his hands away. "Why would you think he would put his arms around you like that?"

Dolors shook her head and her face flushed. "He wouldn't. He was on my mind when you touched me and——." She grew silent, looking at the growing blisters on Josep's palms.

Josep pulled his hands away. "Why is he coming here?"

"For my checkup." She pointed to her lower half. "It's routine after any birth. Especially after what my body's been through."

"Couldn't you just go to his office like everyone else?"

"We're not like everyone else. We're far too close for that."

"I gathered that," Josep said and left before his best friend could arrive. The burn on his hands was like a piercing scream.

***

When little Pau turned one year old, and the girls were nearing the end of their first decade, Dolors felt it was high time for some unifying measures and made an announcement.

"We're taking a holiday," she said to her family gathered around the table, and looked out at the fat snowflakes dashing past the window. "I am closing the bakery on Monday. It's all arranged."

"We can't just close the bakery," Josep said, once again unable to understand his wife. "What will everyone do? Besides, I'm going over the border on Monday. People are relying on me."

"My customers will go elsewhere for just one day. And your people and your trip will wait. People rely on you here." Dolors stood and put her hands on her hips, which had shrunk only slightly since Pau's birth. "Josep, you've been wanting to try it for years, so we're going to do it. We're going skiing. It will be a late birthday celebration for you, before your almost middle-aged body gets too old for it." She looked at Núria and Albert who looked as shocked as all the others. "We'll go to Vall de Núria. You've always wanted to go there, haven't you, Núria?"

Núria shook her head and the carefully formed curls did not budge. "I can't be skiing with this old body and my eyesight. What about the co-op?"

"It is a co-op, isn't it? The others can run it for a day. We can take the rack railway up and you can visit the sanctuary if you want. Plus someone will need to take care of Pau while I ski." She turned to Montse and Rosa who were staring up at her as if expecting the punch line. "Girls, one day out of school won't hurt you. What do you say?"

"Are you going to lie to the nuns?" Montse asked.

"A white lie, pure as snow. Don't worry, it will be worth it. If there's a problem I'll bake them a cake."

Montse nodded. In the year since Pau's birth, Montse had become less concerned about the nuns at her school than with the boys at the school nearby. Rosa, however, still had her sights on one boy in particular. "All of us will be going, won't we?" Rosa asked, glancing at Víctor. "Even though I don't know how to ski."

"Neither do I. Nor does your father, or *Tieta* Àngels, Manel, Víctor, or Dr. Sort, but we're all going to give it a go." Dolors sat down heavily in her chair like a gavel on a desk. "And we're going to have fun."

Although he was loath to admit it, Josep was indeed excited about the thought of going skiing. He had been watching the city dwellers do it for years. Now that people had a little extra money and the foreign powers had decided that the Franco regime was less evil than the communists that were sweeping through Asia and elsewhere, more foreign tourists were also swarming Spain's beaches and ski hills. While he was excited to feel the cold wind on his face, the free feeling it would bring, he was afraid Dolors might be right: His body might already not be able to handle the strain. Every time he carried a loaded sack through the mountains, his back punished him until it was time for his next trip. It was reacting against his years of hauling ice, chopping wood, and acting like a pack mule. Since the flooding of Adiol, they had been trying to make up for lost orders at the co-op by selling extra bread and treats and he had more work than he could carry. What he needed was a strong, young back. He also had a new address burning in his pocket, though he didn't know if his conscience would take him there. While the men told him it was the best bordello in Languedoc-Roussillon, in the past such places had only brought him horrible luck. Although he had been very near it many times, he had managed to resist alleviating an itch that lately only he had been able to scratch. Dolors' announcement of the family holiday had saved him from temptation, for now. Still he refused to be Dolors' blatant second choice. Other family and friends, even Baltasar, told him that his pride would make him a very lonely man. Josep, however, knew that he would never let himself be lonely. His days alone and feeling abandoned in Canada had taught him how to seek out company. He thought that now could be the perfect time.

CHAPTER NINE

THE FAMILY HOLIDAY had arrived, and Josep, Dolors, Rosa, Montse, Pau, Núria, Sr. Palau, Baltasar, Àngels, Manel, and Víctor all squished into Sr. Palau's car and drove to the Núria Valley. Above them at the rack railway station the mountain loomed, like the stomach of a prostrate, large-breasted woman. Pine trees like stubble framed it and stopped at the base of the snowy peaks. The sanctuary and ski resort hid out of view. As the train crawled up the narrow gorge toward it, they all stared out the window in awe, except for Rosa.

"Rosa, leave Víctor alone," Dolors called. "Where's your camera? You should be photographing this." She motioned out the window to the rocky cliffs and dusting of snow.

Rosa was sitting between Montse and Víctor but she was flush against Víctor's side staring at him. "Montse hasn't left me any room," Rosa said and nudged Montse's ample stomach. "Go get your own seat." She shoved Montse and took out the Brownie camera that Josep had brought across the mountains for her as a first communion present. Holding the box-like camera in her lap, she looked through the viewfinder and focused on the silhouette of Víctor against the train window.

Montse slapped Rosa with her mitten. "You're supposed to take pictures of the landscape, or of all of us." She indicated the circle of family around them. "But we all know that you love Víctor."

"I do not." Rosa turned her back to Montse. Yet everyone did know of Rosa's crush on Víctor, despite her vehement denials. She was fascinated by the smooth darkness of his skin, the exotic look of him, quite like the people appearing in the *National Geographic* magazines Josep brought her from France.

Víctor's face turned darker as he blushed. He wore a white woolen hat and his layers of sweaters made him look much larger than he was. Over the years, Àngels and Manel had tried to fatten him up by feeding him the best that they had, but instead he grew in height. Now, at age seventeen, he was a full head and shoulders taller than almost all of them. Other than the time he had used a magnifying glass and the midday sun to burn an ant colony, almost setting fire to Manel's carpentry workshop in the process, he had caused them little trouble. They had all attributed his mix of curiosity and daring to his mother's side, since Carme had revealed nothing about his father's character. Reaching out, Víctor ruffled Rosa's hair with the creamy palm of his hand.

"You're going to record this whole trip on that camera, aren't you?" he asked her, goading her on.

"Yes, I am going to make a photo-reportage," Rosa said, nodding and shaking her curls. "And it will be published in *LIFE* magazine and *Pare* will bring me a copy of it." She turned toward Josep. "Don't forget to bring me the next issue," she said, aiming her camera at him. Josep was at the center of their group and staring at his shoes.

"Yes, of course, I'll bring everything I can," he said. Originally he had brought Asterix and Tintin comics for the girls, until he found that Rosa had greatly matured in the past year and was suddenly very savvy. In secret she had been reading the magazines and newspapers he smuggled in. Despite it being material quite beyond her years, she began to devour it with an uncontrollable appetite that could not be satisfied. She had been badgering him for a camera ever since she found his pictures of Canada: insouciant young men with cigarettes hanging out of their mouths, coy women leaning against small wooden houses, signs with names of towns on them, or one of a boy in the middle of a frozen lake. He finally relented and brought her the camera to make her happy and to have a little peace of his own.

Dolors nudged him. "Look at the scenery. It's breathtaking."

"I have seen more than my share of mountains," he said, but when the whole family sighed in awe, he looked up to see the snow-blanketed valley spread before them. A cloud passed overhead, its blue shadow erasing the brilliant reflection of the morning sun. A moment later the sun was back and blinding. Then the train entered the darkness of a tunnel.

Manel, who so far had been sitting quietly, looked out and took his woolen hat on and off. He shifted in his seat. "Are we really going to do this?" he said to Àngels, who was sitting calmly beside him. "Skiing doesn't seem natural."

Baltasar leaned toward Manel from Àngels' other side. "Don't tell me you're afraid."

Manel scoffed and removed his hat again. "Not afraid, perhaps a little nervous. This should be nothing." He swallowed. "I just think that with all the risks that we have taken in our lives and that we continue to take, that it is perhaps unnatural to risk our lives for fun."

"We don't take as many physical risks as we used to," Baltasar said. "The adrenaline, that's what our body releases when we're at risk, provides a little charge."

"Thank you, Dr. Sort, for the scientific explanation, but unlike yours, my work is physically demanding," Manel said displaying the palms of his scarred and calloused hands. "I take risks. Tell him, Àngels."

"Of course, you do, Manel. Every piece you make involves some risk. The wood is heavy and your tools are sharp," Àngels said softly, not wanting to be cornered into the center of another argument between Manel and Baltasar. They had both been trying to one-up each other to gain her favor, but for now her heart couldn't be persuaded by either of them. She wondered if she would ever give it to anyone.

"But, Manel, you don't take risks like we do." Baltasar squeezed Àngels' arm and rested his hand on her wrist. "We are still trying to change things," he whispered. "Even though I am convinced that the more the international community accepts this situation, the harder it will be to change it."

"I disagree." Àngels looked over her shoulder at the people sitting behind them and turned to face Baltasar, putting her hand on his. This was the one topic she felt passionate about. "I keep telling you this. If Spain is now a member of all these organizations, and with the American military bases here, they can't ignore us. If the people come together and protest they will have to pay attention. Look at all of the student protests. Look at what happened with that tram boycott in Barcelona years ago. People walked for days and finally the regime gave in. That was just the beginning. They will eventually give in. They'll have to," Àngels said, her whisper now much louder. They emerged from the tunnel into blinding sunlight.

Dolors cleared her throat and shifted baby Pau onto her other knee. "No need for this talk here. Besides I must say that the situation has improved with The Caudillo. I cannot complain," she said rather loudly in Spanish rather than Catalan looking at the other passengers.

No one answered her as they emerged from the tunnel and saw a frozen lake on their left, the gray façade of the sanctuary behind it, and the mountain peaks towering beyond. The snowy valley was wide before them like two cupped palms with black dots snaking down it. The train abruptly slowed its pace.

"Doesn't it look fabulous," Núria said. "You know, Dolors, I have always wanted to come here, just to see it. I'm not religious, but I am keen to see the sanctuary and the hermitage. I am glad that they managed to rescue the Virgin during the war. This is our heritage."

Víctor leaned towards Núria. "Are you going to stick your head under Saint Gil's pot and ring the bell?"

Núria giggled. "You sly one. I don't think even Saint Gil could make me fertile again."

"Dolors," Baltasar called. "Don't you even think about it."

Dolors bounced Pau on her knee. "You never know, I just might," she said and nudged Josep.

"Don't even think about it," Josep said as the train screeched to a halt.

Once Núria and Albert, finely dressed with Pau held securely in their arms, began to slide in their best shoes across the snow toward the sanctuary, the rest of the family strapped on the wooden skis and began sliding toward the ski hill.

"I suggest we all try walking up a bit and then skiing down before we try to get on that thing," Dolors said, motioning to the ski tow. Her layers of clothing underneath her white jacket made her look like an enormous snowball. Throwing all of her energy into the hill, Dolors faced her skis straight up and attempted to walk, but instead slid backwards. "Help me, *hòstia*. Don't just stand there," she cried. Baltasar and Víctor moved in beside her and pulled her to her feet. Josep stood watching and shaking his head, thinking how she would do anything for Baltasar's attention.

"Fine, *senyor*, let's see you do it then," Dolors said to him. The rest turned and looked at Josep expectantly.

"How hard can it be," Josep said determinedly. He was in reasonable physical shape; he knew mountains and snow like his own skin and blood. If rich people could manage, so could he. But under his feet, his skis took a life of their own and soon he was lying in the snow. He put a mitten to his back. "*Collons*. This is just what I need." As he pulled himself up, he wondered if it was really worth it. What if he injured himself and couldn't work. He was thinking first of his family, though some would never believe it.

"It's like this," Víctor said, demonstrating by stepping sideways up the hill. They all looked at him in surprise and followed his steps, except Rosa, who was snapping pictures of everyone standing in line like a necklace of multicolored beads. Víctor turned slowly and began a slow snow plough downhill.

"Where did you learn that?" Àngels asked mystified, as if seeing for the first time that the boy she had brought up with such devotion had turned into a capable young man.

"Just now," Víctor said, smiling with teeth as brilliant as the snow. He had a look in his eye that they had seen many a time in Carme's. "Just watch what other people are doing."

"I'd bet you can do it, Baltasar," Dolors said, leading them toward the novice ski hill. Josep looked on as his wife and best friend struggled away as excited as they were awkward. His daughters, sister, and friend followed, leaving him behind. He laughed as Rosa caught Montse's elbow and saved her from falling face first into the snow. They could have their fun while he got his ski legs.

Holding his back, he looked up at the mountain peeled of trees before him. The blue sky was spotted with airy clouds and he felt the cool breeze in his nostrils. He pulled out his cigarettes from inside his jacket, lit one, and took a deep drag as if strength and courage were stored in that one puff. Thinking that his family was probably having a better time without him anyway, he watched the other skiers gliding their way gracefully down the bigger slopes, making it look as easy as walking. Closer to the chairlift, a middle-aged couple with their two teenage boys caught his attention. The couple was in a heated argument, oblivious to those around them. The man was on his feet pointing a gloved finger at the woman, who was sitting in the snow, hunched inside a pink snow suit.

"Tu ne fais que te plaindre," the man shouted and pointed his ski pole. *"Bon Dieu. J'en ai marre de toi et tes bêtises."* His tone was insulting and his choice of words offensive. He abruptly turned toward the ski lift with the two boys in tow, leaving the woman sitting on the ground, a pink stain in the snow. She was covering her face in her hands as Josep carefully slid his skis toward her.

"Are you all right?" he asked and touched her shaking shoulder.

She lowered her hands and looked up at him with honey-hazel eyes rimmed with running black mascara, like they had been dipped in ink. *"Ça ira, merci."* She responded and tried to pull herself to her feet, instead falling clumsily back on her skis and burying her face in her knees. "It's his revenge," she continued in French. "He wants to take the grace out of me. He made me come here."

"Qui?" Josep asked. "Who did? Why don't you sit and relax for a moment? Cigarette?" he offered her his pack.

She sniffed and nodded before taking one and putting it shakily between her lips. Josep bent down with his lighter and as he lit her cigarette he wavered, his balance lost. He thudded to the frozen ground beside her.

Shrugging, he lit another cigarette. "I'm not too thrilled about being here either. Though I've always wanted to come." He looked from the woman to the hill in front of him and all the people skiing down it.

"It's my husband. He knows what my feet have been through, yet he's forced them into these boots. I can't do this at my age." She inhaled her cigarette and wiped her wet cheeks. "He says I'm useless."

"I'm thinking it's not the best for my back either. You don't have to ski to show that you're worth something. In fact it might show you're senseless."

"Exactement. That's what I told him. Besides if I hurt myself, what will all my little students do?"

"You're a teacher?" Josep asked, thinking of his friend Marie-Claude in Canada, although this woman actually reminded him of someone else from those days.

"I'm a dancer. I've just started my own dance school. I was almost a prima ballerina, but then my husband made me quit." She sniffed and Josep handed her his handkerchief. "He once loved my legs and now he wants me to break them. I told him I wouldn't dare risk it."

Josep butted out his cigarette on the ice with a sizzle. "Is that why he was yelling at you?"

"Yes, he does it all the time. Speaking of which, he's waiting to do it again now." She pointed up the hill, where three spots could be seen waving at them. "They won't come down until I go up and meet them."

"Why didn't they take you with them?"

"Jules got tired of waiting and said I was useless and left. My boys agree with him." She looked at him with her black-ringed eyes. "How would you feel about taking me up there?"

"Me?" Josep looked at the hill and the lift and shook his head. "I can't go up there."

She stared at him in silence. Black tears once again rolled over her cheeks. "That's okay. I don't even know you. My own husband won't help me, so why should you?" She looked at him again with the same honey eyes of a woman he had tried to help in Canada. He had failed then, but now he could help. Pushing himself to standing he felt the most confident yet on his skis. He reached for her hands, which were very soft despite their coldness, and pulled her to her skis.

"Let's go," he said and urged her toward the lift before he could come to his senses.

"Thank you, so much," she said with a glimmer in her eye. She almost hugged him but he stopped her, for fear they might collapse.

"You've been on a ski lift before, *n'est ce pas?*" she asked, looking quite concerned. Josep tried to wipe the fright from his brow, but before he could, the platform was empty and the lift operators were motioning urgently for them to approach. Josep slid forward, and before he could panic as to how he had actually got to be here, the chair slammed into the back of his legs and he fell into it. It propelled them into the air. Looking down and seeing that he was sitting firmly in the seat, he grabbed tighter hold of the edge of the chair and laughed. Then he looked down at the great hill below them that seemed to climb forever upward.

"You don't know how much this means to me," the woman said. "I'm Geneviève. When we get to the top, please don't act like you know me. Jules wouldn't understand."

Josep hesitated and looked behind him toward the hill where his family would be. He suddenly felt like an idiot, a very lonely idiot. "I'm Josep Balaguer."

"You speak good French for a Spaniard, but you have a strange accent, if you don't mind me saying so."

"Catalan," he said. "And I spent some time in Quebec. I am sure you know about our situation here. I had to get away. I'm from Pujaforta, a town not far from here."

"I live in Merloin-les-Bains, over the border," she said and pointed over the mountain.

"It's the one with the charming old market place. I pass through that town often for my work. My brother actually lives near there, in Fontsec."

"Really?" Her expression looked brighter than he had seen it yet. She had a soft, innocent face underneath her makeup. "Maybe I know him. Do you work together? Many people work in the spring water at Merloin-les-Bains."

"Eduard and I don't work together. We don't even speak. It's a very long story." He looked at her and raised his eyebrows, which disappeared under his woolen hat. He wasn't sure why he had even mentioned Eduard's name. Perhaps it had to do with being propelled up the mountain toward France with this French woman. "So why did your husband make you stop dancing?"

"That is also a very long story," she said. "I would be happy to tell it to you another time. Sorry, that sounds very forward of me. I'm usually alone. My husband travels and the boys are in boarding school. It's been such a long time since anyone has listened to me."

"I feel the same way, though I do it to myself. I have a way of separating myself from people."

"Maybe it's so that they won't do that to you first."

"Someone who looks a lot like you said the exact same thing to me years ago. But it's become a lot worse since then. Many of my family and friends think I'm my only enemy, though my wife might beg to differ."

"You look like you could use a friend, too." She smiled.

"Perhaps," he said and smiled back.

"So what work takes you to France?"

"A little of everything, really. I'm in imports, let's say."

"Yes, I understand." She lowered her eyes and nodded. "I've heard a lot about that. In fact, my husband dabbles in it. That's why he's always away and that's why we're over here, actually. A client of his suggested we come here for the local flavor." She appeared to size him up out of the corner of her eye. "Maybe you should speak to him. It would give us an excuse to see each other again."

"Perhaps," Josep said thinking that he would enjoy seeing her again. There would be no harm in it. "What area does your husband work in?"

"Jewelry, basically," she said.

"I deal more in local goods, foodstuffs and the like, nothing that elaborate."

She shrugged. "I know I haven't given you a very good impression of Jules. He's a bad husband, but they say he is good at business. If you change your mind, go to the chemist's in Merloin-les-Bains and ask for the house of the Petitpas or even my dance studio. They'll point you in the right direction." She squeezed her hands at her chest. "Please do come to visit. You've helped me so much. I could make you lunch or something to thank you." Then she winced. "We're almost there."

Josep saw that the tip of the mountain was careening towards them.

"And there they are," Geneviève said. Josep followed her look to the three men with their hands on their hips at the top of the hill. "Thank you for distracting me from my holiday. You've done wonders."

Soon they were launched off the lift and Josep was flat on his stomach. Geneviève had managed to stay upright and helped him to his feet. He brushed off the snow and tried to appear calm.

"Thank you and remember Merloin-les-Bains for lunch." She smiled at him and squeezed his arm.

"I would like that," he said, as he watched her pinkness ski awkwardly away. Her husband and sons were scowling at her and took a moment to frown at him as well before pushing Geneviève over the lip of the hill. Peering down before him, Josep realized that from the top it looked even steeper than from down below. He was terrifyingly high up and the reality of his predicament was setting in. He shook his head at himself. Once again his offering a woman a helping hand could get him a broken neck. Then his stomach growled.

***

Across the mountain, on the novice hill, Dolors had her knees locked, her rear out, and a look of exhilaration on her face. "Hee, hee!" she cried as she whizzed down the hill. "This is fabulous," she shouted to Baltasar who was skiing beside her. "Doesn't this feel like absolute freedom? You're catching on, but you always do everything perfectly," she called.

"It feels rather risky to me," he answered as he turned awkwardly away from her and looked back over his shoulder. "But it is thrilling, isn't it? Isn't Àngels doing it splendidly?" He waved toward Àngels, who was gliding with complete ease in front of them. When she stopped at the bottom, she beckoned to Manel, who was perched at the top of the hill like a baby bird peering beyond the nest. He had yet to come down and Víctor, who was standing patiently at his side, had failed to coax him into flight. Àngels had been trying to ignore Dolors' exaggerated enthusiasm, particularly towards Baltasar, but in the end it was slightly infectious. She didn't know if it was the air or the excitement of the activity that was making her feel elated. It had been years since she felt such delight. For a flash of a second she had glanced over the mountaintop toward France and wondered why she hadn't had news of Eduard in so long. She had been so busy working with Manel that she hadn't pushed for news from Eduard's family. She shook away her worry and breathed in another dose of crisp air. Unlike the rest of them, Manel appeared to be hating every moment. Àngels motioned again for Manel to come, but he shook his head energetically. "Give it a go," she shouted to him. "Even the girls can do it," she said as Rosa snow ploughed between them with Montse like a wide shadow behind her.

"I've never had so much fun in my life," Rosa said to Àngels and Dolors when she reached the bottom. "I can't believe we've never tried this before. This ski resort has been here almost since I was born."

"Ever so long ago," Àngels said and straightened Rosa's hat.

"And how do you know?" Montse asked Rosa and jabbed her pole into the snow.

"Because I've read about it."

"With your camera and your books you think you have the answers to everything."

Àngels put a hand on each of the girls' shoulders. "As I'm sure you both know, we have been very busy with other matters to be able to come skiing."

"Like ensuring you have enough food, for instance," Dolors said. She then motioned widely to the other skiers. "We're not like all these foreigners. Imagine having two full weeks of holiday. With what it cost me to take one day."

"Speaking of food, when is lunch?" Montse asked. "I can't wait for you to try the sandwiches I made. Then again, we could eat at that bar." She pointed to a terrace where people were sprawled in chairs facing the sun as if it was a film star. "It looks like there are lots of boys there, too."

Dolors steered her away. "That bar looks far too expensive. You know that we're having a picnic."

"I know. You're going to love my new style of *coca*. You do really like it, don't you, *Mare*?" Montse said, her attention no longer on the terrace or the boys.

Rosa poked her sister. "Maybe you should read more than recipes. It's not normal to be so interested in food."

"I don't use recipes and maybe I'm not a normal girl," Montse said. "Besides, the nuns always said that good cooking was a woman's duty, and a way to snatch a good husband."

"I would beg to differ. You're too young to be thinking about husbands." Dolors slid between them. "Montse, you're perfectly normal. There's nothing wrong with having some extra shape. You don't want to be skinny and sickly. I for one have never felt better." She jutted out her ample middle.

125

A scream of terror came from the top of the hill and they all looked up. Manel was coming towards them.

"Manel, turn," Víctor shouted as he followed after him. Instead he came straight down the hill with his arms flailing at his sides, and a look of fright on his face, which was soon covered in snow as he crashed near the bottom of the hill in a clang of skis.

"Manel," Àngels yelled, taking off her skis and running toward where he was lying twisted and groaning. The sight of him seemed entirely unnatural. What if he was severely injured?

He moaned loudly and clutched his shoulder. "I knew this was a bad idea."

Àngels leaned over him and stroked his immobilized arm. "Baltasar!" she shouted. "Help him."

Baltasar was leaning casually on his poles and wore a tilted grin on his lips. "I'm rather enjoying this."

"*Per l'amor de Déu*," Àngels cried. "What kind of a doctor are you?"

"He's an excellent doctor," Dolors answered.

Baltasar sighed and trudged up the hill to Manel, who was wincing, rocking and clasping his shoulder. Baltasar removed Manel's hand and sweater from his collarbone before declaring it dislocated.

Àngels groaned. "Does it really hurt?"

Manel grasped his shoulder and nodded.

Baltasar wiped the snow off his hands. "Anything for attention." He shook his head. "Take off your skis and let's see what we can do." He turned to the others. "In the meantime, you can have your picnic. I'll tell Núria and Albert to join you. I'm sure I'll find them in the bar."

As Baltasar escorted Manel away, Dolors looked at the girls, Àngels, and Víctor. She gasped and looked behind her as well. "Where's Josep?"

Àngels shook her head. "What do you mean where's Josep? I thought you sent him to check on Pau."

"No." Dolors looked at her skis and whispered, "I've been so enjoying myself that I didn't notice."

"And you meant for this holiday to establish a truce." Àngels raised her eyebrows. She thought that frankly Josep and Dolors were always predictable.

"What's a truce?" Montse asked.

"It's an agreement for peace," Rosa said.

Víctor was putting on his skis, and reached into his jacket where he had been protecting Rosa's camera. He handed it to her and said, "I'll go find him." He skied away.

***

At the top of the hill across the way, Josep was now sitting in the snow shivering and swearing, blaming himself for getting into such a predicament, but mostly blaming Dolors for bringing him here. But then again he also thanked her. If he hadn't come he wouldn't have met Geneviève. He was surprised by how much talking to her made him feel lighter. By now she and her family were long gone and he looked down the hill and now felt very heavy. Perhaps skiing was something he could have done earlier, when he was younger, before a war, exile, and black-marketeering ruined his back. He jutted his pole in the snow and thought of his family and how now they would surely abandon him. They were probably enjoying their picnic without him. Now he was numb rather than hungry.

When later he saw that the sun was edging dangerously close to the snowy peaks, he stood, balanced his skis in one arm and his poles in the other and began climbing down the edge of the hill along the pine trees. He sank almost knee deep in snow, and with each step the nerves in his back pinched. When the people on the esplanade below finally looked like sticks rather than specks, and Josep's face was bursting red with the effort, he heard a swishing behind him. And then he heard his name. When he turned, Víctor was looking down at him with a sweaty brow and a look of both worry and relief in his dark eyes.

"*Hòstia*, Josep. Here you are. *Em cago*," Víctor said and leaned on his poles in exhaustion. "I have been looking everywhere. This hill is the last place I thought you would be."

"Rightly so and I won't be coming here again," Josep snapped, although he was so thrilled to see Víctor he could have done a cartwheel in the snow. Given his aching back, he refrained and instead clasped the boy's gloved hand.

"What are you doing all the way up here anyway?"

"Ironically I was trying to help someone. Sheer stupidity on my part."

"Well, now you're going to learn to ski. There is no choice."

"I'm not putting these back on." Josep rattled his skis at him.

"We'll miss the last train. We'll have to sleep here. I don't know about you, but I'm starving."

"So am I," Josep said and threw his skis to the ground and started fastening them to his feet. He shook his head at Víctor but was really shaking it at himself.

"We'll go down little by little," Víctor said. "You can follow me." Víctor started ever so slowly to ski perpendicular to the hill and Josep followed behind, never removing his gaze from Víctor's back. They crisscrossed the hill, with Josep toppling over a handful of times. Víctor helped him up, brushed him off, and continued to lead him downward. Slowly Josep noticed that the people on the small esplanade appeared bigger. He even thought he recognized Dolors and Montse, two matching snowballs walking toward the bar and was surprised by his joy at the sight of them. By the time they reached the bottom he could hardly stand up straight, let alone ski or walk. His back was screaming at him for his senselessness and now his brain was as well. If the bakery was to function properly, he would have to make a trip to France in the next few days, but the question was how he would carry anything back. Now that he was nearing the bottom and possible safety he wondered how safe Geneviève was. He saw her husband's angry face again and how she had cringed from him. He wished he could check on her. When finally they reached the bottom of the hill, Josep rested his hands on his knees and looked up gratefully at Víctor.

"Thank you, son. I will not forget this." He cleared his throat. "Can we perhaps keep this to ourselves? I think other people won't forget it either."

Víctor nodded shyly. "Certainly. It will be our secret." Víctor put an arm around Josep, helping him support his back as they walked toward their family.

Josep felt Víctor's support and wondered how this boy had become such a strong young man without him even noticing. Then he remembered that half of his blood was Carme's and before taking time to think or to remember the promise made long ago to Àngels, he said, "Do you need a job, son?"

"A job?" Víctor's eyebrows peaked. "Anything in particular?"

"I need a helper. I've needed one for a while now what with my back. You seem fast on your feet. Your reflexes are good." Josep appraised Víctor and nodded. The boy had grown very tall and thin yet seemed sturdy and strong. Àngels had always applauded his conscientiousness, his curiosity, and his thick skin. She said that, unlike her, Víctor would let anything derogatory bounce right off him. Now Víctor wore a particularly knowing look in his dark eyes. Josep whispered, "You know I run goods across the mountain for my wife and others. It's my small contribution to the downfall of the regime. Plus there's good money in it." Josep put an arm around Víctor. "I've also just made a new contact. Perhaps something about jewelry."

"That could work. I have been dying to explore beyond Pujaforta and I could use the money. I can't depend on Àngels and Manel forever," Víctor said and Josep grasped his hand firmly and shook it.

"*Pare*, there you are," Rosa called. "I knew Víctor would find you." She waved at them as they looked at her. "Smile," she called and took their photograph. She continued snapping as Dolors ran toward Josep and wrapped her arms around his shoulders.

"Josep, darling." She looked into his face. "Where have you been? I've been worrying about you all day."

CHAPTER TEN

THE DAY THAT Víctor announced his new job with Josep, Àngels and Josep had a deafening argument.

"I can't believe you would do this to me," Àngels said, trying to remain calm, but taking Josep's reneging on his years-old promise as a personal affront.

"This has nothing to do with you," Josep said. "It's about a very capable young man who has free time and can now start to contribute something. My back has had enough. Don't you want to bring down the regime, package by package?"

"That's what you tell yourself. You could choose any other young man. Not my Víctor." She stood in the middle of Josep's living room, trying to stop herself from trembling. She covered her face with her palms. "Don't you see the irony? Don't you see the danger? Carme smuggled. She smuggled people. Now she's dead." The air seemed to catch in her chest. When she managed to capture a breath she said, "You'll take him away from me."

Josep watched her with his usual guilty expression. He put an arm around her, but she roughly shrugged it away. Still covering her face with her hands, she shook her head and in a muffled voice said, "Don't you try to comfort me."

"But, Àngels, you know I've been doing this for years. That's why my back is shot. The danger isn't that great and I now have a fool-proof system. Víctor won't be at risk," Josep said softly. "Besides, our meetings at Baltasar's are probably more risky."

Àngels' hands fell from her face revealing a coating of tears and she heard her own voice growing louder. She didn't know if she needed to protect Víctor or herself. "That is entirely different. That is about us. It is not about a boy."

"Have you noticed lately that your boy is now quite a young man? Did you see him on the ski trip? He handles himself quite well, reasons like an adult, not like a child. Besides, he sounded keen to get out there beyond this town. Like you said, half of his blood is Carme's and the other half is from another continent. It's no wonder the boy is curious."

"You're pushing him away from me. Tell him you don't want him to do it. Tell him you've changed your mind."

"But he'd be really disappointed."

"If you don't, I'll be more than disappointed." She feared that she was right.

Josep's eyes were full of worry. He raised his palms toward her. "Fine. Maybe you have a point." Josep held Àngels' shoulders, though he was the one now looking disappointed. "I will do it for you." She felt his warm hands on her shoulders as he pulled her head to his chest and stroked her hair. He then rubbed his own back, likely anticipating going back out there alone. "How is Manel's shoulder?"

Àngels sobbed into Josep's shirt, and after a moment she said, "He can't work. He'll need me—and Víctor—to do everything. But Baltasar says it will get better." She pulled away and stroked the damp circle on his shirt. "I should go."

***

That very day Josep gently told Víctor that he wouldn't require his help and refrained from giving a reason. Yet, early the next morning when Josep set off into the woods, he found a dark shadow behind him. As fast as his back would allow, he tried dodging behind trees, over hilltops, hiding in dugouts and caves that only he knew about, but whatever he did, Víctor was on his tail. This both frustrated and fascinated him. This young man was showing incredible skill. Josep dashed around a boulder, slid another aside, and hid inside a cave he had devised himself, only to have Víctor dismantle the door and squat down beside him. Josep finally said, "You can't be here, Víctor. I promised Àngels and you promised me."

"Am I not good enough? Is that it?" Víctor was biting his glove.

"On the contrary." Josep shook his head and slapped Víctor's back. "Fine, you can work for me. You'll put my back out before we even get there." And my sister will never talk to me again, he thought, as he grasped his aching back and tried to catch his breath.

On that first joint outing, once they were over the border, Josep informed Víctor that they were on a special recognizance and possible humanitarian mission. It was as if the teary face of the French woman had followed him home from the ski hill. While he knew he had more than enough to worry about with his own family, he felt a digging concern for her. He only wanted to find her, check on her, and then let his mind forget her. To do so, they had to get to Merloin-les-Bains. After a very long walk, they found themselves first at the chemists and then standing before the immense lilac door of a walled manor. Josep instructed Víctor to wait beyond the gate before he knocked the giant knocker with a shaky hand. Geneviève herself opened the door. He hardly recognized her without the ski hat covering her hair, which was long, loose, and dark, shining on her shoulders as if shellacked there.

"*Bonjour, monsieur. Est-ce qu'ils nous ont encore changé de facteur? Vous avez un colis pour moi?*" she said, not recognizing him either.

"No, I'm not the postman and I'm not delivering anything. In fact, I'm hoping to pick up your spirits." Josep smiled and offered her a cigarette. "Josep Balaguer, from the ski hill at Vall de Núria."

"Yes, it is you." She looked as if he had brought her a gigantic bouquet of flowers rather than a pack of Gitanes. Covering her smiling mouth, she said, "I'm so sorry I didn't recognize you. The post office is always changing our postman. Please do come in." She pulled him inside by the hand and Josep glanced over his shoulder toward where Víctor was waiting. "I've been so hoping you would come to see me," she said, and then a shadow fell over her face. "Unless you've come to see my husband about that business. I'm afraid he's away, *comme d'habitude.*"

"Actually, I have come to see you. Are you well? I left you at the top of that horrific hill and I was concerned. I was nearby and wanted to check on you."

"It took me ages, but I managed. Of course, I wasn't fast enough for Jules. But let's not talk about him. Tell me how you are." She led him into to a small sitting room with a large bay window framed by curtains striped in fuchsia and gold. Opposite the window was a gold settee and on their left were two red velvet arm chairs facing a portrait of a woman on the wall above the fireplace. A green and blue Persian carpet covered the wooden floors.

Josep held his back as he examined the room. "A few aches and pains, but I'm managing. You have a lovely house," he said, the gold reminding him of the Palau mansion as he sat in the chair she offered him.

"Do you think so? It's my mother-in-law's taste. They've never let me touch it." She was hunched in a chair and frowned at the room around her. "Would you like a little drink to go with your cigarette?" She looked up at a clock on the mantelpiece. "In fact, lunch is almost ready. We eat much earlier here. You must stay. Since Jules insisted on sending my boys to boarding school, I would enjoy the company." She leaned in and pointed a pink-nailed finger at him. "I did promise you lunch. I'm so happy you could come. I knew you would. I actually have something to tell you."

Josep took a closer look at this petite woman, whose figure was no longer that of a wispy dancer, though she seemed fragile enough to break.

Her cheek bones were high and creased slightly by the lines that spread from the corner of her eyes when she smiled. Though her make-up was almost as thick as the day he met her, he suspected that it hid a naturally handsome face. He wondered why she wore such a mask with a matching crimson scarf around her neck. Her hazel eyes and loose dark hair were familiarly haunting, both taking him to long ago places and people. Now that he was sitting across from Geneviève, he fidgeted slightly in his chair as he wondered how his life had brought him here. Surely he had learned enough from the ski lift and from all his previous misadventures. She wiggled slightly towards him, her excitement resembling that of a little girl. "Please stay," she said.

"I would love to," he said finally, and she clapped her hands and pulled him to the kitchen where she was stewing a rabbit.

"*Lapin au vin.* I prefer it to the chicken version." She looked up from the pot in front of her. "But I should warn you, I'm not a very good cook. Jules says I can't even boil an egg."

"It looks and smells delicious. Is your husband away on business?"

She shrugged and stirred. "That's what he tells me. I suspect he's keeping good company."

"Why would you think that?"

"Perfume on his shirts. Theatre tickets in his pockets."

"That doesn't mean anything."

"I've followed him and it means something."

Josep swirled his drink in his glass. "What is his business exactly?"

"He supplies gems to jewelers. He is infatuated with his little rubies and sapphires. It is really his only interest these days. I'm sure he would love to talk to you about expanding to Spain, if you're interested." Her glowing look turned sad.

"I don't deal in goods like that. Just staples," he said, and thought of Dolors. He had a sudden feeling of being watched and looked over his shoulder. He scanned the kitchen wondering what on earth he was doing there. Geneviève took his arm and led him to the dining room.

"We had shortages here after the war as well, but now things are much better." She poured him some wine. "I hope the rabbit's not too salty."

"It's delicious," Josep said thinking that it wasn't bad, but Dolors' would be better. "Now you have your dance school."

"Yes, a school with very few students. I'm not very good at promoting myself, but I do have a name in dance circles. I live through the dreams of those small clumsy children. There's little hope for me now with my feet. They say it's arthrosis."

"The toll of time. For me it's my back." Josep looked at her in silence. Despite her obvious years, she seemed afraid of herself. Dolors with all her driven energy would run her over. "It must have been difficult to go from great stages to this little town. You must feel very lonely," Josep said as he watched her eating, lost in what looked like a spell of nostalgia.

She sighed. "I'd rather not dwell on it. It's too late for me now. You make a decision and your life takes a certain tack because of it. I'm trying to make the most of it and find ways to keep busy." She crossed her cutlery on her empty plate and offered Josep a cigarette. "I hope you don't mind," she said and cringed. "I was so sure that you would come, so I've been asking around about your brother."

Josep almost choked on the cigarette he was lighting. "My brother? Eduard?"

"Yes, you said he lived in Fontsec. There are a lot of Spaniards around here, but just one called Eduard Balaguer in that town. Everyone knows everyone around here."

He put down the cigarette and almost burned himself. "So what did you find out?" he said, thinking how strange it was to hear the name of his brother on the lips of this woman, who despite her vulnerability had managed to find his own.

"Not much, really. You probably know it all already. He has a very tall wife called Francine who works at the post office. He has a very handsome young son called Gaspard. I suspect he looks a lot like his uncle. Eduard is a very quiet man, very reserved, they tell me. He's probably not quite like his brother. You know all this already, don't you?" She pouted and looked at him.

"No, go on," he said and emptied his wine glass.

"They say he has a bit of a drinking problem. When he drinks, his true personality comes out and it's nothing like his everyday sober personality. Apparently the problem is that he has quite easy access to this at the PMU bar where he works placing bets on the horses. They say he likes to do a lot of betting himself." She drew in her breath. "And the injury to his hand must have been very painful." She shook her own hands and tilted her head at him. "I'm sorry. I've said too much. I always say too much."

"No, you haven't." Josep was looking at her and listening in silence. He had a surreal feeling of watching the two of them from above, sitting at this table in France talking about his brother who had deserted him. "But can I ask why you bothered to find out?"

She stood and walked behind him and softly rested her hands on his shoulders. "You helped me so much at the ski hill. You paid attention to me, more attention than anyone has paid in years. We connected and I knew you would come. I wanted to pay you back." She removed a hand from his shoulder. "Are you angry?"

"No, I'm not angry, I'm just surprised," he said, but he didn't tell her that he hadn't known about Eduard's job, or about his apparent problem with the drink, although his last encounter with Eduard could have been an indication. What he couldn't fathom was why Eduard would be working in a busy bar when he had taken such pains to hide away. He also hadn't known that Francine was working at the post office. That could actually be quite a useful contact. But then he would have to swallow the inedible lump of pride that seemed as large as the Pyrenees between them and contact Eduard as well. All of this news delivered by this woman surged through him like an electric force. It had been so many years since he had given up on Eduard and he couldn't wait to tell Àngels what he'd learned. Maybe she would also begin to believe his outings were important.

Geneviève seemed to feel the excitement running through his back. "I can find out more if you want me to." She looked at him shyly. "It would be my pleasure and it would give me something to do."

Josep nodded and looked again at this gentle woman who could fill his emotional void with her company and with information about Eduard. "I would like that. But all in secrecy. He can't know that I'm asking. He did some horrible things to me and I shouldn't even care what happens to him."

"But you do. He's your brother," Geneviève said. "I knew you were a good person from the moment I saw you."

He looked at her over his shoulder and motioned for her to go back to her chair. "Maybe I can help you. Do you mind?" Reaching down he gently took her foot in his lap. He carefully removed the shoe and began to rub. "I hope I'm not being too forward. Does that feel any better?"

She grinned and let her head rest on the back of her chair. "It feels marvelous. Your hands are so warm."

Josep could feel her bony feet in his fingers and felt her perfume sweet in his throat. He was beginning to feel dizzy from digestion, the wine, or the unlikeliness of it all that he didn't hear the doorbell ring until Geneviève kicked him.

"The door." She shook her foot free. "I'm sorry. That felt so nice but I must get that. This time it could be the postman."

Josep watched from the living room as she opened the door. She took a step back and gave Josep a surprised look. "It's for you."

"Me?" Josep stepped forward. "Víctor, what are you doing here? I told you to wait." Josep dashed towards him then remembered Geneviève and his manners. "Sorry, Madame Petitpas, this is my business associate, Víctor Munt. He's also one of the family."

Geneviève covered her mouth and then swatted Josep. "You should have told me you weren't alone. He could have stayed for lunch as well. Please do come in. There's some left. I can heat it up in a moment." She moved toward the kitchen.

"No, but thank you," Josep said. "Víctor and I must get across the mountain before dark."

"Let me get you something for the road then." She scurried away, and while Josep was glaring at Víctor, she returned with a bundle in brown paper. "I'm sorry that it's lukewarm." She handed it to Víctor who stepped back in surprise.

"Thank you. That's very kind."

"It's a shame that you have to go, but I do hope to see you again soon." She took Josep's hand. "We can finish our," she began.

"Business," Josep said and shook her hand. "I'd like that very much." He looked into her watery eyes for a few extra seconds before stepping outside with Víctor. Gripping the back of Víctor's neck, he guided him down the front walk and when they were beyond the gate, Josep slapped him across the head with his glove.

"Rule One. Never interrupt." The peaceful feeling he had earlier was now frustration.

Víctor raised his palms. "Fine, I'm sorry. It was getting so late and I found some information you might want to know."

"You found information out here?"

Víctor guided him to a bench across from the house that was slightly behind an old tree. Josep sat down. "I was observing from here," Víctor said, sitting next to him and pointing to the side of the house. "They appear to be very well off. Looking at the garage, they seem to have two cars. Imagine having not just one car, but two." Víctor flapped his hand up and down. "The house looks like it's been in the family for generations, yet it has been freshly painted, at least last year, although the choice of color is odd. All the hedges and bushes are sculpted, so they must have a gardener."

Josep sighed and shook his head. "Those aren't facts. It's just observation."

"I asked around," Víctor continued and raised an eyebrow. "The woman, Geneviève, runs a new dance academy, so income doesn't likely come from her. The two children go to boarding school. Everyone raves about her, but they also seem to feel sorry for her. They don't know much about her husband other than his comings and goings, with significantly more goings. Geneviève has been known to fall into bouts of depression. She doesn't open the curtains or turn on the lights for days. The husband, Jules, does work in jewelry, just like she told you." Víctor rubbed his hands together.

Josep looked silently at Víctor and was beginning to forgive him for the interruption. Geneviève's state of mind was worse than he'd thought. In his thick jacket and woolen hat Víctor still looked too young to have such gumption. Víctor was looking back at him with his dark eyes wide, clearly hoping for some form of approval or recognition. Josep slapped his shoulder and thought that he could really use this boy, as long as he knew when to start and stop his investigations. "You have been busy. I hope that you asked your questions discreetly."

"Yes, definitely," Víctor said nodding. "Everything arose naturally. It's amazing how much people in small towns like to talk about their neighbors, particularly the older folks. And I did have quite a long time to do my research. You seem to really like her."

"Yes, I do." Josep looked at Víctor and saw Dolors' face reflected in his eyes. "But it's just business. I'll have to come back when her husband returns." Josep put an arm around Víctor. "I must say, I'm impressed by your first day. But remember, when I tell you to wait, you wait." He pulled his ear closer. "We'll have to make an agreement that everything that happens in the field remains a secret, a sort of pact between partners. Àngels particularly has no need to know, and probably Dolors shouldn't either."

"Partners?" Víctor grinned.

Josep slapped his back. "Maybe not yet, but if everything goes well and we keep our agreement, we could discuss it."

Víctor smiled and nodded. "A pact, I agree." As the men shook gloved hands, Víctor motioned to the house in front of them. "There goes Geneviève. She must be in a hurry. She's in stocking feet."

Josep quickly pulled Víctor behind the tree and they watched in the light of dusk as Geneviève, with her hair now neatly in a bun on the back of her head and white socks on her feet, opened the main gate and reached into the post box hanging there. She took out a parcel the size of brick, turned in over in her hands, then reached in and removed some envelopes, which she shuffled with urgency. She pulled one envelope out and frowned at it then ran back into the house. The door closed behind her. Josep couldn't help but think the envelope could contain more news about Eduard.

"It looks like it was something important," Víctor said.

"It was just the post. People receive it every day. She did tell me she was expecting the postman," Josep said, intending to demystify this woman who had managed to slip under his skin. If Geneviève was to be a regular visit on his list, both for her company and the news of Eduard, it would be best to put Víctor's curiosity to rest.

"There was something in that post box." Víctor looked sadly at Josep. "I failed. I'm sorry. That should have been the first place I looked. I'll get better. I promise."

"Relax, it's fine. I hired you to help me carry the goods. I don't need a detective," Josep said, and led Víctor away from the house.

***

Across the mountains in Pujaforta, Dolors was sizing up the garden area just outside her bakery with unrestrained energy. Rosa and Montse, holding their brother's hands between them, were trying to follow behind as Dolors measured the area with long strides. The ground was almost flat with a thin blanket of grass and weeds upon a thick base of stubborn rock. They watched as Dolors grinned, took a deep breath, and looked over the cliff edge toward the mountains. "I don't know why I never thought of it before, but this will make the perfect terrace. We can open a bar, a café. It could be like the one at the ski resort but better."

Rosa looked at Montse and then her mother. "How will it be better?"

"Because it will have my bread, my *coca*, my *flam* and *crema*, and many other simple dishes I will think of." She waved to the mountains beyond. "And it will have a breathtaking view. I haven't actually looked at it in such a long time. That's what tourists want." They all stood on the edge of the property and looked across the valley to the height of the snow-encrusted Pyrenees in the distance.

"Won't it be too cold for a terrace?" Rosa asked. "Plus I've never noticed any tourists in Pujaforta."

Dolors sighed and shook her head. "It would be just for summertime, for the good weather. We'll need a few months to get it ready anyway. The permissions from the town hall will be the hardest." She seemed to be talking to herself, then she looked at Montse. "Tourists, and people from all over will come once they hear about my *truita*. Won't they, Montse?"

Montse's eyes brightened. She loved to help make the omelet, the classic version with the eggs and potato and just a little chopped onion. "Yes, yours is the best."

"After school, you girls can help me. Montse can take care of the *truita*. We can make some with spinach from the garden and with wild mushrooms if we find some."

Montse nodded eagerly.

"I'd rather take care of Pau." Rosa looked at him walking gracefully along the edge of the property. He was very sure on his feet for a toddler. "I hate cooking," she said, and shuddered.

***

From across the garden, Àngels spotted Dolors admiring the mountain view and marched purposefully toward her. When Dolors spotted her coming, she waved the children inside.

"Àngels," Dolors said, "What's going on? Is it Manel? I need to talk to him. Once his shoulder is better I'm going to need him to build the terrace for my bar." Dolors appeared to wait for Àngels' reaction, but she wasn't listening to anything but her own panic.

"Where's your husband?" Àngels demanded. "He ignored my feelings and took Víctor with him, didn't he?" She slapped her thigh as the familiar hopeless feeling returned. She was convinced that everyone was out to undermine her. Didn't they see that Víctor was all she had? He was all she had left of Carme. Her two brothers were on another plane, one across the mountains and one obsessed with crossing them, even if it divided the family. Her mother and Sr. Palau were getting on splendidly, so her visits were scattered. Her greatest satisfaction came from Víctor and their almost daily conversations at her table, where he had begun to share his aspirations about using the co-op to help others. He was sure that there were people out there who needed proper clothing. Now she feared that Víctor had been lying, only trying to please her. Otherwise, why would he accept so readily to become a pack mule for her brother?

Now Dolors looked surprised. "Víctor will surely turn up later. When Josep left the house he was alone. Just be patient. Speaking of patients, how is Manel?"

Àngels' face perked up. She hadn't thought of that. "Maybe Víctor is with Manel. He's the one who needs Víctor's help right now." With Manel's broken collarbone he was trying to do everything single-handedly. She insisted on helping him, carefully turning trees into functional works of art. That was another source of satisfaction and she knew that Manel had something to do with it as well.

"You and Manel seem to be getting on much better than you used to. Now he's going to need your help more than ever. All those years, I thought you couldn't stand him."

"He's changed. That was so long ago," Àngels said, looking across to the mountains. "Or perhaps I have. I see him differently now. If Carme was willing to accept him, then I must be as well. Besides, he's lost everyone. He's even lost his town. We're all he has."

"And he did carve you that lovely bed," Dolors said with a hint of mischief in her voice.

"Yes, it's absolutely beautiful." Àngels thought of how peacefully she slept in that bed, on her first real mattress.

"I think he's been waiting all this time to share it with you. I'm sure of it."

"No, absolutely not." Àngels stepped forward. She had grown tired of everyone's insinuations. Why did everyone insist that every woman needs a man? "That is not on his mind. Even if it is, it is the furthest thing from mine." Àngels glanced away from Dolors.

"Your bed could probably use some warming," Dolors said, and added very quietly, "You're not thinking of warming it with Baltasar, are you?"

Àngels' mouth fell open. After all these years, Dolors was still able to dismay her. Maybe Josep had been right. Dolors had never let her desire for Baltasar and his status burn out. "You're married to Josep now, Dolors. You have three children." She added very loudly, "The day you said yes to my brother you lost all rights to Baltasar. Leave the man in peace. He certainly deserves it after all those years with you." Àngels stepped closer. "It will be my business whom I choose to warm my bed."

Dolors huffed and turned on her heels. As she strutted towards the house, she said, "When you see Manel, tell him that when he's better I have a job for him."

"When you see Josep or Víctor, tell them that I am expecting them."

Àngels was waiting up when Víctor finally returned, carrying an enormously full pack on his back. Despite every urge to the contrary, she sent him back to where he came from.

"You did go with Josep," she said pointing to the door. "You can stay with him. Both of you knew how I felt about this and decided to ignore me." She tried to mask the tears in her voice. "You're not welcome here anymore. You can tell Josep that he isn't either."

"But, the contraband, I'm good at it," Víctor began to protest.

"You can never be good enough," Àngels said, and gently pushed Víctor toward the door, which she shut behind him before falling shattered to the floor. After all these years of caring for him, she could not believe that he would purposely abandon her and that her brother was ready to shove her back over the edge.

***

Minutes later, when Víctor knocked on the door at Josep's house, Josep was crawling into Dolors' bed, something he hadn't done since before Pau was born. The room was black and he could feel Dolors' heat under the covers. He put a hand on her shoulder and kissed her cheek. During the entire walk back from France, Josep could still feel Geneviève's feet in his hands and her fingers on his back and felt growing remorse for the thoughts of her in his head. Surely he would feel better if he'd just gone to the bordello like the others had suggested. The unexpected guilt made him decide that it was time to remedy his marriage. He hoped that some of that old fire from his wife could shoot Geneviève's sad face out of his mind. Yet at that point, he would have settled for a cuddle. As he kissed Dolors' sleeping cheek, she moaned and turned on her side so that her back was to Josep. He put his body along the length of hers and at that moment there was a banging on the door. Dolors awoke with a start, kicked Josep away and looked at him as if he were an intruder.

"What are you doing? What was that?" Her eyes were unfocused and she was breathing heavily from the fright.

"I just wanted a hug. It's been so long."

"Now you've decided? After all this time? In the middle of the night?"

"It's as good a time as any, isn't it?"

"No." She was shaking her head and pulling the covers closer to her chin. "I have to start making plans for the bar tomorrow. I have a meeting at the town hall."

"What bar?" Josep asked looking down at her.

The door pounded again.

"What's that noise?" Dolors asked. "Who could be here now?"

Josep groaned and padded toward the window. He looked down and saw Víctor standing at the door in the moonlight.

"The boy has incredible timing," he said heading for the stairs. "I think we might have some company for a while."

"Company? Who?" Dolors sat up in bed.

"Víctor. Àngels must have kicked him out."

"Víctor?" Dolors said. "Tell him he's welcome here," she called. "Maybe he can convince Àngels that Baltasar is not a suitable bed partner," she added softly, but Josep was already downstairs.

***

From the moment Rosa learned that Víctor had moved into the attic, she did not put down her camera. She followed him and snapped pictures as he pushed dusty crates, chests full of old clothing, and Josep's suitcases into a corner and began to set up a bed. She handed him her favorite blanket.

"I'm making a report of your move, in case some day you want to look back on it." She took a photo of Víctor's face streaked with dust and sweat and thought how she would love to frame it.

"There's probably not enough light in here," Víctor said, gesturing to the damp stone walls before putting some straw on top of the crates. "Besides, I don't think I'm going to want to remember this."

"Don't you want to live here with us?" Rosa asked, preparing to argue with him if she didn't like what she heard.

"*Clar que sí.* Of course I want to live here with you," he said, and patted her head with his large hand. "It's just that your *Tieta* Àngels is upset and I should really be with her."

"Yes, I heard she was *cabrejada*, really pissed off."

Víctor smirked and sat on his makeshift bed. "Who told you that?"

"She did, basically." Rosa sat down beside him. "I overheard her tell *Mare* that she was angry at you, but even angrier at *Pare*." Rosa lowered her voice. "I followed her home and saw her through the window. She started throwing clothes from the loft into the kitchen then she came down and sat in the pile. She was crying hysterically. I have a picture." She held up her camera. "Then she started to fold and smooth the clothes ever so carefully and stacked them on the table."

"It's worse than I thought," Víctor said. "She has to realize that she can't protect me forever. I have to live." Víctor was gazing toward the attic's single window, covered in years of grime and dirt. "She's been trying to protect me for so long and now it's causing a rift in her own family."

"They say she's pretty fragile," Rosa said nodding.

"Who said she's fragile?"

"Everybody, *Mare*, *Pare*, *Iaia* Núria. Everybody. Even Dr. Sort. He's really concerned about her. He's always asking about her, wanting to know if she's keeping busy. They say that ever since your mother, *Tieta* Carme, died," Rosa leaned toward Víctor and hugged him, "*Tieta* Àngels has been on the edge. I don't think Dr. Sort likes her to spend so much time with Manel. But he keeps her busy. I think he's good for her."

"You do, do you?" Víctor shook his head as he smiled down at her. "Not much gets by you, does it?"

"No, not much." She smiled and took another picture.

"Montse doesn't seem to be very pleased that I'm here."

"She's not," Rosa said. "I think she's just a little jealous."

"Of what?"

"She thinks that with you here, I won't pay attention to her anymore."

"That's ridiculous."

"Not really." Rosa stood, believing that frankness was the best approach. "I have to go to school. The nuns will be waiting. So will Montse. Will you come tuck me in tonight? My room is right downstairs." She pointed to the bottom of the stairwell. "I want you to tuck me in every night."

"I know where your room is. Of course, I'll come and say goodnight. Now get back to school, though I don't know what they can possibly teach you."

"That's what I tell them." She waved and disappeared down the stairs.

***

Some weeks later, Josep found himself heading back to Merloin-les-Bains with the purpose of brightening Geneviève's day. She was still so much in his thoughts that he had tried to erase her by finding dirt about her family. However, according to his contacts everything appeared to be spotless. Even Jules, despite all his wife's criticism, had come back sparkling. The man appeared to be well appreciated in business circles. He was also said to be devoted to his wife and children. While the news was comforting for his business inclinations, it didn't help him justify needing to protect Geneviève. Yet he knew that many put on one face for strangers and another for those close to them. He had witnessed the man's temper at the ski hill. He was more than certain that the bruise that Geneviève had shown him was not the first of its kind.

So very early one morning he set out into the woods without a word to Dolors or any of the family. With Víctor now living under his roof, he didn't want to be followed. Yet when he was just steps into the woods, Josep heard the ice crunching behind him. Hiding behind a tree, he soon saw that it was not a border guard as he had feared but Víctor, dressed entirely in black. Josep waved him toward him.

"*Collons*, you gave me a fright, man," Josep said breathing heavily, his body a dark gray shadow against the night.

"You almost left without me," Víctor accused.

"I did leave without you."

"Why? I knew you didn't think I was good enough." Víctor kicked a stone.

"On the contrary, you were very good." Josep thought reluctantly that in fact he was too good. "I have a special mission. Besides, you're supposed to be helping Dolors and Manel. Now they won't be talking to me either."

"Manel's shoulder is getting better, so he doesn't need me so much." Víctor touched Josep's arm. "Forgive me for saying so, but your wife is a bit bossy. I need a break."

"Indeed she is." Josep chuckled. "When she has something on her mind, no one can stop her. Now she's obsessed with this terrace idea." Josep glanced into the darkness and at the bare trees encircling them as if tuned to their conversation. He shook the eerie feeling in his spine and said, "Enough chatting for now. If you're coming with me, let's go."

"I'm coming," Víctor said and put his feet in Josep's footsteps.

When finally they were across the border but still among the identical trees and rocks that had no sense of territory or nation, Víctor asked, "So what's the mission? Guns? Drugs? Jewelry?"

Josep shook his head. The sun filtered through the trees, making the pine needles underfoot look like a soft, rose-colored carpet. "Your vivid imagination may disappoint you. You know that my deals are more about booze and chocolate. I do have to go back to Merloin-les-Bains, but I have another mission for you. I need you to go to Fontsec, not far from here. Go to the post office, ask for Francine Balaguer and give her this." Josep handed Víctor a thin blue envelope. "Don't read it and don't tell anyone who sent you. *M'entens?*"

Víctor turned the envelope over and examined the seal, which was still damp with Josep's saliva. He tucked it inside his jacket and nodded at Josep. "I understand."

"Don't get curious and start investigating. If there is anything you want to know, you ask me directly. *M'entens?*"

"Yes, I understand." Víctor looked somewhat offended then turned and started walking in the direction of Fontsec.

Josep, for his part, headed to Merloin-les-Bains with a bounce in his step and a vision of Geneviève in his mind. As he approached the house it looked more grand than he remembered. At the great wooden door he raised his fist and knocked. He knocked again, and again, until his knuckles stung. There seemed to be no movement inside. He had come all this way, thinking about seeing Geneviève's face when she opened the door. Her hazel eyes. Her bright lips. He banged again. When the disappointment began to ache more than his fist, he turned and walked down the front walk. As he approached the giant gate, he heard a click of the door and a smile replaced the sadness on his face. He turned and his smile vanished. A man was looking questioningly at him.

"*Oui*, what is it?" he said. He was wearing a dark sweater and slacks and was holding a pair of spectacles in his raised hand. His glare drilled through Josep.

Josep vaguely recognized Geneviève's husband from the ski slope, and he wasn't about to be trapped beyond his ability this time. He waved and shook his head. "No, thank you."

"But you were so insistent. I thought you would knock a hole through the door," the man said, stepping out the door in slippered feet. "What is it about?"

Josep exhaled and looked at his shoes. Then he walked toward this man and offered his hand to shake. The man had put on his glasses, and eyes that were hard and round as pebbles were peering suspiciously over top of them. "Jules Petitpas," he said and shook Josep's hand very slowly.

"My name is Josep Balaguer. I met your wife at a ski hill and we talked about some possible business ventures."

The man took off his spectacles and bit the end of the arm. "Yes, Geneviève has spoken highly of you." He nodded and gave Josep an appraising look, as if determining whether he was coal or a precious stone needing a serious buffing. "You make deliveries to Spain, is that right?"

Josep looked over either shoulder and he nodded. He couldn't admit that he was really only there to see the man's wife. In fact, he was quite surprised that Geneviève had even mentioned him.

Jules gestured inside. "Come in then. It will be more comfortable talking in the house."

Josep followed Jules into the sitting room where Geneviève had first welcomed him. Jules motioned toward the armchair, where Josep sat and reexamined the oil painting of the woman hanging on the wall. The woman looked like a feminine version of this man, with the same dark eyes, tubercular nose, and narrow lips pursed in disapproval.

"So what is it you deliver?" Jules said and motioned to a glass and crystal decanter.

Josep glanced at the clock on the wall and shook his head. "Mostly primary necessities, flour, sugar, coffee, a few luxury goods—luxury for Spain at this moment—chocolate, tobacco, and alcohol," he said as Jules placed a full glass of whisky in his hand and sat on the sofa across from him.

Jules took a long draw from his own glass and said, "Geneviève told you what I deal in?"

"Yes, but I don't necessarily want to get into anything new right now."

"You might change your mind when you see this." Jules opened a small case and held out his palm for Josep to see. Tiny diamonds glittered like raindrops in the seat of his hand. "The main part of my business involves importing gemstones, diamonds, rubies, emeralds, sapphires. I supply jewelers, but I'm always looking for other places to sell."

Josep watched as the stones drew in the sunlight and sparkled at him. Rather than sparking temptation they cried a warning. It was too drastic a step for him to go from bringing his people essential goods to smuggling adornments for the rich. Although he knew he could eventually find buyers, he could not justify it. Josep pretended to nod his appreciation. "They are spectacular, but I don't think people are ready for that in Spain, at least not people that I deal with. We have other needs right now."

Jules closed his palm and the diamonds disappeared. "That is entirely understandable, though I hear that Franco's wife is quite an admirer of jewels." He tucked the stones back into the case. "I said that this was my main business, but I do deal in other areas." He stood and left the room. He came back holding a leather-bound book, which he handed to Josep.

Josep fondled the supple leather and read the embossed cover. *L'Ingénu*, by Voltaire. He opened it and felt the coolness of its fine paper and the darkness of its ink. Jules placed more books on the table in front of him. *Les Trois Mousquetaires* by Alexandre Dumas, *Leviatán* by Thomas Hobbes, *El origen de las especies* by Charles Darwin. He picked them up slowly and turned them over in his hands.

"You could find buyers for those," Jules said standing over him. "I could get you more Spanish translations. You won't find them in any bookshops around here."

Josep held the Spanish version of Darwin and looked up at Jules. "Do you know how dangerous that would be? If I'm caught I would be imprisoned or worse, and I don't know what they would do to my family."

"The risk always makes it more exciting and lucrative, *n'est ce pas*? I deal in books, first and special editions, which are entirely legal in France. For me gems are much more stimulating."

"Yes, indeed." Josep nodded. "There would be a certain thrill in the challenge, and in the risk for me. I can see that." He reluctantly returned the book to the table beside the others.

"Name any banned book and I can acquire it in Spanish for you, perhaps even in Catalan."

"Let me think about it. First I need to see if anyone would buy them," Josep said while trying not to reveal the eagerness tingling inside him. He could bring knowledge and culture rather than luxury. It could be his own underground attack on the regime.

"Surely you'll find many buyers. All those books were burnt, were they not?"

"Those that the fascists were able to find," Josep said and stood up. "I would like to have a word with Geneviève before I go back. Do you expect her soon?"

"She won't return until late this evening," Jules said. "She is away with the boys. You are going to finish your drink, aren't you?"

Josep looked at the full glass of whisky on the table in front of him. "Sorry," he said. "I need to keep a clear head. It's essential in this business."

"Fair enough." Jules shook Josep's hand and led him to the door. "Let me know what you decide."

As Josep walked down the front walk and heard the door close behind him, his spine ran with the thrill. Though slightly formal, Jules seemed like quite a reasonable man, not nearly the ogre Geneviève spoke of. As he opened the gate, Josep could still feel the smoothness of the leather on his fingertips and smell the dust in the paper. He felt a flutter under his ribcage. Smuggling banned books would really help him thumb his nose at the regime, much more than smuggling flour. There was hunger for food, but surely there was desire for learning. He felt an urge to tell Eduard about it, sure that he would appreciate these tactics. As he crossed the road a car approached. He stopped and stared. Geneviève's crimson scarf was fluttering at the wheel. Once again he felt a thrill run up his aching back. With this new venture he could also spend more time with Geneviève.

CHAPTER ELEVEN

"WHAT ARE YOU doing here?" Josep was standing in Geneviève's driveway watching her get out of her car. She straightened her scarf, turned her back, and began applying scarlet lipstick using the mirror of her compact.

"I'm very glad that I am," she said over her shoulder. "What a wonderful surprise." She grinned at him.

"Your husband said you wouldn't be back until late," Josep said, though he was also very pleased that she wasn't.

Her mouth dropped open. "You've been talking to Jules?"

"Yes, and he seems like an agreeable fellow, not the monster I expected."

She slammed the car door. "He's just a monster to me." She raised her sleeve and showed him her yellowing bruise. "He's charming to everyone else. I told you that he's a business man." She lowered her arm "He told you I wasn't coming because he doesn't want me to have contact with anyone, particularly not a man." Her hazel eyes grew large. She nudged him. "So did you talk about any business?"

"With everything you say, why would you want me to do business with him?"

She looked at her feet and twisted her scarf around her finger. "For selfish reasons. You would have to come here more often. That could give me a real reason to get up every morning." She glanced upward again. "You're looking rather handsome today." She smiled at him and they both turned towards the bay window at the front of the house, where they could see a dark shadow looking out. Geneviève waved.

"Is there somewhere we could talk? I want to tell you about Jules' proposal," Josep said. "I'm quite excited about it, for a number of reasons." He glanced at her arm, thinking there were even more reasons not to get involved.

Geneviève turned her back towards the house. She took something out of her bag and handed it to him. "Rue des Crusades, number 12. I'll meet you there in an hour." She stepped away, waving shyly at him as she approached the house. Once she was inside, Josep discreetly put the keys she had handed him into his pocket. He noticed they were still warm from her touch and ran in search of directions.

***

In the woods below Pujaforta, Àngels was helping Manel in his workshop, now lined with workbenches fashioned from the surrounding trees. The far end of the workshop contained a few pieces of carefully carved furniture—a bookshelf, a bedside table—although generally Manel worked to fill specific orders. The place smelled like sawdust and pine and Àngels' skin always felt dry, as if the wood absorbed the moisture from it. Manel insisted that she was imagining it, since her skin looked unbearably soft to him. Manel was now bent over half of a giant chest of drawers and was furiously intent on building the other half. Àngels found that Manel was just as upset as she was that Víctor had ditched them for Josep.

"Manel, you're going to hurt your shoulder," Àngels said, trying to slow his hammering arm with her hand.

"If Víctor had shown up, I wouldn't be doing this." He looked up at her and wiped his forehead with his forearm. "He knows that this piece has to be delivered next week."

"I know. I don't understand how he could have been so selfish." Àngels took the hammer from Manel's hand and started tapping a fine nail into the edge of the drawer he was making. She was also so angry that she had to try not to bang too hard. "My brother must be responsible. He only thinks of himself."

"Don't start again. I can't hear another word about Josep. If you're still angry with him you need to tell him about it, not me."

"He's trying to make up for it, but I won't let him. You know he even told me that he had news of Eduard, but he wouldn't say where he had got it, so I didn't feel inclined to share mine either." So far any news she had about Eduard did not tell her Eduard's side of what had happened between the two brothers, but she was beginning to suspect that Eduard had a good reason.

Manel shook his head. "The two of you—no, the three of you—are exasperating. You still have each other yet you do everything to stay apart. What I would do to be so lucky."

"Although he is my least favorite person right now, from what Josep says, he may be justified in waiting for Eduard to contact him. That said, I think he can't wait forever. It's all just lost time in the end."

"Why don't you go to see Eduard? I would take you," Manel said.

Àngels thought of going into the forest without Carme to guide her and shook her head. "I'm not ready for a trip. I tried that once and it was terrifying. I ended up facing Carles Puig at the station. We'll have to meet some other way."

"I think you're getting stronger, don't you?" Manel asked. "I am, thanks to you."

"Yes, I feel fine most of the time," Àngels said truthfully. The years she had spent working with Manel had slowly helped her forget the shadows of the past.

"We have to be really strong now, particularly since Víctor has abandoned us," Manel said and rested his hands on his hips. "We have to get this finished. You know it's the only order I've had all year."

"That's why I'm helping," she said, and hammered in the last nail. The two of them lifted the drawer and inserted it in the empty slot. "It's going to be beautiful." She stood back and admired the carved wooden fronts on the drawers and the smooth surface of the top of the chest. Slowly she opened the tiny compartments inlaid into the drawer's base. "It's a shame it's for the mayor's family. Maybe he'll tell everyone to get one. You'll have many more orders. I know it. I have faith in you."

"You don't know how pleased I feel every time you say that." He smiled at her and tilted his head. "I wish you had enough faith in me to marry me."

"A lot of faith is needed for that, but there's more than faith." She stroked the top of the chest of drawers. He had asked her the question so many times that now she hardly heard it. "Manel, you know that you're dear to me."

"Just not dear enough." Manel grasped one of the remaining drawers and once again started hammering loudly. "When I see Víctor, I'm going to give him a piece of my mind."

"I'm just as angry as you are, but don't take out your other frustrations on him."

"Then alleviate my frustrations and just let me hold you."

Àngels jumped backward as if he had hit her with the hammer. She shook her head. "No, you can't do that." She reached for her jacket and headed for the door. "I'm going to see Dolors. She probably has Víctor working on her terrace."

"Run away. Escape, just like you always do." Manel called after her, adding on just as the door slammed behind her, "My regards to Baltasar."

As Àngels made her way up the hill, her anger and embarrassment mounted. Why was there always this physical demand, this expectation? She enjoyed Manel's company and would rather spend her day with him than with anyone else, but she didn't want him to touch her. The idea of his hands on her body was repulsive. It didn't matter whose hands. For now the only relationship that she considered safe was a mother-son relationship, like the one she had with Víctor.

Once at the top of the hill, Àngels found Dolors on her hands and knees hammering a plank of wood to the terrace. Most of the floor was in place and a heavy wooden railing ran along the mountain side of it. Dolors looked up at her, clearly surprised. They hadn't spoken since the last time Àngels had been looking for Víctor, nor since Víctor had moved in to their attic.

"He's not here," Dolors said sitting back on her calves and putting the hammer down beside her. "*Estic de mala llet.*"

"I'm also in a nasty mood and so is Manel. Víctor was meant to help him finish an important piece."

"And he was to help me finish this." She motioned to the remaining small gap in the deck. "I've had to take the girls out of school to do the baking." Dolors stood up and dusted off the front of her smock with her hands. "I've been meaning to apologize to you for Víctor moving in here," she said, but her voice did not sound apologetic. "I actually had nothing to do with it."

"He can come back when he assures me that he won't be working with Josep."

"Do you think he'll do that? He seems pleased to fit in and to be good at something. Josep says he's got talent."

"He surely has talent for safer things."

"Like building," Dolors said. Then she smiled and motioned to her patio. "So, what do you think?"

Àngels stepped on to the wooden deck and flexed her knees, bouncing slightly. "Looks good and sturdy." She gazed out over the mountains where the snow was beginning to dissolve. "And the view is superb. Funny I've never noticed it."

"We have no time for it." Dolors dropped to her knees again and continued hammering. "This has to be ready by Easter. That's when the tourists arrive."

"I've never seen any tourists here," Àngels said, before adding hastily, "but I'm sure they'll come."

"They'd better. We're ready for them. Your mother has all the women making sweaters and ski hats to sell to them, which you would know if you spent more time at the co-op. Then again, Manel does need your help, doesn't he? And I think you like to be around him. He definitely likes to be around you."

"I enjoy his company, but you can leave it at that. Don't keep pushing with your silly ideas."

Dolors stopped hammering and looked up at Àngels. "What about Baltasar?" she asked quietly.

"You know what I wish, Dolors? That you would want something for me because you think I need it. Because you care about me. Not because of what you might get out of it. That's what I wish." Àngels walked away without seeing Dolors sitting on her haunches, biting her lip and blinking back the tears.

***

Josep stood outside a newer single-story house with the façade painted white. A sign outside the door read *Geneviève Petitpas École de Danse* with a drawing of a bunny in a tutu. Using the key that Geneviève had given him, he let himself inside. Switching on the electric light revealed a small foyer with a reception desk. The bright pink walls were decorated in Degas reprints. Nothing was out of place.

As he waited, two purple doors behind the desk beckoned him. He opened one and peeked inside a small change room with hooks and a bench, and another door leading out the other side. This one led to the dance room, with a wooden floor, a barre, and a mirror stretching along one side. As Josep approached the mirror, he straightened his hair and examined his teeth, noticing the reflection of a white door on the wall behind him. He tiptoed towards it, opened it with a squeak and peeked inside. The light from the room behind him revealed an office with a wooden desk. A coat rack and hooks were covered in cardigans, leotards, and leg warmers, and in the corner were several boxes of pointe shoes in various sizes. He scuttled towards the desk, not sure why he was snooping. He was so drawn towards Geneviève, perhaps he hoped that this place and these objects would help him know her and understand her better. On the desk were various letters. One jutted out from underneath the stack. While the other papers were white, this one was a single piece of blue paper, folded once, with no envelope. Josep flattened it out and realized that the curly French handwriting stopped midway down the first page. It had to be Geneviève's. It was dated yesterday.

Chère Mme Balaguer,

You cannot know how pleased I was to receive your response to my letter. After all these years, I did not think you would remember me. I am so thrilled to hear that your family

The letter stopped there. Josep folded it again and put it back on the desk. For a moment he squinted at it, as if hoping it would fill in the enormous blank at the bottom of the page. How could Geneviève know Francine? He then remembered her saying that everyone knew each other in the area. He felt heat rush from his toes to his head, which he shook in an attempt to concentrate on the most important part of all. She was trying to find out more about Eduard. His own personal spy. This could definitely be a relationship to foster for a variety of reasons. Not wanting to get caught, Josep returned to the dance studio and wandered over to the barre where he awkwardly lifted his leg and tried to rest his ankle. His back jarred. Yet when he heard the echo of applause and a giggle behind him he almost leaped to the ceiling. Reflected in the mirror behind him Geneviève stood clapping. She was clutching her handbag under her arm and her eyes were sparkling at him. Josep quickly disengaged his foot and approached her.

"You're doing that rather well," she said. "But why would that surprise me?"

Josep rubbed his back. "It's not really my thing."

"Men dance, too, you know."

Josep shrugged. "You won't catch me in those tight leotards."

"That could be interesting." She looked first at his legs and then around the room. "So what do you think of the place? It's a bit small and dark, isn't it? Jules told me no one would sign up for classes anyway. I used to teach when I first came here, but he still thinks I'm incapable."

"I'm sure you're more than capable. You shouldn't let him drag you down like that."

"So he didn't frighten you away?"

"Of course not. I don't frighten easily. But after what you told me maybe I should." He hesitated then decided to address his business concerns before finding out what she might do for his family. "I actually found your husband's proposal quite intriguing. What can you tell me about his books?"

Geneviève led him to a chair in the corner and sat down beside him. "I know that he has book dealers in Paris and other places. It's usually for rare editions and such. Why? Are you interested in books?"

"This could be a way to filter banned books into my country. But while it all sounds very heroic, I don't know if it's for me."

"Of course, it is. You know what I think of Jules, but it does sound perfect. I'd bet your brother would be proud of you." She gripped his arm in obvious excitement and released it. "But what do I know?"

"I have no idea what my brother thinks." He put his hand on hers. "I do like the thought of being able to see you regularly. But first I need to know something. Where did you get that information about Eduard?"

She looked at her knees and her face flushed. "When I asked around about him I found out that his wife is someone I used to know. I wrote to her thinking she wouldn't likely remember me. But she did and wrote back." She rubbed her eye and streaked some black eyeliner onto her cheek. "Are you angry?"

"It's all very odd, but no." Josep bit his lip. "Listen, please don't tell her that you know me, and see what else you can find out."

"What a relief. I was afraid you would never talk to me again. It will be our secret." She smiled. "I have learned a little more since the last time. I know that Eduard can't go back to Spain until Franco is gone."

Josep nodded slowly leaning toward her. "What else did she say?"

She looked at him shyly. "I have a number of sources and they say that he's wanted by the police. Or so he thinks and that terrifies him. It debilitates him and his relationships with everyone around him." She pulled on his sleeve. "And his son is rather intelligent. He's jumped ahead in school. He devours books, they say."

"Books?" Josep said, thinking of the fine leather editions that were so smooth in his hands.

"Yes, that's all I know. For now. Are you happy with what I found it out? I hope so." Geneviève's eyes had a frightened look. "You do have a way of working yourself into people's thoughts. I can't get you out of mine."

Josep felt strangely closer to Eduard, his family, and to this woman beside him. She knew almost as much about his brother as he did. "Yes, I'm glad you found that out." He rubbed the smudge near Geneviève's eye with the tip of his fingers. "We're practically strangers, yet the same has happened to me."

"It's my instinct. I feel it right in here." She touched her chest between her breasts, then she reached out and touched Josep's chest. "From the moment I saw you, I had a good feeling about you."

"You hardly know me. I've done lots of horrible things. If I told you I'd killed a woman, would you believe me?" He didn't know why he said this, but felt compelled to test her.

She swatted him. "Not for a minute. We've all done things we've regretted, but I don't think you could hurt anyone."

"Not intentionally." He edged closer and noted that her perfume was strong and magnetic. She jumped up and pulled him to his feet, dragging him by both hands until they were in the center of the room looking at each other in the long mirror. She held his arm out straight at his side.

"Let me show you how it's done. Just some of the basics."

He clicked his tongue and waved his arm in the air. "I'm no dancer. Besides, I thought you had sore feet." He looked down at her sensible shoes.

"My days on pointe and in high heels are over. That woman is long gone."

"I quite like the one who's here right now." He pulled her back to the chair, where he made her sit and took her foot in his hand. "Isn't this where we left off the last time?" He began to massage the awkward boniness of her foot and she rested her head against the wall behind her. The sole of her foot felt rough in his hands, but her ankle was so soft. As she relaxed, he slowly moved upward to her calf, which under the smooth skin was hard with muscle. When she sighed, he kneaded even higher, feeling her delicate knee and her rather fleshy thigh. When they were both breathing faster, she looked at him through one eye. "Is this a good idea?"

He nodded. "Best I've had in ages."

She stood and slowly pulled him into her little office, where she spread an exercise mat and some blankets on the floor beside the desk covered in letters. She giggled and pulled him down beside her. He slid his body up against hers and felt her softness cushion the length of his torso. It was as if they melded together perfectly. He kissed her and ran his hands over her fleshy buttocks.

Not that many minutes later, lying under a tousled blanket, with Geneviève's lipstick blurred around both of their mouths, she said, "I'd heard you Spaniards could be surprised like school boys." She ran a hand through the thick hair on Josep's chest as he sat up in wonder. He felt his confidence plummet. After all his years of marriage and practical celibacy of late, he feared he had lost his well-honed skills in the bedroom.

"Who says that? I'm no schoolboy. It's just been a while." Josep leaned on his elbow and looked down at her, trying to appear unruffled by her comment. Geneviève's dark hair was curving down over her shoulder and as he pushed a loose lock into place, he thought how familiar it seemed.

"What would I know personally? The women around here like to talk. And now there are lots of Spaniards. But you're the one I like." She grinned and handed him a cigarette. "I hope I was all right."

"You were fabulous." He studied the perfect edge of her full lips. "But can I ask you why you wear so much makeup? You're lovely. You don't need it."

"Really?" She touched the circles under her eyes. I suppose I got used to wearing it on stage. Jules tells me I'm a fright without it."

"That can't be true." He cupped her face in his palm. "Jules wouldn't be very happy about this, would he?"

She drew in her breath, almost choking on the cigarette smoke. "No, he can't know. I don't even want to think what he would do to me. I would need more than make-up. It's so unfair. He does this all the time. What about your wife?" Geneviève snuggled closer. "What's she like? She's probably prettier than I am."

Josep pictured Dolors' face and there she was on the ceiling again looking down at them. Her expression was flat with disappointment and as she turned her back her image evaporated. He stroked Geneviève's hair. "You're different. And this will be another secret of ours, even if my wife's heart has always been with someone else." He sat up. "What time is it?"

"Almost five."

"Five o'clock?" Josep thought of Víctor and jumped from the floor. He would be back from Fontsec by now. "I'm sorry, but I have to run."

"Please don't leave yet." She pulled him back down. "I knew that you wouldn't want to stay with me for long."

"It's not that. Víctor is waiting for me." He leaned down and kissed her. "I will definitely be back."

Geneviève sat up and held the blanket against her breasts which hung like twin pears on a tree. "I'll see what I can find out about your brother before you come again." She grasped his shoulder. "You will come again, won't you?" She looked down. "I hope you'll come for me, not for my information. Then again, I don't mind." She hugged him to her. "I don't know how, but you already matter to me."

Josep kissed her on the top of her head and whispered, "You also matter to me." He found he wasn't only talking about her ability to acquire information.

When Josep arrived at the bar, Víctor was already pacing in front of it.

"*Cony*, where have you been?" Víctor said, as Josep whisked him inside to a free table in the corner. The small bar was full of men and women, but the cigarette smoke was so thick that no one seemed to notice them.

"Don't talk to me like that. Don't ask me questions." Josep leaned across the table until his nose was almost touching Víctor's. "And the biggest rule of all: don't draw attention to yourself, or to me."

Víctor lowered his head. "But I've been waiting here for hours."

"Did I ask you to come?"

Víctor shook his head.

"Well, then, you have to take what you get. Maybe you'd rather be working with Dolors."

Víctor shook his head even more adamantly. "No, no. I'm happy to be here. I'll wait. You're right. I have no right to complain. Maybe next time you can give me a longer mission."

"So did you see Francine?"

Víctor nodded.

"How was she?"

"She's gigantic. She seemed well, healthy. But she doesn't seem very pleased with you."

"Why? How do you know? You weren't supposed to mention my name," Josep whispered forcefully. Now he feared that everyone in the post office would know that he had contacted her and then Eduard would find out as well. He wasn't ready to let down his guard. Not yet.

"I didn't mention any names. I just gave her your letter. When she opened it her face flushed and her eyes became so angry. She has this one eyebrow." Víctor drew a line between his eyes with his index finger. "It was peaking and creasing. She scribbled a note and handed me this." Víctor took an envelope out of his pocket. Josep tore it open and read the handwriting scrawled across La Poste letterhead.

Josep,

Contact Eduard before asking me for favors.

Francine

Josep refolded the paper and put it in his pocket. "I should have known. No use having contacts at the post office if they're not speaking to you. It looks like I'll be making the deliveries myself." Josep motioned for Víctor to stay in his chair. "I say we have a drink or two before we head back."

Josep and Víctor returned to Pujaforta in the middle of the night, after more than a couple of drinks. Their late arrival was to keep them safe from the border guards and from the angry family. Josep was convinced that the band in favor of Víctor and against him as his corruptor would be growing. They crept into the house without the help of any lights and Josep carefully closed himself in his bedroom. Once again, he was glad to have a room to himself, not having to disturb Dolors in his early morning departures or late night arrivals. More than not disturbing her, he was relieved that she would not disturb him. Instead he went to sleep with Geneviève swirling in his head.

***

When Víctor passed through the girls' room to get to the attic, Rosa was lying in wait.

"*Hola*, Víctor." Her voice cut through the dark.

"Rosa? Why are you awake?" He put his fingers to his lips and whispered. "Quiet, you'll wake Montse."

"You said you would tuck me in."

"That was days ago."

"And I'm still waiting."

Rosa heard him sigh and his footsteps approach her bed. She was lying under the covers, her body forming barely a lump.

"You've been away with *Pare*, haven't you?"

"Yes, how do you know?"

"Because everyone is in a foul mood because of it. *Mare* is really peeved. She was working on the terrace alone until she went crying to Dr. Sort. Manel was angry because he had to finish a piece all by himself, though he did have Àngels' help. Àngels was upset for the same old reasons. I should be angry, too, but I'm not." She sat up in bed.

"Why would you be angry?"

"Because instead of going to school I had to work in the bakery. I had to serve customers. I had to serve the mayor. Usually we deliver to him, but this time he came on his own. I think he wanted to check what *Mare* is up to. He sort of looked suspicious and intrigued. *Mare* had to do your job. But I'm not angry with you."

"You're allowed to be. I deserve it. I just needed to get away for a while. Sometimes people are just a little too demanding around here."

"Precisely. That's why I prefer to go to school. The nuns are a pain, but sometimes *Mare* is worse. Montse was glad to work in the bakery because she loves it and she saw one of the boys she likes. She'll be happy to see you."

"She's likely the only one."

"I'm always happy to see you."

"You should get some sleep."

She shook her head on the pillow. "Not before you tuck me in."

Rosa felt Víctor so near as he tightened the blankets around her and kissed her on the forehead. "Good night. Go to sleep." She could still feel his lips on her forehead when he was well out the door.

***

The next morning it was clear that Rosa was right. Only the children were happy to see Víctor and Josep. For Dolors, Àngels, and Manel they may as well have never returned. The kitchen table was laden with plates of toasted *pa de pagès* that Dolors had made fresh that morning, ripe tomatoes, garlic buds, olive oil, sliced *embotits* from the local butcher. Josep was cutting into his blood sausage, convinced that it would replenish his energy and improve his mood. The girls were sprinkling red wine and sugar onto their bread when Víctor entered. Dolors looked up in surprise from feeding Pau as he approached the table, as if she had forgotten that he lived there. Rosa shuffled toward Montse to make room for him.

"So you come and go as you please now, do you, Víctor?" Dolors said. "I'm wounded because of you." She put Pau down and displayed a bandaged finger. "Now how am I to bake and make all the chocolate *mones* for Easter? Are you happy?"

"I'm sorry, I should have warned you, but I didn't know that Josep would be leaving."

"You see, it is your fault." Dolors waved her finger at Josep.

"I didn't invite Víctor, did I, Víctor?" Josep said, determined to defend himself.

"No, he didn't. In fact, when I caught up with him he told me not to come."

"But you went," Dolors said. "And where did you go? What are you hiding?"

"I'm not permitted to speak of our missions," Víctor answered.

"I may have a chance to bring in some extra money, but it could be risky," Josep said, trying to calm the excitement in his voice. "First I want to discuss it with Baltasar."

Dolors nodded enthusiastically. "Baltasar will know. Thanks to him I was able to finish the terrace yesterday, on schedule. You see, he's around when I need him." She looked pointedly at Josep and Víctor.

"But that hasn't always been the case, has it?" Josep said, but the comment didn't seem to reach her.

"He was here to bandage my finger. Plus he approves of my venture. He thinks it's going to be a great success. Unlike others around here, he believes in me. Someone like him, the town doctor, actually believes in me."

"And the regime. I don't even want to think about what you've had to pay them this time."

"You don't have to think about it because I won't tell you," Dolors said and ran to the corner where Pau was crying in pain. She lifted him up, "Where's the pupa?" she asked and blew on his fingers that he had just jammed in a drawer.

"Don't pamper him," Josep said. "He knows he's not supposed to touch that. You're turning him into a sissy. He's afraid of his own shadow."

"He's afraid of you and I don't blame him. He's only a little boy with plenty of time to become a man." She hugged Pau and handed him to Montse. "Go give him a treat and you can take a little one for yourself."

Montse ran with Pau into the bakery.

"You shouldn't let her eat so much either," Josep said as he finished his sausage. His family was becoming all the more difficult to understand. "She's getting enormous. It can't be healthy."

"All my children are going to be well nourished, not like these children surviving on nothing but powdered American milk. We are privileged to live up here in Pujaforta and my children will benefit. Besides, don't you think I look better now?" She patted her wide middle that was now touching the table. "You don't want a woman who's skin and bones. There would be nothing to hold onto." Then ever so softly she said, "Not that it gets held very often."

"Next week I have to make another trip to France," Josep announced, and pushed his chair back from the table. It made a screeching noise.

"So soon?" Dolors said. "You will be here for the inauguration of the bar at Easter."

"I'll try. It depends on who you're inviting," Josep answered and turned to Víctor. "I don't need you this time, so don't even think about following me. And you can tell Àngels and Manel that I said so."

Before returning to Merloin-les-Bains, Josep wanted to gather some opinions on the prospect of becoming a smuggler of books. He felt suddenly very erudite at the thought of it, as if it would bring him a notch above smugglers of alcohol and dirty magazines. He decided to explore his options with his political group at their meeting at Baltasar's office. Baltasar, Àngels, and the rest of the group had gathered, and were seated in their usual circle, but Àngels had angled her chair so that her back was to Josep. The recent flux of emigration from Spain and immigration to Catalonia was a subject of group discord and Josep was waiting for an interlude to ask for their advice.

"It's like the end of the war all over again. All those people exiled. Now they're leaving in search of work, in Switzerland, Germany. Maybe they'll never come back and we'll lose even more people," Baltasar said.

"If they're *Feixistes* let them stay away," Salvador said. "But many of the unemployed are being sent here to Catalonia. Have you seen them? Building houses any which way outside the cities. It's shameful. You realize that any money they make here will just be sent back to their provinces."

"Sounds like you're with the regime, not the *Maquis*," Àngels said. "Those people have every right to work, just as we do. Some of us in this room have done well working in other countries."

"I don't wish that on anyone," Josep said, thinking of the cold remoteness of northern Quebec. "Different languages, customs. But we do what we have to do."

"I'm just trying to protect our region. Someone has to," Salvador said.

"I might have a way, not to protect but to enlighten," Josep said. "What if I were to say I could get us a copy of Darwin. Do you think people might buy it?"

"I'd buy it," Baltasar said.

"But I couldn't charge you," Josep said. "I could have access to a slew of books in Spanish, maybe even Catalan, if I could find the right buyers. Discreet buyers, of course."

Àngels huffed, slapped her thighs and said her first direct words to Josep in weeks. "If you get Víctor involved in this, I'll never forgive you. In fact, I might turn you in myself."

Josep was stunned that she could say something so harsh after everything they'd all been through. "You would never do that. I've already told Víctor he can't participate in this." He looked at Àngels and silently pleaded for her to understand him. "In fact, I've told him a million times that he can't participate in any of it, but he keeps following me. He's as stubborn as his mother."

"And we all saw how she ended up." Àngels stood and starting walking for the door. She hid her face.

Baltasar sprang from his seat and put an arm around her shoulder. "Àngels, none of us wants anything to happen to Víctor. Why don't you at least listen to Josep?"

She shook her head and the tears flooded her eyes, "I can't." Then she glared toward where Josep was sitting. "I'll never understand you. You're corrupting a teenager and you're letting your own brother destroy himself."

Josep jumped from his chair. What else did Àngels know about Eduard? But before he could ask he had his answer.

"Francine. I'm in touch with Francine and I know you were, too. And frankly, I'm disgusted that you would try to use her. Sometimes I'm ashamed to be your sister." Àngels ran for the door and slammed it behind her.

"Àngels," Josep called, while Baltasar glared at him and shook his head.

"Do you think you could get some Rabelais or Antonio Machado?" Salvador asked.

Josep sat in his chair and looked at his lap. He couldn't understand how he was managing to alienate all those close to him. He felt misunderstood and suddenly lonelier than he had felt in years. An image of Geneviève's brightening face seemed to appear out of the crease in his lap. She was reflected several-fold in the full length of the dance room mirror and was leaping straight for him. Even though they spoke a different language, he needed to believe that she could understand him.

CHAPTER TWELVE

"I KNEW HE would miss it," Dolors said, standing on her newly inaugurated terrace, sagging with the weight of all the guests. The entire town had come to admire the mountain view, to sit in the new wooden chairs and above all to taste the free food: Dolors' bread with tomato, *coca*, pastries, sandwiches and *truita*, plus an array of chocolate egg-shaped *mones* on display for Easter. The wooden patio stretched the length of what had been the cornfield between the Hereu and Balaguer family houses. While one side overlooked the mountain, the other reached the side of the stone farm house and one of the bakery doors, with a large-silled window beside it. That way Dolors could peer out and check on her customers and ensure that all their orders were filled.

Àngels watched, feeling very doubtful and strangely sorry for her sister-in-law. She had long ago realized that Josep was not a very good brother; she hated to imagine being his wife. Then again, Dolors was a case apart. Before Àngels could utter a word of encouragement, her mother piped up.

"He'll be here," Núria assured Dolors. She was wearing a sweater knit of bright green and gray wool and was standing before a table of similar sweaters, socks, hats, scarves, gloves, and mittens. "Josep won't let you down. What I want to know is where are the tourists?"

Dolors glanced nervously at the crowd. "Of course he would let me down. I don't know why I expect him not to."

"I hear that you sent Víctor to put up notices at the ski hill and in towns nearby," Àngels said, finding it difficult not to get drawn into the excitement. "Some tourists will come, you'll see."

Don Albert appeared beside Núria and looked down at his wife from his towering height, despite the growing stoop in his back. The once taught skin across his face now clung to his sharp cheekbones and the extra skin seemed to pleat on his neck. While now he shuffled rather than walked, his tongue had not lost its speed. "Dolors, you once again have done a marvelous job. I'm pleased that my cancelling your loan allowed you to do this."

"But Albert, I paid you back. Every peseta."

"Yes, I'm sure you did, dear." He patted her head and shrugged at Núria and Àngels.

"Dolors has done this all on her own," Núria said, appearing stronger than ever. Àngels thought that she even seemed to be seeing clearly today.

"Exactly. On my own," Dolors said. "With help from Baltasar, some help from Víctor, and no help whatsoever from my husband, who is away at every opportunity. Never mind. Come and see the fabulous counter Manel built me for the bakery, which I'm sure you had something to do with, Àngels."

Àngels followed Dolors inside, where Montse was manning the delicately sculpted counter. Its miniature bread baskets and loaves mirrored the real ones behind it. The counter marked the division between the small sitting area for customers and the cash box and baskets of bread ready to be bought. With a wide grin and conspiratorial glances at her mother, Montse sold bread, pastries and *coca* and swiftly took the money. When her customers had gone, she said to Dolors, "We're making a killing today. We might even need to bake more bread."

"There's no time. Why isn't your sister helping?"

"She was taking pictures, as usual. Now she's gone with Víctor to try to attract some tourists."

"Splendid," Núria said.

Àngels heard some voices and saw Dolors dash toward the door.

"Baltasar," Dolors called, darting into the yard and grabbing Baltasar's arm. Àngels joined them and rolled her eyes at Manel, who was standing on Baltasar's other side. She looked around at the mix of people, which to her liking included too many members of the regime.

"Hasn't Baltasar done a superb job with the terrace?" Dolors asked her, as if she had just arrived. Knowing that the question was not meant for her ears, Àngels heard Dolors add, "Of course, it's hard to see the workmanship with all those customers standing on it."

Baltasar raised his hands in protest. "I cannot take the credit."

"Yes, of course. I did do much of it myself. But Baltasar, you saved me." Dolors wiggled her injured finger, now wrapped in a light bandage. "And Manel, I'm thrilled with the counter you made. Everyone is complementing it. Àngels did you help with it? I know you two have become very close."

Manel stepped toward Àngels. "I don't know what I would have done without Àngels while my shoulder was healing. In fact, I don't know what I would ever do without her, and I've asked her an important question in that regard."

"I had something I wanted to ask you as well, Àngels," Baltasar added leaning closer on her other side. Dolors clung tightly to his arm.

Àngels glanced at the men, whose company she was thankful for but whose demands she was becoming tired of hearing. She glared at Dolors. She's wasn't going to let her engineer her love life or any other matter. "So where did you say your husband was? Not that I care to see him, mind you." She was still far from forgiving Josep.

"He'll be here soon, and so will all the tourists Víctor has gone to fetch," Dolors said and they all looked skyward, as uninvited coin-sized snowflakes drifted down upon them. Dolors dashed into the crowd. "Don't go. Please stay. Surely it can't last long. It's almost May," she called to the guests. A group in uniform began to leave and Dolors blocked their path.

"Mayor Vidal, you mustn't leave before trying my *truita*, or before allowing me to thank you for, you know." Dolors nodded toward the terrace and Àngels shook her head.

"With the snow, I think we can trust you to bring us some of that omelet to the town hall," the mayor said, the buttons of his uniform still pulled tightly over his expanding belly. "Where is your husband?"

"He's on his way. He'll be here any moment," Dolors said and again looked at the sky.

***

Josep emerged from the woods and could hear the murmur of voices growing to a loud rumble as he approached his house. He felt relief to arrive before the event was over, more to spare himself Dolors' nagging than to attend the event itself. He also felt relief and elation: he had just completed his first mission. After a heavenly hour with Geneviève, he had hidden his first banned book in his trousers and smuggled it over the hills. It was now warm in his left breast pocket. This made his heart feel closer to Geneviève, even though he didn't need a book from her husband for that. As he approached the house, he brushed the snowflakes from his shoulders and the sprinkling from his hair. The voices were now beginning to spread and as the terrace came into view, he saw that only a few clusters of people remained. He drew closer and squinted. Àngels and Manel were against the railing watching the snow floating into the valley. Montse was carrying platters of food toward the house. Núria and Albert were barely visible behind towering piles of sweaters and other knitwear. The Vidal family was hunched over the food table. At that moment he spotted Dolors. She was standing with a group of men in uniform with her head thrown back in laughter. When the man turned in profile, Josep recognized the paunch of Mayor Vidal himself. He put a hand on the book at his chest and quietly took a few steps backward until he felt a body against his back and cold hands covering his eyes.

"Guess who?" a young female voice asked.

The air returned to Josep's lungs and he exhaled in relief. "Is it Don Albert?" he asked.

"No," the voice giggled.

"Is it Víctor?"

"Almost," Rosa cried and dropped her hands from his eyes. He turned to see that beside his younger daughter, Víctor was standing smiling.

"Where have you two been?"

"We went to Adiol la Nova and then to the bus station to hand out pamphlets for *Mare*'s terrace."

Josep nodded. "No officials saw you handing anything out, did they?"

Víctor shook his head. "I checked that there was no one around. We're not looking for trouble."

"What's wrong with handing out pamphlets?" Rosa asked.

"Nothing. You just might be questioned about what they say."

"I think we should be able to say whatever we want," Rosa said.

"So do I, *petita*. But the reality is different." Josep reached inside his jacket. "I want you to do me a favor. Put this book inside your coat and go and hide it in your room somewhere. Somewhere where no one will find it. And don't tell anyone that you have it. No one, not even your mother. Especially not your mother," Josep added thinking that Dolors' contacts were becoming increasingly undesirable.

Rosa nodded and stuck *Ingénu* inside her skirt waist. "I can do that. For how long?"

"Until I ask you for it. Go on. Be discreet." Josep patted Rosa lightly on the back and she ran off toward the house.

"Why didn't you give it to me to hide? I could have done that," Víctor said.

"Because no one will suspect her of having it. It's perfect, don't you see?"

"If you say so, but I wouldn't tell Dolors, Àngels, or anyone about this. You saw what happened when I got involved."

"Absolutely. Not a word of this to Dolors. Or to anyone." Josep shook his head at himself wishing he knew why the road he chose was always the riskiest.

"So you're finally here," a voice said behind him. "Better never than late," Dolors said and stomped away.

***

The book smuggling and the bar, two ventures inaugurated on the same day, proceeded first at an equally slovenly pace and then shot into action. As the days, months, and years passed, Josep managed his book trade and his afternoons with his dealer's wife with extreme precision and discretion, since his life and others depended on it. Despite his thinning hair and widening middle, Geneviève still seemed hooked on him, so much so that every time he left, tears would stream down her cheeks and she would beg him not to go.

Dolors' terrace went from initial desertion to almost constant full occupancy, half of which was by men in uniform and those overtly sympathetic to the regime. Gradually alienated by this presence, the other half of her customers dwindled, until to Dolors' and Núria's delight, a spattering of foreign tourists, oblivious to the political issues, replaced it. They were attracted by the delicious *truita* that melted on the tongue. Yet even the most succulent omelets or tangy tomato bread could not tempt an ever-single Àngels into keeping company with the officials on the terrace right beside her house. Nor could Dolors convince her to join the party line on her new, highly coveted possession: a telephone. It was a shared line and was surely tapped by the authorities listening for illicit Red activities. Nonetheless, Dolors was ecstatic with the acquisition, until she realized that its rarity meant there were few people to telephone. Luckily, the two people they could reach were Núria and Sr. Palau. Their telephone in the tower was free from spying ears, since the connection, like the electricity, was pinched from France.

Between the telephone, the terrace, and the extra temptations that Josep smuggled in, the bakery was flourishing. With the help of Víctor, Josep ensured the flow of quality flour, sugar, and other supplies, while also meeting the growing demand for books, which Rosa continued to stash in her bedroom. He was convinced that his agreement with Geneviève's husband was ingenious. As Josep upped his book orders, Jules increased the frequency of his trips, leaving Geneviève alone and very needy of attention. With great care and coordination, Josep had managed to keep Víctor away from Geneviève. Every time Josep saw her she thanked him profusely for giving her a new reason to live. She made him feel necessary. Sometimes she also gave him news of Eduard, though it was usually disappointing. She did say that Eduard and Francine had given up on the idea of having other children. One brilliant son would be enough for them. Eduard, however, seemed to show little interest in his family in Pujaforta. His daily energy went to the bar where he worked and a good part of his wages went to the horses. Josep found this news highly discouraging. So many of their birthdays had gone by without so much as a word that if it weren't for Geneviève he would fear that Eduard was no longer alive to celebrate. He counted on Geneviève's news, however brief and uneventful. Josep had begun to trust her with so much of himself, and every time she mentioned Eduard's name he felt their bond tighten. While he knew his feelings for Geneviève ran primarily from his heart, he wondered if they weren't also influenced by the fact that most of the women in his own family still failed to speak to him.

The only females who seemed not to judge him were his daughters, who were the highlight of his stays in Pujaforta, like the chocolate filling in day-old croissants. Pau was also growing up, but Josep saw him only rarely since he was usually stuck to Dolors' side or playing alone in his bedroom. While Josep constantly criticized Dolors' overprotection of their son, she blamed Josep for the boy's shyness, insisting that Josep terrified him. Josep tried to reach out to him, sometimes suggesting a game of pachisi, but the boy would cower and run away.

As the child who most resembled Dolors, Montse spent her free time seeking her mother's approval in the kitchen, while Rosa would shut herself in her room awaiting Josep's irregular returns. With each visit home, Josep found that Rosa grew in height, in confidence, and as his confidante, particularly given her role as a hider of his banned books. She had bloomed later than Montse had, and was more tidy and compact. Her curiosity also sprouted like an overfertilized garden and she was always asking Josep to tell her about the adventures of his early years, particularly those involving hauling ice and counting tobacco with a little boy in Canada. As Rosa's body and mind changed, her fixation on Víctor was replaced by an obsession with the school rules with which she did not agree. It became a true family crisis when Dolors waved a letter under Josep's nose right as he came in the door after a rather prolonged trip away. He put down his bag, hung up his jacket, and gave Dolors a nasty glare.

"Surely this is something that can wait until I piss," he said.

Slapping him with the envelope in question, she said, "It is urgent. Our daughter is turning into a dissident and it's your fault. You're a horrific influence and you bought her that camera."

"And you think that the crew of fascists that you deal with are a good influence?"

"They are the authorities. Without them we can't do anything. When are you going to accept that?"

"Never. Frankly it disgusts me. Why do you think I'm never here?"

"Why do you think you're able to come and go as you please? You would be dead if it weren't for me." She sat down heavily. "I'm so unappreciated. Now I'm going to have to use my influence to keep Rosa out of trouble at school as well."

Josep also took a seat at the table and began untying his boots. "What's the trouble? Did she speak to one of the nuns without being spoken to?"

"No. She handed them a written list of demands."

"Really?" Josep nodded, quite impressed with his daughter. "What kind of demands?"

"She wants classes in sports, football, basketball. She wants a full library and to choose the books for the curriculum. In Catalan. She wants classes in Catalan. Mixed classes. Boys and girls haven't studied together since the Republic. The list goes on." Dolors put the letter on the table. "They have banned her camera from the school. They don't like her taking pictures during classes."

"She's just a teenager."

"Who they will expel and report to the authorities if she doesn't change her ways. These nuns are serious." Dolors stuck out her chest. "Since Rosa's father was unavailable, as usual, I went to see them. I brought them *coca* and *truita*."

"As usual. Food bribery is your answer to everything."

"Nowadays it's what seems to work." Dolors stood and smoothed her apron. "But it doesn't work with your daughter. She doesn't want anything to do with the bakery and she won't listen to me. I suggest you have a word with her."

"I will try to talk to her before I leave tomorrow."

"Tomorrow? But you've just got back."

"If you supply the nuns with pastries, I'll have to be away even more to bring you more flour."

"That's not what's keeping you away. Just what are you up to anyway?"

"It's better if you just take the money and not ask questions. You've always been good at that." Josep picked up his bag of goods and headed for his bedroom.

The next day, Josep got up early to see Manel at his workshop before Àngels arrived. He had some business to propose. Some customers were interested in handcrafted furniture. It would be much cheaper in Spain given the low labor costs and general desperation. First, though, he had to have a word with Rosa before she left for school. When he sat down to eat his blood sausage, Dolors, Montse, and Víctor immediately stood as if on cue and left him with Rosa, who was still finishing her bread with wine and sugar.

"How's school?" he asked her.

"Un pal. Everything's prohibited." She rolled her eyes at him.

"Do you need any film developed?"

Rosa nodded. "Wouldn't it be easier if you set up the dark room you've been promising me?" She had a bag prepared on her lap and handed it to him. "Any new books come in?"

Josep nodded. "A few, but they're hidden. I'll get the ones you have before I go tonight."

"You're going again already? I feel like you're never here." She dropped her spoon into her bowl. "Remember when you told me about your father and the rose bushes? You told me you would plant some. You also promised you would tell me what happened to that boy you were with in Canada and that woman you almost married."

"I told you I have no idea what became of him or her for that matter, nor do I plan to find out. I don't intend to tell you about me and a woman who is not your mother. That was all so long ago and though I did care a lot about them, that boy was a little hard to handle."

"Maybe he had his reasons. You told me he was really attached to you."

Josep looked down towards his cup of coffee laced with anise liqueur.

"We are, too, you know," Rosa said. "I'm not the only one upset that you're leaving again. You'll be away for the anniversary of the bar. Again."

Josep winced and slapped his thigh. "I entirely forgot about that. She didn't even say anything."

"Why would she bother now?"

Josep sighed. "You're right, *petita*." He ate his last bite of sausage and patted Rosa's curls. "Try to be good at school. Otherwise it will only cause trouble for all of us."

"I'd rather go with you," she said sticking out her newly formed chest. "I am almost sixteen."

"It's no place for you. You have school. Besides your mother would kill me."

"What you could teach me is far more important than what the nuns try to teach me."

"You're far too young. And you may never be old enough for this." He put a consoling arm around her when he felt he needed one himself. Of everyone, he regretted leaving Rosa behind every time he went into the forest.

"Are you sure you have to go?" Her eyes were pleading.

"You think we should be able to read whatever we choose, right?" He kissed the top of her head. "Well, that's what I'm working on. And I'm going to see to those rose bushes."

***

"What can I do?" Núria said. "My table is all ready with the sweaters and I can't just sit and wait." She had just entered the bakery where Dolors was carefully decorating a castle built of chocolate and Montse was delicately flipping a fat potato omelet onto a plate and sliding it back into the pan. The counters were covered in trays of food, bread, sausage, and *truita*, which Rosa was rather savagely stabbing with toothpicks. Dolors looked at Núria in surprise since her visits were rare these days. She was always at the co-op knitting.

"You can supervise Rosa," Dolors said. "She's destroying the omelet so that I'll fire her."

"She's just a little energetic. It looks fabulous." Núria kissed Rosa on her raised cheek and turned to Dolors. "Your chocolate *mones* get fancier every year. I hope they attract lots of people. We've knit so much stock and I have to sell it before it gets too hot. We have many townspeople contributing wool and they want to earn some extra money. Everyone is excited about it, except perhaps for Albert. He's been so absorbed lately. He sits around all day reading those books that Josep sells him for half price."

"Surely Josep doesn't make him pay. He's family." Dolors looked up from her castle and rolled her eyes.

"Family or not, Albert won't take charity. He complains that I'm always at the co-op, but when I'm home he hardly notices me. But he does notice the money the co-op brings in, not that it's much."

"Men. Josep's the same. While my bakery and bar make money he doesn't complain."

Montse flipped a perfectly rounded *truita* onto a plate. "But you do. You complain."

Dolors huffed. "Of course. I have everything to complain about. My husband is never home. My daughter may be expelled from school. And my other daughter ignores my instructions. Pau is my only hope." She watched her son sitting quietly in the corner playing pachisi by himself.

Dolors pointed to a little dish that Montse had begun to fill with olives. "Not so many. Do you want to ruin us, Montse? How many olive trees have you seen up in these mountains?"

"You're never happy. You make me think that no one is ever going to want me. You don't." Montse put down the dish and left the kitchen.

"Why do you always do this? All she needs is a little encouragement." Rosa jabbed a piece of *truita* with a toothpick. "Maybe we need to make a list of demands for this house. You're worse than the nuns." She ran toward the stairs. "Montse, wait for me."

"Teenagers are so sensitive." Dolors stopped spreading the oil and looked at Núria with watery eyes. "No one seems to understand how hard it is to run this place. If I don't keep a close eye on everything, it could all fall apart." She picked up a round loaf and started sawing off a piece with a serrated knife. "It's been so much work getting to this point."

"All the Easter baking and the opening days of the terrace are always a strain on you. On everybody," Núria said. "You do realize that everyone has been helping you. Víctor, Manel, even Àngels. You'll have to learn to actually trust other people with all of this. They are your family."

"I know I get all worked up with the reopening. But Montse and Rosa are just children."

"Not for much longer."

Dolors looked toward the door. "I think people are starting to arrive." A grin appeared on her face. "It's Baltasar. He said he would come early to help."

Núria glanced at Dolors. "You should be this happy when your husband comes home."

"*Senyora*, can I have a menu, please," Baltasar was calling. So far just a few tables along the mountain edge were taken. The rest were set with simple cutlery and a wild flower in the center of each table. Rosa had insisted on the decorations and had even picked them herself. The petals were fluttering in the crisp breeze coming from the distant peaks. The bright sun fortunately dulled its bite.

"So good of you to come," Dolors said to Baltasar, handing him a menu. She nodded at Àngels and Manel. "You already know all my specialties, don't you, Baltasar?"

"We don't over here," a voice said from a table nearby. "But we might like to."

The mayor was patting his belly and winking at Dolors.

"Mayor Vidal, I think you've tried everything." She gave him a menu. "But this year we have added a few even tastier items."

"I hope they are local products. Where is your husband today?"

"Is your wife well? I haven't seen her in the bakery lately."

"She's been a little under the weather." The mayor folded his hands over his stomach. "Why don't you bring me the bread instead. We always appreciate your deliveries."

The chairs scraped across the floor at the next table. Àngels was standing and pulling Manel and Baltasar to their feet. She was clearly not about to sit next to Carles Puig's successor and listen to Dolors butter him up as well. "I have no appetite." She walked away and the two men followed slowly after her, leaving an extra table for paying customers.

Right beside the door to the bakery was a stand piled with brightly colored knitwear, the stacks tottering in the breeze. Inside, Montse, Rosa, and Núria were standing behind the counter when Dolors came in. It smelled of a blend of baked goods, chocolate, egg, and vanilla. "Don't just stand here. Montse, be a dear and go take some orders," Dolors said. "Rosa, you get ready to fill them. Núria, there are three tall blond people standing at your stall."

Montse and Núria ran off leaving Dolors panicking and Rosa sulking in the kitchen. After Montse had brought in numerous orders, they filled them and the cash register, finally towards the end of the service, Montse, with her face blotchy red from running back and forth, came in and said, "*Mare*, there's a woman out there who only speaks French. You'll have to take her order."

Dolors didn't look up from the *coca* she was carefully decorating. "French people. That's excellent. Montse, if you studied more you could talk to her."

"She asked for you."

Dolors looked up from the pine nuts she was sprinkling. "Me? By name?"

"No, she wants to see the *'propriétaire'*."

"She asked for the owner?" Dolors quickly took off her apron. "Did she look angry? Did you do something?"

Montse shrugged. "She hasn't even ordered yet."

Dolors dashed out to the terrace and saw a woman at a far table with her hand waving shyly beside her apologetic face.

"Bonjour Madame," Dolors said. "Have you chosen what you would like?"

"*Je voudrais essayer votre omelette.* They say it is marvelous." The woman was looking at her through hazel eyes lined in black. Her hair was wrapped into a knot on the back of her head and her light pink jacket gave her a calm, peaceful look.

"They say that my omelet is marvelous? Where do they say that?"

"Partout. All around." She motioned to the mountain and the valley around them and sighed. "What an exceptional view. You are very lucky."

Dolors nodded and smiled. "My flam and crema are quite well known in France, so why not my omelet? Have you been here before?" Dolors noticeably relaxed.

"No, I've never had the pleasure. It looks different from this side of the mountain. Our side isn't as magnificent. You've done a lovely job here. And that woman over there is selling some beautiful items."

"That's my mother-in-law. You should take a look at her goods before you leave. We accept Francs, of course."

"I've already got something." The woman pulled a mauve sweater, a hat, some gloves and some socks from her bag. "Or a few things, though I don't know if I'll do them justice." She smiled, revealing a smudge of pink lipstick on her front tooth. "In fact, I have put in an order for some leg warmers."

Dolors looked at her questioningly.

"I'm a dancer. We wear them over our calves."

"Really?" Dolors signaled to Montse. "What kind of dancer?"

"I do ballet and contemporary, jazz and the like." She carefully folded each knitted item and tucked them into her bag. "To tell you the truth, I did dance. I really danced, but now I basically teach. It's my age."

"You're not that old," Dolors said, although the lines around the woman's eyes said that she was not that young. "So why did you stop?"

"For my husband. For love. You know how silly we women can be in giving up everything. It's almost as if it's expected of us and we don't even question it. Now my husband is never home, he treats me horrendously when he is, and I am no longer a dancer." She pursed her lips and Montse placed a triangle of *truita* before her and a small plate of tomato bread. "Gracias, *señorita*," she said in Spanish with a very heavy accent and with a look of surprise on her face.

"It's my specialty and it's on the house," Dolors said.

The woman smiled and blushed while motioning to Dolors and the empty chair in front of her. "Then you must join me. I hate eating alone. I am always eating alone. But you must be too busy."

Dolors looked around the terrace. The three tables that were still occupied appeared close to finishing. It was getting late. She pulled out the chair, sat down and sighed. "What a relief. I feel like I've been on my feet for days."

"My name is Geneviève." She extended a delicate hand across her *truita*.

"I'm Dolors." Dolors' hand was red and nicked with scars.

"Dolors, they are right. Your *truita*—is that how you say it in this Catalan language of yours? It is heavenly, far better than any omelet I could make," Geneviève said and took another bite. "I'm not surprised your feet are tired. I have a foot cream that works wonders. I'll bring it next time I come."

"Thank you," Dolors said, somewhat surprised by this strange woman's overly friendly gesture. "When your husband is away, where does he go?"

"On business, to the north. To Paris, for example. That is where I am from."

"Paris? Wouldn't I love to go to Paris. I once took a day off to go skiing but I've never been to Paris. I've never really been anywhere, except for Barcelona, but that was many years ago."

"It's a lovely city, Barcelona. Paris is so full of tourists, though I haven't been there in at least a decade. Barcelona still has charm. When I was young, between the wars, Paris was more like that. My father had a tiny bookshop, a bookstand, really, and we lived in a very simple two room flat. My mother cleaned houses in the rich neighborhoods." She looked north as if searching for Paris in the distance. "Sometimes I would go with her and admire all the magnificent things these people displayed. One of the ladies my mother cleaned for suggested I dance. At first no one believed I was capable, especially me." She took a bite of bread and licked her lips. "My mother worked many hours—I remember her hands were red and chafed—just so that I could dance. When my parents realized that I was good at it, they worked even harder to pay for the lessons. I danced till my toes were so calloused. I have the ugliest feet. No shoes ever fit me now." Geneviève shook her head. "When I met Jules, he was older than me. I

172

found him intriguing, distinguished, and I was flattered that he seemed interested in me." She covered her mouth and nodded. "He seemed to really know what he wanted. And he wanted me. I had thought that I wanted nothing other than dancing, but then there was him. I'd never felt like that before. So I left the dance company without saying goodbye to anyone or telling my parents. I ran off with a man they hated and abandoned their dream. In the end I was the disappointment that they had expected. I couldn't face them, so I didn't." She lit a cigarette and puffed quickly. "My mother died soon after that. Paris was occupied and my father decided to close his bookstand. He started working as a cleaner for the Germans. After the liberation, all his old friends and neighbors refused to talk to him, even though many had collaborated in one way or another." She shook her head. "That killed him." Geneviève sighed. "I'm sorry. I don't know why I'm telling you all this. I don't even know you. You'll have to forgive me. I must be lonelier than I thought."

"Don't worry," Dolors said. "I would be lonely too, if I had time. My husband is always away working, too."

"Really?" Geneviève leaned forward. "What does he do?"

"Business. It's difficult to explain. You know we have quite a different situation here. He is often traveling." Dolors wiped some crumbs off the table with the flat of her hand.

"Do you miss him when he goes?"

Dolors looked at the mountains and did not answer.

"I'm sorry," Geneviève said. "That's such a personal question. It's just that I miss my husband so much. I've even followed him to see where he goes. Have you ever done that?"

Dolors clicked her tongue and shook her head. "I'm too busy to be following him around. My husband is full of talk, but I can't imagine him doing anything wrong." Dolors shifted in her chair. "So you still dance then? You said you ordered your special socks."

"Leg warmers. Yes, I do. I've started teaching again. I have a dance school. I had to do something."

"A school, really? For children?"

"Yes, mostly children. It is just new. Do you have children?"

"Yes, three." Dolors leaned in. "Where exactly is your school?"

"Merloin-les-Bains, not far over the border."

"In France. That wouldn't work."

"Why? What are you thinking?"

"My daughters won't be interested. One is just too tough, and the other is, well, very attached to my kitchen. But I have been trying to think of a way to help my son. He's very shy and introverted. Do you think dancing could work?"

"Definitely," Geneviève said. "It did wonders for me. I was always so timid and look at me telling you my entire life story in an instant."

Dolors nodded. "I might like him to try it, but we can't be traveling back and forth over the border. Maybe I can find a school or other activity near here."

"Or I could come here."

"You would do that?" Dolors shook her head. "I can't ask you to do that. Besides, it would be impossible. My husband can't know anything about this. He would never understand. You see, he is always complaining that I'm too protective of Pau. He thinks it weakens him. Ballet would be too much. I'll tell you, though, my idea is for him to ski. But I have no time to take him. Maybe in the meantime, dancing would give him confidence and help him be flexible and graceful in a masculine way. Perhaps you know someone nearby."

"I could teach him personally. I do know someone in a town just up the mountain, in Adiol la Nova, who has a flat I could use."

"But that would be such an effort on your part. And I'm sure we could never afford it."

"I can give you a special price. You see, I'm a woman with too much time on my hands. The school is small and it's only starting. We can try a few classes. Then you can decide."

"Let me think about it. Do you have a telephone? I do. I can call you to confirm, but only a quick call since it's international and would cost an eye from my face." Dolors jumped from her chair. "I'll go get Pau so you can meet him. But if ever you have the opportunity to meet my husband, Josep Balaguer, do not mention a word."

When Dolors returned from the kitchen holding Pau by the hand, Geneviève smoothed her sweater and stood up to greet him. His gray eyes peered up at her from under his heavy bangs and he cowered slightly as she came nearer. She smiled at him and gently lifted one of his thin arms from his side, supporting it with her two hands.

"Graceful as a bird, I'd say," Geneviève said in French. In broken Spanish she added, "What do say young man, do you want to dance?"

Pau shrugged his bony shoulders.

"I'm Mme Petitpas and I can teach you. Just tell your mother to ring me to confirm the time."

Pau smiled widely and hid his face in Dolors' side.

"I'm not sure of much, but I can definitely help with this. You'll see," Geneviève said, and patted the crown of Pau's head.

***

A few days later the weather turned cold again and Josep felt the comfort of Geneviève's foyer as he stepped inside. The warmth seemed to hug him as strongly as Geneviève did when she saw him.

"I'm so happy you're here, *mon amour*," she said. "I've been waiting and was afraid that you would never come."

"I did come and you weren't here," he said as he pulled out of her embrace.

"When? I've been here this whole time." Her joy shattered visibly. "I can't believe I missed you."

"It was on Saturday."

"Saturday? Oh yes, I did go out for a bit." She kissed his cheek leaving a blurry red lip mark. "If only I'd known you were coming." She squeezed his hand and peeked quickly out the window beside the door. "Wait here just a moment." She scurried outside in her stocking feet and returned carrying a package and some letters.

Josep squinted at the box covered in brown paper and followed Geneviève into the living room. "When will Jules be back?" he asked as she put the post on the table.

"Not for a couple of days." She looked up from the envelope in her hand and smiled. "Can you stay?"

He shook his head. "What's in those?" he pointed to the package.

"This?" She shook the box. "Just pointe shoes for my students." She ripped open the paper revealing a thin shoe box which held a pair of pink ballet slippers. A sliver of light fell across her face as she stroked the satin. "To be able to break in new shoes. They would only break my feet." She shut the lid to the box as if her dreams were locked inside it. She put her arms around Josep's waist and he held her against him feeling her cushiness along his front. He felt protected and safe. He looked up and also felt observed. The face in the portrait seemed to be watching them with its features so similar to Jules'.

"Would you like to go upstairs for a bit?" he whispered into her hair. She nodded enthusiastically and led him up the stairs.

"Just a minute. Wait here," Geneviève said suddenly and left him standing outside the bedroom door.

"We'll just mess it up anyway," he said and followed her. The red bedspread was dotted with some pieces of clothing, which Geneviève scooped up before rushing for the closet. Most of it was knitwear.

"What's all that?" he asked stopping her and taking one of the mittens. He examined it and took a sock and then the sweater from her arms. "Where did you get these?"

"I bought them. It's still rather cool out."

"Where did you buy them?" He examined the knit more closely, stroked the wool, and felt his worlds coming together.

"I bought it from a very pleasant woman, one who doesn't see very well, at a stand outside a terrace café." She looked at him with mascara puddling in her crow's feet.

"You bought that from my mother," he said and tried to pull the other items from her arms. The thought of Núria and Geneviève exchanging words, exchanging money. It all felt so filthy. "When were you there? What did you tell her?"

"Calm down," Geneviève said trying to pull the knit back to its original shape. "I didn't tell her anything. And I didn't tell Dolors anything either. None of them know I know you." She giggled. "Josep, they seem like such wonderful people."

Josep paced around her as he imagined Dolors and Geneviève face to face, right outside his family home. He knew that his allegiances were blurred, but now they seemed to come into pristine focus. "Yes they are wonderful. Tell me why the hell you would go there."

"Because they're a part of you. A big part of you. I was so jealous. I know about your brother and I wanted to understand the other part of you, the part that's over that mountain, in another country, another language." She sat down on the bed and covered her face. "I wanted to feel closer to you."

"You are close to me. You're closer than anyone: my wife, my mother, my sister, my brother. You're the only one who seems to understand me. You'll probably abandon me, too."

"Unless you abandon me first. That seems to be your usual line of action. Put up a wall and walk away." As she said it she gripped his arm like she meant to keep it.

"Maybe I should." He tried to pull free. "Don't go back there. I beg you. Stay away from Pujaforta and my family."

"I will. I'm so sorry. Sometimes I can't stop myself. Please don't go." She gripped his arm again. "Tell me something. I'm prettier than Dolors, aren't I? You do love me more, don't you?"

"I'm not about to compare you." He pulled away and headed for the door.

"I do have some news of Eduard," she said. "Just sit here beside me for a moment." She wiped a tear from her face and patted the bed beside her.

Josep turned ever so slowly and sat on the edge of the bed without looking at her. He needed some time to think about all this. "What?"

"He was arrested."

Josep turned to look at her full on. "Arrested? Where? When? By whom? Was it the Guardia Civil? Why didn't you tell me this earlier?"

"No, it's nothing like that. It was the local police. He was unruly and loud. He was apparently very drunk and he started a fight in the middle of the street." She was twisting one of Núria's scarves.

"In the street?" Josep shook his head. "This is horrible. Last time I saw him he was convinced that they would come to arrest him. It was almost paranoia. I thought he was losing grip. Why would he change and start making an open spectacle of himself?"

"It's the alcohol surely. They say he becomes belligerent, but also delusional. He calls people by other names. I heard that he calls people your name. It's just the local police. It can't be that dangerous. Can it?"

"In theory, no. It's not like our days in the beach camps when they wanted to send us back. I don't think they would do it now. But it draws attention to him. In my country he is wanted for murdering that guard." Josep was pacing. "What else did Francine tell you?"

"Nothing. Promise me you'll be careful going back home. I forget how dangerous all this is." She begged with her eyes.

"I will. And you stay on this side of the border. Do you hear me?" Josep held her chin and kissed her on the lips as she nodded. He went out the door. He had to find out more about this. Where was Eduard being held this time? Why would he draw such attention to himself? More than anything he wanted to find out if the Spanish authorities were still after Eduard. Maybe it would finally be safe for him to come home. He shook his head, surprised at himself and his sudden feeling of forgiveness. Josep sat for a moment on the bench outside Geneviève's house and looked at the sky. Night had fallen as fast as a ball dropping. The sun was now over the mountains, in Spain. He would have to walk towards it. As his did, he thought he had to get Àngels to talk to him. She must have news of Eduard. Josep increased his pace and lost himself in the forest.

CHAPTER THIRTEEN

WHEN JOSEP ARRIVED at his usual time in the middle of the night, he was shocked to find Dolors sitting in the kitchen waiting for him. Everything was neatly put away, the counters were sparkling, the bread baskets were awaiting their next batch, but the baker wore a sour look on her face. During Josep's entire trek back across the mountain he had worried ceaselessly about Eduard and about Geneviève's expedition into Dolors' territory. Now his trepidation mounted.

"What are you doing up? How did you know I would be home tonight?" As he took off his coat, he tried to hide the genuine surprise and any guilt on his face.

"Víctor told me." She was glaring at him.

Josep nodded, thinking of Geneviève and the sweater. "So why are you up? Couldn't you sleep?"

"No, I couldn't and I'll tell you why." She took something off the table and showed it to him. It was a book. A very weathered Spanish copy of Zola's *Germinal.*

"Yes, a book. What's the problem?"

"I found Rosa reading it. A teenager shouldn't be reading such filth."

"Have you read it?"

"No. I just skimmed it a little."

"How do you know it's filth then?"

"The Church. The Caudillo. They've banned it. She could be excommunicated or worse. So could we all for having it here in this house." She stood up and began to pace. They all knew far too well what getting caught could mean, particularly for the bakery.

"So now you think it's acceptable for the Church and Franco to decide what we can and cannot read? Have you really let them get that far into your head?"

"You make them sound like the Devil himself. They're not so bad. They're just people. If you sat down one day with one of them out there you would see that."

"I have sat down with them. But at the town hall, not on your terrace, and frankly I didn't care much for it." Josep thought of the mayor's taught stomach before him and the excruciating effort it took for him to remain unruffled by his questioning. He reckoned he had been quite successful so far.

"If they find out about these books, the Guardia Civil could take you away. They could send all of us away. There is only so much I can do to protect us. You don't seem to be concerned at all about that. You don't appreciate all that I do for this family." Dolors leaned over him. "You have to talk to Rosa and you have to make sure that she or any of the children never find your books." Her eyes had turned from angry to pleading.

"I'll talk to Rosa, but you know how strong-minded she is. Besides, it's not a good idea to protect them so much. Look at Pau and that shell you've built around him."

"It's not my fault, but I am doing something about that. I've enrolled him in some classes, but I won't bore you with the details." She shook the book by Zola at him. "Rosa is just like you. Her head is as hard as year-old bread. If you can't convince her, just make sure she doesn't have access to your books. I'm not demanding that you give it up entirely. I think I'm being reasonable."

"Fine," Josep took a step closer. "I'll talk to Rosa. Listen, your contacts haven't mentioned anything about Eduard, have they? Directly or indirectly?"

Dolors looked toward the patio, where empty tables were awaiting new customers and all of the signs of the opening celebration were gone. "No, thank God. I wouldn't have the nerves for it. If they bring all that up again they could take away my terrace and everything else."

"I'm glad to hear that you're concerned for my brother, who by the way is in jail in France."

Dolors put the book on the table and looked like she was trying to sort out a riddle. "How do you know about this?"

"I have my sources, my contacts. Just like you have yours. Tomorrow I have to talk to Àngels." Josep's look softened as he remembered how busy Dolors had been. "How was the re-opening the other day? I'm sorry I missed it."

Dolors raised her eyebrows and crossed her arms. "I doubt that."

"No, really. How did it go? Were there many tourists? I know Mother was counting on it."

"It went fine. The terrace was packed. There were a few tourists."

"Any from France?"

"No, I don't recall any from France."

"All right. No French." Josep shrugged and looked at his wife, unsure if she was oblivious or lying.

"Whatever you're up to, Josep, be careful. And be sure to talk to Rosa. Leave her out of any of this."

"You were supposed to hide them not read them," Josep said early the next morning when he was standing next to Rosa's bed. "And, no one was to know, particularly not your mother."

Rosa was sitting on the edge of her bed with her crumpled sheets around her waist. Beyond the window the sky was still light gray and she reached toward the bedside table and turned on the lamp, which emitted a warm circle of light. "I know. *Mare's* the one who's always nosing around. I caught her digging into my things. Yesterday she came in without knocking." Rosa gestured towards the door of her room as angry tears slowly began to streak her face. Josep sat down beside her and put an arm around her. She wiped her cheeks briskly. "I have been so good at hiding them all. Not even Montse knows they're here." Montse's hastily made bed was right beside them.

"I know," Josep soothed. "You did a good job. But, really, that's not the point. You weren't meant to read the books."

"You never said that." She dug under the bed, dragged out a suitcase, lifted a top compartment full of socks and underwear, pulled out some worn magazines, and showed him the row of pristine, hardcover books. "You said to hide them, not to tell anyone, but you never said not to read them."

"Didn't I? That's because it's logical. You don't bite into an apple you're selling or taste a bottle of wine before delivering it. So you don't read the merchandise."

"It's not the same. I've learned far more from those books than I will ever learn in school."

"Which one did you like the most?" Josep looked with longing at the books before them. He never seemed to find the time to read any of them.

"I was really enjoying *Germinal*. And I would like to finish it. It's such a tragic story. That family crushed by the owners, the landowners, the wealth. They are enslaved and it makes me think of what you and *Tieta* Àngels have told me about what happened here, about what happened between my grandfathers, your father and *Mare's*. Is that what it was like?"

"I don't know, *petita*. I haven't read the book."

"But you can tell me about how life was here, can't you? I found more pictures of you in Canada and I want you to tell me about them, too." She got up and started making the bed. "There are some of you by a tent on a lake surrounded by boulders, a bit like Turtle Rock." She paused and sat down on the bedspread. "The woman who is with you has this distant look in her eyes. The sun is reflecting off the ripples in the lake and her eyelashes are glistening. She looks absolutely peaceful. I would love to be able to take pictures like that. That was who you were supposed to marry, wasn't it?"

Josep sat beside Rosa and patted her shoulder, thinking of Marie-Claude perched on a rock on the lake edge. That was when she was just the school teacher to him and his boss's daughter. Henri had so many daughters to choose from.

Rosa was all wound up. "And there are pictures of that boy. He'd be even older than I am now." She yanked on his sleeve bringing him back. "Don't you want to go back there to visit some day? You can take me."

Josep shook his head. "That's out of the question. You know how I told you about your Uncle Eduard and how he can't come back here? Not that he seems to want to, mind you. Well, I can't go back to Canada. It all ended very badly. So I want you to erase it from your mind. It was ages ago and now I'm concentrating on trying to make a living."

She huffed. "There are other, safer ways to make a living. You love the excitement and you are unable to stay here. We bore you." Rosa crossed her arms.

Josep shrugged. "Perhaps, but you don't. I do like to feel that what I'm doing is undermining a bit of Franco's power, getting a little revenge for what happened all those years ago."

"If you won't take me to Canada, let me help you here." Rosa bounced on the bed and her curly hair moved with her. She had cut it short, in a modern hairstyle she must have seen in one of the magazines he brought her. "I'm sure I can help you more than just by hiding these books. Summer holidays are coming. I won't miss any school. You can take me to France instead."

Josep shook his head. He then looked at Rosa and began to see a young woman other than his daughter sitting beside him on the crumpled pink bedspread. Her gray eyes had turned smoky and looked at him as if she were reading him like a classic. Her figure had taken shape. She was sitting on her rounded hips and her now full breasts were heaving up and down as she watched him expectantly for his answer. No one would question her being in the woods. Since he would never leave her alone, they would never suspect a family on an outing. It was perfect and she was a fine example of how much people desired his books. "I'll think about it," he said. "I do worry about all of you, you know. I'm particularly worried about Pau. The boy doesn't speak."

"*Mare* is working on that. Don't worry. She has a plan."

"I don't dare ask what that could be." He shook his head, as if adding oxygen to the issue that had been burning in his mind. "Now, tell me something. Were there any French people at the bar opening?"

"One woman. Why?"

"Did your mother talk to her?"

"For ages. Why?"

"I was just wondering," Josep said, wondering why Dolors had lied to him and what Geneviève and his wife had talked about for so long.

"So when will you decide if I can come?" She wiggled towards him.

"Later. In the meantime, stop reading those books, or if you do, don't let anyone see you." Josep stood and rested a hand on the top of Rosa's head then pulled it away. "I have to go. Something has happened with your uncle and I have to talk to Àngels."

"You said he can't come here, so why don't you ever go and see him? If Montse lived far away, I would visit her." Rosa was tilting her head at him and looked at him with such certainty. "Don't you want to go?"

Josep shuffled the books in his hand. "Of course I do. You don't know how much."

"Then why don't you?"

"He doesn't need me. When he does, I'll go see him."

"We also need you, but you're never here."

Josep thumbed the pages of *Germinal* and they suddenly seemed much less important. "You must understand that I have to do this for myself. If I worked here doing just any job, I would become another cog in Franco's wheel. I can't let myself do that, but I can't let myself leave for good. I need my family. I do need you. It's a shame that your mother doesn't seem to need me."

"Of course she does. You're too sensitive. And far too proud." Rosa clicked her tongue in disapproval.

Josep handed the book back to Rosa. "Tell me how it finishes. We'll be leaving early in the morning before your mother gets up. You can come, but just once. I'll find a small job for you. But you mustn't mention a word to your mother or to anyone."

"Not even to Víctor?"

"Not even to him. I will be the one to tell him. It will be a secret. Your mother is already beside herself over this book. Have you seen her yet this morning?"

Rosa shook her tousled head. "She was leaving early to take Pau to Adiol la Nova on an errand. They should be back soon."

***

Àngels was sitting at her kitchen table, which was scattered with envelopes and papers. She had just begun writing a letter and as she searched for the words, she looked at Manel sitting across the table from her reading the local newspaper. She felt comforted to see him there. He was as familiar as her mother's chair in front of the fireplace and her brother's ancient corduroy jacket still hanging near the door. She looked back at the paper and continued writing: "You must take control of your life, for your health and for your family. Gaspard seems like such a nice young man. You should be proud. I can't help but think that my Joana would be about his age right now. However, there is no sense in dwelling on that. You say I should let down my guard like you have, but Manel and I are fine as we are." She glanced up at Manel. "He has done a wonderful job fixing up his little house. We are the best of friends and I'm not sure I'm meant to be a wife. Manel says I could never disappoint him and he says he wants to protect me. There is nothing left to protect me from, other than myself. The Puigs are gone and so is almost everyone who was dear to me, like you, for instance." She heard a knock at the door and it opened.

"*Bon dia,*" Josep said and nodded at Manel. "Àngels, could I have a word?"

She folded the letter and slipped it under the papers on the table. "You can say it in front of Manel."

"Yes, Manel, you are like family, aren't you?" Josep turned to Àngels and lowered his voice even though they were alone. "Have you heard about Eduard?"

"Heard what?" Àngels said, first wanting to know what Josep knew.

Josep's eyes held hers. "My sources tell me that he was arrested in France. They wouldn't be able to turn him in to the authorities here, would they?"

"No." Àngels stacked some of the envelopes on the table and put her half-written letter to the bottom of the pile. "Regardless, my sources tell me he's been released." She pushed her chair back and stood. Though Manel had been trying to convince her to lighten up with Josep, she didn't feel ready. She wanted to hear more of Eduard's side of the story first.

"Who told you?" Josep asked, before answering his own question. "It was Francine, wasn't it? What a relief." He collapsed into Àngels' chair.

"It is and it isn't. Apparently they released him to take him to hospital." She paced, looking at her feet and not at her brother. "He's home now and he's fine. I don't know what's got into him. He drinks too much and he's ill all the time. And now he gets arrested."

"He's unreasonable."

"He's not the only one." She looked him in the eye.

"You're not comparing us. We are not at all alike. Not anymore."

"How would you even know?"

"I have had more than my share of grief for him. He needs to appreciate me."

"Like Dolors appreciates you for that matter. Do you presume to be as good a brother as you are a husband? You're never here. If you haven't noticed, Dolors has begun to appreciate Baltasar again."

"You're trying to stick your finger in my old wounds. But those are healed. I've managed to salve them myself. I don't know why you are so worried about Baltasar if Manel is practically family." He glanced at Manel. "You said I could say anything in front of him. I for one am no longer worried about Dolors and Baltasar." Josep's eyebrows lifted. "I'm more worried about Dolors and the mayor."

"Aren't we all," Àngels said, opening the door and ushering Josep outside. She watched him walk in the direction of the co-op.

"Why don't you let up on him?" Manel asked. "You're lucky to have one brother nearby."

Àngels sighed and shuffled her letters, thinking how far away they all seemed, when Josep was right next door. "One day soon, I will have to forgive him."

***

At four in the morning, right before Dolors would be getting up to start her baking, Josep went down to the side of the house, where he found Rosa dressed in black from head to toe with a small pack on her back. Although it was still impenetrably dark out, the spring air was unseasonably warm mixed with a slight damp chill. They left footprints in the frost as they headed out of town the back way, but by the time their tracks melted they would be long gone. Víctor had left an hour earlier and was to wait for them inside their hideout, although he had made it clear to Josep that he was not in favor of Rosa tagging along.

Josep covered his lips and motioned for Rosa to stick closely behind him. He couldn't help but think that Víctor had been right. Together they weaved in and out of the trees, dodging rocks and branches that would appear underfoot as if suddenly ejected by the earth. It was still dark when they reached Turtle Rock. It hovered ahead of them in the dark, the clump of moss-covered boulders that to Josep signified safety. He whistled and slid aside the rock blocking the door. He lit his candle and saw that Víctor had dug a deeper pit inside, but that except for the shovel the burrow was empty. He looked over his shoulders and he listened.

"Where is Víctor now?" Josep whispered and crawled inside the pit with Rosa following him. Josep struck a match and lit a candle. It illuminated a small circle around them, but the edges of the cavern remained in darkness. Crouching, he held Rosa close beside him. They listened to the silence of the woods like a giant pillow of calm around them. As their breathing returned to normal the noises of the forest grew louder. The breeze in the trees, the cawing and chirping of birds, a sudden crack of a branch. Rosa started and sucked in her breath.

"It's just a tree, its bark settling," Josep said, putting a calming hand on her arm. "One eventually manages to distinguish the normal noises of the forest from the dangerous ones. There is something comforting in those normal sounds." He tried to reassure her but he was shaking his head at himself for allowing his emotions to overtake him. It made no sense to have Rosa here. "Where the hell is Víctor?" He reached into a hole in the corner where a large tin was buried. "Do you want something to eat while we wait?" There were dried sausage, nuts, dried figs and apricots, all wrapped in a cloth. Taking a similar bundle out of his pack, he placed it inside the tin. "This is the emergency supply. We have to freshen it up every so often." He cut a piece of *fuet* and handed it to Rosa who bit into the dried sausage and chewed.

"What kind of emergency?" she asked.

"If the border guards get on our trail, or if there's a storm. I once spent three days in here. That's why I put this here. I learned the hard way."

"Three days? What for?"

"It was just before Montse was born. Things were much tougher then."

"I know. That's when people were being arrested. Like *Tieta* Carme. I wish I could have met her."

Josep raised a hand and leaned his ear toward the door. Footsteps were approaching. He was so much more nervous than usual. He drew his pistol and pointed it toward the opening. The stone slid across and Víctor was squatting in the doorway. Josep put away his gun as Víctor held up a hare by the ears.

"Fine specimen," Víctor said. "Who else were you expecting?"

"No one, but one can never lower one's guard. You were supposed to be here waiting."

"I know. Then I heard something go by. Nothing gets away from me." He shook the rabbit at them. "So, Rosa," he whispered. "How's the adventure so far?"

She nodded.

"I think we've managed to give her enough of a fright. And myself. Let's go before dawn sneaks up on us," Josep said.

Víctor wrapped the hare in a cloth and stashed it in the metal box. "I'll fetch it on the way back. Dolors can make us rabbit with garlic sauce. Something to look forward to tonight. It's also a good cover for the guards. Hunting."

***

When they finally emerged from the woods, Rosa's face brightened as they entered her first French town. She thought that it looked familiar yet different, like a shoe in an odd style and size. Everything felt roomier. All the stone façades were crisp and clean, while others were freshly painted with flowers lining the balconies. It was like Pujaforta, but the streets were somehow neater with more breathing space. She wondered if that's what having money meant.

"I'll leave you two here," Josep said. "I have some things to pick up. Then I'll be back. Don't worry."

"What?" Rosa said feeling slight panic. "I thought that we were going with you."

Josep shook his head. "Not today. You're just getting your feet wet. Don't you want to stay with Víctor?"

Rosa looked at Víctor, who was her real reason for wanting to come. His dark eyes were looking down at her and she smiled. "Of course I don't mind staying with Víctor." She took his arm.

"It would appear that I am the babysitter," Víctor said and Rosa pouted. Then he said, "Why don't we take a look at the newsagents? All those magazines and newspapers."

"Newsagents?" Rosa said with her eyes glowing. She took her camera out of her back pack. "Víctor, stand here beside *Pare*." She motioned for Josep to join them, but his back was already disappearing across the square. Rosa took a picture.

"You probably shouldn't take too many of those," Víctor said and ruffled her hair.

Later the two of them sat at a simple table in a plain bar. Rosa felt so grown-up being in an establishment for adults, across from Víctor, even though she was sipping an Orangina. She didn't know what excited her more, having free access to printed matter or having Víctor all to herself. Besides them, there was only a handful of older men in a corner playing cards under a cloud of cigarette smoke.

"I hate to admit it, but my mother was right. I'll have to improve my French to be able to read all of these magazines and newspapers," she said, and tried to make her excitement sound intellectual rather than naïve.

"I don't know why you want to read Le Monde and all of these, when I know you prefer the ones with the pictures," Víctor said, referring to the latest issue of *LIFE* Rosa had rolled up in her pack.

"I am a photographer. My father learned English reading the newspapers in Ontario, so I reckon I can do the same with my French." She leaned in and whispered. "Since when has *Pare* carried a pistol?" She always knew that her father was in the mountains but had never truly considered the peril this presented to him, and to Víctor. Perhaps Àngels had reason to be angry.

Víctor approached until their noses were almost touching. "Since the war. He's always carried a gun on these missions as far as I know. And he needs one." He cleared his throat. "Listen, Rosa. I know you suggested this and your father agreed to it for some reason of his own, but do you know how dangerous this is? This is no game." His dark eyes flashed at her as if she was still a child.

"I know it isn't," she said and pushed her Orangina aside. "But when I saw *Pare*'s reaction when you were approaching the hideout, I really realized it." Now that she had felt the danger under her skin, she would have to convince her father to let her accompany them regularly. She had to keep an eye on Víctor and surely there was safety in numbers.

"You still want to do it?"

"Of course." She sat up straight. "We have to do what we can against this regime. I want to be able to read all those books out in the open and buy magazines from newsstands like here. I especially don't want to work in *Mare*'s bakery. And you know that I always want to spend time with you." She rested her hand on top of his, which was comfortingly warm. The contrast made hers appear whiter and his darker.

Víctor gently withdrew his hand. "In my opinion, you're far too young for any of this."

"I'm not so young. Besides, *Pare* doesn't think so." She jutted out her chest.

"I think he does. I think that's the point. No one would suspect you."

***

Josep was in Merloin-les-Bains, under a thin blanket with Geneviève's head resting on his chest. The cool morning air drifted in the open window and he took a deep breath and a drag on a cigarette. He wanted to give himself just a minute, since that was all they had. Geneviève wasn't even meant to be there and Rosa wasn't supposed to be waiting for him either. Geneviève stood with her bare buttocks facing him and tried to cover herself. As the sun reflected off the mirror, it turned her skin stark white. He admired her profile and in his mind sculpted out her younger dancer's body from her current curves and folds. Stopping, he realized he loved each and every bump and bulge just as she was now. She pulled on her slacks and blouse then wrapped her hair in a knot on the back of her head. When she turned to look at Josep, he was staring at her. He motioned to her face.

"You're smudged. You should fix that before Jules gets home. When will that be by the way?"

"Any minute." She waved him urgently out of the bed. "I'm sorry. I shouldn't have risked it, but I couldn't resist you." Geneviève opened a tin of candies and offered him one. "You're not disappointed, are you?"

"Of course not," he said and buttoned his trousers. "I wish you wouldn't eat those sweets. They can be dangerous."

"I'm trying to quit smoking, darling. Which could be more dangerous?" She wiped the edge of her mouth. "Besides, your smuggling is even worse. You love it too much."

He looked at her and became close to saying something very compromising. Instead he turned to business. "I wouldn't say I love it. But I wouldn't love working under the regime." He shivered.

Geneviève led Josep downstairs into the living room, where they sat opposite each other at a good distance. As she reached for the water jug, she looked out the front window. "Here comes Jules now. He looks happy, luckily. That was close." She looked very relieved. "He has a huge parcel."

Josep looked outside and, indeed, Jules was practically staggering up the front walk. When he came in his enthusiasm followed him like a cloud and made him positively buoyant. He put down a large box and straightened his hair before kissing his wife and shaking Josep's hand dynamically.

"You are here. You'll be glad you waited. Take a look at this." He lifted the package onto the table and peeled it open as if it were the skin of a rare, exotic fruit. Reaching inside, he pulled out a leather-bound book. He then displayed it on his palm like he would the finest wine.

"You found it?" Josep took the book gently from his hands. It was an original edition of Antonio Machado's last poems.

"They told me that he had it with him in Collioure when he died." Jules shook his head. "But I don't believe it. I think they said it to fetch a higher price. I have others, just wait till you see." Jules delved into the box again like a child into a bag of sweets. He put all the books on the table. Balzac. Gandhi. Lorca. *El libro de buen amor.* Jules and Josep leaned over them. "Don't drool on them now," Jules said and pointed to the side of Josep's mouth. "You've got something red there. Tomato sauce or something."

Josep wiped his mouth with his handkerchief and glanced at Geneviève, whose bright red lips winced at him. Josep turned his attention back to the books. "This is fantastic," he said. He couldn't wait to see the look on Rosa's face. Painstakingly he wrapped the books and put them inside his bag. "People are waiting for me today, so I have to go." Josep put the bag over his shoulder. "They will be thrilled to see these." Josep waved goodbye, leaving Geneviève and Jules linked by the arm. As he went down the front walk he wiped his mouth again and examined the red tips of his fingers.

That evening Josep, Víctor, and Rosa returned to Pujaforta with Josep's books and Dolors' supplies and enjoyed the tastiest wild rabbit in garlic sauce, roasted with just the right amount of fresh cream and crushed almonds. The exercise and mountain air made it all the more succulent. Although Rosa had to hide her earlier whereabouts from Dolors and everyone, she seemed beside herself from the adventure of the day and with the books that Josep had managed to acquire. Even though Josep required no persuasion, Rosa continued to convince them that his book ventures were the key to opening the closed minds of the regime. Or at least of empowering its people. She was so devoted to his cause that through the rest of the summer Josep allowed her to accompany them on two other occasions, both of which she spent with Víctor at the newsagents and the local bar. Rosa had also reminded Josep of his unfulfilled promises and urged him to bring back some baby rose bushes. She even offered to carry them herself, though Josep would not have it. If she was to come, it would be a father–daughter excursion and she would be allowed to carry no goods, no matter how innocuous or thorny. Víctor agreed that this was wise, just in case they were caught. It was as if the three of them were bound by their special secret.

***

Late one summer afternoon Àngels decided that while they could do nothing about the regime, it was time to make peace with her family next door. Manel had helped her see that grudges were a waste of precious time. Àngels spotted Josep digging in the garden behind her house and saw her chance to finally put things right. She walked toward him, first stopping at the shrine to Carme and Artur and bowing her head. Looking surprised to see her there, Josep silently joined her at her side, his shoulder touching hers.

"I'll bet you're shocked to see me," Àngels finally said, afraid that if she looked at him she might change her mind. She stared at the rock marking the shrine. "You know what Carme once said to me?" she finally asked. "She said she didn't deserve to live. Her whole family was gone and she hadn't saved them. I don't dare think what that would be like." Josep tried to put an arm around her, but she stepped away. "But she had Víctor, you see. When my baby died, it was as if she gave him to me. She made me promise I would take care of him." She shrugged. "And he's the one who's taken care of me."

"And I took him away."

"No, I took myself away. And I can't do it anymore. I'm losing everyone." She shoved her hands into the pockets of her sweater. "Both Manel and Víctor have made me see that."

Josep put an arm around her gently, as if she might break. "Àngels, I'm so sorry you have had to live with all of this. I'm sorry about Víctor. I'm sorry that I let this come between us." She tilted her head up toward him, ready to hear his version. "At first I convinced myself that work would help bring down the regime," Josep continued. "I let myself use it as an excuse. Then I couldn't stop. And I suppose it's a way to distance myself from everyone."

"It must run in the family. But can I ask why you would do that?"

"Because I would be destined to disappoint them, just like I did with you." He looked to the ground where a young rose bush was lying with its roots exposed. Àngels once again saw the face of a devastated boy so many years ago. Josep looked down at her with the same sad expression. "I'll never forget the look in father's eyes as he fell. He was so angry at me."

"You've been carrying this with you all these years? Josep, it wasn't your fault. He wouldn't blame you for the ruined flowers. He would know that in his heart."

"His broken heart," Josep said as he walked to the same spot in the garden where the rose bushes had been planted and started digging. Àngels bent down beside him and scooped the cool earth. Once the hole was almost knee-deep, Josep sat back on his heels and said, "I suppose I tend to blame myself for a lot. Much of it I do deserve."

At first Àngels didn't respond and instead gently stuck her trowel in the pile of soil, now ready to give in. "I know that Víctor didn't give you any choice about taking him with you."

"No, he didn't. He is very good at it though. He has a gift. Deep down he loves it. I think it makes him feel closer to her, to Carme." Josep's look was trying to convince her. "But, regardless, I should have refused."

Àngels felt the wall around her disintegrating. She sighed. "I lost so much over the years and I couldn't lose Víctor too. Now he's an adult and he can do what he chooses. I, of course, would rather see him work at the co-op or something." Àngels looked toward the house. "Manel made me see I'm not being fair with you. You know he's been waiting for me to marry him."

"He's a good, honest man, despite my earlier impressions. So why don't you?"

Àngels shrugged. "I don't want to depend on anyone."

"What would be wrong with that?"

She shrugged again, feeling the wall mounting.

"Àngels." Josep hugged her and rocked her back and forth holding her hair in his fingers. "How have we let this happen? Between the three of us, how could we have become so divided?"

"I don't know. This wasn't the life we chose." She rubbed his back.

Josep pulled away. "If you had news of Eduard, you would share it with me, wouldn't you?"

Àngels nodded, knowing that she had already told him everything she knew.

"See what I have here?" Josep pointed to two rose bushes. "I've been telling Rosa I would plant these for ages, but never got around to it. Will you give me a hand?"

The plants lay beside the hole as if begging her to let them thrive. She took Josep's hand in hers before the two of them placed the tangled roots of the rose bushes into the soil and packed the earth around them. Josep kissed Àngels' cheek. "I am so glad to have my sister back. You are back, aren't you?"

Àngels nodded. "And I am delighted to have my brother," Àngels said, feeling more at peace than she had been in years. "Now we just have to work on Eduard." She brushed the soil off her hands.

***

Before they knew it, school was to start again and Dolors began to plan to close the terrace for the winter. The season had gone unexpectedly well and she had been stashing away some extra pesetas to buy one of those new television sets everyone was talking about. She told the family that it could take a few more years of savings, but the wait would be worth it. A television plus her famous *truita* would ensure the terrace was always packed. The terrace's last day of business was a lovely sunny Sunday and every chair was full. Clearly the townsfolk, those from surrounding towns, and even tourists knew that this would be their last chance to savor Dolors' omelet in such a spectacular view. Núria had spent days helping Dolors prepare. Josep was away, as usual. Dolors had even arranged for Pau to have daily dance lessons to keep him out of her hair. They were expecting him to return with his teacher any moment. Núria was also trying to get a start on the next winter season by selling as much knitwear as she could. Her table at the entrance was stacked with sweaters, socks, hats, gloves, mittens, and was in perfect earshot of everything. Albert sat beside her, although he hardly rose from his chair.

Later in the day when they were all run ragged, Núria saw Pau and Geneviève, wearing one of her recent sweater creations, come around the corner. Pau appeared to float towards them, looking entirely at peace. Dolors ran to him and kissed him.

"*Fill*, you're back. How did it go?" Dolors said and kissed Geneviève on either powdered cheek. "Is he getting any better?"

"He's doing fantastically. And he does seem to enjoy it." Geneviève nodded and cringed. "Your husband isn't here today, is he?"

"He's never here. I'm starving," Pau said, kissing Núria on the cheek and then going inside as Montse came out, carrying a tray to one of the only tables left.

Dolors pulled Geneviève towards a table right in front of Núria's knitwear. Dolors sat down and called out, "Montse, you can take care of it all, right? This is what you say you want. Consider it a test." She then turned her full attention to Geneviève. "My mother-in-law's sweater looks lovely on you."

The pink knit pullover was a perfect match with Geneviève's cheeks as she blushed. "Merci. Sorry I was late this morning. I had some trouble getting away. My husband," she sighed. "You know how it is."

"I know. Mine never seems to be here for the opening or closing. But I do have something to thank him for."

192

"What's that?"

"I asked him to talk to our daughter Rosa about school. Remember how I told you she was causing trouble with the nuns? She still has difficulty realizing that we must abide by the regime. She gets it from her father and her aunt, for that matter." Dolors shook her head. "But this year Rosa's so excited to go back to school. She wants to learn French. Before she was never interested. I know that she and her father are up to something, and whatever it is seems to be working." Dolors smiled but then she sighed. "And now I have another problem."

"What's that?" Geneviève leaned forward and took her hand looking genuinely worried.

"It's Montse. She's just told me that she wants to quit school entirely. She wants to bake with me."

"That's flattering, isn't it? I wish my sons wanted to spend time with me."

"Of course, I would be thrilled to have the help, though she still has much to learn. But I would rather she finish school, then she can work in the bakery if she wants to. Besides, she's always complaining that our town is too small for her. She says she'll never find a husband here. She may never find one anywhere." Dolors sighed and leaned in. "Our friend, Baltasar—well, he's more than just a friend—he's been trying to convince Rosa to go to university in Barcelona. I think she might even be considering it. But with Montse it's different." Dolors sat back. "Have I ever told you about Baltasar, the town doctor? That I almost married him?"

"Really? Why didn't you?" Geneviève edged closer.

"It's a long story. There was the war. Our war and then your war. Baltasar will always hold a special place in my heart. It may be a spot that no one else will ever reach. In fact, sometimes I still dream of him."

"Is he married?"

"No. But he seems to fancy my sister-in-law."

"But they've never married? Maybe he still holds you in a special place in his heart. Maybe that's why he's never married anyone else." Geneviève was shredding the edge of her omelet with her fork.

"I had considered that." Dolors wiggled in her seat. "He is very attentive. He helped me build this terrace." She caressed the wood with her foot. "When everyone else abandoned me he was there to help. Baltasar is really very special, too special for anyone else to have him."

"You've never tried to, you know." Geneviève raised her eyebrows as she chewed. "Maybe you should."

Dolors held her hands to her chest. "Good heavens, no. I'm a married woman. Over here we're not like you French people. We still have scruples."

Geneviève frowned. "Most of us still have scruples. Everyone but my husband, I suppose."

"I'm sorry, I forgot about that." Dolors took Geneviève's hand. "He hasn't hurt you again, has he?"

Geneviève looked at her plate. "Not physically." She looked up and smiled. "Let's not talk about that today. Today I wanted to talk to you about Pau." She rested her fork. "I've told you this before, but I think he's really talented. His dancing comes from inside him. Like he has something to say. It's like it's his way of expressing himself."

"That's a relief since he doesn't use words very often. Just how talented do you think he is?"

"You could forget the skiing and concentrate on dancing. He just needs continued instruction. It's like he's got it in his genes. Is your husband particularly graceful?"

"Ha." Dolors threw back her head. "As graceful as a lumberjack, which he was once, in fact."

"So, he still has no idea about Pau? Pau really loves it."

Dolors' eyes were wide and she shook her head. "Pau twirls around the house and I have to remind him to stop in case his father sees him. My husband would never understand."

A shadow appeared over the table as a body blocked the light and warmth of the sun.

"Montse," Dolors said without looking up. "Not now."

"I am not Montse." It was a man's voice and it sounded angry. A green uniform moved closer.

Dolors jumped to her feet. "Sr. Mayor, I'm sorry. Is there something I can get you?"

"I came to pick up my order. Normally I prefer you to deliver it, but I need it now. Right now."

"Certainly, please come with me." Dolors waved at Geneviève before leading the mayor toward her kitchen.

Dolors pointed to a window with a sill half a meter wide that gave onto the terrace. "That's where I plan to put a television. That way we can all watch The Caudillo's speeches on the NO-DO from the comfort of the patio. Isn't that a fabulous idea?"

Núria watched them go by, smiled and shook her head. Albert grunted and awoke, lifting his chin from his chest.

"What was that?" he said.

"Just Dolors keeping all sides of her bread buttered."

"One day your son may be very grateful that she does," Albert said, his mind still frightfully sharp.

CHAPTER FOURTEEN

ANOTHER COUPLE OF years passed before Dolors had enough savings for a television. When she had Josep install it on the window ledge, it was as if the Barça football team was playing on the terrace itself rather than on a small black and white screen. So many people came to gather around it. Josep scowled at it stating that with the regime's grip on the programming of both channels, and even on the soccer teams, it was a pure propaganda machine. Dolors seemed ambivalent since she was too busy feeding her customers to watch it. She ran around on swollen ankles in the heat and called out orders to Montse, who was now helping her full time. Montse had taken to baking and carefully perfecting her mother's recipes, but received only occasional praise from Dolors, who seemed afraid to relinquish any of her control.

Pau had become rather friendly with Vicenç Vidal, one of the mayor's sons, and when they weren't playing soccer themselves, Pau was practicing his dance steps in private. He was becoming particularly devoted to the more contemporary choreographies that Geneviève told him were the buzz in Paris. She even bought him a red leotard to wear to enhance the effect of a special routine of a raging flame. Sometimes when Josep was away, Dolors and the girls would gather in Geneviève's studio in Adiol la Nova for an impromptu performance, where they would all end up dancing and floating around Pau like he was the rising sun.

Rosa used Pau's dance lessons to practice her French with his teacher. Her grasp of the language had also greatly improved from all the reading matter she brought back on her occasional jaunts to France with her father, which they still hid from Dolors. During the trips, Rosa was content to spend every moment with Víctor and never asked where Josep went to collect his books. While it was hardly challenging for Víctor, he didn't complain. Even Àngels now believed that their missions were no longer that risky. She, however, had yet to take on the risk of matrimony. She said that she was happy with her life as it was. The Balaguer lives continued on with relative calm, until a storm appeared from over the mountaintop.

One afternoon during a particularly tense Barça match, Josep received an urgent call to meet Geneviève at her dance school. Josep went at the set time, worrying all the way, thinking that she must have received some news about Eduard. He also thought about Geneviève, her panicked voice and the fact she had never telephoned him at home. When he arrived at the pink door, he anxiously let himself in with his own key.

"*Chérie*, I'm here," Josep called as he burst through the door and tried to catch his breath.

"Hello, *chéri*. How did your customers like those books I got you?"

"Jules," Josep said, his breath catching again in his throat. "They loved them, of course. I'm surprised to see you here. Geneviève asked me to come."

"Yes. I know." Jules put on his spectacles and stepped forward as if for inspection. "I asked her to have you come here. I have an interesting business proposal for you."

Josep nodded, wondering why Jules wouldn't just contact him himself. "And you thought it would be better to discuss it at the dance studio?" Josep was panicked that Jules had found out about their affair. More to the point, he was afraid to think about what Jules might do to him or Geneviève, and what that could do to their mutual amorous and business relationships.

Jules appeared to ignore him. "You recall my diamonds."

Josep nodded slowly.

"I'm going to need your help with something."

The little door in the wall of the studio opened and Geneviève came through it. Her face was lined with mascara that looked as thick as melting tar. One look between them confirmed to Josep that Jules had found out.

Jules stepped closer. He gruffly held out his hand to Geneviève, staking his territory. She silently went to him and took it. "What do you say we talk about my business proposal?" Jules went toward the little office and Josep followed, as if entering a cage. They sat down around the desk, still stacked with papers. Jules straightened them and rested his interlinking hands on top of them. "I think you'll find this very interesting," he began. "I have jewels, a good number of them. And I have a buyer, a reliable one, in Marbella. I'd like you to help me get the jewels to him."

"Marbella? Why don't you just send them or ship them?" Josep asked. "Unless," he sucked in his breath.

"No." Jules clicked his tongue. "It's not like that. Everything is legal on our end. It's the buyer, you see. He doesn't want the purchase known."

"How do you expect me to get the jewels all the way down to Marbella? That's the other end of Spain. I only know the Pujaforta area."

"It's simple. My client also collects fine furniture." Jules smiled and nodded. "If I'm right, your sister works with Manel Masplà, the furniture maker. It's only a matter of making a few secret compartments."

"I can't ask my sister or Manel to do that."

"Perhaps you'd like me to ask Dolors?" Jules raised an eyebrow.

"You know my wife's name?"

"It's nothing compared to what you know about my wife." Jules looked first at Geneviève and then at Josep. "So, my business associate and my wife." Jules leaned forward. "It's a little cliché, *n'est ce pas?*"

Josep swallowed and shook his head. He felt the nerves tingling in his face and feared that if he had to run right now, his legs might collapse underneath him. He steadied himself against the stack of shoe boxes along the wall. After all these years the seriousness of the situation came careening towards him. He could lose absolutely everything.

"The jewels will be here next week," Jules said. "That should give you plenty of time to arrange it all with Monsieur Masplà. You will have to pick a fine piece of furniture. I think all the details are clear. If they're not, Geneviève will take care of it, won't you, *chérie?*"

"Yes, *chéri,*" Geneviève nodded at Jules, but her eyes were apologizing to Josep.

Josep put up his hands. "I haven't agreed to this yet."

"But you will," Jules said. "I trust the two of you to behave from now on."

Josep nodded and went towards the door. "Don't even think of putting a hand on her."

Jules looked toward Geneviève. "On her? Don't worry. She's safe with me."

On his way back to Pujaforta Josep climbed blindly through the dark across the mountain. He was far too distracted for the matter at hand. Not only was jewelry smuggling beyond his ability, it went against the grain of his beliefs, which were based on the fact that food and knowledge were fair game. Jewelry was for rich folks. He shook his head at himself. Even the two books hidden inside his coat and the prospect of their sale could not distract him from his new dilemma. He didn't know which was worse: to tell Dolors about his affair or to ask Manel to help him with the smuggling. Both sounded equally perilous. As he weighed his options, the scale gradually tipped in favor of not telling Dolors. That option had too many overlapping risks. While he didn't expect that Dolors was a vindictive woman, she was very jealous and driven. The whole scenario unraveled before him. Dolors would collapse on hearing the news and would use it to run to the arms of Baltasar. Josep would not only lose his wife but also his best friend. Then to make sure that he stayed out of their way, Dolors would set the mayor and his people on him, like a hound after a fox. He would spend his last days in Franco's jails, alone with no wife, friends, or family. Angels would abandon him as well.

Josep sniffed and shook his head. Then he hit his thighs with his fist. When would he learn? Women had already caused him too much misery. A large rock appeared in his path and he kicked it with all his might. The rock did not budge, but the pain shot from his toe to his brain. He grabbed his foot with both hands and fell to his side, where he sat rocking, cradling his injured limb and his growing feeling of helplessness. In such circumstances an injury was potentially fatal. *"Estic fotut,"* he muttered. Then he pulled himself to his knees. "Boy am I screwed," he repeated, and began to look for sticks that would serve as crutches. He was taking far too long and every minute he wasted brought him closer to being caught, so he hopped to Turtle Rock and stashed his books and other suspicious objects in the tin inside. In the time it took him to carefully hobble down the hill to the edge of the forest behind the house, he had made his decision: telling Dolors was out of the question.

As he limped out of the trees he heard a "Psst," and looked into the barrel of a gun. While the guard dragged him to the station, Josep was thankful for the excruciating pain in his foot. Without it he would have had two banned books in his jacket pocket. After he had waited interminable hours, he found himself sitting in the mayor's office. As Mayor Vidal stared at him for minutes on end, it became clear that he could find no reason to keep him there, other than to make him suffer. Josep couldn't stop thinking about his throbbing foot and how it had saved him. He then thought of Jules and his current predicament.

"They tell me you had nothing on you. Today. Just be thankful that our sons are close friends, and that you have a charming wife."

Josep didn't respond. He only nodded and hobbled homeward.

When he limped inside, Dolors marched to the table and waved a letter at him. Her face was dusted with flour and all the baskets were full of bread ready to be bought. He hopped in further and said, "Dolors, I'm in no mood or state to talk about Rosa's problems at school. I've just spent hours at the mayor's office and I'm injured."

"The mayor?" Dolors dropped the letter. "Now we are in trouble. Luckily he's a very nice man. It's your back again, isn't it. I knew that it would be our end."

"Our end? Why must you always be the victim?" Josep said, as she pulled a chair out for him and carefully sat him in it. "The man let me go this time. And it's not my back, it's my foot."

"Serves you right for gallivanting."

"What?" Josep scowled at her. There was no way that she could already know about Geneviève.

"The letter is not about Rosa. It's from that Marie-Claude in Quebec." Dolors raised her eyebrows and nodded knowingly, while slapping the palm of her hand with the letter.

"Marie-Claude? Don't tell me you're still jealous of her. She lives thousands of kilometers away across an ocean."

"Greater obstacles have been overcome."

"I am in agony. Give me that letter and call Baltasar for my foot, would you. Talk about the pot calling the kettle black. Baltasar lives right down the hill."

"Thank God. You would be in a fine mess otherwise." She held the letter to her chest and shook her head. "This time I haven't tried to read it. She wrote in English for some reason. You are going to translate it. Then and only then will I call the doctor."

Josep ripped the letter from her hands. Dolors was this upset about a letter from a distant woman whom he'd slept with once a few decades ago. He made the right decision in not telling her about a woman in much closer proximity in a variety of ways. Josep scanned the English before making a generic translation. "She says that her father, the one who wrote to me last time, is very ill. But he still insists on delivering the ice himself, to the few people who still want it."

"It says a lot more than that, all those paragraphs."

"Her husband," he emphasized, "is going on a fishing trip. And her son wants to come to visit." He lowered the letter. "I don't think that's a good idea," he said thinking that the last thing he needed was to have an adult Luc blaming him for events that occurred in another lifetime and that were mostly beyond his control. On the other hand, he might be curious to see how Luc, the foul-mouthed boy, turned out. He looked around the basic kitchen, at the marble sinks and pipes running in front of the ceramic tiles. "Besides with the way they live in Canada, I'd rather he not see us here."

Dolors tore the letter from his hand. "What's wrong with the way we live? You can say anything you want about The Caudillo, but I for one am proud. Look what I've managed to do with the bakery." She glanced at the letter again. "You're sure that's all it says? I don't think I can believe you."

"I'm sure." Josep was very thankful that Dolors' English was nonexistent. While the sound of Marie-Claude's words was a welcome trip through time to some memorably romantic moments, he had to hope that Luc would stay away. Josep grasped his foot. "Now will you call Baltasar?"

"Why? Are you in pain, dear?"

"Excruciating."

"Good." She slammed the door.

Baltasar plastered Josep's broken foot, but could do nothing about his nearly ruptured life. Josep asked him to send Manel and Víctor in that order. Víctor didn't know it yet, but he would have to make the mission alone. In the meantime, Josep lay in bed with his leg raised and stared out the window towards the mountains counting the errors of his ways. When Manel arrived he was dressed in a shirt that accentuated the new muscles in his arms and across his chest. His hair was graying, but his face was still boyish and thin. Josep was anchored to the middle of his bed and the cast on his leg seemed to weigh almost as much as his troubles.

"That must have hurt." Manel pointed to Josep's leg and winced. "Baltasar told me you wanted to see me, and I'm intrigued to find out what for."

"How's the carpentry business going?"

"I'm just finishing an enormous cabinet for an important customer. I've been working on it for months. Other than that, it's rather slow."

"I hear that you're very skilled." Josep tried to sit up slightly. "Listen, Manel. I need a favor."

"Of course. I remember what it was like when I dislocated my shoulder. If it hadn't been for your sister I don't know what I would have done."

"Àngels can't know about this," Josep said, and motioned for Manel to take a seat in the old armchair beside his bed. If Àngels found out, any chances of maintaining their truce would disintegrate. He had decided that his only way was to deal with Manel alone.

Manel swallowed and sat quietly. "I can't imagine hiding anything from Àngels."

"Surely you haven't always told her the truth. You'll have to remember how to lie," Josep said and shook his head. "I'm sorry, I shouldn't have said that."

"Not if you want a favor," Manel said, but didn't move from his seat.

"It's a big one, you see. I'm in a bit of a bind. You know what I do, right? The goods I bring across have always been for the business or for people around town. I've never smuggled goods of value. Only what I consider necessities." He paused. "I have a client who is insisting I bring some other goods over and I can't say no."

"I don't see what it has to do with me."

"They want you to hide it in one of your pieces of furniture and ship it to Marbella."

"Me? Marbella?" Manel's eyes glazed slightly. He got up and slowly walked towards the window, from which there was a view of the side of Àngels' cottage. He stood and stared, his forehead resting on the pane. Josep waited patiently until Manel finally turned and said, "How much money is in it?"

"It's quite lucrative. Much more than your furniture, I imagine. You would be paid very generously for the piece with the compartments. Imagine what you could do with the money. You could buy more wood, or more land. You could lavish some on my sister. You did say business was slow."

"No, I couldn't possibly. What if Àngels found out?" Manel bit his lip and sank his hands deep into his pockets. "Unless you think that if I had more money, Àngels would finally agree to marry me."

Josep shrugged. "You know Àngels isn't all that fussed by money. But she is a woman, isn't she? Don't tell her I said that."

Manel removed his hand from his pocket and began twirling a wood chip in his fingers, staring at it like it held the answer. He sank into the chair and examined his calloused palms. "I've been trying to convince her to marry me for so long. I could help fix up Àngels' house, maybe get her some new shoes. I think she'd like that." Looking up, he said, "Do you know what we would be shipping?"

Josep slapped him on the back. "The less you know the better. It's safer for everyone."

With Manel taken care of and Víctor briefed on his upcoming mission to Merloin-les-Bains, Josep was unable to move from his bed when the bakery party line rang its three short rings. Josep told them to take a message, which was: your order is ready for pick up.

***

In the middle of the night Víctor left all alone, being extra careful under the light of the full moon. As he vanished among the tree trunks, a dark shadow followed him until it was on his heels. Rosa knew that he had sensed her presence the moment that he hid behind a tree. It had been so difficult to follow him, since he walked so stealthily and quickly up the hill, in and around the trees, as if tracing a well-worn path; yet she knew that they changed their routes to avoid exactly that from occurring. She kept her eye on the tree where he had disappeared and continued as silently as she could. When she was right outside his hiding place, she whispered, "Víctor, it's just me."

He grabbed her by the arm and pulled her behind the tree. Then he shook her through his fury. "You're not supposed to be here. I could have shot you."

Rosa looked at him from under her black toque and was saddened by the angry look in his eyes. She had thought he would be glad to see her. "You carry a gun, too?"

"Somebody has to," he said, and pulled her further up the hill by the hand. "It's too late to go back now, so it looks like you're coming with me."

Rosa shook her arm free. "I'm sorry to be such a nuisance. I am perfectly capable of walking by myself."

He held his fingers over his lips and gave her a punishing look. Rosa followed silently after him, placing her feet inside his large footsteps and watching his tall back in front of her. He seemed to climb with such certainty and confidence. With his height and slenderness he blended easily with the tree trunks in front of them. Rosa thought she would follow him anywhere, no matter how he tried to hide. When they came to Josep's first cave and squatted inside it, Rosa looked at Víctor's face as it turned amber in the candlelight. "I'm sorry. I should have asked you first," she said, although she did not regret being alone with him in such a confined space.

"Yes, you should have. What you did is dangerous for both of us. Now we both have to get across and back without getting caught. My trip was supposed to be a secret."

"I know. I heard," Rosa said and felt a slight wave of worry when she thought of the real danger before them.

"It's going to be quick. Besides you shouldn't be missing school."

"I'd rather be here with you."

Víctor shook his head and dug his heel into the dirt before looking slowly towards her. "I do have to admit that part of me is glad not to have to do this alone."

"Are you glad just to have the company or because it's me?"

Víctor looked away. He put out the candle and darkness fell upon them. "Bundle up. It's getting chilly. Let's go." He crawled out of the cave.

***

As Josep lay in bed worrying about Víctor and debating whether or not to respond to Marie-Claude's letter, Dolors and Pau slid out the front door. Pau, who was now a head taller than his mother and much leaner, appeared to float along beside her. He had spent the morning with the Vidal boy and had returned smelling of what she initially thought was tobacco. Dolors had swatted him and dragged him stumbling along beside her. When they arrived at the flat in Adiol la Nova, Geneviève was waiting. Dolors kissed her on both cheeks. Her own were flushed and clammy from the walk and from worrying about her son's experimenting with noxious substances. Geneviève put a steadying arm around Pau and led them into the living room, where all the furniture was pushed back and a large mirror was propped against the wall reflecting Geneviève's darkly rouged profile and Dolors' perspiring temple.

"I'm so glad that you could come on such short notice. I had an opening," Geneviève said. "I hope it wasn't too inconvenient."

"No, but it was a bit risky. You see, my husband is bedridden. I was afraid he'd see us leaving. Then I had to drag this one from Lord knows where." She slapped the back of Pau's head.

"Bedridden? What happened to him?" Geneviève asked, her penciled brow arching. She motioned for Pau to start warming up as her face flushed and her voice became higher. "Wasn't he supposed to go away? I hope it's nothing serious."

"Broken foot. He sent my nephew instead."

"A broken foot? The poor man. How long will he be out of commission?"

"Another six weeks at least. Dr. Sort, my Baltasar," Dolors nodded proudly, "says he'll have to stay in bed until well after the Saint Jean festival. Later he'll be able to walk on crutches. I am not looking forward to having Josep stuck in bed. He's going to drive me mad." Dolors took a step closer to Geneviève and whispered, "How is your English?"

Geneviève frowned. "*Ça va*. Why?"

"When you've finished the lesson I have something I have to read and I need your help. It's from a floozy." Dolors showed her the letter postmarked in Canada and addressed to Josep Balaguer.

"Why don't we take a look now." Geneviève turned to Pau and clapped her hands. "*Première, seconde, plié.*"

"Do you have anything to eat?" Pau asked.

"Pau, how rude. I'm very sorry," Dolors said.

Geneviève steered Pau into the kitchen. "There may be something. Help yourself." She shut the door and motioned for Dolors to sit beside her on the settee. Geneviève held the envelope in her hands and hastily pulled out the letter. She bit her red lip and her eyes dodged back and forth. Slowly she began to translate:

"Dear Josep, Many years have passed now since you left. There have been a number of wars in between and this Cold War, which has managed to freeze out a good number of our people. You will know who I am referring to. You know that Thomas, the other school teacher, is my husband. He and some of the others are going on a special fishing expedition this weekend, but he has not told me what they are aiming to catch. I will not ask, since I have not been involved in all that for decades. My father is ailing. He found out about our tendencies but it didn't destroy him like we expected it would. Instead he's suffering from repeated bouts of pneumonia. But he still insists on delivering the ice, to the few people who still want it."

Dolors nodded and interrupted. "He did tell me she said that. Her father is ill."

Geneviève hushed her with a wave of her pink fingernails. "I have my hands full with my children, and with my teaching. I have been studying

English and am able to use it to write to you like you asked. I know you will wonder why I would finally write after all this time, all the frozen water under the bridge. It's because of Luc. For the past while, he has been asking a lot of questions about who his real father is. He remembers all those early years with you, and quite fondly at that. We have told him the truth, but he still wants to come to see you. He says he has some questions that only you can answer."

Dolors grabbed the letter from her hands. "Father? *Père?* Does this say what I think it says? Why did he tell her to write in English?" A look of sheer horror flooded Dolors' face and she handed the letter back. "Keep reading."

"I would be quite intrigued to hear from you myself. As one grows older somehow those early memories seem brighter, perhaps because we lived with such intensity and were not so distracted by the routine of living day to day. I do think about you quite often, and wonder what it might have been like living in your dear town of Pujaforta. Please write, if not to me, at least to Luc. Your friend from afar, Marie-Claude."

"Her living in Pujaforta?" Dolors looked like she'd swallowed poison. "Geneviève, what is she saying?"

"First of all, who is Marie-Claude?" Her eyes were large and frightened.

"A woman Josep knew in Quebec. In Canada. He did say he had some secrets that he wouldn't share. I was pregnant at the time and didn't want to hear anything about these people."

"Perhaps the secret is his son." Geneviève held the letter to her chest. "You see, I told you. Men cannot be trusted. Look at your husband. Look at my Jules. We should just lock them away and keep the key to ourselves."

Dolors put her hand to her forehead. "I don't feel well. I feel faint."

Geneviève fanned her with the letter and fetched a glass of water, which Dolors drank in gulps. She wiped her lips and stood up. "Pau," she called. "Get out of the kitchen."

"Sit and relax a bit. This has all been such a shock," Geneviève said.

"I can't stay. I have to go. Pau, Josep's other son, who he pays no attention to, needs to go home."

Pau leaned gracefully in the doorway wearing his trousers over his leotard and gave her an adolescent frown. "You dragged me here to dance."

"It's your father's fault," Dolors said and whispered to Geneviève, "Let's keep this between the two of us, *d'accord?*"

"Of course. Who would I tell?" As Geneviève accompanied them to the door, she said, "Just one more thing. You did say that your nephew was making a trip today?"

Dolors nodded and kissed Geneviève on either cheek. As Dolors and Pau went out the door, Geneviève wiped the black tears that were streaming over her cheeks.

***

"Sit," Rosa told Víctor. "Take a look at this." They were at the table in the bar where he had insisted she wait while he went to Merloin-les-Bains to fetch the jewels.

"Here, near the back, after pages of pictures of Robert Kennedy's funeral and stories about the student protests, there's an article." Rosa showed him a column of type. "It's about Spain, about some Basque terrorists killing somebody."

Víctor scanned the article and frowned. "A Guardia Civil." He sighed. "I don't like the sounds of this at all. Do you know what this could mean?"

Rosa looked at him over the newspaper. "That people are finally resisting Franco? I have heard of a few different groups. FRAP, GRAPO. Plus some former Marxists and these Basques."

"This means we are not away at a good time. We're going to have to be extremely careful. If a Guardia Civil is down, even if it happened further north, there will definitely be more guards in the mountains. Plus it's a full moon." Víctor stood up. "We can't sit here."

"It's not dusk yet and where is the package?"

He frowned at her and patted his gray jacket at chest level. "We'll get to the edge of the woods and start as soon as it's dark. Will you be able to handle this?"

Rosa nodded and thought that as long as she was with him she would be fine. "You're probably worrying about nothing."

When the sun had fallen to the Spanish side of the mountain and the forest turned the blue-gray of dusk, Víctor and Rosa tried to lose themselves in it. Rosa imitated Víctor's every move as he attempted to blend with the trees, the low-lying bushes, the boulders and rocks, every time a suspicious noise crossed their path. Huddling together, they would sit and wait until Víctor dismissed the noise as non-human. He was clearly on edge. Rosa was unsure if it was due to the increased risk or because she was with him. At the slightest little sound he would form a rock or meld with a tree and signal for Rosa to copy him. At one point she whispered, "It's just a bird."

Víctor drew his finger across his throat and looked at her in such anger that instead of a rock or a tree she wished that she had a hole she could bury herself in. In one swift movement he rolled behind a rock and Rosa followed him. The moon was now out in its full shining splendor and may as well have been a spotlight. The noise drew closer. Footsteps in the dirt. Rosa thought of their own footprints and looked at Víctor in panic right as his eyes filled with fright. A Guardia Civil in full uniform with a torch in one hand and a rifle in the other passed between them and their destination. Turtle Rock was not far away but they would have to dodge this man and any others to get to it. Rosa could feel the warmth of Víctor's arms take the night chill out of her shoulders. She felt both terrified and safe. In one swift movement, Víctor grabbed her hand and ran again until the two of them were inside the shelter breathing like they would never catch their breath. From inside their cave of rocks Rosa listened. There were the usual sounds of birds and animals, settling and cracking branches. Víctor was lying on the dirt floor with his long legs drawn toward his stomach. Rosa lay down beside him and felt his warmth along the front of her body. Putting her mouth just inches from his ear, she whispered, "Maybe we should have waited for a day or two for things to calm down."

"Sometimes it's like this. Besides, your father needs the goods delivered now." Víctor's breath tickled in her ear.

"Do you like doing this? You're very good at it."

"It's in my blood. Doing this actually makes me feel closer to my mother."

"Doesn't it frighten you that this is what she was doing when she got caught?"

"Don't say that. You could bring us bad luck." Víctor rolled away and carefully took the tin of food out of its hiding place. He put it between them in the dark.

"Do you know anything about your father?"

"No one has ever told me a thing. I only know that he gave me the color of my skin. Try growing up in Pujaforta with a face like mine. And a bastard on top of it."

Rosa felt him put something round in her hand. When she bit through the leathery skin she tasted the sweet fruit of a dried fig and cracked the tiny seeds between her teeth. Rosa put her lips to Víctor's ear. "You're the most wonderful bastard I know. I wish I could have met your mother." She pulled away. "So you don't want to know more about your father?"

"On the contrary. Why do you think I'm doing this? If I get enough money and experience, I might be able to go find him, or at least find out more about his people."

"So you plan to leave." She looked at him in surprise. "I was afraid you were going to do this forever."

"Change will come soon and I won't have to. Franco is getting older."

"But not old enough."

"Change will come," Víctor said. "And then I plan to help people. People who look like my father. People who look like me."

"You would be perfect at that." She looked at him feeling even greater admiration than usual. He put his fingers over her lips and she felt their warmness on her skin. They both lay there listening to the woods, but Rosa couldn't stop listening to the comforting beat of Víctor's heart until he started moving slowly towards her.

"I have a plan," Víctor whispered in her ear. "It sounds calm now. I am going to go alone. It's too risky."

"Alone?" she said too loudly. He put a hand over her mouth.

"You will wait here and in the very early morning, when you're sure that everything is calm, that there is no one out there, you come down. They have nothing on you. You're young, you're not suspicious."

Rosa shook her head and said through his hand, "What if something happens to you?"

"I will be fine. I've done this many times. I can't be looking behind me all the time. With two of us it's too dangerous."

"You're angry I came."

"I was, but now I'm not angry, I'm worried. If they stop you, tell them you're looking for pine cones or hunting. You have your camera, don't you? Tell them you're taking pictures of nature. Then again, don't. They may confiscate it." Reaching into the back corner, he found a rectangular package and slipped it inside his coat. "Your father's books," he whispered. He patted the other small package in his breast pocket.

"Show me what you've got. Have you seen it? You must want to know what it is."

"I don't ask questions."

"Which is precisely the problem in our country today." She reached inside his jacket and pulled out the package and put it in his gloved hand. In the flash of her camera, she saw individual gems glow against the dark leather. "My father sent you to get these?"

Víctor closed the package and put it back in his pocket. "Apparently it's a long story. This is all highly unusual."

"Next we know he'll be bringing in drugs. Just wait till I see him."

"Not a word. You didn't see it. You weren't here." He held either side of her head in his hands. "Will you be all right?"

Rosa nodded and tried to concentrate on the warmth of his hands embracing her face. "I'm more worried about you."

"I'll be fine." He moved towards the door.

"Víctor," she said sitting up. "You know I love you."

He looked back at her from where he was squatting. "I love you, too."

She reached for his hand. "No, I mean that I'm in love with you."

He squeezed her hand and let it go. "Rosa, you're too young for that. One day you'll meet someone more like you."

"You're like me."

He shook his head. "You are like a little sister to me." He crawled out the door. "Be careful," he said before closing her inside the rock.

As Rosa heard his footsteps growing distant, the dark become darker and her sadness and humiliation turned to loneliness and fear. She breathed in the musty air and hid her sobbing face in her arms. Of course he said she was like a sister. She had acted like a child. A stupid, naïve child. Víctor was so timid that she should have known that she would only send him running. But she never imagined he could leave her alone up here like this. She needed some time to think about her future and at the same time she could get his attention, get everyone's attention. Alone in a rock cave in the cool hills above Pujaforta, she was in the ideal place to decide where her life should take her. Of one thing she was certain, her future was not on this mountain.

***

In Pujaforta the streets were filled with their usual summer activity, as was the bar and Dolors' bakery. The townsfolk seemed to be out enjoying the early June weather. Indoors, Josep was lying with his foot elevated and was trying to scratch inside the plaster with a pencil. Baltasar had told him about the terrorist attack, but so far he hadn't seen it in the newspaper. At one of their recent political meetings they had been discussing these new groups, with acronyms reminiscent of the war. ETA. GRAPO. FRAP. One was for independence and two were anti-fascist, yet none had ever resorted to violence. Josep wondered why one had to do so the day he had sent Víctor out on his most risky mission yet. Now he couldn't sleep, he couldn't read, and he couldn't walk. Plus Dolors had snubbed him again. He didn't know what he'd done this time, since he hadn't budged enough to be a nuisance. She was likely fed up with him being in the house. His worries circled in his head until finally after hours of shifting and turning, he fell asleep under the picture of Robert Kennedy's coffin. He awoke abruptly to a whisper in his ear.

"Josep, I'm back."

Josep shook his head, and the newspaper fell to the floor. He saw Víctor sitting beside him and threw his arms around him. "Thank Jesus," he said. "*Mecachis*. I've been worried to death."

"You seemed really worried." Víctor slapped his back. "It's done. I got them."

Josep hugged him again. "You did. You are wonderful. Thank you, son. Manel will also be so pleased. He's got the cabinet ready and even suggested doing this again."

"You might reconsider that. I have something else to tell you." Víctor pulled himself from Josep's embrace. "It's Rosa. She followed me. It was too late to turn back."

Josep shook his head at the ceiling. "She didn't go for the jewels, did she?"

"No, I left her in the bar, as usual."

208

"And where is she now?" Josep was looking into Víctor's worried eyes. This mission seemed to be threatening too many of his friends and family members.

"She's on her way back. I had to leave her in Turtle Rock. The moon was full and the guards were out. With the two of us we would have been caught."

"You left her up there?" Josep's face turned white and then red. This was so much worse than he had imagined.

"It's safer for her to come down alone. She has nothing on her. No goods, no record. She's just a young woman."

"Precisely." Josep put his hands to his forehead. His daughter, his Rosa out in the woods alone. "Don't you see how risky this is? What were you thinking?" He tried to jump from the bed and instead held his foot and shouted in both anger and agony. "Don't you dare breathe a word of this to her mother, or to Àngels. We have enough problems."

When the next day Rosa had yet to return and Dolors and the whole family were climbing the walls with worry, Víctor headed into the woods and returned, unable to find her. Josep was then forced to tell them she was not on a photography expedition but another type of mission. Dolors hit the roof, clawing at Josep and Víctor. Once they restrained her she said, "You take a teenage girl on your excursions. I don't think I can ever forgive you for this. And I already have plenty not to forgive you for." Then she grabbed her handbag.

"You can't go looking for her now," Josep said. "Besides, Víctor has already searched everywhere." Josep felt helpless, caught like a child, and angrier than ever at the political situation. If they just had a normal government, none of this would have happened.

"It's none of your business where I'm going," Dolors said. "All I can say is you are lucky someone has been insuring the future of this family. Do you have so many children you think they are disposable?" She didn't wait for an answer and slammed the door.

When she ran into the house about an hour later, she said, "Is she back yet?"

By now all the family and friends had gathered around the table. Everyone shook their head.

"Well, she hasn't been arrested, but we have some convincing and appeasing to do. After all my hard work, they're still not sure if they can trust me." Dolors huffed and strutted to her storage area. She came back carrying an enormous framed portrait of Franco. "I've had this on hand for ages and hoped I would never have to use it." They followed her to the bakery, and watched her hang the portrait on the empty wall. Josep watched from the top of the stairs and couldn't believe they had been brought to this. Now the eyes of The Caudillo would follow them everywhere.

Later in the afternoon, they were all eating the special paella that Núria had made to celebrate Sant Joan and Rosa's return, but she still wasn't back. The atmosphere was very subdued for an occasion warranting a paella. Dolors was not speaking to anyone until halfway through her rice, when she rested her cutlery and said, "Josep, I blame you entirely for this."

"So do I," Àngels piped in. She was sitting between Manel and Víctor and she grasped Víctor's hand in hers. "You should never have involved anyone else in this, especially Víctor."

"But Víctor's a man now. Rosa is just a girl," Dolors said and held her temples.

"I've tried to find her everywhere. It's my fault, not Josep's." Víctor swallowed his mouthful.

"It's partly your fault, but it's mostly mine," a voice said from the door.

Everyone turned as if the Sant Joan fireworks had already started. Rosa was in the doorway. Her black outfit and her face were dirt-stained and her hair was in a knotted mess. She looked as if she had been living in the woods for months, not days. She was so relieved to see everyone around the table, everyone but Víctor. "You can't blame *Pare* for this. He didn't know I was going," she said.

Dolors jumped to her feet and smothered her in her arms. Then she examined her face. "Are you all right? Did anything happen to you?" Dolors was rubbing the dirt from her cheeks.

"I'm fine," Rosa said and it was true. Now.

Dolors shook her shoulders. "Then where have you been?"

"In the cave, up at Turtle Rock." She glanced at Víctor. "And wandering a bit."

"Turtle Rock?" Baltasar said. Everyone else looked equally intrigued.

"The hideout. At first I kept hearing things and was afraid to leave. Besides, I was in no hurry to come back." She thought of the dark inside of the cave and the eerie noises outside. She glanced at Víctor who looked at his empty shellfish. "You'll have to restock the food up there," she said.

"Darling, you must be starving." Dolors pulled her into a chair. "Sit, there's still some paella left. *Iaia* made it especially for you."

Rosa noticed that Víctor had moved his chair to make room at the table, but instead she squeezed in beside Montse. She took a sip of water and saw all the faces examining her. "While I was up there, I was also doing a lot of thinking." She looked at Baltasar. "I've made a decision. I'm going to take Baltasar's advice. I'm going to apply to study in Barcelona." She nodded at him. "I'm going to do it. I'm going to become a journalist."

Baltasar slapped his hands together. "Wonderful news. I will call everyone I know. You can lodge with my friends, just like I suggested."

Josep saw the confidence on his daughter's dirty face and his earlier worry melted away. He felt both sad and proud. Somehow she had grown up. He liked to think that he had played a hand in it. "That suits you perfectly. You should be reading and writing books. Smuggling is clearly not your forte." He saw her eyes turn sad and so did his. "But I will miss you. So much."

"You're going to let her go just like that?" Dolors said. "A young woman alone in the city? What about all those student protests? The violence?"

"Someone will have to take pictures, won't they?" Rosa glanced at Víctor, searching for a hint of a reaction either way, but he was still staring at his plate.

The lunch that had been cooked as a celebration finally became one, and when everyone could hardly move due to their overstuffed stomachs, Josep said, "Dolors, now that Rosa is back, surely we can take down the portrait of Franco."

"Not with the likes of you around here." She shook her head. "While he's alive, consider him our guardian angel."

CHAPTER FIFTEEN

WITH THE ARRIVAL of autumn, Dolors closed the terrace and turned away all the mushroom-picking customers from the city so that she could throw a small farewell party for Rosa. The rain and winds came and threatened to blow the yellow leaves and scatter the pine needles and cones from their branches. It was the end of a season and a time for beginnings. Even Josep was excited about Rosa's new adventure, although he dreaded her departure so much that he lost his appetite. He was also slightly hurt by the enthusiasm with which Rosa was planning her life without them. Her energy bounced from wall to wall and infected the rest of the household. While Rosa kept packing and unpacking the one suitcase she would take to her first big city, Montse followed her like a trembling shadow. She seemed even more nervous about Rosa's leaving than Rosa did herself. She baked cake after cake for the occasion, most of which were fluffy and golden and for once received Dolors' unfettered praise.

When the party began, everyone seemed to make an effort to smile, except for Núria. She sat in a chair and cried into her handkerchief. Àngels stroked her hair, while Josep held her hand.

"It's like all those years ago. When you all went away. Some of you have come back, some never will, and others have yet to return. And now our little Rosa," Núria said.

"*Mare*," Àngels said. "It's not the same. Rosa is choosing to go away. Maybe she won't return to Pujaforta to live, but she'll visit. You should be pleased for her." Àngels crouched until her eyes were level with her mother's. "Eduard is well. He's happy in his own way. I have it from a good source."

"You do?" Josep said.

Núria blew her nose. "Why doesn't he just come and visit me? He did all those years ago. Remember, the day that Dolors and Baltasar were supposed to get married?" She covered her face. "It's been far too long. That seems like a lifetime ago."

"*Mare*, you know that if he hadn't come all those years ago, he never would have had a run in with the guard. Maybe he'd be living here right now," Àngels said.

Núria looked up and nodded. "If it weren't for Franco, of course. You're so right, as usual. Whoever your contacts are, tell them he should wait. This regime can't go on forever."

"And tell Francine to have Eduard write to me," Josep said, wondering how much information Àngels had about Eduard, and how much it differed from the news Geneviève brought him.

"Well, my lovelies. And Josep." Sr. Palau was stooped over them shining his smile. "You mustn't fret. Rosa is the pride of us all. She will be fine. Barcelona is only a few hours away."

"But it's the city. A big city, with all its dangers," Núria said.

"And all its opportunities," Sr. Palau said. "You forget, my dear, how smitten you were with your co-op, so much so that you did anything to get it back. Even marry me."

"Albert." Núria flicked her handkerchief at him. "You know that I haven't regretted it for a minute." She hesitated. "Well, maybe a minute, but that's as long as it lasted." She grasped her husband's hand.

"Rosa will be fine," Josep said as much to them as to himself. "It's healthy to get away. We all had to do it."

"I didn't," Àngels said quietly. "I've never gone anywhere. And my stay in Barcelona doesn't count. That wasn't really me."

Josep thought how Àngels now looked confident, which he would have liked to attribute to her newfound relationship with him. However, he suspected it was the influence of working with Manel.

"May I have a word," Sr. Palau said, and steered Josep away by the elbow before he could react.

"What is it?" Josep looked at the concern on his face. "Is it *Mare*? Is she ill?"

"No, she's as strong as ever. Luckily her eyesight has stabilized and now that she's at the co-op less, we have more time together." Don Albert rested an arm on Josep's shoulder. "Son, the other day I went for a little horse ride. Like me, my horse is almost on its last legs." Sr. Palau shook his head. "Ten minutes, it was all we could handle, but it got me to thinking about you. All that time you spent running around in the mountains. It's dangerous. Look what happened to your foot. Josep, this is none of my business, but now that you're better, don't you think you should stay here and dedicate more time to your family? To your wife? I'd bet you've enjoyed these last few months here in the house. Besides with the economy opening up, there is really little need for black market goods."

Josep felt asphyxiated at Albert's suggestion. "Albert, don't you appreciate the books I bring you? Besides, the months I've been stranded here because of my foot have been stifling. I can't wait to get back out there."

"I have enjoyed every written word. Don't get me wrong. It's just that now that your mother and I are spending more time together, it occurred to me that you might benefit from the same with your wife. You could work at the co-op and stay around here."

"I see what this is about. You need someone to run the co-op." Josep stepped backward. "That's not for me. Besides, it's a failing business." Josep squeezed Albert's bony shoulder. "There is someone who might need an extra job. Why don't you ask Víctor?"

"But he works with you."

Josep sighed. "I've been looking for a way to steer Víctor away from smuggling. It's a dead-end road, as I know too well. We both know that Àngels would be in favor."

As the words left Josep's mouth, he realized he had spoken the truth. Maybe Albert had a point. Maybe he was getting a bit too old for this. And now that Jules had found out about his affair with Geneviève, he didn't feel quite the same pull to continue his treks over the border.

Albert nodded and raised his eyebrows, looking beyond Josep. "Here's the lady of the hour."

Rosa was standing beside them with a glass of *xampany* in her hand.

"Are you ready for the city?" Albert asked. "Or do you think it's ready for you? I remember your mother saying that years ago before she went to Barcelona, when she was not much older than you are now. Things have changed a lot since then."

"Not enough," Rosa and Josep answered simultaneously. Josep smiled and squeezed Rosa's hand. "What am I going to do without you, *petita*? Are you sure you would rather just Baltasar take you? I do want to go, you know."

"You and *Mare* have enough work here. Baltasar wants to introduce me to his friends. Àngels has told me all about them. I'll be staying in the same room as she did."

"Under better circumstances at least," Albert added.

"Have you seen Montse? She's been following me around all week and now I can't find her. I'll have to be leaving soon."

"I think that all of this is quite upsetting for her," Albert said.

"I know," Rosa said. "I'm going to look for her. I'll see you in a minute." She hugged Josep.

***

215

As Rosa squeezed through the crowd toward the house she felt the energy of her friends and family combust with her own until she could hardly contain her excitement about the future. She walked into the kitchen and her energy level plummeted. She was looking straight into Víctor's chest. He'd hardly spoken to her since their day together in Turtle Rock. Now he tried to skirt her and when she dodged him in the same direction, they both smiled nervously.

"I have actually been looking for you," Víctor said. "I want you to know that I'll miss you."

"Like a brother misses a sister." Rosa looked at his shirt buttons.

"And like a friend misses another friend. A dear, dear friend." He reached behind his back. "I couldn't let you go without giving you this." He held out a box wrapped in red paper.

Rosa took it, feeling her face turn the same color as the present.

"Open it," Víctor told her.

Slowly Rosa began to peel it open until she was holding the fanciest camera she had ever seen. "Víctor, you shouldn't have done this. I can't." She turned the camera over in her hands, her eyes eating every detail of it. "It's too beautiful. It's too expensive."

"It's for you. It's loaded and ready to go. Every time you take a shot I want you to think of us here in Pujaforta."

"I will. Thank you." She went on tiptoe to kiss him on both cheeks.

"Don't let your head get too big down in the city." He squeezed her shoulder. "And don't forget about us or where you come from."

"How could I ever forget you?" She looked into his familiar face, but she didn't regret her decision. "Víctor, please take care of *Pare*. And take care of yourself."

***

Àngels watched the exchange between Rosa and Víctor, noting a newfound awkwardness between them. She knew that other than herself, Rosa was the most devoted to Víctor and always had been. Yet now she wouldn't look him in the eye. When Àngels saw Rosa go inside, leaving Víctor standing alone in the doorway, she headed towards him. She had some news that would cheer him up. Of anyone, he deserved to hear it from her first.

"Víctor," she held his arm. "You're looking a bit sad. Rosa will come back to visit, you know."

He nodded but didn't answer.

"We'll all miss her," Àngels said. "Don't worry, she'll have to come back for my wedding."

"No, she's gone," he said before registering what she had said. Víctor shook his head and stepped backward. As he looked into her face, his sad expression disappeared and joy replaced it. He jumped forward and hugged her, almost spinning her around. "You don't know how long I've been waiting for you to say that."

"Almost as long as Manel," she said, and covered her laughing mouth with her hand. "After all this time, he says he'll still take me."

"Of course he will." Víctor stepped back and held her shoulders. "You know it would make me happier than almost anything for the two of you to finally be together. It's like my parents are finally getting married." He squeezed her shoulders. "But are you sure that it will make you happy?"

Àngels nodded. "It's time. I can't cut myself off forever." She had come to realize that by refusing to let Manel come any closer, she was letting the regime win. It was as if in addition to the horror Carles Puig had put her through all those years back, she had allowed him to take away her future. She couldn't do it anymore. "Víctor, taking care of you saved me from myself. Now I've decided that it's time I let someone take care of me."

"It is high time," Víctor said and pulled her face to his chest and stroked her hair. He looked down at her. "So have you set a date?"

Àngels patted his chest. "Let's not rush things now. I need to take one big step at a time." It had taken her this long to realize that this was what she needed. While she didn't want a large affair, such a grand occasion would require that everyone she loved be there. Such an event could bring Eduard back to her.

Víctor looked around. "So where is Manel? He must be elated. Who else knows?"

"He'll be here any minute. He's set on finishing a piece of furniture today. And no one else knows. We're waiting to tell everyone. This is Rosa's day. I think she deserves all the attention, don't you?"

Víctor nodded. "She's also decided to move on. I suppose we have to join her in celebrating."

***

After searching for Montse everywhere, Rosa found both her and her brother in their bedroom upstairs. The room was quiet except for the murmur from downstairs and Montse's sniffling. She was lying face up on her bed with tears running into her ears. The bed beside her was neatly made, as if for safekeeping. Pau was sitting on the floor leaning against Montse's bed.

"I've been looking for you for ages," Rosa said. "What are you doing in here?"

"Nothing," Montse said, and covered her eyes with her forearm.

"Hiding," Pau said in his newly deepened voice.

"Hiding from what?"

"From everyone." Montse wiped her face. "From *Mare*, from *Pare*, from you."

"Why would you hide from me? Soon I'll be gone anyway." Rosa sat on the edge of the bed with Pau's chin at her knees and rested a hand on Montse's leg.

"Exactly," Montse said and snorted loudly. She sat up and the tears ran along the edges of her nose. "You're so happy to be leaving us. I never go anywhere or meet anyone."

"I'm happy to be leaving, but not happy to be leaving you."

"You'll get to the city and forget all about us up here in the middle of nowhere. I'll be left to die an old spinster in Pujaforta."

"You will not." Rosa went over to her own bed and reached under it. "And I will come to visit all the time. Holidays and birthdays. You'll get sick of seeing me." Rosa returned to Montse's bed. "In case you don't, I want you to take care of these for me while I'm away." She handed Montse a large biscuit tin.

Montse wiped her eyes again and looked at the tin. Then she looked up. "Your pictures? All your pictures? You'll let me keep them for you?"

Rosa nodded. "You can even look at them if you like, but don't do it out in the open."

Pau tried to take the tin. "Can I look at them, too?"

"Yes. You two and no one else. Especially not that Vicenç Vidal friend of yours. I don't dare ask what you get up to with the mayor's son. Keep my pictures here and safe," Rosa said. "Now help me bring down my case. Baltasar and I have to leave."

Pau stood tall and leapt across the room toward Rosa's belongings. Rosa pulled Montse to her feet and hugged her, feeling safe one last time in her sponginess. Then they all went downstairs to join the others.

After an hour of goodbyes, Rosa got into the passenger seat of Baltasar's new Seat 600 and all her family and friends gathered near the window. As they pulled away, she took their picture with her new camera and the image lodged in her memory: the sun through the autumn leaves in the trees, and the blur of her childhood and their waving hands.

***

In the end, Josep took Albert's advice and stayed in Pujaforta, trying to live simply and be an attentive husband and father. He gave up the smuggling and promised himself he wouldn't see Geneviève for a while, hoping his absence would make Jules think they had ended their affair. Instead he tried to help Dolors and Montse in the bakery. But his years away had made him feel like an intruder in his own home. When Montse took trays from the oven, he would find himself between the oven and the counter and she would be forced to dance around him. "*Pare*," she would say, "You're always in the way."

At nighttime, when Josep tried to join Dolors in her bed, she swatted him away.

"After all these years you can't just come in here all randy and expect me to roll over and take it. No, *senyor*. I'll remind you who moved his sleeping quarters down the hall. Besides, you keep so many secrets, I hardly even know you. I certainly don't understand you."

"But Dolors, I'm trying to be a good husband," Josep said, almost falling to his knees. He was also fighting every urge to flee and avoid dealing with any of it.

"It's a bit late for that. You rejected me ages ago. For me that loaf is baked. Keep your secrets. They don't concern me anymore."

"But Dolors," Josep said, but she shoved him gently from the room and shut the door.

His next attempt was to make himself useful at the co-op, but soon he saw that Víctor was already fulfilling that duty. Since business was reduced to making knitwear for tourists, Josep's skills in running a large knitting mill were not required. Finally, his uselessness overcame him and when he tried to list his reasons for abandoning the black market, he found only one: Jules. He didn't need him. Even if he did, he began to think that the lucrative and exciting nature of the business made it worth it. Josep had thought that at his age, he would finally feel ready to stay at home, but he realized that he wasn't ready to lie down and die in Pujaforta.

Instead of going over the border, Josep met Geneviève in Adiol la Nova. She had begged him to meet her in a flat there. Initially he was reluctant, but hearing her voice on the telephone made him realize how much he truly missed her. When she opened the door and smiled shyly at him, she was wearing only a light layer of make-up. He could see her true hazel eyes and her fleshy lips. She took his hands and gently pulled him inside and into her arms.

"I've missed you so much," she said. "I'm glad you're better. How is your foot? Poor darling."

Josep peeled her arms from his neck. "We can't pretend that nothing happened."

She pouted at him. "We can't let Jules win. Don't you see? He's trying to scare us away from each other. But what scares me more is not being able to see you."

"But he forced me to take those jewels and was going to tell Dolors about us."

"You did find it exciting, didn't you?"

"I was bedridden the whole time." He stepped closer to her. "And, yes, it was exciting. Even Manel found it quite the thrill."

Geneviève took his hand and pulled Josep to the sofa but stopped to admire their reflections in the long mirror on the wall. "Don't you look handsome," she said as she stroked the thinning hair at his temples. "We'll just have to be careful," she continued. Her face reddened suddenly. "It's your wife, isn't it? After all these weeks together, you've mended things with her, haven't you? I knew you would ditch me. I'll just become another one of the women of your past." She buried her face in her hands.

Josep gently lowered her hands from her face and his resolve dissolved at the sight of her. "What are you talking about? I don't think you could ever become my past."

"Really?" Her voice squeaked slightly. "You know I can't live without seeing you."

"You won't have to." He pulled her close to his chest and rocked her. He looked around the flat at the sofa, the long mirror, and the makeshift barre along the edge. "What is this place anyway?"

"It's just a spot I use sometimes."

"Who with?" Josep looked at her in surprise. "I've never been here before."

She smiled. "Now you're jealous." She looked thrilled. Then she ran a finger from the tip of his nose across his lips and to his chin. He could smell musky perfume on her fingertips.

He pulled back. "I'm not jealous. I only wanted to know who you bring here."

"Just some dance students who can't come to my studio." She turned away from him and the mirror. "I do have a little news of your brother. I hope that if you don't come for me, you'll at least come for that."

"Don't be ridiculous." He stroked her hair patiently, though he really was anxious to hear what she had to say. "While I was home all these weeks, I began to think I should just write to him or go to see him myself."

"I thought you wanted him to make the first step."

"And each day we're a step closer to our graves."

"That is true." She pulled him to the sofa. "It may actually be quite true for Eduard. I'm so sorry."

"What are you talking about?" He almost jumped to his feet but she urged him to sit.

"He's not well. He's been hospitalized a number of times. They say it's ulcerative colitis."

"What the heck is that?"

"Some sort of severe intestinal trouble."

"Can it be treated?"

"He's on medication for now. I heard about his horrible experience in the prisons at the end of the war. No wonder he has so many problems. I'm so glad that didn't happen to you."

"Maybe it should have been me." Josep took a step toward the door. He couldn't believe what he was hearing. What if Eduard was seriously ill? "I should go to see him. I'll have to contact Francine myself."

"I can try to arrange a meeting for you. I would love to be able to help you. She lives nearby and I can use the post much easier than you can. Unless you plan to go back and see Jules about more books."

"After what happened I don't think I could do that." He tilted his head. "But how do you think he would react?"

"Jules always puts business first." Her eyes glowed. "He'll be thrilled and so will I."

He looked around the flat again. "For the time being, would you be able to meet me here on occasion?"

"Of course, *mon amour*. I'll come whenever you want. That way I won't have to worry about you risking your neck so often in the woods. Your neck is far too adorable for that." As she nibbled it gently, his thoughts of Jules, books, Dolors, and an ailing Eduard disappeared momentarily.

***

"I'm so glad you finally had the sense to put in a telephone," Núria said as she entered Àngels' house. "Otherwise you would have had no way to contact me way up at the mansion."

Àngels was sitting at the table and had a stack of letters in front of her. "I know. Now it's like you're right next door. But I didn't think we should talk about this on the phone."

"So what's happened with Eduard? Is it bad?" Núria sat down holding her fists to her chin.

"No, he'll be fine," Àngels said more to calm her fears than anything. There was nothing they could do for him in Pujaforta, except worry. "It can be treated, although Francine tells me that the medication is rather expensive."

"Really? We can send money if he needs it. Between all of us we should be able to put something together." Núria squeezed Àngels' hand. "In fact, I think you should take it to him. You and Manel could go on a holiday together. It could be your honeymoon. It would do you both some good to get out of this town. I'd go if I could."

Àngels shook her head. "Why can't you?"

Núria clicked her tongue. "There's the co-op and Albert is not in good shape for traveling. Tell me, at one point you did say that Eduard wanted to come here to visit. He's healthy enough for that, isn't he?"

"Yes, absolutely. He even says he wants to. And one day soon he will." Àngels arranged the letters in front of her, some from France, some from her nephew Gaspard, who was turning into a true intellectual, and ever fewer from Eduard. His notes to her appeared written by a distracted hand,

221

but one whose focus remained on politics and how he didn't intend to set foot on soil still governed by Franco's hand. Eduard did say that the last thing he wanted to do before he died was return to Pujaforta. Àngels hoped for a significant gap between the two.

"He can come to your wedding." Núria clasped her hands together as if the idea had just occurred to her. "When will that be, by the way?"

Àngels sighed. "When we decide on a date. Manel wants to have a proper wedding, but I told him that it's a waste of money. I just want all of us to be together."

"I think those are excuses, dear. Manel would marry you in a cave wearing a potato sack."

"I'm not so sure about that," Àngels said. "I'm going to need a while to adjust to the idea of a wedding, but when I do, Eduard will definitely be the guest of honor."

***

As the months went by, the rose bushes grew and bloomed each spring, but Àngels had yet to set a date and no word came from Eduard. The family did receive visits from Rosa, which were like an injection of oxygen into their asphyxiating daily routines. She had grown her hair long so it hung along either side of her face like a curtain. She wore blue jeans tight and low at the hips and flaring at the knee and she no longer wore a bra. With her photography she had joined clandestine political groups and while she studied, she volunteered on some of their underground publications. She raved about her course, the speakers who came to inspire them and the trips they would make. Soon she would be going to Madrid, where she said that if she saw Franco she would shoot him, at least with her camera. She had turned into a true Barcelonina, and appeared transformed whenever she came home to Pujaforta, yet every time she was home she would look at Víctor and say that she hadn't changed at all. Between her visits, Josep would sporadically receive photographs. They would come alone with no notes. Most were of students protesting, with their faces contorted and shouting, in the streets of Barcelona. In one such photo Rosa was in its center waving a placard reading *"Franquisme ha mort."* However, *Franquisme* and Franco were far from dead, although the dictator was aging poorly.

As for Josep, except for his back, he felt younger than ever, which he attributed to occasional surges of adrenaline from his renewed book smuggling missions plus two impromptu jewel deliveries that Manel had instigated. Manel had said that he'd enjoyed the challenge of crafting secret compartments in his furniture and the extra money would go to his wedding fund, for whenever it finally happened. He insisted that as each day passed Àngels got closer to becoming his wife.

For his part, Josep was spending more time away from Dolors and had rather regular visits with Geneviève, mostly in Adiol la Nova and sometimes at her studio in France. Despite his attempts to improve relations at home, the cold front in Pujaforta had not risen. Dolors was dedicated to her bakery and her dreams of Baltasar. Montse helped her daily, and if she was happy doing so, she was very clever at hiding it. Pau, meanwhile, remained introverted, even secretive, and he was acting strangely. He was now going to his dance classes alone, claiming that if at his age his sister had been helping their father smuggle, he could go to a neighboring town without the help of his mother. While Josep knew nothing of the dance lessons, they all knew that Pau continued to spend his time with Vicenç Vidal, son of the mayor, but no one, not even Dolors, knew if the friendship was beneficial to the family. They soon began to suspect that it was not good for Pau's health: he often returned home with eyes red as *guindilla* and clothing smelling of sweet tobacco.

Àngels continued to work with Manel, who had spent months crafting a unique cabinet the size of the local bus, and she appeared to be finally on the verge of setting a wedding date. Àngels also helped in the co-op with Núria and was relieved to see Víctor working in the safety of the sewing machines rather than amongst the pine trees.

Right before Christmas in 1973, Josep suggested going to visit Rosa in Barcelona. They could make it a family holiday. Rosa was thrilled with the idea but said that it would have to wait until the new year, after she had returned from a photography seminar in Madrid. So Josep decided to go to Adiol la Nova instead. As he was leaving, he found Manel on his doorstep asking for a private word. Both had kept their earlier episodes of jewelry smuggling a secret, and that secret hung between them like a stolen kiss. Josep led him inside and into his room.

"What's so urgent?" Josep asked. "I was just leaving."

Manel was pacing and clearly hesitant to speak. Finally he looked Josep in the eye. "Àngels wants to get married on February 14th. She's finally given me a date."

Josep hugged him, feeling excitement at the news as well as disappointment not to hear it directly from his sister. "You should be happy. Why aren't you happy?"

"Do you know what that date is?" Manel's eyes drilled into his and Josep shook his head. "That's the day Carme died." He cut the air with his hand. "What kind of wedding will that be? I hate to think what it could mean for our marriage."

"Don't be so sure. You've been waiting all this time. Maybe it's what she needs to mark a new beginning." Josep slapped his shoulder. "Start smiling."

Manel sighed. "I can't yet. It's not just the date. I know she's going to change her mind. She will when she finds out."

"Finds out what, man?"

Manel looked out the window. "That I can't afford a special wedding. You know that enormous cabinet I've been working on? It really turned out beautifully." He bit his lip. "It was my only order and they've cancelled it."

"Who would do such a thing?" Josep frowned.

"Mayor Vidal. It was a custom fit." They both raised their eyebrows.

"The bastard," Josep said. "What do you want me to do? Maybe Dolors can talk to him. Àngels will understand."

"Dolors has already tried. I owe my wood cutters, my suppliers. I'll never be able to pay for a wedding. I have no family to help me. I know that Àngels would understand, but that's not the point." Manel looked towards the window.

"We're family. We can help." Josep nodded, thinking that he would pay anything to finally see his sister at peace.

"I can't ask you to do that." Manel leaned in with a spark in his eye. "What if we did another jewelry run?"

Josep jumped to his feet and sat down again shaking his head. "We can't do that again."

Manel looked Josep straight in the eye. "If I had a little extra cash, I could save my business, do more to the house, and have enough for wedding expenses. That's why over the past few months I've been building some perfect pieces of furniture, with little secret drawers, little compartments. It's quite an ingenious system, whoever thought of it." He pointed at Josep. "I'm sure you could use the thrill. I know I could."

"Yes, but," Josep shook his head. "I'm all in favor of your plan but there must be a better way. I'm telling you, Àngels doesn't care about money."

"It's important. We all deny it. Look what you've been doing all these years. Look at Dolors. Look at your mother. It's money and power." Manel tried another tactic. "Don't you want to help Eduard?"

"Eduard? How am I supposed to help him?"

"With money for his treatment. Àngels says it's very expensive."

"But he lives in France."

"The French system doesn't cover foreigners."

"He's married to a French woman. Besides, he would just gamble any money away. I've heard all this before."

"Eduard and Francine aren't married."

Josep stood up and put a hand on Manel's shoulder. He looked out the window and imagined the early mountain air on his skin, his heart pounding in his chest. "I'll tell you what." He stood. "I'll ask Jules hypothetically if such a shipment is possible."

Manel sighed and grasped his hand. "You're the best brother-in-law ever. It will only be one shipment, nothing more. I just need to get back on my feet."

Josep squinted at him for a moment. Then he extended his hand. "I will talk to Jules, but I'm not making any promises."

Manel shook his hand. "If he says yes, I'd like to come with you."

"Out of the question. This is not for novices. I could do this alone, but I know that Víctor is a little bored at the co-op. This will make his day."

"Fine, and not a word to Àngels."

"Not a word."

Josep went to the flat in Adiol la Nova where Geneviève was waiting as they had planned. When he told her about Manel's proposition she first looked skeptical and then excited. Josep gave her a letter for Jules and asked her to post it from France, since he couldn't send it from Spain. Nor could Jules know that Josep was still seeing his wife.

Josep waited for more than a week for a response, during which time he visited Víctor at the co-op and hinted that they had a new mission. He was almost as enthusiastic as Manel, who asked him every day if he had received any word. Finally, Jules confirmed the deal with an eager call to Josep at Sr. Palau's safe telephone. A few days later at home, Josep received another phone call in code. "The cakes are baked and ready for pick-up." He recognized Jules' voice through the crackling line. After he told Manel the mission was officially on, he told Víctor to get ready and to bring his gun, just in case.

Well into the night, Josep and Víctor climbed through the dark, over the mountain, just as they had done years earlier. When the sun had risen and they were standing in front of the Petitpas mansion, only Josep went inside and found that Jules was at home alone. He had aged considerably and Josep realized just how much time had passed since he'd last seen him. Jules' normally bright eyes had a thin film of cataracts and the bags below them were deep and dark. The sight of Josep seemed to awaken him and he led him into the living room at what was almost a run.

"You don't know how glad I was to hear from you. And my client in Marbella is even more pleased." Jules had almost begun to dance. "Maybe later we can talk about shipping something other than books and jewels."

"I draw the line there." Josep glanced around the room, which looked exactly the same, except that the portrait of the disapproving matriarch was missing. In its place was what looked like a very fine reproduction of a Miró painting. Josep thought it was as busy as the overcharged living room, but then again, he had no eye for art or decorating. What he did know was that he wanted to get his goods and run. Geneviève had reminded him to be careful with Jules. He was still not to be trusted.

"Books and jewels." Jules waved his hand dismissively. "There are so many more lucrative substances nowadays. I deal much less with the southern Spain now. I have suppliers up in the north, in Galicia."

"The drug trade doesn't interest me at all."

"Does my wife still interest you?"

"From what she always told me, you're not interested in her anyway. I probably shouldn't say this, but I know all about your affairs, so don't try and use that one time against us."

Jules smirked and offered Josep a glass of whisky. "I see she's managed to make you as delusional as she is." He clicked Josep's glass with his own. "I've never cheated a single moment on that woman. I admit to taking her away from her career as a dancer, but she lost her chance anyway when she broke her foot. She got this idea that I was cheating and drove herself mad with it. At one time I considered having her committed."

Josep put down his glass and the liquid sloshed onto the table. "You mean locked up? There's nothing wrong with her. At least there wasn't last time I saw her...which was ages ago," he hastily tried to cover up his blunder but he was so angry. "Maybe if you didn't hit her and grind her down all the time she would be more stable."

"I've never touched her. And I know you saw her last week. In fact, I think she's waiting for you at her studio right now. Isn't that right?"

"How do you know that?" Josep stood and pointed at him. "You've treated her horribly. Years ago I saw you yelling at her at the ski hill."

"Because she was accusing me of wanting to break her feet. You can have her." Jules stood up again. "Regardless, I still want to do business."

"That is where your heart lies, isn't it?"

"And yours? What are you doing here?"

"I'm doing someone a favor. So where are the jewels?"

"Geneviève has them at the studio. If your house had a safer line of communication I would have told you that. When are you going to get rid of that Franco anyway? Aren't you sick of him?"

Josep turned away saying nothing because his chest and head were pounding. Instead he took it out on the door, slamming it so loudly that The Caudillo himself could have heard it as far away as Madrid.

Josep was still fuming when he and Víctor were standing in front of Geneviève's studio. Josep told Víctor to wait for him on a bench across the street. He would only be a moment. Then, when there was no answer, Josep used his key to let himself in. Josep called her name but saw only his lone reflection in the horizontal mirror. He paced back and forth in front of it and wove circles in the floor, trying to calm his nerves and his anger, even though he was sure that Jules had intentionally tried to rile him, and successfully at that. Geneviève was slightly volatile and very dependent, but he didn't think she was that inventive or that good a liar. In the mirror he noticed the office door behind him was slightly ajar and thought that maybe she was hiding away, scared by Josep's fiery mood. Inside, the small desk was piled with its usual papers, the leg warmers and sweaters hanging on their hook, but there was no Geneviève. There was a ledger open on the desk. Giving the doors a wiggle, he found that they were all locked, and among the papers there was no note from Geneviève, no letters from Eduard or Francine. He turned away from the desk and extracted a shoe box from the stack. Inside, satin pointe shoes lay like two palms clasped in prayer. As he examined them, the door squeaked.

"You are here, *chéri*. I've been looking for you." Geneviève was in the doorway, her ample chest heaving. "You could have waited for me out there." She pointed to the dance room with a shaking finger.

Josep lowered the shoes. "I did." He peered inside, wiggling a finger into the toe. That was when it hit him. "I've never understood these things. How do you actually stand on your toes?"

"*Mon amour*, come outside. I'll show you if you like. I'll get my shoes, though my feet might not handle it." She kissed him and tried to pull him outside.

"Show me with these." He displayed the shoes on his palm.

She waved her hand. "Those won't fit me."

"You've got plenty to choose from." He motioned to the array of boxes on the back wall. There were so many stacked there they looked like they were about to collapse. "Funny how Jules has never told me how he ships his jewels. Maybe it's time you did." He felt his face reddening.

She shook her head.

"Isn't there supposed to be a box in the toe? The ones you showed me had a box in the toe." He held the shoe under her nose. "I'm no dancer, but I'm not stupid. All those packages of shoes you received for your handful of students. That's how he did it."

Geneviève hesitated and Josep saw her wilt before him. "Yes. Jules made me," she said. "Besides he was doing nothing wrong."

"He hides the jewels in ballet slippers to make legitimate shipments? And what about that new Miró painting in your living room? I don't believe any of this for a second." At the thought and its implications, Josep felt as if his bones were melting and leaned against the desk. "It's always been illegal." He stared at her. "It's always been a lie." Three times they had smuggled stones, and three times they could have been caught. The magnitude of the risk hit him like a blow to the groin. He looked up and Geneviève was kneeling before him.

"I'm so sorry. Jules made me do it. He sent them through the post and said no one would ever know. And they don't. No one besides you." The black liner around her eyes dissolved across her cheeks.

Josep looked through the smudge into her eyes and he finally read the truth in them. His heart twisted. "Stolen goods. Stolen moments. It has all been a lie. Not just the jewels. Jules never had an affair. He never hit you. You were just trying to reel me in."

"That's not true." She grasped his leg and looked at his foot planted firmly on the floor. "Not entirely. Jules isn't a bad husband. But he took everything away from me. My dancing, my boys. And now that we have each other, he's going to take you."

"Why did you go to my home and visit my wife, buy a sweater from my mother?"

Geneviève hid her face in his thigh. "I was curious." She looked up at him. "I was jealous. I had to know what she was like. She gets to sleep beside you every night. She gets to live with you. And silly me, I found that I liked her. I liked your whole family and I wish I was a part of it."

He felt like he was standing naked, stripped of his sense of self, his reality. His whole family was bare before her. Who was this woman? After all these years? He leaned down over her and pushed her head backward so that she was looking at the ceiling, looking at him. "Don't go near them. And all your news of Eduard, was it all really from Francine?"

She shook her head in his hand. "And from his son Gaspard. He was a student of mine."

"You taught Eduard's son?" Josep said and she tried to nod her head. Then he let go. "My brother would never let his son dance. You're lying. Again."

"He was good, but I've seen better. Now he's a handsome young man, too old for my classes. We just meet and talk." Geneviève tried to stand. "I did it for you. I knew how important your brother was to you, how you were desperate for the information."

"Desperate is a word I reserve for you," Josep said, although he was realizing that his own desperation verged on the pathetic. "How could you do all these things? I can only wonder what else you've done."

Geneviève shook her head. "Nothing. What else could I have done? You don't think this is enough?"

"It's too much. And it's all over. No more books. No more jewels. No more us."

"Are you trying to kill me?" Geneviève grasped his hands. "All I ask is you think about it. That Spanish temper of yours is clouding your mind. You'll see that we have to be together."

"There's nothing to think about." Josep shook her hands off of his and headed for the door.

"So you're not going to take the shipment?"

Josep didn't turnaround. "No," he said firmly.

"But you have to. It has to get to Marbella. It's all arranged and you could put Jules in danger."

"You actually think I'd let you put me and all my family in danger instead?" He went out the office door.

"I'll go to Dolors."

"Go ahead," he said.

"I hope that Eduard never speaks to you again," she shouted after him. "Gaspard told me that Eduard will never forgive you. I don't blame him. You abandon everyone. You've abandoned your wife all these years. Now you're abandoning me."

But Josep was already walking out the front door.

"You were right all those years ago," Josep said as he approached Víctor, who was pacing across the street. "They were never to be trusted and now we've come all this way for nothing." Josep felt a mixture of anger, heartache, and stupidity for having believed everything Geneviève told him. He felt hurt to the bone as if she had broken every limb in his body.

"So there are no goods to take back?" Víctor had a relieved look on his face. "Thank God. Look at this."

"What?"

"As usual I had a long wait." Víctor showed him a newspaper picture of a war zone. The street was a giant hole surrounded by debris and crushed automobiles.

"Where is that? What happened?"

"Madrid." Víctor turned the page and showed him another picture of a railing with a car folded over it as if it were made of wax. "Carrero Blanco's car."

"The Prime Minister?" Josep grabbed the paper from him. "Was he in it?"

"Yes. The explosion was so big it blew his car five stories high."

"It was ETA, the terrorists, wasn't it?"

"It doesn't say. It just says a terrorist attack. It could be ETA, GRAPO, FRAP."

"The regime has many enemies." Josep tried not to smile since it was spectacularly horrific, but he couldn't help saying, "What will this do to Franco?" Then his face turned deathly serious. "And now what will Franco do? Thank God we have nothing illegal to take back with us. There could be police and guards all over the mountain now."

"This is much worse than the time I was with Rosa. The guards will be sealing all the borders."

Suddenly something dawned on Josep. "Rosa is at that seminar. In Madrid." Josep looked at Víctor with worry clearly written on his face.

"It's a big city," Víctor reassured him. "Besides, you told me she was coming home."

"I hope she's already there. Maybe we should wait and see what happens before going back."

"We're not doing anything illegal," Víctor said. "If we don't go now, we may get stuck here for a while. I have things to do at the co-op. But to tell you the truth, I don't want to miss Rosa's visit. And Dolors was planning a little party for Àngels and Manel."

Josep looked into Víctor's dark, begging eyes and then looked across the street where Geneviève was coming out the studio door. "Maybe you're right. We don't want to get stuck here. But we'll wait until nightfall."

So they returned the way they came and waited for dark. When the moon was high and the cold night air numbed their faces, each man began to put his years of tree dodging and rock simulating to the test. The woods seemed relatively calm and uneventful until they were deep inside them and the shouting started. Josep paused and listened. The Guardia Civil were scuttling through the trees like fleas through the finest hairs, mixing their footprints together. Josep scurried with Víctor behind him into a cave right over the border, near Turtle Rock. Leaning his back against the cold stone inside, Josep looked at Víctor and sighed.

"They didn't see us," Víctor said.

Josep put his hands over his lips and listened. The shouting and the crunching in the snow had stopped. "Not yet. If it's like this here, further down it will be infested." Josep lit a cigarette with shaky hands. This was too much for his nerves.

"What if they smell it?" Víctor warned, putting his flask on the floor between them.

"They're gone." Josep handed the pack to Víctor who lit one of his own. "Tobacco helps relax my back." Right now he felt as if Geneviève had kicked him in the kidneys in addition to everywhere else. They sat quietly smoking, listening. The steam of their breaths in the cold mixed with the exhaled smoke of their cigarettes. "I think you're as thrilled to be back out here as I am."

Víctor inhaled. "My blood is pumping again."

"It's a rush that's hard to give up. Just like these things." Josep flicked his cigarette.

"It starts by taunting you, enticing you until you're hooked for good. Last time I was in a situation like this I was with Rosa." Víctor took a swig from his flask and passed it to Josep.

Josep nodded slowly. "She's much better off in the city. We can't keep a young woman like that hiding in caves like these. She's got something to say and she makes sure people listen." Josep put his fingers over his mouth and they waited, the silence flowing around them.

Víctor crushed the glow of his cigarette into the ground. "She's changed so much and I'm sure she's forgotten about me. I don't blame her. I forced her away. Now I realize I miss her more than anything. I was thinking about spending some time in the city."

"Why would a young man like you stay in Pujaforta? She's still the same Rosa inside. She'll never forget you. You're family. You're like a brother to her." Josep buttoned his jacket tight and took a breath before whispering, "We should move. Are you ready to run?"

Víctor nodded and followed him. Josep dashed ahead and crouched behind a log before waving Víctor forward. Behind them, Josep saw the familiar line of trees at the border that appeared no different from the rest, but to him they were like a beacon to danger or safety, depending on the direction he was traveling. Now they were heading into calamitous territory, where each tree and rock represented shelter and each unexpected noise and movement was like a flare gun shot in warning, every reverberation resounding under his skin. While he knew that they had nothing to hide, it was better not to be noticed.

As he squatted behind a tree stump to listen, instead of shouts of the Guardia Civil, he heard the pleading and then the irate screams of Geneviève rebounding between his ears. He shook his head to clear his ears and listened again. He couldn't let himself become distracted now. Then again, without his smuggling, his comforting afternoons with Geneviève, and without her news of Eduard, what did he have left? Life with a wife whose apathy toward him was as strong as her love for her business. No job. No hope of reconciling with his brother. If he was caught tonight no one would care. If he was shot, no one would miss him.

Josep jumped to his feet and with the rush of blood from his head he stumbled. Víctor grabbed him and seemed to shout at him with the whites of his eyes. With his black glove he pointed below and behind. The guards were everywhere. Just meters away was a stack of rocks like two cupped palms. Víctor pointed to it and Josep felt himself being dragged by the back of his trousers until he was diving towards it. Josep pulled up his knees to make room for Víctor. There was a whistle, a shot and then a shout "¡Alto!" Josep could hear the boots on snow as loud as a train approaching until they were right outside his rock.

"I'm just hunting. I haven't done anything wrong," he heard Víctor say. Then he heard him grunt, the air forced out of him, and the sound of his body being ground into the snow.

"I don't have anything."

"*Calla. Terrorista.*"

Josep heard Víctor go silent then he saw the torches flashing around him, saw one skim over his boot.

"Where are the others?"

"I'm alone."

"You terrorists are never alone."

"I'm no terrorist. I told you I'm hunting."

"In the dark? With a pistol?"

"Do I look like a Basque terrorist? *Sóc català.*"

"That what all the FRAP say." Josep heard the clicking of metal and more shuffling in the snow as the voices of the Guards grew fainter. "I bet you've come down from Paris like the rest of the Marxists. You don't look Basque or Catalan and you are definitely a liar," was the last he heard. Then the forest grew quiet, Víctor was gone and Josep was alone. He covered his face in his gloves. He should have gone to help him. Maybe he could have saved him. As he pulled into a tighter ball, he realized that his will to live was greater than he thought.

In Pujaforta the streets were empty, as were the bar and Dolors' bakery, where the television was blasting the scenes from Madrid into their sitting room. Everyone seemed to be waiting for Franco's wrath to fall. Dolors was wrapping the fare she had enthusiastically prepared to celebrate Àngels having finally set a date. Though she had seemed even more excited than the bride at the prospect of a wedding, it was clearly not a time for parties. When Josep crawled into the house, he saw the face of Carrero Blanco, the murdered prime minister. His portrait covered the front page of *La Vanguardia*, the Barcelona daily, which Manel lowered as Josep approached the table. As the others put down their newspapers and looked away from the blaring television, Josep looked straight into the eyes of Àngels. He looked away.

"You're a fright." Dolors turned down the volume and helped Josep off with his coat. "Look at your trousers. The knees are almost worn through. What have you been up to?"

Manel showed him the headlines. "You weren't out in this panorama? Have you heard the news? The police must be everywhere."

"I have and they are." Josep grunted partly from the pain of taking off his boots and partly in reaction to Manel, who knew full well where he had been.

"The poor Admiral," Dolors said. "Blown practically to the heavens. At least he had just been to mass. He must have felt some peace and absolution."

"I doubt he felt a thing," Àngels said. "Dolors, you really can't believe that a mass can absolve him of being an instrument of Franco."

Dolors looked horrified. "Are you saying he deserved it? A death like that?"

"No one deserves such a death," Àngels said and she stared at Josep with a sinking look in her eyes. "Isn't Víctor with you? The ladies at the co-op said he left with you yesterday."

"No, he's not with me." Josep sat beside the fire. He tried to prolong the announcement, but he was at a crossroads. "Dolors, we are going to need some extra favors. That portrait of Franco may not be enough."

"What are you saying?" Àngels was now standing over him, clearly trying not to tremble.

"The guards were everywhere."

"And?" She had stopped breathing.

Josep covered his face. "And they took him."

Àngels pried his hands from his face until he could do nothing but look at her eyes just centimeters away. "They took him? You let them take him? My Víctor?"

"He had no goods on him, just his pistol. They arrested him for just being there."

"He was carrying a gun? *Ai Déu.*" Àngels collapsed into the chair.

Dolors stood beside Àngels. "If you knew about the attack, why didn't you wait before coming home?"

Josep looked back and forth between his sister and his wife. He tried to hold in the sob that was stuck in his throat but couldn't. "It's almost Christmas. It was Víctor. He didn't want to miss Rosa's visit or the party."

***

A few days later, on Christmas Eve, Rosa returned and was so excited to be home she appeared to float through the door. She was wearing a wool coat, flared to the knee and boots with a heavy heel that made her taller and secure. Feeling so confident and excited she had no idea of the imposing effect she gave. Everyone gathered around as her enthusiasm filled the vacuum of their silence. She had so much to tell them.

"It was spectacular and horrific," she said while pacing the room. The news in Madrid had fused with her adrenaline and fed her hunger for more. "Sickening, devastating, and an incredible opportunity for me." She put her pictures of the scene on the table. The giant hole blasted into the ground as if carved by a meteor, the cars crushed like aluminum, and the shattered storefronts. "Unlike some, I was in the right place at the right time," Rosa continued, oblivious to the sadness around her.

"The further away the better," Montse said, reaching for a picture of a particularly mutilated car. "Can I keep this one?"

"You haven't got it in your blood like I have. You have flour in your blood. Go ahead, that picture is yours. You know where to keep it." Rosa beamed at them all. She was thrilled with the thought of her future and of being back at home. "I can't wait to tell Víctor that I took those pictures with his camera. It's thanks to him. Where is he?"

Everyone looked at the table.

"Where is he?" Rosa dropped the picture. At that moment she noticed that she was the only one smiling.

"*Petita*, he's not here." Josep slowly stood. "There's some bad news." He put a hand on Rosa's shoulder. "They've arrested him."

"Arrested him? But for what? Where is he?" She stood at the end of the table with her arms stiff at her sides. The array of photos before her blurred and their meaning evaporated.

"When they were sweeping the woods for terrorists. We don't know where he is exactly, but we think he's been taken to Barcelona, to the Modelo," Manel said.

Rosa's earlier excitement curdled and she fell into the chair. "It can't be. He's no terrorist." She looked at them all with begging eyes, tears streaming from their corners. He was her reason for coming home. "I know cases like this. If they think he's a terrorist, they'll never release him. They may even shoot him."

A chair scraped on the floor and there was a sob of pain. Àngels stumbled past them and out the door.

CHAPTER SIXTEEN

CHRISTMAS DAY AND Saint Stephen's were somber rather than festive occasions as the family picked at the traditional *carn d'olla* and *canelons*. There were three empty places at the table: for Víctor, Àngels and Rosa. Rosa had left on Christmas Day for Barcelona and Àngels hadn't left her house. After the meal, Manel invited Josep to his cottage, where every piece of furniture had been meticulously carved by his own hands: a narrow bed against the wall, an elaborate table in the middle of the room, and a tiny counter supporting a single butane burner with a traditional coffee maker perched on it. Josep took a seat in a high-backed chair and watched as Manel poured strong black coffee and a hefty splash of cognac into a small glass and handed it to him.

"I'm sorry the jewel deal fell through," Josep said, sipping the *carajillo* and savoring the cognac that Josep had smuggled in himself. He swore it made it even tastier. "Now what will you do?"

"That's not the only deal I'm afraid will fall through." Manel straddled a chair and the pain was clear in his eyes. "Everyone is blaming you for all of this, but I'll have you know I'm blaming myself. I'm so worried about Àngels. I haven't seen her like this since Carme died. She had Víctor to pull her out of it then, but now she has no one."

"She has you. I'll keep taking the blame if it will help her get better. I'm used to it by now," Josep said and took a sip of his drink. He couldn't watch his sister break again and had to do something to pull her back. In turn it might soothe his own conscience. After he had exhausted all his contacts and Dolors had baked all the bribery cakes she could, they had to accept that Víctor's detention was part of the larger picture, where a town like Pujaforta was but a speck. With her contacts in the city, Rosa was the only one with a chance of getting information or pushing for his release. Josep insisted that the regime had no proof that Víctor was a terrorist. The only issue was the gun. In the meantime, he tried to relieve Manel's concern about Àngels, while trying to hide his own. "They can't keep Víctor indefinitely."

"He was in the wrong place at the wrong time, and I can't help but feel that I put him there. A boy like my own son." Manel edged his chair closer. "Listen, Àngels still has no idea of my involvement in those other Marbella runs."

"And she won't. There's no reason for her to know. Especially not now. There will be no more jewels, books or anything for that matter."

"It's a shame. Since I had no orders, I was working on more cabinets with the most ingenious compartments. I'll have to try to sell them as plain furniture, I suppose."

"I'll help if I can. Has Àngels said anything about your wedding plans?"

"I knew that date was unlucky." Manel lowered his eyes. "She won't talk about it. With Víctor's predicament the wedding is the furthest thing from her mind."

"But it's just what she needs." Josep jumped in his seat spilling his coffee. This could be the answer. "Planning the wedding would keep her mind off of all of this. Dolors would make sure of that. We've got to try to convince her. I'll talk to Dolors and my mother as well."

"What if she uses it as an excuse not to marry me?" Manel looked up shyly. "Maybe that's her real reason. Look how long it's been. Besides, she'll want Víctor to be there."

"But you'd set the date. We were even going to celebrate. Dolors was more ecstatic than anyone."

"Àngels did seem rather excited." Manel's face brightened. "With the help of the family maybe she will actually do it."

"Let's not mention this to Baltasar." Josep grasped Manel's shoulder. "I have to admit that at first I didn't trust you. But now I think I couldn't find a better brother-in-law." He was surprised to feel that he meant what he said. Surely Manel was the ideal medicine for his sister.

***

As the new year approached, and as a distraction from their own worries about Víctor, the whole family was intent on creating romantic opportunities for Manel and Àngels to be alone. Yet Àngels' attention could not be drawn away from the realization of her worst fear. With Víctor's arrest, she was reliving it all. Carme's detention, her own, and the death of both her daughter and her best friend. At first she was determined to do as she had in the past and fight to have Víctor released. When she saw that with their influence in Pujaforta they may as well have been in Gibraltar, she resigned herself to letting Rosa pull what strings she could from Barcelona. Until then, Víctor was foremost on Àngels' mind and everything was put on hold until she had word of him. However, when Rosa returned from Barcelona with news, it appeared that the postponement would be a long one.

"Víctor is in the Modelo," she told them. "I brought him some clothes and some food and he looks thin, although relatively healthy. But he's shattered. He thinks they'll never release him. They've officially charged him with terrorism, but he hasn't been convicted."

"So there's still plenty of hope," Manel said and smiled, nodding at Àngels.

"Yes, there is." Rosa stood before them at the table as if delivering a speech to the masses. "There's hope because I am going to do everything I can to get him out. I've taken a job at a new weekly newspaper in Barcelona. One that can turn heads and change the system. If we can get enough international exposure, foreign governments may put on some pressure. The newspaper may send me to France. I stretched the truth and said I'd worked there before."

Montse sighed and shook her head. "So you're not coming home?"

Rosa's look softened but her determination didn't. "No. For now, I'm staying in the city. I'm not going anywhere until Víctor is free."

***

Despite the attempts to switch Àngels' attention from Víctor's imprisonment to the joys of celebrating nuptials with Manel, Àngels had made up her mind. "I will not marry anyone until Víctor can be at my wedding," she insisted and told everyone who tried to convince her to the contrary. Her position did not budge over the year to come and neither did Víctor's. Yet when Rosa tried to convince Àngels to visit him in prison, the response was always silence. She hadn't the strength to see him through those bars.

Nonetheless, everyone was relieved in knowing that Rosa and Víctor were together in the same city. She called home regularly to report on Víctor's pendulous state of mind and health. Yet the time wore on. Rosa vowed that every word she wrote and every picture she took had one purpose: to capture the attention of the right people and not that of the wrong people. However, by now she and everyone had begun to believe that Franco's attention was nothing to fear since his mental and physical state were failing. From her room near the prison Rosa still wrote articles and letters to anyone and everyone. Each time she visited Víctor she had to force herself to walk through the doors as if she were crossing into enemy territory.

This day when she entered the cacophony of the visiting room and saw Víctor through the bars, his face was swollen and he had a gash above his eyebrow. It had begun to form a dark scab that would likely leave a scar, though not as large as the one already inside him. Rosa clutched the bars as she leaned into them. Her whole body ached in her helplessness and she felt caged herself. Her eyes searched his lost expression. "Víctor, what happened to you? *Estàs bé?*"

He looked from the floor and into her gaze and nodded his head. "I'm fine." He tilted his head. "Have you made any progress in getting me out of here?" His voice broke at the end and he cleared his throat to disguise it.

"Víctor, I can't see you like this." Rosa covered her mouth with her hands but she didn't take her eyes off of him. "You look thinner than the last time, but I wouldn't have thought it possible." She sighed and swallowed. She couldn't cry here. Her whole purpose of coming was to keep his spirits from sinking. She couldn't let him see that she was a wreck herself. "Everything is moving along. I've written and published articles. I've written, sent, and even hand delivered letters to contacts here, Madrid, Paris. Some of the old Republicans are still up there. I've interviewed them personally. You remember the Minister of Health? She was Catalan." Rosa was nodding, listing everything she had done, just as she did on every visit, even though each and every person she had spoken to had promised her nothing. She looked at Víctor, but he was shaking his head at the floor.

"At this point, the Republicans can't do a thing for me. That was decades ago. Maybe I need some terrorists to vouch that they've never heard of me."

"They know that you're no Basque terrorist. I think I've managed to convince them that you're not with the FRAP either."

"Then why am I still here?" His honey-brown eyes looked large and lost.

"It can't be much longer. Besides Franco is still in hospital. With any luck he won't leave there alive, unlike you. I have a perfect article planned for the next issue. It will be the clincher. I'm sure of it. You can't lose hope now."

"Rosa, I don't know why you're doing this for me."

She leaned against the barrier. "*Vida meva*, why wouldn't I?"

"Because you bared it all to me. And I ignored you and I mocked you." He swallowed. "But you are my life. Don't you see? You always have been."

"I know, Víctor." Rosa bit her lip. "I've known all along." She smiled slightly. "But even if I hadn't, I would never abandon you here. I would be doing exactly as I am now. Just you wait. This article will do it. I promise." She stroked his fingers through the bars.

***

At the end of August, Josep received a telephone call in code from Rosa. "It's me. Paco's shut us down. Call you at the Palace." The whole family and Baltasar then climbed up to the Palau mansion's safe telephone and waited for a call from Rosa. Baltasar had already told them the news of

Franco's new anti-terrorism law that was closing newspapers and handing out death sentences. They were all standing in Albert's tower, except for Albert, who could no longer climb the stairs. The decades' worth of stacked papers were now gone, leaving room for them to circle the telephone, staring at it, willing it to ring.

When it did, Rosa said, "Franco has closed the newspaper. Part of his anti-terrorism act." Josep heard her sadness and anger charge along the phone line. She continued, "We don't write about terrorism. Or perhaps we do: the terrorism of Franco himself."

"Yes, we've heard. What are you going to do, *petita?* Are you going to come home?" he asked. While he knew the importance of what she was doing, he couldn't help but feel hopeful. Without Rosa or Víctor, or Geneviève and his smuggling, he was feeling isolated. Baltasar was his only outlet. They were at least on the same plane, while Dolors, Montse, and Pau were on another. He looked at his wife and daughter. Dolors was standing with her ear almost to the receiver and with her hands praying at her chest. Montse was squeezing Dolors' elbow with one hand and was holding Rosa's biscuit tin under the other arm. She carried it everywhere.

Rosa's voice was breaking with the poor connection. "I can't come home now. I have to keep writing. My editor wants me to go to France because we could reach more people there. I could tell them what's happening here. It's 1975. It's unfathomable. Before I decide anything I have to see Víctor."

"How is he?" Josep felt his usual guilt for not having gone to visit him.

Her voice softened. "Surviving. But barely. I'm trying to keep his morale high. I see him whenever I can and I send him warm thoughts when we're not together. Go ahead and laugh, but he says that he receives them and that's what keeps him going."

"Can you send him messages from as far away as France?"

"In France my message will be different. I will be sending them to the highest powers. I'll make them listen this time. Then I'll be able to send him my thoughts directly to Pujaforta because they'll release him and I'll be able to see his whole face, not a face sectioned by the bars between us. You can tell Àngels that she can start planning her wedding." Rosa sounded very optimistic considering the situation. "We have to believe it. If we all just curl up and let ourselves fade away, Víctor will do the same. *Pare*, I have to go. Someone might be listening." The receiver clicked in his ear.

***

A few weeks later any headway Rosa made for Víctor and Manel made with Àngels was lost when five young men were sentenced to death. When Àngels heard the news she burst into Josep's kitchen like an erupting storm.

She was holding her head and her curls protruded like wings. When she saw Josep she shoved him with all her anger.

"Àngels, calm down. What's happened?" Josep was holding his arms up in defense. She knew that everyone thought that she had one toe over the edge.

"It's all your fault." She poked his chest and covered her mouth with her hand. The room seemed to spin around her. "You and your contraband. I told you from the beginning. Don't you see?"

"No, I don't." Josep moved to grasp her shoulders but she pulled away.

"They're going to shoot those five boys."

Josep held her firmly and shook her lightly. "Yes, but none of them is Víctor and all of them have been convicted of murder, of terrorism. Víctor hasn't."

"But if they're going as far as killing them, what are the chances that they will free the others?" Àngels wiped the tears from her cheeks. The room had stilled but she couldn't get her bearings.

"It could be good, though, don't you see? This will get people's attention. There will be protests. Rosa will see to it." Josep's voice was soft and coaxing, as if he was speaking to a child.

"I don't know." She shook her head. "Do you really think so?"

Josep put an arm around her and pulled her head to his chest. "I do think so. And I think that you're driving yourself mad with all this worry. You have to think about other things. Hasn't Manel been able to distract you a little?"

"I know what you're doing and it won't make me miss Víctor less." She pulled away, the ache still dull within her, and walked out the door.

As predicted, uproar surged across Europe and around the world in reaction to the death sentences. Even the Pope begged Franco for mercy, but Franco's spirit was still strong and his ears were intentionally deaf. It would seem that he wanted to go out with a bang instead. Franco was now out of hospital, the Maker having granted him clemency, for now. The day of the executions, everyone gathered around the television at Dolors' terrace to hear the final verdict. At the moment that they all realized that the sentence would hold and the bodies would fall, they received word that an official car had entered Pujaforta's main square. The people stood around as an officer in uniform emerged and raised his head toward the church and the town hall, reflecting, as if searching the stones for memories.

A while later, when Àngels heard the news of a car arriving, she almost fainted in excitement. They had to be delivering Víctor; she was sure of it. Rosa's plan had worked. She ran to Josep's house to find out what he knew. But when she got to the doorway of the bakery, she came face to face with the official himself and fainted in earnest. She collapsed into the arms of

Manel, who had run after her trying to warn her. Manel stretched Àngels out on the floor of the terrace, brushed off the sawdust that had fallen from his coveralls, and the whole family proceeded to fan her. When she opened her eyes she was looking into the face of Carles Puig framed by the light of the afternoon sun. His dark eyes looked puzzled as he took off his cloak and wrapped it around her shoulders. Removing his hat, he revealed his cowlick, now thinning and gray. He reached for Àngels' hand. She shook her head in an attempt to erase the vision and put her hand to her temple where she had hit it in her fall.

"Àngels." It was Manel's voice. She saw his face beside hers and felt calm and relief. "Are you hurt?" he said. "Can you stand?"

She nodded and slowly stood. Feeling the heat of the sun, she noticed the cape around her shoulders and shook it off.

"Àngels, I'm sorry to cause you such a fright." This time it was not Manel's voice and Àngels looked toward it. Again it was the blurry face of Carles Puig. "I need a word with all of you." With the sound of the voice itself, Àngels' head began to turn again. She felt as if she had four walls compressing her, squeezing the information and life out of her. Then she heard herself whimper.

Dolors rushed forward and took Carles by the elbow. "Come have a seat on the terrace. I hope you like what I've done here. I would have liked to have shown you the bakery personally, but I'm sure that Montse gave you a good tour."

Àngels, Manel, and Josep stayed back as Dolors led Carles to a seat. He stood beside Dolors' favorite table with a view of the mountaintop splayed before them. Àngels grasped Josep's and Manel's arms to hold herself up. Her breathing was fast. "What is he doing here? Why has he come after all this time? Just when I thought I'd finally forgotten about him."

"I can't imagine it's a friendly visit," Manel said.

"I'll go fetch Baltasar. He should be here," Josep said and kissed the side of her head, before running down the hill.

Carles was still standing at the table but was now facing them, beckoning them closer. Àngels and Manel slowly approached.

"I need a word with the two of you. Alone," he said, and undid his jacket button as he sat down, releasing his now round stomach.

"Why are you here?" Àngels said. She didn't look him in the eye and she didn't really want to know the answer. She and Manel sat down.

"It's odd to be back here and to have no family to visit." Carles looked toward the town center before clearing his throat and sitting up. "I am here because I received some worrying news on my desk in Madrid and I was concerned when I saw the name of the town involved. I thought I should come and warn you."

"Warn us? Why would you do that?" Àngels asked.

"I feel I owe it to you." Carles turned towards Manel. "Have you been shipping furniture to Marbella?"

Àngels looked at Manel whose eyes flew open and she said, "I don't remember any shipments that far away."

"What did it look like?" Manel said.

"It's not what it looked like, but what it had in it," Carles said. "In secret compartments in the back of the lower left cupboard. I think you know what I'm talking about."

Àngels turned to Manel again. "Secret compartments? Manel?"

They all looked up as Josep and Baltasar approached, squinting warily at Carles. Josep looked calm and determined, with his dear friend at his side, still ready to take on the entire Puig family. Nearby the church bell rang repeatedly, calling them all to mass, but only Manel jumped to his feet. He whispered in Josep's ear and Josep's face paled. It looked like the worst possible case scenario for all of them. He stepped backward and stared at Carles as if he was aiming a rifle at his chest. The chiming bells ceased.

"This is exactly as I suspected," Carles said. "I didn't imagine that Manel could do this alone, but then again Manel is capable of a lot more than you would think."

Josep sat down. "Let's talk about this rationally. What do you know? Why do you think we are involved?"

"A cabinet with a secret compartment hiding jewelry reported stolen by Interpol was intercepted during its delivery to Marbella. This is what I know, but I haven't passed it on to the authorities in question. It's clear that it was you."

"Why would you come here now?" Josep asked.

"Because I wanted to confirm my suspicions."

"Suspicions they will remain. What proof do you have? Manel makes furniture, but it doesn't mean he put the jewelry inside it."

Carles pushed his chair back. "I thought I had enough evidence with the file." He went into the bakery and returned carrying a biscuit tin. "But it's all here in this box. You should really watch what you leave lying around."

"Montse's biscuits?" Josep looked at it like he hadn't noticed it before. "What can be incriminating in that?"

Àngels watched as Carles opened it and lined up some pictures on the table. Víctor and Josep climbing through the woods. Josep walking across a square in France. Jewels in the palm of a gloved hand.

"This doesn't prove anything," Josep said.

"I'll remind you I've come here to help you. Manel could be in big trouble. The cabinet bears his signature."

Àngels pushed back her chair and ran from the table. She felt her life tripping her again. And again. She had already lost her trust in Josep, but she would have trusted Manel with her entire future.

"Àngels, it's not what you think," Manel called after her. "I did it for you. For the wedding." He tried to stand up but Carles held him in his seat.

Baltasar followed Àngels. She was by the side of the house where she still had a view of the table. She had to see it for herself, since now no one could be trusted. Looking at the triangle before her, Josep, Manel, and Carles Puig, the whole story was unbelievable, yet it wasn't. Now she understood why Manel had been carving so secretly. For some pieces he hadn't wanted her help at all. She paced and turned to Baltasar. "Did you know about this? That not only Víctor but Manel was involved in Josep's smuggling?"

Baltasar's eyes looked equally hurt and he looked at his feet. "I didn't know. Frankly, I'd like to know why they didn't tell me."

"I know why they didn't tell me. All this time everyone has been pressuring me to marry Manel. Meanwhile he's been smuggling stolen jewels with my brother."

"I wasn't pressuring you. I'm as shocked as you are."

Carles was approaching them and Àngels stepped backward, as if forced by her feeling of repulsion. He was right in front of her. "I need a word with Àngels alone." His voice was commanding but also had a gentle lilt. He rested a hand on his closely shaven chin.

Although he was the last person she wanted to be alone with, she nodded slowly and Baltasar backed away. Before he could speak, Àngels stepped closer to Carles. "Have you come to ruin my life again? Is that your intention?"

"Not at all. I've come to save it. If you'd stayed you would have heard that I destroyed the file."

"You did?" She stepped back. "Why would you do that?"

"I thought I owed it to you. I owed it to Manel. After all he was the one who brought you to me all those years ago. He did just as I asked him."

Àngels turned away. "What are you talking about?"

"Manel arranged all the details of your arrest. He knew how much I admired you." Carles reached for her hand. "I thank him for that. I also want to apologize to you. For what I put you through. I was very young and drunk with all the power. Now that I see you again I realize why."

Àngels felt a chill run up her back and swatted his hand away. "I can never forgive you. Ever. It was decades ago, but in my mind it was just days ago. You tried to apologize before just as you are now, but I will never forgive you. You ruined my life."

"I'll find a way to make it up to you."

"Never."

"I will. You'll see." Carles stepped away.

She shook her head. Nothing he could do could repair the damage done. But then, maybe there was something. She gasped and turned to look at him. "There may be one way." She saw hope in his eyes. "Get Víctor Munt out of prison," she said. "But I'm not making any promises where you're concerned."

"Víctor Munt, Carme's son? He's the one in the pictures, the dark one." Àngels nodded.

"You don't want him shot like the ones they executed today." Carles' eyes were serious. "I will look into it. Then I'll come back and we'll talk." Carles started to walk away, then turned around with a final warning. "If I were you, I'd tell your brother to get rid of those pictures."

***

At the table on the terrace, Josep was fuming. Dark clouds appeared overhead, reflecting his angry mood. He had just skirted one of the greatest dangers he had ever encountered. The fact that his daughters could be so careless, one for taking the pictures and the other for exposing them, made him doubt they were all made of the same substance. He picked up the tin of photographs and went into the bakery where Montse was flipping a *truita*. When she saw him approach, the omelet slid from the pan to the floor. Josep shook the tin at her.

"Why would you leave these lying around?"

Montse looked at the pictures and shrugged.

Josep shrugged in imitation. "What does that mean? You know this tin is full of compromising photos. Why would you be so careless?" He shuffled them and held some in the air for her to see, stopping at one showing him loaded down with an overstuffed canvas sack.

Dolors put a hand on Josep's arm. "She's been carrying that tin around for ages. None of us knew what was in it."

"She did." He shook a wad of pictures at her.

"When Rosa has those photos she's like a queen," Montse said. "Everyone buzzes around her. I spend my days in here, making cakes and bread and *truita* and *coca* and no one even notices." Montse grabbed the tin and went for the stairs.

Josep and Dolors watched after her and Josep shook his head at his wife. "This is your fault. You've got to appreciate her more."

"Look who's giving the lessons," Dolors said, looking like she would have spat on the ground if she hadn't been in her bakery.

Josep looked at the selection of pictures in his hand. He plucked one from the pile and felt his stomach sink. He examined it more closely. "What is this?" He shook it under Dolors' nose and practically crushed the others in his opposite hand. He squinted at it again and rubbed his eyes. It was his son Pau wearing a red leotard and posing in an arabesque. Geneviève was guiding the curve of his arm. It was like surreal evidence of the crossing of his two parallel worlds. He looked closer and the scenario shot into his mind until he felt he was free falling into the deepest hole the earth could provide. He recognized the sofa, the mirror on the wall. It was as if his face was still reflected in it.

"What is this?" he repeated.

Dolors hesitated then she sighed. "It's obviously Pau. I'll have you know he's an excellent dancer. Everyone says so."

"Everyone?"

"Everyone who's seen him dance. He could even go professional. That's what his teacher says." Dolors grasped the hand holding the picture. "You would never have accepted it. That's why we never told you. You already think your son is a sissy. But you don't even know your son. You've been away most of his life. You've been away most of our marriage."

Josep shook his hand free and showed Dolors the photo. His finger was just under Geneviève's chin. "Is this his teacher?"

"Yes, she's French. She's a customer. She's become a good friend, maybe even my only friend." She looked down. "I even think you'd like her if you met her."

"Where is Pau now?"

"Probably dancing or with that Vidal boy."

Josep's arm was trembling and the picture fell to the floor. He was so angry he could hardly see his wife standing before him. Geneviève's jealousy, her insecurities, all the traits so endearing to him, had made her weave herself into the very fabric of his family. He covered the photo with his boot and ground it into the tiles. Then he stormed out the door and headed for France before his entire life unraveled.

CHAPTER SEVENTEEN

As JOSEP CLIMBED through the woods, he promised himself that he would find Geneviève and ensure that she could never contact his family again. He felt such rage towards her and towards himself. He would have to fix it, and then he could concentrate on the true root of the problem: he had ignored his family. In that, Geneviève had been correct. It was time for him to reclaim them, his wife, his children, his sister, and even his brother. He would have to drop the decades' worth of pride and go and see Eduard. The decision soothed him, but as he crossed onto French soil he thought of Geneviève, all her pointe shoes, and his prancing son. She would never see anyone in his family again. He would have to make sure of it.

When he arrived at Geneviève's door it was Jules who answered. He told Josep that Geneviève had received an urgent call and sped off in her car. While Josep waited outside his anger slowly dissipated and he realized he was misdirecting his energy. Geneviève was a lost cause, but his family wasn't. So he headed back the way he came, his blinding desire to see his family making him risk the woods in the daylight, and he managed to get home before sundown. From on high, Pujaforta bathed in solemn sunlight was a unique sight for his eyes.

Every seat on Dolors' terrace was taken by townsfolk admiring the final view of the sunset reflecting off the mountaintops. Only a few days of the season were left. Josep arrived at almost a run. Of all the times he had returned to this house, now it was finally like he was coming home. From a distance he could see his mother's table with mounds of knitwear blocking the view of the door. A few people were gathered around it examining clothing, holding it up for inspection while Núria pointed out the details of the pattern, the painstaking stitch work. Albert stood behind her, his hooked body hanging over her. Josep felt pride at the sight of them, their

247

harmony and their passion for their garments. Josep approached and squeezed his mother's hand. "Where is everyone?" he whispered.

Núria kissed him on the cheek. "We've been just too busy to notice."

Albert shook Josep's hand. "They'd be inside, on the terrace, or at home. Àngels is still moping at her house. I told her we'd fetch her later."

"I can't wait to see her," Josep said, and saw Pau come around the corner. His eyes were hidden under thick bangs and his hands were deep inside his front pockets. When Pau saw him he did a quick pirouette and headed in the other direction, but Josep managed to catch him by the elbow. "*Fill*, I'm so glad to see you. I'd like to spend some time together."

Pau shook back his hair and looked at him with surprised eyes, which were also blood red and seemed to have trouble focusing.

"Maybe later. Vicenç Vidal is waiting for me."

"What could you and the mayor's son have in common to spend so much time together? Is he a dancer too?"

Pau almost stumbled. "No."

"Right now you couldn't dance a straight line to save your life. What's going on with you?"

"The question comes a little late, don't you think?" Pau turned and walked away. Josep watched him disappear but was determined to not let his son sink his mood. He was truly pleased to be home. He dashed for the bakery door, which Montse was exiting with plates of *truita* in either hand. He hugged her.

"Montse, I'm so glad to see you." He rocked her back and forth.

"What are you doing?" Montse said. "I'll drop my dishes."

"I'm so pleased to be home with all of you." Josep drew away and looked around eagerly. "Where's your mother?"

"Over there, talking to the French lady. You know the one." Montse smiled slightly as she turned away.

That was when Josep saw them sitting on the terrace. Geneviève had her hand on Dolors' and her red lips were laughing. At that very moment Geneviève looked toward him and her laughing stopped. Suppressing the urge to kick the wall with his healed foot, he stormed away until he was standing beside the rose bushes that he and Àngels had planted. He couldn't watch his wife and former lover and he couldn't confront Geneviève in front of Dolors. For the first time he believed in Geneviève's madness and how it could ruin his life. Somehow her tentacles reached everyone he knew, while they almost pushed him over the edge. He looked toward the cliff and shivered. When he turned she was standing right in front of him.

"It's not safe for you here," he said and turned away. "I don't want to talk to you. I just want to strangle you."

"Go ahead. I don't have anything to live for." Geneviève's hazel eyes were no longer sparkling.

"You have a wonderful friendship with my wife. You know my son better than I do. I hope you haven't been supplying the drugs he and half the kids in town are on."

"Of course not." Geneviève bounded forward and wrapped her arms around him. "I also think I know you better than you do. I've missed you so much."

He pushed her away. "Get off of me. Do you want my whole family to see you?" His face paled. "Unless you've already told them."

"You told me I could. But no, I haven't. They trust me and they wouldn't understand." She reached for his hand. "I've been so worried about you, given the news."

"I trusted you, too." Josep grabbed her wrist and twisted it. "What news have you got now?"

"You're hurting me." She tried to pull her hand away. "It's about Eduard."

"What now?"

"So you haven't heard?" Her eyes grew large and watery. "Eduard's been gambling again. The family is ruined. No house, no medicine."

Josep hesitated then twisted her arm again. "Why would I believe you? This could just be another fabrication. Besides, we would have heard if this were true. We're his family." He looked down into her face and could see the lie in her eyes. "Listen, you are going to leave here today and you are never coming back. You will never contact Dolors, my son, or any of my family again. That includes Eduard's family."

"But Dolors will be devastated," Geneviève said, trying to pull away. Josep twisted her wrist all the more.

"She'll get over it, just as I have. If I see you again, I swear I'll kill you."

Geneviève laughed. "You could never do such a thing."

"Yes, I could. I once killed a woman. I told you I did. I'm capable of more than you would think."

"So am I and so is your wife." Geneviève was looking at the rose bushes. "You're wife made an interesting confession to me a while ago. She said that when you were children someone destroyed your father's rose bushes. You always thought it was her father. But she did it. It was her. It's not a confession of murder, but for some reason she was very upset about it."

Josep looked at the roses he'd planted and saw the childhood face of his wife ready for mass with her recently combed hair, heard the sound of his father's scream as he fell. When he looked up Geneviève was no longer there, and Sr. Palau was standing in front of him.

"Are you all right, son?" Don Albert asked. "That looked like quite a heated dispute. If I didn't know better, I would call it a lovers' quarrel."

"Don't be ridiculous."

"With that hug she looked rather intent on making up." Don Albert leaned over him. "Son, my advice to you is not to do it. But if you do, have the decency to do it far away from here. Have a little respect for your wife and your mother. Haven't you already brought enough misery on this family? And right when I thought you would take my advice and spend more time with your wife." His stooped body turned away. "I'm going to see if Àngels is coming. She hasn't quite been the same since all this trouble with Víctor and Manel and we know who's responsible for that." He shook his head and shuffled towards Àngels' door.

Josep stared at his rose bushes until the beat of his heart slowed to normal. He took a deep breath and looked across the mountains to where he had been trekking just hours before and to where Eduard lived. It was now almost lost in darkness. Geneviève gave him every reason not to believe anything she said, but he had to check for himself. Àngels would know about Eduard and later he would deal with Dolors. He ran to Àngels' door, which he found wide open. On the threshold, in a stream of light, he saw Àngels leaning over Sr. Palau, shaking him. Josep rushed to her side. Albert's face was locked in a state of shock. His already delicate skin appeared paper thin and clung to the bones of his face. His pallid complexion and his wide open eyes and mouth gave him a particularly ghoulish appearance.

"What happened?" Josep asked Àngels, who stopped shaking him and looked up.

"He came in the door and collapsed. I can't revive him." Àngels looked at Josep with such fear and panic in her eyes that she appeared to forget her anger towards him.

"I'll stay with him. Run and get Baltasar. He was on the terrace. Don't tell mother. Not yet."

As Àngels ran off, Josep leaned over Sr. Palau's bald head. His open eyes seemed to be staring inward. This is all my fault, Josep thought. Again. The shock of seeing him with Geneviève had clearly sent a clot straight to Albert's brain. Softly tapping his cheeks, Josep said, "Albert, wake up. Don't do this now. Don't do this to me."

At that moment Baltasar pushed Josep aside and began listening for Albert's breath and pulse and tried a myriad of ways of reviving him until he sat back on his heels and looked at the ground.

Àngels put a hand on his shoulder. "Baltasar, is he?"

Baltasar nodded and closed Don Albert's eyes. "You should go tell your mother. Or if you prefer, I can tell her."

Àngels shook her head and glanced at Josep as he stood up.

"We'll go together," he said, taking Àngels' hand. This time she let him. It saddened him that only tragedy seemed to bring them together. They walked towards their mother's stand of knitwear, which was piled only half as high as at the beginning of the day. Núria was still standing behind it, showing a red ski sock to a customer. Josep looked at her shining face and dreaded having to take the joy out of it. Albert, who had once signified the enemy, had become one of the family. Even Josep felt it. He watched his mother laugh at something as she put the socks into a bag. The news would crush her. So would the news of Eduard, which he still didn't know was true. He pulled Àngels to a stop and looked into her sad eyes.

"Are you still in touch with Francine?" he asked. "Are they having money troubles? Severe money troubles?"

Àngels shook her head. "No. In fact, Eduard's started back at work. He's doing much better. You should really go and see him. Your priorities need to change. When are you going to realize that you just end up hurting people?"

Josep nodded and closed his eyes. "I do. Everything you say is true." Then he opened his eyes. "Don Albert, before he collapsed, did he say anything?"

Àngels shook her head. "No, he didn't have a chance. The poor man."

"Yes," Josep said, trying not to show his relief. "And poor *Mare*."

When they pulled Núria to the side, made her sit down and told her the devastating news that she was once again a widow, at first she didn't react. She looked at them and then at the empty chair beside her as if expecting her husband to be sitting in it. Then she threw back her head and emitted a strange whine that seemed to come from her very core. She ran to Àngels' house, where Don Albert was lying on the table with his arms crossed over his chest. She put a shaking hand on his cheek and rested her own cheek on his chest. Josep was standing in the doorway holding up Àngels by her shoulders. It seemed that everybody was collapsing around him. Núria took one of Albert's hands and sat beside him. She looked toward them and said, "Will you give us some time alone?" As her tears ran down her face she waved them all towards the door. "Albert and I need a moment. I need to say farewell to my husband."

The next day as they gathered in the cemetery to lay Sr. Palau to rest, a *Tramontana* wind flew across the mountain and brought with it horizontal rain. Despite the storm, everyone came to show their last respects for a man who had earned the praise of townspeople of all political tones. They stood in shadow behind Núria, dressed in black, her face hidden behind her black *mocador*. Àngels and Josep were on either side of her and watched as the Palau family tomb was opened and Don Albert was put to rest.

Àngels held Núria's elbow. "You can stay with me. No need for you to go back to that mausoleum of a house."

"I've grown to love that house, just as I'd grown to love its owner." Núria wiped her eye. "I don't know if I have five years left in me. If not, you'll have to put me with your father and Pau. Without Albert, now what am I going to do with myself?"

"You've never had any trouble keeping busy. But first let's say our goodbyes to Sr. Palau."

Once they had all had a private moment, they gathered at Josep's house, where Dolors and Montse were busy filling plates of tomato bread, *truita*, and *coca*. Given Don Albert's prominent position, they broke with custom and welcomed the townsfolk into the living room to escape from the rain, to have a bite and pay their condolences to the widow. There was the family of Salvador the *Maquis*, the whole Vidal family, and even all the Guardia Civil. Josep watched as the whole town with their hats in hand filed past his mother. When a tall fair young man stopped before her and Núria's sad face filled with joy, Josep approached for a closer look. The man was in his late twenties and stood confidently, although his height and slight weight made him appear gangly. As he reached up to straighten the spectacles on his nose, Núria grasped both his hands.

"I didn't plan for us to meet on such a sad occasion," the young man said in Catalan with a very French accent, while smiling apologetically at her. "It is an unfortunate coincidence."

Núria did not let go of him. "Finally I meet my grandson. You have turned this sad day into one of the happiest in my life." She looked behind him. "Has Eduard come?"

"Not this time, no."

Núria met Josep's gaze and called him over. "Josep, you won't believe it," she said. The young man looked at him through spectacles and smoky eyes.

"Gaspard." Josep slapped his back and pumped his hand. "I would recognize your face anywhere. You still look so much like Francine." The young man had a wide forehead framed by plentiful dark blond hair. The balance of Francine's forehead with Eduard's bone structure made for a harmonious and handsome face.

"They also say I look like my father," Gaspard said. "I was very young the last time I saw you, but I too would recognize you. It's those Balaguer traits." He turned. "And here is my favorite Balaguer of all."

Àngels grasped his arm and kissed him on either cheek. Hers were uncommonly rosy and she wore her first smile in weeks. Baltasar was right behind her.

"Gaspard, I'm so happy that we're finally able to meet you," Àngels said.

"It's not the best day," he said, shrugging his shoulders exactly same way his father had in his younger years.

"Nonsense," Núria said. "There is never a bad day for my grandson."

Josep stood observing the familiarity and was perplexed. "I didn't realize that you knew each other," he said and no sooner had he spoken did a grand realization seize him. "Àngels, is this how you get news of Eduard?"

"Why don't I answer that," Gaspard said. "I've actually come to talk to you, Josep. Could we have a word alone?"

"Of course." Josep nodded at the others and led Gaspard into one of the back rooms. He was intrigued why his nephew would want to talk to him and no one else. Then he drew in his breath. "Your father is well, isn't he? He's not gambling again, is he?"

"No. Father is quite well and the news is good. He's actually the one who sent me."

"Eduard sent you here to talk to me?" Josep sat slowly in a chair.

"That surprises you?"

"Of course, I haven't heard a word from him in decades and now he sends his adult son to see me. I'm thrilled."

"He told me that the two of you write regularly, but that because of the regime and because of his past he can't come and see you."

Josep shook his head. "I see that he's still very confused. I have written to him a number of times, and more recently I have written to your mother, but I have never received a single word from your father. He threw me out, among other disappointments."

Gaspard shrugged. "Now he wants to see you. He wants to come here to Pujaforta."

"He does?" Josep's felt his pulse soar and jumped to his feet. "I can't believe it. He must need money or something."

Gaspard shook his head. "I have a good job. He would come to me."

Josep clutched his hands together and began to pace. "He'll have to wait. Franco's had a heart attack but he keeps hanging on. It may still be too dangerous for him." He looked up. "I could go to him instead."

"Father said that he himself cannot leave this world without returning to Pujaforta. That's why he wants to come here."

"But you said he was well."

"He is, but we don't know how long that will last."

"That disease." Josep pointed to his abdomen.

Gaspard nodded. "So I came for him and also because I wanted to see you again, or to meet you really. Over the years I've heard so much about *oncle* Josep."

"Mostly bad, I imagine."

"Mostly." Gaspard smiled. "So can I tell Father that he can come?"

"Of course, though it's not my permission he needs. While Franco's still alive he should either wait or be very careful. One of ours is already in prison and we couldn't survive another. It would destroy me, but it would kill Àngels." Josep put a hand on Gaspard's shoulder and began to lead him back toward the main room. "Let's not tell anyone about this yet," Josep said. "It will be a wonderful surprise if he comes and a crushing disappointment if he doesn't."

As they reentered the crowd, Josep felt like he was afloat. He saw the people as if from above and pictured Eduard's head among them. He then realized that he didn't even know what such a picture would look like. Perhaps now, like Josep, Eduard would have only a thin coating of hair and a round belly, instead of the visible ribs he had when they last met. As they approached the others, Josep saw his mother across the room talking with some gentlemen in dark suits. By the time they joined Àngels and Baltasar, Josep felt someone nudge him and everyone gasped. Rosa was standing beside him wearing a grin.

"Surprise." She then seemed to remember the occasion and said, "Poor Don Albert."

"Rosa." Josep kissed his daughter, who they now saw infrequently since she was working from France, even though it was closer than Barcelona. "I didn't think you would be able to come."

"I was actually in Villefranche, just over the border. I can only stay for a while, then I have to get back. But I had to come for *Iaia* and to say goodbye to Don Albert. *Iaia* seems surprisingly calm considering. She was talking to some strange men about 'business,' or so she told me." Rosa made quotes in the air and raised her eyebrows.

A plate of *truita* appeared between them as Montse pushed into the circle. "Omelet?" she said. "I made it myself." She smiled warmly at Gaspard and edged a little closer.

"Montse, Rosa," Josep said. "This is your cousin, Gaspard. My brother's son."

"Eduard's son?" Montse stepped backward and then forward again. "It's a pleasure. Please try some." She jutted the plate toward him. "You must be famished after such a long trip. Will you be here long?"

"No, not long. But I will be back." He took a piece of *truita* on a toothpick.

"I do hope so," Rosa said and turned to the rest of the family. "I know this sounds a little presumptuous and immodest, but I wanted to show all of you the pictures I've had published." She smiled and looked at Àngels, who was standing very close to Baltasar. "Where's Manel? He should see them, too." Rosa looked around the room.

Àngels only grunted. Instead Baltasar spoke in a whisper. "There's been a bit of a falling out."

Josep sighed. "And frankly, I've seen enough of your photographs lately." He sounded more abrupt than he intended but he couldn't hide his disappointment. The discovery of Rosa's pictures had hurt him in more ways than one: not only had she been careless in taking compromising pictures, she had kept Pau's dance lessons from him. That Dolors or even Montse could do this was no great surprise to him, but that after all their years of shared secrets, Rosa being a part of the conspiracy hurt him like a finger through his heart.

"I have to go by Villefranche. I could drive you back," Gaspard said as he took another piece of *truita*.

The plate tilted in Montse's hand. "You have a car?"

Rosa smiled. "If it's no bother, it would save me a lot of time."

"No bother at all. And we cousins can get better acquainted." Gaspard's smoky eyes turned from Rosa to Josep just as Dolors approached carrying a plate of *coca*.

Josep ignored his wife and slapped Gaspard on the back. "What a pleasure it is to meet you after all these years. We must get to know each other better as well."

"Àngels can fill you in." Gaspard looked at Àngels. "If she wants to, that is. She probably knows me as well as anyone."

"Yes, she's managed to keep that a secret all this time, haven't you, Àngels?" Josep said.

Àngels glared at him. "So says the man of secrets himself."

Gaspard pulled on Josep's sleeve. "I feel like I already know you, Josep. Geneviève has told me all about you. All these years she hasn't stopped. She says she's one of your greatest admirers."

"Geneviève?" Dolors' tray wobbled. "Geneviève Petitpas, the dance teacher?" Her face looked stricken amidst the wisps of hair that had escaped the knot on the back of her head.

Gaspard nodded. "Yes, do you know her as well?"

"I do." Dolors turned her red face towards Josep. "I'd like to know how she's become such an admirer of my husband."

Josep's face was a similar shade of red. The surreal crossing of his worlds was happening again. "Gaspard, this is my wife." Josep gestured towards Dolors, but she was already running from the room.

Gaspard was biting his lips. "I'm sorry I should have been more careful. They had warned me about you." Gaspard sucked in his breath. "I think I've done all I can here. Rosa, shall we go?"

"Yes, let's," Rosa said.

Soon all the family, excluding Dolors, waved at Rosa and Gaspard as they disappeared up the hill in his little Renault. Montse remained well after everyone else with one hand waving and her face looking both hopeful and dejected.

With a giant burst of energy, Núria ran towards them. Her enormous smile was not fitting for a widow at her husband's funeral. "You won't believe it," she said. "I've just been speaking to the lawyers. The ones in the black suits over there." She pointed to two men across the room. "Albert has left me everything." She shook her head. "After all these years of not spending a cent on the house, of living in two rooms, it turns out the man had a little nest egg. The lawyers said he put it away for me."

"He's had money all this time and he let us risk our necks?" Josep asked.

"You should be angry not happy," Àngels admonished her mother.

"I know." She looked at her hands and looked back up at them. "But I'm just pleased that we can all use it. It could make our lives so much easier."

Josep and Àngels looked at each other.

"What use is it now?" Josep asked.

"*Mare*, you should use it," Àngels said.

"What can I possibly do with it?"

"You can fix the house. You can go somewhere." Àngels pointed toward France. "You can go to see Eduard. Remember, that's what you wanted me to do."

She squinted at them. "I would love to see Eduard, but I couldn't go by myself. Why don't you come with me?"

"I'm not feeling up to a trip right now," Àngels said. "Besides, I have to be here when Víctor returns."

Josep shook his head. "I've been away too long already. I have much fixing to do." He glanced toward the stairs and Dolors' shadow. "Besides, I'm waiting for Eduard to come here. But I'd bet Gaspard would take you to see him."

"That's an excellent idea. I can suggest it to him for you," Àngels said.

Núria looked over the mountain towards France. "It would be a thrill to have my grandson take me there. I suppose I should see something of this world while I still can. I've already wasted too much time."

"Speaking of which, I have to go find my wife." Josep kissed his mother and left in search of Dolors, although he was unsure what he would tell her once he found her.

1975-1982

CHAPTER EIGHTEEN

As the days and weeks went on after Sr. Palau's funeral, Josep rose less and less from his bed, wallowing in a bitter mix of deception, broken promises, and guilt, interspersed with blinding stomach pains. He was convinced that all the bitterness had formed a tumor in his gut. Baltasar's regular check-ups assuring his clean bill of physical health did little to convince him otherwise.

Meanwhile Dolors left Montse in charge of the bakery and closed herself in her room to digest the reality of the last decade of her life. Her only words before shutting her door were to blame Josep for both the loss of her best friend and her trust in her husband. Yet Dolors' silence did not concern Josep greatly: in his eyes she was his murderous wife. His imagination had transformed his childhood memories in such a way that Dolors, in her church clothes, was not only trampling his father's rose bushes, she was shoving Josep's father directly off the cliff. Other images haunted Josep. There was Pau secretly dancing to the beat of Geneviève's clapping hands while the rest of the family looked on. There was Sr. Palau wagging a finger in Josep's guilty face before lying face up on Àngels' floor, and his mother grinning from Gaspard's Renault as she left on her adventure. Josep was also disappointed that Gaspard's promise remained unfulfilled. Josep had yet to hear a word from Eduard, let alone see his face at his door. And tomorrow was their birthday.

Very early the next morning, at 5:20 am, Josep awoke feeling like he had been kicked in the stomach. He felt shorn in two and was convinced that he had reached his end. As he lay in bed, he drifted into a dream-like state, where he saw images of Eduard charging toward him on a horse. He was a young Eduard, before the war, who still had both his hands and whose full hair was bouncing with the movement of the animal. He came to a braying stop and threw something at his feet before trotting back over the hill.

Reaching down, Josep picked up the bundle of muddy, unopened letters and saw that they bore Eduard's address written in Josep's hand. Then he found himself standing on a frozen lake looking into the exhaling nostrils of a workhorse, much like the one Henri Bouchon had up in northern Quebec so many decades before. He heard a loud crack from beneath his feet and felt the ice swell underneath him. Shaking his head back and forth on his pillow, he felt a sharp pain drive into the crux of his ribs. He was done for, but he no longer cared.

"*Pare*," Montse said from the doorway. "What's the matter? You're making so much noise. You're neighing like a horse."

Josep groaned. "I'm going to die."

"I'll get Dr. Sort and some chamomile tea," she said and left, but before she could return, he had fallen into more disturbing dreams.

***

That same morning when Àngels awoke, her usual feeling of loss was no lighter. Baltasar's attempts to lift her spirits with his company and then with chemical substances had been unsuccessful. On the rare occasion that she did leave her house, she felt that people were staring at her reddened eyes and could read her sleeplessness in them. But how could she sleep in a bed made by Manel? And how could he have smuggled her brother's jewels past the Guardia Civil right under her nose and have been party to Carles Puig's twisted desires? After all the years of scrubbing herself clean, she still felt dirtied. She once again felt the cold water in her face, the cold floor under her back and Carles' hard body smothering her.

She remembered all of Manel's conniving, his swindling them out of the co-op. And she had almost married him. Víctor's imprisonment had stopped her, though she now realized that it was likely not the only reason. Looking above her in bed toward the birds carved by Manel's hands, she felt the hollow feeling return. Now each one seemed like a diving vulture. Getting up, she felt the cold floor on her stocking feet as she walked to her old wireless radio. She turned it on as she did every morning since Franco had been ailing. There was a crack and a buzz and finally a solemn voice announcing the news she had been awaiting for almost four decades. She dropped to her knees and put her ear to the speaker.

"*Españoles, Franco ha muerto*," the prime minister's voice was saying between sniffs. Àngels collapsed to a ball on the floor and covered her face when she heard it. Francisco Franco, the Generalísimo, The Caudillo, was no more. It was finally here and she couldn't believe it. It had taken so very long. And it had taken too many people from her in the process. Immediately she thought of Víctor and sucked in her breath. Turning up the radio, she listened for news of the political prisoners. But every wave and every station was solemnly making the same announcement. It was like an ax had fallen, dividing their lives into a past and a future. And the future was starting now. As Àngels listened for word of amnesty, her heart fell when she remembered that Víctor was considered a terrorist, not a political prisoner. They could keep him locked up for good. She lay on the cold floor hardly hearing the echo of the radio in the silence of her house. When the news and the reality had actually registered, she sat up and felt an urge to see Josep, even though she had every reason not to be speaking to him.

Rising to her knees, she looked to the table where an open envelope was leaning against a candle stick. It was as if it was calling her name in Eduard's low, pained voice. Àngels pulled herself up and held the letter in her hands. While she hadn't liked what it said, she felt her worry subside. With Franco gone, the barrier between Pujaforta and Eduard would have to crumble. If Eduard didn't crumble first.

***

Josep awoke from his fitful sleep to see not a cup of chamomile tea but a pillow in front of his nose. Panicking, he swept it aside and Àngels' face appeared in its place.

"Josep, you're awake," Àngels said.

"And you're here." Josep released the gasp from his chest. "I thought you were going to smother me."

"Don't give me any ideas." She leaned toward him. "I've come to tell you something. It's the day we've been waiting for."

Josep belched, pushed himself forward in bed, and searched behind her. "Has Eduard come home?"

"No, but he might soon." She squeezed his hand. "Franco is dead."

"What?" Josep attempted to shake the dreams from his head. "Finally? It's official?"

She nodded. "It is over."

Josep threw back the covers and hugged Àngels, holding her against him for endless minutes while waiting for the reality to hit. "You've cured me." He squeezed her again. "Franco's gone and you're here." Gently pushing her away, he saw her strangely sad expression. "This means that Eduard can come home. Do you have any news of him?"

Àngels closed her eyes and nodded. "I do. And I have something to tell you."

At that moment, Josep heard stomping on the stairs and both he and Àngels turned toward the door. In came Baltasar and Dolors. Baltasar's eyes were alight and he clutched his instrument bag in one hand. Dolors was looking up at him with teary eyes while clutching a handkerchief to her chest. Josep noticed she hardly glanced at him. As Baltasar approached, Josep could smell the *xampany* on his breath, despite the early hour.

"The ladies tell me that your stomach is acting up again," he said, heading for the window and opening it. He waved his hand in front of his face as the cold air rushed in. "You have heard the news, haven't you?"

Josep sat forward in bed. "Baltasar, do you think we can believe it?"

"Yes, after all his agonizing, Franco is finally dead," he said. "When Montse called me, I was afraid that you'd had a heart attack from the news."

Dolors brushed by and took a seat in Josep's armchair. "But now what? What will happen to the mayor, to all my contacts?" She was still wearing her flour-smeared apron, the news having interrupted her baking.

"They can all drop dead as well for all I care." Josep thought of the mayor sitting on the terrace like he owned it. All the green uniforms always hovering. He had a quick thought: with no more regime his job became superfluous. If they weren't already, his smuggling days were definitely numbered. The thought actually excited him. "This can be a new start for everyone, for all of us." He looked first at Dolors and then at Àngels.

"It would be nice if you started getting along." Baltasar shook his head. "Now let me look at your imaginary tumor again."

Josep reached for his tobacco on the bedside table. "I feel fine now." He said it and meant it, intending to live a long life, although his death would come as a shock to him as much as anyone.

Ignoring him, Baltasar pulled some instruments out of his bag and began poking. "You are blown up like a balloon," he announced. "I've never seen so much gas in a human." He took out a box of tablets. "These will do the trick, but you'll have to show some restraint with the alcohol, which incidentally, is being served at my house. Some of the fellows are already celebrating." He backed towards the door. "Josep, join me later? Àngels, will you join me now?" With a spin he was gone and Àngels shrugged and followed him out the door. Josep and Dolors were left alone in his bedroom, a first in a very long time.

"Àngels, what did you want to tell me? Just give me a minute," Josep called after her, intent on not missing a moment.

"But it could be too dangerous out there. Besides, don't you want to see Rosa?" Dolors asked, pointing to the kitchen downstairs.

"Rosa's home?" Josep asked. "I can't wait to see her, but first there are some things I have to do." After swallowing the tablets, and jumping into his trousers, he dashed down the stairs before any of them could stop him from what he had to do next.

He needed to breathe some free Pujaforta air, to walk in his town knowing that Franco was finally defeated and their country was now technically liberated. As he made his way through the street toward the main square, he shivered and realized he should have brought a heavier coat. It was still early morning and while the sun had begun to turn everything a buttery yellow, it had yet to heat the town, to melt the ice off the slate roofs and the frost off his neighbors' windows. In the openings above the lace curtains, Josep saw no faces or peering eyes, but he knew that inside the townsfolk were not asleep: they were lying in wait and more than a few would be gathered around a bottle of *xampany* or *cava* as it was now officially called. Josep had been having a hard time adapting to the new name. Now he thought it would be fitting to mark this new start with a glass of cava or even a bottle. He had let the others run on ahead because he needed a moment to take stock, to put the pieces of his past in order so that they could help him chart an onward path. A path that could lead him to Eduard's house, although Josep wasn't sure if he was ready to forgive Eduard yet.

As Josep entered the main square, he looked at the centuries-old tree in the middle of the square as if it was silently observing him, just as it had through the great events of his life. Its gnarled and intertwining branches were a reminder of how complicated family could be. This square was where his family had come together and where it had fallen apart. Around him the square remained empty and calm; even the guards outside the town hall were gone. The Spanish flag above was at half-mast, snapping at him in the wind. That very spot before the town hall had witnessed Àngels' unraveling, as she had stood in her nightdress, barefoot on the ice, shouting insults at the guards.

Josep breathed in, smelling the pine logs burning in neighboring fireplaces, and turned his back on the square and the memories of his past. There were so many events in it that he wished he could undo and a number he was afraid would come back to get him. Now it was time for a new future. He held his stomach, burped again and nodded to himself. He began the well-traveled route through the twisting streets toward Baltasar Sort's house. The time had finally come to celebrate.

***

As Àngels made her way homeward from Baltasar's place, she passed corners, doorways, and cobblestoned alleys that seemed to hide the souls of others gone in distance and time. Once Josep had arrived at Baltasar's house, the celebrations had picked up their pace. She ducked out, intent to celebrate in due time when she had news of Víctor. So far the news she had of Eduard was worrisome and she touched the letter in her pocket. She would have to talk to Josep when the moment was right.

The bell above the bakery door jingled as she entered, but she could hardly hear it over the blast of the television set. As she crossed between the counter that Manel had so intricately carved on her left and the empty chairs for customers on her right, she spotted Dolors, a dark lump on the armchair in the sitting room beyond. She was perched before the television and its images of Franco and the thousands of people queuing outside the Palacio de Oriente in Madrid. Dolors kept glancing from the screen to the portrait of Franco on the wall. Àngels stood still, observing, after so many decades still unable to comprehend the stark contrast of ideas between her brother and his wife. They at least had each other, whereas she, as always, had no one. Abruptly Àngels switched on the light, making Dolors jump in her chair.

"Àngels, you're back." Dolors turned toward her. "Josep certainly recovered quickly from his tumor this time. He couldn't get out of here fast enough."

Àngels did not dare to answer. Instead she pointed to the portrait on the wall. "Maybe now you could take that down." Franco stared down from inside the cheap frame, his insipid face and combed moustache, all the medals on his lapel.

"But it may not be safe yet." Dolors sat on the edge of her chair and clasped her hands together. "It's managed to keep us safe so far—at least most of us. I don't dare take it down yet."

Àngels shrugged, thinking that perhaps she was right. Even she would accept having Franco on the wall for a while longer if it meant having Víctor come home. "Are the girls in the kitchen? I hear that Rosa is here. I'm dying to see if she has any news." Àngels saw the light in the back, put her nose in the air and could smell the familiar sweetness of bread in the making. She followed the scent to the bakery kitchen, where rows of round pa de pages sat rising on the far counter. Beside it was a bowl, its inside white with flour, and on the table in the middle of the room was the sour dough base that they took from and added to daily. The natural yeast made it grow and ferment, much like the worries in Àngels' head. She turned to the marble countertop on her left to see Montse putting her full weight into kneading some dough in front of her. Standing at her side was Rosa, hands on the wide belt at her hips and not a speck of flour on her. Her dark hair was parted in the middle and draped on either side of her long face. When their eyes met, Rosa's face came alight.

"Àngels, you're here," Rosa said. "I thought you were at Baltasar's celebrating."

"I was. And I thought you would be in Barcelona covering this great day." Àngels hugged her, rocking her thin shoulders, feeling her earlier thoughts and memories dissipating. Àngels felt Rosa slowly pull away.

"After dying for so long, Franco had to do it on my day off." Rosa shrugged. "I wanted to come for *Pare*'s birthday. I was afraid he might be a bit down."

Àngels sighed. "He's making up for it now. But I couldn't stay. I can't celebrate. Not yet."

"I know. Soon we will. Víctor and Eduard will be home. I know it," Rosa said. "By the way, *Mare*'s been looking for Pau everywhere. He wasn't at Baltasar's, was he?"

Àngels shook her head.

"He's the smart one." Montse looked up from her kneading, brushing a streak of flour across her forehead. "You want everyone to come back and all I want is to get away from here."

"But how would *Mare* run the bakery without you?" Rosa asked. Montse shrugged and became absorbed with pounding the dough flat on the counter in front of her.

"*Mare* wants me to make a special *coca* for The Caudillo," Montse said, raising her eyebrows as she began rolling out the dough into long, narrow tongues. "She said we can sell them whether people are happy or sad. It's all fine as long as they pay for them," she added, dotting them with candied fruit colored bright red and yellow for both the Spanish flag and the Catalan flag. Given the now uncertain situation, it would be safer to cover all sides.

Àngels sighed. "I think it's time I went home." She slowly backed away. "When your father comes in, please tell him I need to see him."

Rosa grabbed her arm and said, "Don't go yet. Give me one minute." Rosa ran to her bag and took out her camera. She pulled Dolors into the kitchen and arranged the three women in front of the counter.

"This is a day I have to capture. Say Lluis," Rosa said, as the women hugged, Dolors wiping her reddened eyes, Montse brushing flour from her cheek into her hair, and Àngels wearing her first smile in what seemed like decades.

***

Josep came stumbling up the hill, holding his aching back, the earlier view of his town blurred by uncountable glasses of cava. He stopped, burped, and held his stomach. As he passed in front of the town hall, he held himself upright, trying to walk straight past it, while scoping for guards out of the corner of his eye. When he saw none, he remembered the reason for his current inebriated state, and relaxed his shoulders. He continued trying to walk straight nonetheless. Franco or not, now was not the time to be arrested. As he approached his house, he saw Àngels' cottage, the house that had once been home to their whole family. Now that their mother was gone, Àngels was always there alone, wallowing in her self-made misery, or so it seemed to him. He stumbled towards the door and knocked, sure that after Àngels' earlier overture toward him, now would be the perfect time to clear the air between them. Over the years it had become so thick and cloudy that he was sure that neither could see the truth through it. One thing he knew for certain: she had been in contact with Eduard but had kept it hidden from him. He deserved to know what she knew. He was his brother too. Maybe that was what she had wanted to talk to him about. Josep knocked harder, and jumped when the door moved under his fist.

"So you got my message," Àngels said, standing aside so that he could come in.

"What message?" he said as he slid past her holding his breath to spare her a whiff of the alcohol. He felt his pasty tongue against the roof of his mouth and thought that perhaps it was not the best time for confrontations. "I'm very happy you left me a message in any case. It's been a great day for me. Franco's gone and you're talking to me."

Àngels gestured for him to take a seat at the table. The old wireless was blaring garbled voices and static from across the room. Àngels went to the radio and with a turn of a giant knob, silenced it. Then she went over to the window and pushed open the wooden shutters, letting in the late afternoon light. Josep shivered, feeling a cool breeze against his back. Stroking the table where Don Albert's body had been not so long ago and his father's body had lain more than forty years before, Josep shivered again and shifted in his chair. "So, Àngels, earlier this morning you said you had something to tell me."

Àngels nodded, standing over him with her hands folded behind her back. "It's something I should have told you long ago. About Eduard. I've been in touch with him."

"I know you have," Josep said, attempting to hide the resentment in his voice. "And I really wish you had told me."

"I'm telling you now. And I've heard from him recently." Àngels stiffened beside him and she looked from the floor into his eyes. "I'm very worried about him."

He looked up at her expectantly.

"Usually Gaspard sends me news, but I haven't heard from him since he took *Mare* to Eduard's. She hasn't sent any news either. Now I've just received a letter from Eduard himself." She swallowed. "What I've needed to tell you is that, back during the war in France, Eduard gave me this." She showed him a small key on the flat of her palm.

"But that was ages ago." He pushed the chair back and attempted to stand.

Àngels put a hand on his shoulder, holding him in place. "I've tried to tell you. Most of the time you weren't particularly deserving. It was a secret."

"You say I'm the man of secrets." Josep shook his head, staring at the tarnished key. "Well, what the heck is it for? Or is that still a secret?"

"That's what worries me." She held her fist over her mouth. "When he gave it to me he said we should use it upon his death." She collapsed into a chair beside him. "And now, so many years later, he writes to me and asks me if I still have the key. He said to keep it handy."

Josep sighed. "That doesn't mean anything." He grasped her hand and it folded over the key. "Eduard is fine. Gaspard told me that Eduard's planning to come here. I even wrote to him asking him to."

Àngels shook her head. "He said he can't travel."

Josep stood up this time. "We could go to him then."

"And he doesn't want to see anyone besides *Mare*." Àngels looked at her clasped hands. "And he wouldn't give me a reason."

"I don't think we should jump to conclusions. You've had enough upset lately, mostly all my fault." Josep looked down at Àngels. "So do you know what the key opens? Did Eduard at least tell you that?"

"No, but I know that what it opens is at his house."

"And he doesn't want to see anybody. So much for our joint birthday celebration. Again." Josep shook his head then put an arm around Àngels and squeezed. "Don't worry. I'm sure it's not as bad as you think." He kissed her on the cheek.

***

In the Balaguer kitchen, Montse was taking a new batch of Dolors' bittersweet *coca* out of the oven. The base had risen, engulfing the candied cherries and orange, and smelled of bread and bubbling sugar. Dolors wiped away the streaks from her earlier tears and squeezed Montse's shoulder.

"That looks almost as good as my pine nut *coca*. What a fantastic idea. I think that even The Caudillo would be proud," Dolors said. "Not that I care, of course."

Rosa had been standing back watching the exchange, preferring to remain a silent observer in her mother's kitchen for fear that she might get drawn into baking. But now she couldn't hold her tongue. "*Mare*, you'd better not care. Besides, we will have days of enforced mourning ahead of us and you won't be able to sell a crumb."

"But people need to eat, surely. The *coca* will either console them or help them celebrate: it goes perfectly with cava. Maybe we should bring some down to Baltasar's house. We can check if Pau is with them." Dolors looked livelier than she had all day.

"We should stay put," Rosa said, although all she wanted to do was dash back to the city now that Franco was gone and find out when Víctor could be freed.

Montse slid some *coca* off of the tray. "Pau always gets to go and do whatever he wants. I'm betting he's with Vicenç Vidal."

Rosa rolled her eyes. "He wouldn't dare. The last place he should be right now is with the *Franquistes*. Lord knows how this is all going to pan out." Rosa leaned a low-belted hip against the counter and crossed her arms. "*Mare*, not even mayor Vidal and your other friends at the town hall will be able to tell you that. They're probably all afraid to show their faces now. Speaking of which," she pointed out beyond the kitchen to the sitting area, "surely you can take down that horrid portrait out there. I've been back and safe for years."

"You and Àngels." Dolors wiped her hands on her apron. "You don't realize why you've been safe all these years. All of you but Víctor, of course." Dolors shook her head. "With your father's antics, not even I have been any help there."

Out beyond the kitchen, the bell over the bakery door jingled and they all looked at each other in a mix of excitement, surprise, and alarm.

"Víctor," Rosa whispered.

"Pau," Dolors called and ran out into the bakery.

Rosa heard her mother gasp and ran out behind her. Standing on their doormat was not Víctor or Pau but a foreign-looking man. He had straw-like hair that reached the back of his collar and a moustache that curved around his startled but smiling mouth. He was looking at them through amber eyes, much like the golden crust of Dolors' *coques*. Montse appeared from behind and seemed to devour them with her own eyes, while Rosa looked upon him in curiosity. He seemed to have a glow about him, like a brilliant aura. Rosa watched as he put down his suitcase and shot straight toward them with an outstretched hand.

"Soy Luc, Amigo de Josep de Quebec," he said in choppy Castilian with a strange French accent.

As Rosa felt his hand warm and strong in hers, Montse appeared between them. She reached for his hand as well, while Dolors held her head with her fists.

"A friend of Josep's from Canada? Today?" Dolors shook her head. "*Estic fins al gorro,*" she said under her breath, attempting to be polite. She headed for the stairs, repeating, "I've had it up to here."

"You'll have to excuse our mother," Rosa said, switching to French. "She's a bit out of sorts today." She tilted her head at him and his familiar-sounding name.

"Most days, really. But the rest of us are entirely normal." Montse gazed at him.

"Is my father expecting you?" Rosa asked.

"Not in the slightest." Luc bit his lip. "He is here, isn't he? I've taken several planes, a bus, and now a car to get here and I haven't slept in days. But I had to come immediately. I can't wait another moment."

Rosa looked at this fellow again, trying to guess his age. He had slight creases at the corner of his eyes and they deepened when he smiled at her. There was something intriguingly exotic about him. There was also something slightly familiar. And then she knew. He was the grown version of the boy standing on the frozen lake in her father's pictures in Canada.

Now she wondered what brought him so many years later to their bakery at the top of the Pyrenees.

***

As Josep made his way the few steps from Àngels' house to his own front door, he was still thinking about the news Àngels had dropped on him, and what he was supposed to do with it. Eduard was unwell. Eduard was stubborn. Eduard was likely, more than anything, a liar. That was when Josep saw the small Renault parked in front of his house. Blinking repeatedly, he looked at it again and ran towards it. It was Gaspard's car. Eduard had come. Eduard was here. He was sure of it.

He ran as quickly as he could but stopped short at the bakery door. If it was Eduard he couldn't show such elation and eagerness. They both knew that Eduard didn't deserve it. Despite his misgivings and his cava-blurred vision, he pushed the bakery door open, the bell above it ringing shrilly. Taking a tentative step inside, he saw the back of a younger man with fair, almost yellow hair. The man turned and Josep focused on this apparition from his past. The toasty skin, the amber eyes so much like his mother's. This time they did not belong to an eight-year-old boy but to an almost middle-aged man. Josep felt his head spin and stomach-ache return. He thought he had shut away the pain of those years. Now here was Luc, standing between his two daughters in his home, his different lives converging once again. Josep saw his own future take on a more perilous shape. He stepped forward, smiling nervously.

CHAPTER NINETEEN

"HAPPY BIRTHDAY, JOSEP," Luc said in French with an accent that brought ancient tunes to Josep's head. "Or can I still call you Papa?"

Josep offered his hand, faltering slightly. He was relieved that he had asked his daughters to give them a moment alone. When Luc's thick grip was in his and he was barely a foot away, he said, "You remember my birthday after all this time." He slapped his shoulder. "Luc, let me take a look at you."

Luc stepped away and turned in a circle, displaying his solid body.

"You've grown into quite the man," Josep said and took his hand again. He examined the fingers. The tip was missing from his left pinkie. Josep once again saw the blood and heard the screaming boy. "It is you. I take it you learned not to touch things you shouldn't." He then wondered what an adult Luc was now doing in his home. "How did you find me?"

"After all your pining over Pujaforta, I figured there was just one place you could be. It is a steep climb, indeed." Luc smoothed his moustache. "Surprised to see me?" He started taking off his corduroy jacket.

Josep gestured to a chair and tried to keep his calm. "Have a seat. So will I. This is all a bit too much for me. How have you been?"

"Since 1946? Well enough, I suppose. Although I'm still waiting for a letter from my so-called father."

"I know. Marie-Claude wrote to say that you were asking questions. But I think you've come a long way for nothing." Josep tried to sound discouraging, while his mind revisited the 1940s and how in addition to the war, this boy had been one of his reasons for staying away so long. He was beginning to feel weak and closed his eyes for a moment. "I'm a bit out of sorts today. It's all been out of the ordinary. Have you heard that our dictator is dead?"

"I wouldn't know what an ordinary life is," Luc said.

"Has it been that bad?" Josep asked, although he didn't want to hear the answer. The guilty part of his conscience was already overflowing. He felt a sharp pain in his stomach.

Luc shrugged. "So you have two daughters."

"And a son. Although apparently no one knows where he is." Josep tried to stand up, but couldn't and collapsed into his chair holding his stomach. He was not up to handling this. Not today. Too much had already happened.

"You're not well. You've had a lot of upset," Luc said, standing. "And I see by the look on your face that I'm not helping." He gave him a sad glance and held up his hands when Josep tried to stand up again. "Don't worry. We will have plenty of time. I'm staying in Adiol la Nova for a while. I think we both need to rest. Then I'll be back with some questions for you." Luc offered Josep his hand to shake. "Happy birthday."

"Thank you for remembering. Not everyone has." Josep shook Luc's broad hand before Luc backed toward the door, where Rosa and Montse were waiting for him.

Josep pushed himself up and slowly climbed the stairs to his bed. Between the excitement of Franco's demise, Àngels' news about Eduard, and Luc's sudden arrival, he was sure that his stomach was bursting with nervous gas as he crawled under the blankets. Now he reckoned would be a good time to smother himself. There he lay attempting both to sleep and to figure out what he could possibly tell Luc that he didn't already know. What could Marie-Claude have told him and why would he come all the way to Pujaforta? Perhaps Luc was working for the Canadian police. Or perhaps he just wanted to get caught up. As Josep turned over all the options in his head, his taxed brain became all the more fatigued, and the scenarios blended into more vivid dreams.

Ever since he had taken to bed, his mind had been skirting from dreams to reality. This time the face of a child-sized Luc appeared from underneath a bed with his cheeks swollen with sweets. Josep was carrying him on his back, running and running, but his feet were sliding and he was getting nowhere. He looked down to see his bare feet on blue ice, which opened to a gaping crack beneath him. A horse's head bobbed to the surface and disappeared. Then a human head emerged. It was Marie-Claude's. Then it was Esmeralda's and then Geneviève's. Each one was gasping for air. Finally a whole body bobbed upward and it was Dolors', but an enormous baguette batted it down until it disappeared beneath the surface. Josep followed the length of the bread from the hole to the hands gripping its end. The face of Franco grinned at him and raised the baguette to clobber him. When he awoke, Josep's hair and shirt were soaked with what he swore was freezing water. He rubbed his arms, caught his breath and remembered the pain in his stomach.

"You're finally awake," Rosa said from the doorway.

"Is he gone?" he asked, sitting up in panic.

"For today," Rosa said. "You've hardly even said hello to me. Today of all days."

"Thank you for coming all this way for my birthday."

"I did come for your birthday, but I was referring to Franco." She sat down on the edge of his bed and took his hand. "Can you believe that after all our efforts it's finally over? And now what? I can't help but think that the regime is all I've ever known."

"Me too, pretty much," Josep said. "We'll have to see what this King Juan Carlos plans to do."

"I hope that you'll keep a low profile until we find out," Rosa said. "No crazy political activities."

"Look who's talking," he said squeezing her hand. "Don't you do anything that calls attention to yourself."

There were footsteps on the stairs.

"At least now we will be saved from listening to all those so-called medical reports," Àngels said from the doorway. Montse and Dolors were behind her and Josep and Rosa waved them inside. Josep could not believe his good fortune in having almost his whole family with him. He thought that maybe he should keep quiet lest he scare them away.

"At the magazine some of us were beginning to think that Franco's son-in-law was covering up. That he'd died ages ago," Rosa said, making room around the bed for the other women of the family. Her voice was quick and her cheeks were reddening.

Dolors held her handkerchief to her chest. "But since he's going to be on display at the Palacio de Oriente, it must be real. That's what they're showing on television, and all those people lining up to see him." Dolors' eyes brightened, the morbid curiosity clear on her face.

"Don't even think of it," Rosa snapped. She was starting to get all worked up. "The endless articles and the protests, maybe they didn't work to change Franco, but it's now that it all counts. Now is the time for the changes. Gawking at a dead man is not going to get us there faster."

"What will these changes mean for Víctor?" Àngels said edging closer. "I have been waiting for this day since I was much younger than you are now. But it means nothing to me if they don't let Víctor go."

Rosa sighed and her bright expression dimmed. "I know. It's meaningless if he's still in there. I've been working for ages on this story about all the families that have been separated, husbands and wives, mothers and children. It was all highly orchestrated. They can't keep doing this to us." Rosa's eyes were burning. "I've heard rumors that they'll free the political prisoners. There have been protests for months."

"But he wouldn't be considered a political prisoner. You saw it with your own eyes. Those people who killed Carrero Blanco wouldn't be considered plain left wing prisoners," Àngels said.

Rosa pointed out the window. "To them left wing would be bad enough. There will be plenty of people out there who fear a communist revolution." She stood up and took Àngels' hands. "Àngels, you have to live your life. We all have to live our lives. I've dedicated years to having Víctor freed." Rosa stroked Àngels' arm. "And I'm not going to stop now. You know what I really wish though?"

Àngels shook her head.

"I wish that you would let Manel come back."

They all nodded emphatically.

Àngels turned her back. "He will never be welcome in my house. He did it himself, with a little help from your father." She ignored Josep, who was now convinced that silence from him was the best strategy. Àngels added, "I don't know where Manel is and I don't care. He is like a Puig to me."

"Personally, I'd like to find Pau," Dolors said. "He should be here with his family on such a day, not with the Vidals." She headed for the door. "I'm going to try to find him and to check on the new batch of bittersweet *coca*."

"You know I don't like *coca*," Josep said. "Don't I get something special for my birthday?" he dared to ask.

"No. Besides, how would you know if you like it or not? It's been years since you tried it. Maybe your lover or your long-lost son will bake something for you," Dolors said and stomped out.

"None of you has brought any cava, have you?" Josep said. "I think we all could use a glass or two. Especially me." The women shook their heads at him as they backed toward the door and shut him in.

The next day was the second of thirty official days of mourning for Francisco Franco. Dolors was in a state of worry, which soon began to spread to the rest of the family. Not only was she not permitted to bake, she still could not find Pau anywhere. When Rosa and the others went in search of him, Rosa was not keen to take the news she learned back to her mother. When she entered the kitchen, she found the counters covered in baking trays, pots and pans, and her mother's hind end sticking out of a cupboard. Dolors pulled her face out from between the empty shelves and looked eagerly at Rosa.

"You told me to keep busy and I can't bake." She wiped her hands. "So where is he?"

"Apparently he's gone over the border." Rosa sighed, brushing off her mother's knees and sitting her in a chair. "He's gone to dance."

"Dance?" Dolors looked bewildered. "With her?"

Rosa nodded. "You should be happy. This is what you've wanted." Rosa pointed toward France. "Geneviève has found him a place in a contemporary dance company."

"Yes, but that was before, when I didn't know what a whore she was." Then Dolors' red face suddenly turned upward. "My son, Pau, is a real danseur?"

"In France. Imagine."

"Why wouldn't he tell us? Why wouldn't he say goodbye?"

"Because not only is he an excellent dancer, he is very smart."

Dolors hid her face. "Now I officially am in mourning." She uncovered her eyes and said, "He is excellent, isn't he?"

Outside the house, car brakes squeaked and Rosa's and Dolors' eyes met. "Maybe he's come back." Before either of them could reach the door, Montse had run in front of them and was opening it and grasping Luc's shoulders in each hand. Rosa noticed that rather than the usual bun, her sister's hair was wrapped in an elaborate twist on the back of her head and her face was velvety with powder, some of which rubbed onto Luc's cheeks when she greeted him.

"Luc, you're back. Did you have a comfortable night? I've heard that the hotel in Adiol la Nova is nice but very expensive," Montse said.

Dolors groaned and Rosa watched her mother escape up the stairs. She then went to the kitchen drawer to fetch an old, curled photograph that she had hidden there earlier. She had been very busy investigating recently. Finding out about her family was almost as challenging as getting information from the fascist regime. As she felt the photograph's corrugated edges, her fingers tingled. Stepping eagerly towards Luc, she noticed that under his coat, the top two buttons of his shirt were open revealing a sprinkling of very soft-looking chest hair. Slowly she approached to give him two kisses. When he leaned down she found that his sideburns were soft and his odor was spicy. She held up the picture so that he could see it.

"Is this you?" she asked.

Luc squinted and took the picture from her, staring at it in silence. A fair-haired boy stood on the edge of a frozen lake clutching a toque to his chest. He nodded slowly. "So Josep kept this," he said looking up. "What has he told you about me?"

"Nothing. Well, very little," Rosa said and shrugged. "He kept the picture hidden away. I found it when I was really young, since I've always been a tad curious." When she saw his expression she was afraid that she might have hurt his feelings. "In fact, I've always been very curious about you," she added.

"You have?" Luc stepped closer to Rosa and gently held the picture between his chest and the palm of his hand. "You were interested in knowing about me?" He sounded surprised.

"Yes, I was, and I still am," Rosa said. "Really, though, I think I was hoping to learn more about my father."

"Which is why I've come here as well." Luc nodded and held Rosa's look. "I'm also hoping he will help me understand some things about myself. Is he here?"

"He's here and he said to send you up to see him. Good luck to you, though," Montse said. "Getting our father to talk about those days is like teaching a deaf man to sing, but I'm sure you can persuade him. You may have to stay a while." She helped Luc take off his coat. "In my opinion, *Pare* never mentioned you for our mother's sake." She folded his jacket over her arm and stroked it. "She tends to be jealous."

"Your father was always a bit stubborn and was a bit of a womanizer," Luc said and shook his head. "That I do remember." As he looked up, Rosa raised her camera and took his picture, which was what she tended to do when she was nervous. The camera provided a perfect barrier between her and her subject. She recognized this in herself, but failed to know why Luc's presence would make her nervous. Perhaps it was the way he looked straight into her.

"You're an artist," Luc said, and nodded as if he had found an answer to a puzzle.

Rosa lowered her camera and clicked her tongue. "I'm no artist. I record events. I told you I'm curious by nature."

"Maybe one day you can show me your photographs."

"That has not panned out well in the past." Montse took Luc's arm and guided him to the stairs toward Josep's room. "But that must mean that you will be staying for a while." Her look and her voice indicated that she hoped he would.

"Perhaps," Luc said. "I'm in no hurry."

"Well, then, you should stay here with us." Montse turned to Rosa. "He could stay in the attic, in Víctor's bed."

"No, not Víctor's room. No one can stay in Víctor's room but Víctor." Rosa knew her face was red and could hear the snap in her tone. "Luc could stay in Pau's room until he returns. Or mine. I have to go back to Barcelona in a few days."

"That's very kind of you," Luc said and stepped closer. "It's a shame that you have to go, since I thought that we could all get to know each other. If I had such a family, I wouldn't be so keen to leave it."

"And Manel's house is empty," Rosa said quietly.

"Yes," Montse said almost jumping up and down. "Luc can stay there. That's perfect. No one's using it."

"Maybe we should ask Àngels first," Rosa said, thinking of what a delicate state Àngels was still in.

"I'm tired of asking for permission around here," Montse said. "Pau didn't even say goodbye, never mind ask anyone's opinion. Besides, Àngels hardly leaves her house and all the men in this family up and leave."

"Some haven't been given a choice," Rosa said, while also thinking that with Manel and Víctor away, and with Uncle Eduard still not surfacing, it might be nice to have someone new around the house to spice up the Balaguer lives. She reckoned her father could use it, and was excited to see what such a mix might reveal.

***

"What now?" Josep said when Luc knocked on his door. He was sitting on the edge of his bed trying to put on his shoes but was unable to bend over.

"You said to come back today. Is this a good time?" Luc said.

"I suppose it's now or never, though never would be better." He glanced up at Luc. "Sorry. Listen, would you help me put my shoes on? All these years have been hard on my back. Then we can sit by the window. I need to get out of this bed."

Luc knelt at Josep's feet and slid his shoes over his socks. "I've been chatting with your daughters," he said. "Rosa said she won't be staying long. I suppose she has to go back to her family in the city."

"She's with her family now. Her work is in the city."

"Her work? Is she a photographer?"

Josep nodded. "Yes and a journalist, and an activist. She's been trying to have a family member released from prison. With Franco's death, we hope things will change. I'm telling you this so that you realize that life here is not just free time." Josep patted Luc on the back and led him to the armchair by the window. "So how about you, are you married?" They sat across from each other. The morning sun filtered through the lace curtains and splashed their pattern across Luc's face. It made his cheekbones all the more prominent and his eyes more penetrating.

Luc shook his head. "I've never had any luck with women. Unlike you, I hear."

"I have had anything but luck. Women only bring me misery. You should be thankful. Life is less complicated without them."

"But boring," Luc said and slowly raised the black and white photograph of himself as a boy. "Your daughter showed me this. She said she was curious about me."

Josep glanced at the old picture and shook his head. "That's my Rosa. For years she's been hounding me to tell her about those days."

"But you haven't."

"What's there to tell?"

"I'm hoping that you will tell me."

Josep smirked. "There's really not much to say. First, tell me about life in Walamagou." He had hardly thought of that place for decades, but was feeling slightly nostalgic. Ever since his blow-out with Geneviève, he had done nothing but lie alone in his bed. He then thought of one of the first women who had mattered greatly to him. "How is Marie-Claude? I haven't heard from her in quite some time."

"Marie-Claude still lives in Walamagou and I visit her occasionally. That town was too small for me." Luc leaned forward. "Last time I saw her was not long after Thomas' funeral. I helped her sort through his things."

"Thomas' funeral? Last time she wrote she said her husband was going on a fishing trip."

Luc looked at his hands crossed in his lap. "I told him not to go. I knew that those trips were lies. They would go down to Party meetings in the States. This time he didn't come back." Luc looked out the window and back at Josep. "He was like a father to me. I seem to have a lot of those."

Josep sucked in his breath. "Before we dig up any old stories, tell me why they're important to you."

"They're about my life. They may help me with some things. I'm almost in my forties and I have never managed to have a lasting relationship with anyone. Well, women, really. They eventually turn away. So I lose myself in my work, the result of which people strangely do like. I seem to become one with the wood, stone, or whatever I'm sculpting. I've had a lot of success. Then I got a commission for a sculpture and I drew a blank. I was no longer even in tune with my work. The theme was 'mother as a girl' and I realized that I didn't even know my mother as a woman." Luc leaned forward and put his elbows on his knees. "Marie-Claude said you might be able to help me."

"Why couldn't you have just based it on Marie-Claude? She must have been the closest you had to a mother."

Luc nodded. "But she's not my real mother." He looked up. "Marie-Claude is the one who sent me to see you. For me and for herself."

Josep frowned. "Why would she do that?"

"She said that at one time you almost brought her back here with you. Her life would have been entirely different. She also said that ever since Thomas died you've been on her mind."

"We knew each other decades ago." Josep shook his head, thinking that he had enough problems with Dolors.

"She said she has dreams and you keep appearing in them. And I've been having nightmares. Mainly to do with my mother. I think you have the answers that can make them all stop."

"You already know what happened to your mother. Why didn't you just send me a letter? I could have told you that there's nothing to say." Josep was starting to feel his life collapsing around him. His mind was going down a tunnel into his past, a tunnel that until now he had managed to keep air tight. His stay in Canada belonged to another life, to another Josep Balaguer. Surely they couldn't hold him responsible for events occurring in another lifetime. Plus now Dolors and his family would be asking him plenty of questions. Rosa wasn't the only curious one.

"I had to see you in person. I needed to understand who is guilty of what." Luc stopped and stood. "Long ago I had also hoped that you would bring me back here rather than abandoning me." He looked toward the window. "I'll let you rest for now. You look exhausted. We can talk about this later. I don't plan on giving up."

Josep slowly led Luc downstairs with the intention of heading off any of his family's speculations. He was also dreading any discussions with Dolors, with whom he had yet to address the matter of his affair or much else for months. When he entered the kitchen, he found his wife standing in the middle of the room like a round paper weight intent on fixing all the loose elements in place. Dolors' earlier cleaning spree had turned the kitchen upside down. All of the cooking implements were stacked on the countertop, many of them dating from before the war. One large iron pot in particular Josep knew had been a wedding present to their joint grandparents. When Josep saw Dolors he stopped short and didn't even notice Luc vanish out the door. Montse broke the spell.

"It's all arranged," Montse said and clasped her fingers under her chin. "Luc is going to stay here. In Manel's shack. Isn't that wonderful?"

Josep and Dolors stood staring at each other. Josep grasped his back and fell into a chair. "What's wonderful about it? Why didn't you ask me first?" he said.

"Frankly, I'm sick and tired of asking."

"I'll tell you about sick and tired," Dolors said and as she raised her finger at Josep, their daughters escaped out the door. "You see," Dolors continued, wagging her finger. "This will give you plenty of time to get caught up with one of your sons, while the other has left us to dance with your lover."

"What are you talking about?" Josep held up his hands. "I know Pau's gone and I'm sorry. But it's not my fault. I didn't even know he was a dancer, did I? You can't blame me for your entire miserable life." He took a deep breath. "For as much as it's worth, I had no idea that Geneviève had befriended you."

"Well, not all my life is miserable, just the parts involving you." Dolors covered her face. "That explains everything, why you were never interested in me." She was weeping and would not lower her hands.

"That's not true. You're the one who wasn't interested in me. A man can only last so long."

Dolors' hands dropped to the table. "And women, what do you think we're made of? Do you think we're impenetrable stone? Well, we're not." Dolors pointed upstairs. "And how do you explain this Luc character? What other affairs have you been hiding over the years?"

Josep frowned. "I'm not hiding anything."

"Marie-Claude."

"There is nothing to hide. All that happened before we were married, before we were even a couple, when we were just cousins."

"And since then I always thought that above all we were friends. As a friend you would have told me all of this." Dolors looked him in the eye.

"Friends don't get so jealous," Josep said. "You were angry every time I mentioned Canada, every time I received a letter."

"I've read your letters, so don't you dare look innocent with me."

Josep frowned, shrugged, and although he could not think of what letters she could be referring to, he still felt suddenly very guilty.

***

Knowing enough not to be caught in the parental crossfire, Rosa and Montse dashed from the kitchen and took cover in Manel's cabin. For now, both seemed equally excited that Luc had agreed to come and stay with them. Rosa could still feel the grip of his hands on hers and the luster in his eyes when she said she had wanted to know more about him. She assumed that it was knowing that he was the key to finally filling in some of the blanks in her father's life that captivated her so. Montse, on the other hand, was more than captivated. She was flush with excitement and Rosa had never seen her so enthused about anything, even baking.

As they stepped into Manel's living area, it looked just like it had before Àngels sent him away, except that Manel wasn't in it. An empty coffee cup sat on the table beside an old newspaper announcing that the Generalísimo was fighting his illness like a warrior. A half-full bottle of cognac sat beside the coffee maker. As Rosa and Montse began to remove the months of dust from Manel's hand-carved furniture, hide away his personal effects, and strip the single bed, Montse shook out the clean sheet with such flourish that Rosa could feel Montse's excitement in the snap. Luc's arrival seemed to supersede any feelings about Manel, Pau's, or even Franco's departure.

"You seem awfully keen on Luc," Rosa said. "Don't get too excited yet. We hardly know him."

"I know." Montse tucked the top sheet tightly across the narrow bed. "He's just so handsome, foreign, different. You seem to like him as well."

"Anything is different outside Pujaforta."

"Listen to the great world traveler. Between you and Pau, I obviously am not as worldly. I never leave the kitchen."

"That's not what I'm saying."

"You're saying for me not to jump at the first fellow who comes through the door."

"Or the second," Rosa said. "First there was our cousin Gaspard."

"I didn't know he was our cousin. And I didn't jump on him." Montse pulled a blanket from Rosa's hands.

"You were rather eager, but with our parents being cousins, you'd better look further afield."

"Like Canada," Montse said. "It's easy for you in the city with so many to choose from. Not many men walk through this door and then Luc did."

"I only want one man to walk through it," Rosa said and she really meant it.

"I know." Montse nodded in encouragement. "Now they'll probably release him."

"They're saying they might, so I'm praying, so to speak. I've also sent more letters." Rosa sat on the edge of the bed. "Last time I saw Víctor he looked so helpless and I'm sure he doesn't tell me half of what goes on in there. He's lost so much weight that his eyes seem even bigger. He looks at me imploringly and I feel so helpless. And guilty."

"What do you have to feel guilty about?" Montse looked panicked.

"Because I'm living a normal life. I'm free."

"So Luc has nothing to do with it?" Montse asked softly.

"Luc? What would he have to do with it? We've only just met."

"Can I ask you a favor?"

"Of course." Rosa stood and gently put her hand on Montse's shoulder.

"Let me have Luc, if he wants me, that is." Montse looked at the bulk of her bosom and held out her wide leg. "I've got to do something."

"You're fine. You're lovely." Rosa shook her slightly. "You're also lovely in here." She pointed to Montse's chest. "You don't need a man to prove that."

"Maybe I do." Montse thrust out her breasts. "One thing I am not is a shadow. Nothing I do can ever compare to your accomplishments. But I'm going to make them see."

"Montse, we're different people. No one can compare us."

"But they do. You haven't promised." Montse took Rosa's hand. "Give me a chance with Luc."

Rosa kissed Montse on the cheek. "I promise. We hardly even know him. But he's all yours if you want him."

Montse returned the kiss to Rosa's cheek. "I'll be back in a couple of hours. I'm going for a walk up the mountain."

"What for?"

"Exercise. Why, did you need anything?"

"Let's be thankful that's all over with. We've had too many casualties up there. Speaking of which, before you go, why don't we see how the duel has turned out."

Rosa and Montse made their way back to the house, through the garden and a fresh sprinkling of snow. They both cringed as they opened the door. Inside there was silence. Josep was sitting at the table with his shoulders at his ears and Dolors was covering her face with her hands. They both looked up when the door squeaked.

"Luc's gone to get his things and Manel's house is all ready," Montse said inching towards them.

Both Josep and Dolors sighed, for likely different reasons.

"For once we have people coming to visit, not leaving," Montse said. "Why don't you want him to stay here?"

Josep looked at the floor, while Dolors grunted and tilted her head at Josep. "Don't you think it's time you told us? I know what you've been up to."

"You do?" Josep said, looking back into his memory for any possible information leaks to his wife. "And what would that be exactly?"

Dolors dropped her hands to her lap and sighed. "I know he's your secret son." She nodded at her daughters as if to prove a point, then she scowled at Josep. "I read that letter from Marie-Claude. I've known all this time."

"Who? Luc?" Montse looked horrified.

Josep looked at his wife's reddening face. "You couldn't read that. Besides, your facts are wrong."

"I had it translated. Geneviève helped me."

"So what are the facts?" Rosa said frowning at Josep, while Montse looked about to faint.

"He is not my son." Josep stood as if to deliver his final word. "He's the son of a woman I knew. His mother asked me to take care of him for her and I did. Are you satisfied?"

"I am extremely relieved," Montse said and ran for the door. "I'm going out to get some exercise."

***

Meanwhile, Àngels continued to shut herself away in her house. Even the death of Franco and her momentary truce with Josep had failed to pull her out of doors for any length of time. She kept Eduard's key and letter like a centerpiece on her table, a constant reminder of her worries about his declining health. She was spending too much time thinking. Perhaps Josep was right and she was reading too much between the lines. Eduard's words and her circumstances spun together in her head and she began to fear they were once again running off with her mind. Her uncomfortable nights did not help. She had taken to sleeping on the love seat rather than tossing and turning in the bed made by Manel.

One day she noticed movement outside her window near Manel's house. How could he have the nerve to come back? As she carefully peered outside, daring not to be seen, she saw that it was actually Rosa, Montse, and that Luc fellow. She had yet to know what had brought that man here. But Luc was the least of her concerns. Now, even with Franco gone, it was not clear what course things were taking. There seemed to be no talk of what mattered most to her. Her expression soured as she thought of having to rely on Carles Puig to fulfil a favor and bring her any hopes for Víctor.

As she peeked out the window again at Luc, she found that something about him reminded her of Víctor. Perhaps it was his height or the way he kept his hands in his front pockets as he walked. Like Víctor, his genes were clearly a mixed ensemble. Luc's skin was toasty but his eyes were light, at least that is how she remembered them gazing at Rosa the first time she had seen him. Àngels let the curtain fall between them and stepped away from the window. If they had found a use for Manel's house, all the power to them, she thought. It would at least keep Manel out of it. In the meantime, she was sure that Rosa would find out exactly what Luc was doing here and just how it involved Josep. As Àngels sat firmly in her chair, she knew that she would not be the one to worry about it. Her brother had already involved Víctor and Manel in his antics, and now too many of them were paying.

***

When Rosa left for the city, Luc was well settled in at Manel's little house. His presence had lightened the heavy atmosphere since the departures of Pau and Manel. Even Dolors' mood had lifted, perhaps due to Montse's infectious glee. Montse ran up and down the mountain every day and had stopped sampling the baked goods or practically eating anything at all. Rosa felt drawn to the new energy at home and came back to Pujaforta each weekend. Every time she opened the door she felt the newness in the air and wondered if she had let her work and her quest for Víctor's release prevent her from enjoying her own life.

Meanwhile, in the city the protests continued; the King had sworn allegiance to the remaining *Franquista* government, thus turning Spain back into a monarchy and dashing any Republican hopes. However, as the new King and the old regime clashed, hopes for democracy were rekindled. Most people were just keen for peace, with many subtly switching sides and counting on ephemeral memory. With the Pact of Forgetting, many were willing to turn a blind eye and move onward, while others had new demands. As ETA and GRAPO stepped up their terrorist activities, Rosa hoped that it would not jeopardize Víctor's chances for release. On every prison visit, she found that both her patience and Víctor's were growing thin. Her regular trips to Pujaforta served as a hiatus, as if the town on the top of the mountain was an island parked far away from the troubles of the day.

As time went on, Luc would come and go from Pujaforta, but he would always be there when Rosa came home. On one occasion she returned to find Luc kneeling before the base of a thick log he had begun to sculpt into a soft curve, which he was stroking with his large but delicate hands. Each time she returned the sculpture had grown, gradually taking the form of a woman floating into a pronounced S shape. The wood of her skin was worn smooth by Luc's files and hands. As Rosa stroked its softness and glanced at the hands that had made it so, she touched her blushing cheek and turned away. She could not let herself be tempted by this man who had managed to fill a gap that most of them hadn't even realized existed. Rosa nonetheless knew deep down that while exotic and artistically gifted, Luc could never take the place of her Víctor. Plus she had a budding premonition that Víctor would soon be free. He would return to Pujaforta and they could all look forward rather than back. Of all the Balaguers, however, it was Josep who did not seem uplifted by Luc's presence. It was clear that after endless conversations, he was not interested in looking back at all.

***

With Luc staying right outside their door, Josep and he had long conversations over the weeks and months, but so far Josep had managed to avoid the details of Josep's sojourn in Quebec. Instead, Josep shared his stories of smuggling across the mountains and even found himself telling Luc about his visit so long ago with Eduard. He had already admitted to Geneviève that he had killed a woman, but he could not confess to this boy, or rather man, the person it most affected. Josep hoped that Luc would grow bored and abandon this journey into the past.

They were sitting across from each other in the armchairs by the window in his bedroom. Each man wore a blanket across his thighs due to the chilliness of the early spring air outside and the dampness of the old farm house's stone walls.

Luc was shaking his head. "You're telling me that after all your years of pining to come back, all your stories about having to find your brother, you actually found him and you haven't spoken since?"

"You wouldn't understand."

"Why wouldn't I? I know all about family turmoil."

"Eduard doesn't understand and he doesn't want to understand. I gave up years of my life to set him free. He has never even acknowledged it."

"Does it really matter? I was with you during those years you say you gave up. It wasn't that bad, was it?"

Josep shook his head and looked out the window as if into his past. Although he had not wanted to get into it, he thought that if he co-operated a little, Luc might actually go away. "No, it wasn't. You need to know that. The worst part was when I had to leave you in Montreal."

"Yet you never tried to find out what happened to me."

"I couldn't. I had to leave it behind me. When my ship sailed I left that life on the other side of the ocean. Everywhere I went I brought disaster. I told you that I don't intend to bring that all up now."

"So you left me, just like the rest of my family did."

"Your mother didn't want to leave you. She was a simple woman with a complicated life."

"And bad choice in men."

Josep shrugged. "Perhaps."

"So what do you know about my real father?"

"I can't know much more than you do. Your mother was scared to death of him. She even asked me to take you to Marie-Claude. Since she was the schoolteacher she thought she would protect you."

"I remember always being afraid of my father. Maybe I still am since I have yet to see him." Luc sighed. "When they let him out of prison, he wanted to visit me. But he's the real reason why I left Walamagou. When he was released, the scandal was in the newspapers again and I felt like everyone was judging me, the son of the whore who was murdered by her husband. So I left."

Josep leaned forward. He was trying to put all the information into place. "So they thought your father killed your mother." When Josep realized that he had said this aloud, he thought it wiser to quickly change the course of the conversation. "When you left, Marie-Claude must have been upset," Josep said, but he was thinking of all those years in prison.

"She was, but she has her own children to worry about and to take care of her."

"She and Thomas had kids?"

"Three. They all moved to Montreal and became doctors and lawyers. They wanted me to go to university, too, but that wasn't for me. I told you how I need to create things and use my hands. Somehow being here has managed to release that block I had, you know, the one about my mother."

Josep again tried to veer the conversation away from the recurring topic. "What about all those exhibitions of your work you were telling me about? Don't you need to go visit them?" Josep hoped that he did. It was like this young man had excavated Josep's former life, his former self, and Josep wanted him to leave before it buried him.

"The exhibitions can do without me. Besides, there is still so much I need to know," Luc said. "And you've probably noticed that I'm quite taken with your daughter."

"Yes, Montse seems quite taken with you. She's slimming down. You're having quite the influence on her."

"I've noticed that she hardly eats a thing." Luc winced slightly. "But I was referring to Rosa. She visits me when I'm sculpting and to tell you the truth, I think she's the one who has managed to dislodge that block I had."

"Rosa? Really? She is an inspiration to many of us, but she definitely has her sights elsewhere." Josep frowned. "Though she has been spending a lot of time at home lately." He felt a sudden flare of heartburn.

***

Weeks later when Rosa came for a visit, she couldn't believe Montse's transformation. Her blouse was baggy around her middle and her cheekbones were well defined. Rosa kept her comments to herself at first but then took Montse's hand, which felt bony rather than puffy, and touched Montse's sallow cheek with her other hand.

"Montse," she said. "What you're doing is unhealthy. Let me get settled and we'll go see Dr. Sort. He can give you a proper diet. You're melting before our eyes, and I'm afraid that one day we'll find you in a puddle on the floor."

Montse pulled away. "I feel fine. I feel better than I've ever felt. You don't want me to be thin because you're afraid that Luc will like me more. How do you expect me to ever find a husband?"

Rosa rolled her eyes. "Don't be ridiculous. I want you to be happy, but I want you to be healthy. No one will want to be with you if you're weak and sickly or if you starve yourself to death." She sighed and sat down. "Speaking of which, I'm worried about Víctor. He says that if they don't let him out soon, he'll start a hunger strike."

"But you said that they would be letting him out."

"It's taking too long."

"Then shouldn't you be in Barcelona rather than here? Or in Madrid? What can you do from Pujaforta?"

"I can see you and recover my sanity a little," Rosa said, although her conscience told her she would be better in Barcelona, where she wouldn't be tempted into being a traitor to both Víctor and her sister. When she was in the city she found herself thinking too much about Luc. Then when she was in Pujaforta she thought about both Luc and Víctor, and much of it was guilt.

"You never used to come so much. Now that Luc's here you come all the time."

"It's nice having him around." Rosa looked at the table. "You would certainly agree."

"I would. But remember your promise."

Rosa squinted and tilted her head. "Yes, the promise. Don't worry. Luc is the farthest from my thoughts."

There were footsteps on the stairs.

"Hello ladies," Luc said and headed straight for Rosa. He was freshly showered and his chin-length hair was fluffy and soft. "I'm so glad you're back. It's almost finished. I can't wait to show you," he said, taking her hands and kissing her on the cheek. When he stepped back he didn't let go of her fingers. Rosa looked down at his strong hands worn smooth and pulled her hands away.

Montse reached over and took him by the finger. "Is this from a sculpting accident?" She held his hand flat on her palm and motioned to his shortened pinkie.

Luc pulled his hand away and held it behind his back. "It's from getting my hands on things I shouldn't. I'm good at that." He glanced at Rosa. "It was a firecracker. Your father was there when it happened and he took me to the hospital. It's all foggy for me. He could probably tell you about it, though he hasn't told me much."

"Our uncle lost a couple of fingers in a similar accident, but our father won't tell us anything about that either," Montse said and then gasped. "I've just remembered. Rosa, we've received a letter from Pau. It's so exciting. He's going to dance in Paris." Montse ran towards the stairs. "I'll get the letter from *Mare*. I'll be right back."

As soon as Montse was up the stairs, Luc grasped Rosa's hands again, but she slowly pulled them away. "I can't wait to see what you think," he said and rested an arm on her shoulder. "I have an idea, but don't say anything yet. I just want you to think about it."

Rosa nodded, feeling him squeeze her shoulder and she found herself leaning into the strength of it. She had been imagining an arm like that around her for so long. She slowly stepped away and faced him, curious to know what he wanted her to think about.

Luc looked her in the eye and took her hand. "I told you how when I've finished this sculpture it will be part of an exhibition in Montreal."

Rosa nodded.

"Your work deserves to be seen as much as mine does," Luc continued. "All those photographs. I could use my contacts with galleries in Canada. What do you think?"

Rosa blinked and clutched his hand. She had had to hide her pictures away for so long she had never considered the idea of being able to show them openly. She sighed. "Montreal is so far away. Besides, I don't think I'm ready to show my work."

"I told you to just think about it." He brushed a fingertip across her lips. "So don't answer yet. There's something else I'd like you to think about. What if I were to come to see you in Barcelona? You could show me the city, maybe even introduce me to some people there. We could even have some time alone."

Rosa shook her head and slowly released his hand. "I'm not ready. And in fact, I never will be." She looked down at his large shoes on either side of hers. "I've made a promise to Montse and to Víctor. I've also made one to myself."

"I'd like to make a promise to you too. Maybe you should think about what you really want." He stepped closer. The sunlight was shining through the window straight into his amber eyes. He touched the tips of her curls and rubbed them between his fingers. "It's because I'm older. Or because I'm from so far away. You think I won't fit in."

"That is actually what I find most intriguing about you. You look nothing like anyone around here." She was looking into his eyes, at his fair eyelashes and at the dark skin across his cheekbones. "Why am I always drawn to things exotic? Why can't I just be simple and normal?" she asked aloud, but the question was for herself.

"I'm drawn to what finally feels so comfortable. I came here hoping that your father would help me understand myself better, and he's hardly budged. Meanwhile you have given me so much."

"Luc, I haven't done anything."

"You listen to me. You're supportive of what I do."

Rosa heard footsteps on the stairs. She jumped back and brushed Luc's hand from her hair. "So, Montse, what does Pau's letter say?" she called.

Montse approached them and unfolded the single sheet of paper. "It says that Pau has joined a jazz dancing company and he's going to be traveling all around France. He's going to Marseille, Toulouse, Bordeaux and then to Paris. Imagine, Paris." She laughed but then she stopped. "He says that Geneviève is accompanying him." She sighed and held the letter to her chest. "At least that keeps him away from the Vidal family. Imagine, little Pau jazz dancing all over the place."

"What exactly is jazz dancing?" Luc asked.

"It's like fast, modern ballet to contemporary music," Rosa said. "I think."

"You don't know?"

Rosa shrugged. "I haven't seen him dance in a long time. It was tricky. We had to keep it a secret from *Pare*."

"And that wasn't easy," Montse said. "Considering he was having an affair with Pau's teacher."

"What? He hasn't told me about that."

"That's why you need to stay longer," Montse said. *"Pare* is full of stories."

Luc stepped between the sisters and took both their hands. "I have an idea. Let's go to see your brother. Toulouse isn't that far from here."

Montse looked suddenly pale. "France? You would take me to France?" Then she collapsed like the oxygen had left her.

"Poor Montse." Rosa knelt beside Montse and slapped her cheek. "I told her she had to start eating."

Luc held Montse's head in the crook of his arm and looked across her at Rosa. "I would love to take you to France. I would take you anywhere you want to go."

Rosa slowly backed away.

***

"So I hear that you like French dance teachers," Luc said to Josep the following morning.

"What? I do not," Josep said. "Not any more. I'm too old for such nonsense."

"Does Dolors know about it?"

"She does." Josep lifted an eyebrow. "And she's still recovering. Here she was jealous of Marie-Claude because she sent me a letter."

"So you ended it because Dolors found out."

"No, I ended it because, like most women I've been mixed up with, she misrepresented herself, to put it lightly."

"Did my mother misrepresent herself, as you put it?"

"Not intentionally." Josep looked at the ceiling for a moment and then looked straight at Luc and sighed. This could be his chance to be rid of him. "Listen, I'll tell you everything I know. You were there and you must remember something. Then I want you to agree to be on your way. I hear that this sculpture you've been working on is finished. After all this time, they must be expecting you somewhere, not here on the top of a mountain in the middle of nowhere."

Luc nodded. "If you tell me, I'll move on for now. I want to know how she died, but first tell me how you met her."

Josep swallowed, looked at his hands, and smiled despite himself. "I met your mother on an ice delivery. She opened the door and she was so strikingly different I almost dropped the ice block from my back. There was a huge chandelier overhead and it seemed to drip light onto her dark hair and to sparkle in her amber eyes, just like yours." He pointed to Luc's face. "It was the mix with native blood. I'd never seen such a thing before. I'd also heard that it was a place where you could pay women for their company." Josep cleared his throat. "We were isolated from everything. This is a metropolis in comparison. There were lots of men working in the lumber business, far away from their families. You get the picture. Anyway, I just wanted to talk to her. I was intrigued by her but I was already in love with Marie-Claude. So I used to spend afternoons chatting with your mother. She had run away from your father to protect herself and above all to protect you. Do you remember that? You were always with her. We all spent so much time together."

"When I was little, my father always told me she was a whore. That I remember. I also remember the day that I learned what that word really means. Then I thought that my father was using it figuratively as an insult. But he wasn't, was he?"

Josep shook his head. "She decided to be what everyone expected her to be. She had some very faithful regular customers, most of all me. I used to think that by taking up her time talking, I was helping to save her."

"I remember that you used to always bring tins of sweets and we used to spend hours playing cards and a board game."

"Pachisi. We did have a lot of fun, didn't we?"

Luc smiled at him and they looked at each other and then out the window, both lost in the train of memories.

Josep sighed. "The rest you must remember, but you have to know that I had intended to take the two of you to Montreal. That's what I suggested that last night. I had the tickets arranged for Marie-Claude and me to get a ship to Europe. We were going to leave you and your mother with some friends in Montreal."

"So why didn't you?" Luc's eyes were damp and drilling into his.

"You were there. I refuse to get into all of that now. You wanted to know about your mother and I've told you." Josep stood and stretched his back. "I think our work here is done, don't you?"

Luc sat staring at the floor in front of Josep's feet. "So you refuse to tell me anything else."

"Luc, listen, we've been through it all a million times. Besides you were there. So if you put it that way, yes. I've told you all I plan to and I think you should be moving on. Please send Marie-Claude my regards."

Slowly Luc stood. "So, that's it then?" He raised his index finger. "Fine, I will move on. But I'll tell you something. I will see my real father after all. I think I'd like to hear what he has to say. Then I just may be back." Luc reached out to shake his hand and when Josep took it, Luc almost crushed his fingers in his grip. Luc nodded, turned and walked out.

Josep sat in his chair with his jaw tight, his eyes fixed on the closed door, and his hand stinging. He also felt the pain in his stomach stronger than ever and looked outside to the sky. Not for the first time he was praying that God would take him long before Luc ever returned.

***

When Luc came down the stairs in a flash, Rosa and Montse were standing at the bottom. Rosa had heard the door upstairs bang and wondered if it was intentional or a draft. Luc's face suggested the former; his look was angry and distracted. A car door slammed outside the house, but no one appeared to hear it.

"What happened?" Montse said.

"What's the matter?" Rosa said and touched Luc's shoulder, but he shook her hand away. Then his eyes seemed to focus, his expression calmed, and he looked serenely into Rosa's face.

"Your father wants me to leave," he said pacing slowly in a circle. "I've already been away from home far too long. I can't stay where I'm not wanted."

"But you are wanted here," Montse said and looked on the verge of tears. "*Pare* has no right to do this to me."

Luc didn't seem to hear her. "I have to find my father," he said, and put a hand on Rosa's cheek. He looked into her eyes. "You could come back with me. Come to Quebec with me. Bring your photographs. We could help each other."

Rosa stepped back. "I can't." She glanced at Montse, who was standing beside the window and fortunately seemed distracted.

"Rosa," Montse said anxiously and Rosa brushed Luc's hand away.

"Rosa," Montse said again and waved Rosa towards her. She was pushing aside the curtain. "You have to come here."

Rosa felt the urgency in her voice pull her toward the window. A face passed in front of it and her heart jumped to her mouth. She threw open the door.

"Víctor!" she cried and stood staring and blinking, unsure if the sight was really him. He was as thin as the last time she had seen him, but now his gray-flecked hair shone under the sun rather than under fluorescent lighting. When he looked at her, she knew it was real. His eyes locked on hers and she threw her arms around his neck. She felt his hands gripping her back and his tall thinness along her front as he rocked her back and forth and breathed into her hair.

"Rosa," he said. "Rosa, Rosa." As they rocked and held each other, Rosa could still not believe it. Finally, she pulled away and looked up at him.

"Víctor, how, when?" She shook her head at him. "How did you get here? I would have come."

He smiled slightly. "I got a lift. After years of hell, they actually gave me the royal treatment. Maybe things are changing."

Rosa held his waist and put her cheek flat against his chest. "It's about time they did. There were times I feared I would never see the day." She pulled away. "But I never entirely lost hope, not even for a second."

"Lucky for me you didn't." He kissed her cheek and held her tightly against him. Rosa inhaled the stale prison smell on his clothes, taking her to that dingy visiting room. But the smell of Víctor's skin brought her back. She felt a light tapping on her shoulder and slowly pulled away.

"Hello, Montse," Víctor said, releasing Rosa and hugging Montse. "You're looking almost as thin as I am."

Montse grinned and pulled away. "Are we ever glad to see you back. I was afraid you might never come home."

"I knew that Rosa would never let that happen," Víctor said looking at Rosa, then his gaze fixed behind her. Luc stepped forward proffering his hand, but his eyebrows were joined in a frown.

"Sóc en Luc," he said in the basic Catalan they had taught him.

Víctor tilted his head at him and said, "Víctor." He gave Rosa an inquiring look and she waved it away. She should have plenty of time to fill Víctor in on the latest drama in Pujaforta.

"I realize this is a big moment and I hate to interrupt," Luc said in French. "But, Rosa, do you mind if we have a quick word about what we were just talking about?" He whispered to her, "So does this mean that you won't come away with me?"

Rosa gripped Víctor's hand and said loudly and confidently, "Yes, I already told you I won't go with you." Rosa glanced at Montse who drew closer.

"I will," Montse said and took Luc's hands. "Tell me that you want me to."

"You would come all the way to Quebec with me?" Luc asked her, looking incredulous and instantly happier.

"I would go anywhere with you," Montse said. "Just tell me when we're leaving."

"Now," he said, freeing his hands. "I'm going to pack my things. If you're coming, I suggest you do the same." He nodded at Rosa and Víctor and went out the door towards Manel's house.

"Montse," Rosa said gripping her arm. "Don't be mad. You can't run off with Luc. We don't even know him that well."

"I know him perfectly. And it's about time I did something, don't you think?" Montse said, trying to break free. "Víctor, I'm really thrilled that you're back, and I apologize for leaving before we've had a chance to catch up, but I can't let him go without me." Montse pulled her arm from Rosa's grip and dashed for the stairs. "I'll explain once I've packed."

As Rosa stood stunned, Víctor put an arm around her. "I see that my timing is not the best."

"Amor, I wouldn't want to wait another millisecond," Rosa said and hugged him again.

"I'll tell you what," he said, stroking her hair and kissing the top of her head. "Àngels doesn't know I'm back. Why don't I go see her? That will give you all a little time together with Montse without my arrival stirring things up. Later I expect you to tell me who that fellow is."

Rosa hugged him more tightly and felt his chest against her cheek. "You're still as thoughtful as ever. Àngels will absolutely die of joy when she sees you." She looked up at him and stroked his chest. "But you'd better be back fast, since you've stirred up far too much already."

He kissed the top of her hair and breathed in before backing away.

Before Montse could return, Rosa called her parents together downstairs. She had to warn them. Montse looked set to leave without a word, something her mother may never recover from. When she told them about Montse's decision, Dolors entered into near hysterics and Josep didn't stop pacing. Given the emotional upheaval of the moment, Rosa postponed sharing the news of Víctor's arrival. One piece of big news at a time would be enough. Everyone was in a state when Montse descended carrying two suitcases with great difficulty. Rosa, Josep, and Dolors were all standing in front of the door in an attempt to block it. Dolors was overcome by tears.

"Montse, you can't leave me," she begged. "First it was Pau and now you. You can't do this to me. No matter what I do, everyone still hates me. How will I run the bakery?" Dolors was gripping her shoulders and trying to tear the suitcases away.

Montse rested her bags at her side. "You can run the bakery. You're the one who's good at it. I have to do this. I refuse to stay holed up here and I'm going to see the world, or at least some of it. I'm finally going to use my passport. All I've needed was the opportunity."

"But you love the bakery, you love baking. You quit school. It was your choice," Dolors said.

"I wanted to bake with you. Now I need, I deserve, a break."

Josep reached for one of the suitcases, but Montse slapped his hand. "You're the one who brought Luc here," she said. "You led me into temptation. And I fell, I fell hard. I love him so much."

"But, Montse," Josep said. "There's much more to him than you know."

"I'd rather hear his side of the story."

"If you stay here, I'll tell you. Just don't go with him," Josep said almost falling to his knees.

Rosa squeezed Montse's arm. "If it's about going somewhere else, I'll take you to Barcelona if you want, or to France. We can see Pau together."

Montse shook off Rosa's hand and picked up her suitcases. "You're lucky you-know-who is back. Otherwise I would have thought you wanted Luc for yourself. I saw how you looked at each other. I'm not stupid."

"Then don't be. Don't go," Rosa said, thinking that her sister's leaving would be so very sad for all of them. And on a day that should have been so joyful for everyone. Rosa felt a twinge of resentment that Montse was taking this moment away from her.

"If you have to go, can't you wait and say a proper goodbye?" Dolors said. "I'll throw you a party."

"Your mother's right." Josep held Montse's arm. "I beg you not to go with that character, but if you must," he said trying to take her suitcase away and towards the stairs, "just wait a while and think it over. You can't leave without saying goodbye to everyone. What about Àngels?"

"I think she's rather busy at the moment." Montse glanced out the door toward the front of the house where Luc was waiting. "I'm not missing this chance." She picked up her suitcase and pushed past them all. The bell over the door echoed after her as if in applause.

CHAPTER TWENTY

IN HER HOUSE Àngels remained oblivious to the uproar next door and to the fact that her life was about to change for the better, finally. While she sat ruminating about the past, about the fact that she was alone, without Víctor or Manel, without even her mother, she realized that if she was to have a future, this was no way to spend it. It was time she stopped blaming Josep for all their misfortune. As she looked for the hundredth time at Eduard's letter on her lap, the truth struck her: her own loneliness or happiness depended solely on herself.

She stood up and put Eduard's letter on the table and went to search for a suitcase. Taking charge and going to see Eduard was the only way. Otherwise she risked drowning in self-pity. She knew she should have gone with her mother when she had the chance. As she put her clothes into a suitcase, she thought she could even ask Baltasar to accompany her. She had been putting off the poor man for too long, plus Eduard might benefit from an additional medical opinion. While reaching for the phone to dial Baltasar's number, she heard a knock on her door. She jumped, startled, because visitors were rare. Looking at the phone in her hand and the suitcase at her feet, she felt suddenly so silly. At her age, how did she expect to make such a trip and arrive unannounced on Eduard's doorstep? The knock grew louder.

When she opened the door, she thought she had really gone mad. It was the most wonderful vision before her eyes, but she couldn't believe it. If Víctor was coming home, someone would have told her; Rosa would have called her; she would have had some sort of warning. Yet when she closed her eyes and opened them again, Víctor was still there. Granted he looked much too old and skinny.

"Àngels, it's me. Aren't you going to say anything?" Víctor said, stepping toward her into the light and gently taking her by the shoulders.

The physical contact was like a jolt and Àngels felt the life surge through her. She fell against him, then jumped back and held his face in her hands. "Víctor. *Per l'amor de Déu.* I never thought I'd see the day. Are you well? Are you sick? Are you hurt?" Àngels pulled him inside, patting his cheeks, his thin arms and ribs before grasping him by the shoulders and looking into his eyes. They were still like dark honey, but they appeared dull and empty.

He shook his head. His graying hair was shaved close to his head making his face more drawn and ghost-like. "I'm fine. I couldn't be better. I'm home. I'm back here with you." He touched her cheek. "We are the survivors."

"I suppose we are," Àngels said, gently pulling him inside and not letting go of his hand. "Come sit, or maybe you want to walk. Are you hungry? Or maybe you're tired. You've come such a long way."

"I just want life as it was," Víctor said sitting down. Then he looked down at his worn-out clothing. "Then again maybe I would like to change."

Àngels pointed to the loft. "You can go up to your room. Your things are still there. They may be too big now and they're likely a little out of fashion."

"Do I look concerned about fashion?" He held his arms out at his sides and smiled.

She smiled and glanced away. "Your other things are over at Josep and Dolors', of course. Maybe you would rather have those."

He took her hand and looked down timidly. "Thank you, but I don't want those things and I don't want to stay there. I want to come home. If you'll have me."

"I thought I would never see the day." Àngels' eyes were shining. "Do the others even know you're here? We'll have to go get Rosa. Wait until she sees you." Àngels jumped toward the door, but Víctor gently urged her back into a chair.

"I've seen her. Briefly. And now I'm staying out of the way since there is a commotion." He raised an eyebrow. "Montse is leaving here with some foreigner. A French-speaking fellow."

"Really?" Àngels said, frowning, since from what she'd been able to see, Luc had seemed more keen on Rosa. "Are you sure? Then again, I don't blame her. It's probably time she got out from under Dolors' thumb. It's not a good idea to stay locked away up here, particularly a young woman like her."

"Or any woman," Víctor said. "Speaking of being locked away. I appreciate all the letters you sent me, but I really wish you had come to visit me. Even just once. It would have made it easier for me."

Àngels blanched. "I know, dear." She reached out and stroked his cheek. "You can say my reasons are selfish. I couldn't bear seeing you in there. Seeing all of us back in there. I had to leave that up to Rosa. You know I never gave up for a second and neither did she."

"I know, and I never gave up on her." Víctor patted her hand and looked around the room. "I haven't heard from Manel in a while. Where is he? Of all people I thought he would be here to greet me."

Àngels pulled her hand away. She was too thrilled with the moment to let the story of Manel drag her back down. "He's not here. And he won't be back," she said.

"What?" Víctor looked more shattered than he already was.

"Please don't ask me any more right now." Àngels tried to keep her voice steady. "Let's enjoy this time together. Later I will explain. We have a lot of catching up to do."

Víctor leaned over and kissed her cheek. "We do and there will be plenty of time from now on." He pulled her to her feet. "Shall we go to see if the storm has calmed? I'd like to see Rosa and show the rest of the family that I am back for good."

"You had better be," Àngels said, putting her arms around his waist and squeezing.

***

Later that evening, the family enjoyed a sweet-and-sour dinner prepared half-heartedly by Dolors. While she appeared thrilled to see Víctor home, she said that his arrival only served to remind her that Montse had run off with a strange man. Although Josep tried to reassure her that Luc was no stranger, she was still convinced that the Balaguers would be the talk of the town. So what else was new, Josep asked her. He for one was clearly relieved to see Víctor, for Rosa's sake and his own. Now he could stroke off one major offense from the list bearing his name, even though Dolors was quick to replace it with his responsibility for Montse's departure. Plus, she added, he was the one who was so keen to see Franco gone. Now that he was, so were all her children.

Throughout the meal, Rosa shook her head at her parents, particularly her mother, but did not take an eye off Víctor. Seeing him sitting across from her was the greatest gift of all, almost as great as it would be to finally have a moment alone together. She gripped the edge of the chair to stop herself from jumping across the table at him. She could still feel his body along her front as he hugged her. It was the closest they had been physically in years, and frankly she was breathless with the anticipation of his long fingers in her hair, his body on top of hers, his quick breath in her ear. She glanced across the table at Víctor, but he wasn't looking. He and her father seemed very absorbed in conversation and the enthralled look on Josep's face indicated they were discussing the good old days of contraband. Rosa gave Àngels a knowing glance and shook her head. Once the dishes were washed and they were standing at the table saying goodnight to Àngels, Rosa thought she had her chance. She touched Víctor's sleeve to tell him to meet her later, but Josep put an arm around his shoulder and steered him away. As she watched the two of them disappear up the stairs, she couldn't believe that her father would get Víctor into his bedroom first. When all the dishes were dry and put away, Rosa switched off the light, the darkness echoing her disappointment. First Montse had to abandon them on such an important day and now her father was delaying their time together. Then again she thought that after such a long wait, a few more hours or days would change little. Unless Víctor himself had changed. Maybe now that he was free she would once again be like a little sister to him. Maybe she was just a means to an end. She felt a breeze and noticed that the door was slightly ajar.

Shivering, Rosa entered the yard between their house and Àngels'. The sky was blue black with a scatter of winking stars. She looked around, hoping to see Víctor standing in the dark waiting for her to join him, but saw only the empty air, the dark silhouettes of bushes and trees. She shook her head at herself. Someone must have just left the door open. As she turned back, she spotted him. His dark form stood out against the gray sky behind him. He was crouched beneath the tree, over the shrine to his mother. He turned his head and even through the dark she could feel him grinning at her. He stood and stretched his hands toward her. They felt warm and strong as they pulled her to him.

"All those years that I took this for granted." He looked around them and looked straight into her eyes. "You don't know how good it feels to breathe this fresh air. To see for miles. And to do it with you."

"I do know how good it feels." Rosa put her arms around his waist and rested her cheek on his chest, feeling his heart next to her ear and his blood flowing near her skin. "I've thought about this every day for all these years, but I never imagined it would feel this perfect." She looked up at him. "I was afraid you'd changed your mind. That you were more interested in my father." She squeezed his waist.

Víctor laughed. "He was very tempting and very insistent, but I let him down easily." He kissed the top of her head and looked down at her. "You've never let me down. I have everything to thank you for. All those years you tried to have me released. You must have made an impression because they said I should be thankful to have friends in high places."

"I'm not that influential but I am persistent." Rosa hugged him. "I'm also selfish. I couldn't live knowing you were in there."

"I owe you everything." He gently pulled her head from his chest and raised her chin towards him. "Rosa, you can't know how grateful I am."

She felt his warm lips on hers and his thin but sturdy body against hers. She wanted to fold into him, but his ancient words were in her head. Pulling away she said, "I hope this is not solely out of gratitude."

He smiled and laughed. "Of course it's not. Silly woman." This time when he kissed her she let herself drift with his body as if they were floating together over the mountaintop as part of a passing cloud. Above them the stars were circling. Rosa shivered and Víctor rubbed her arms.

"You're cold," he said. "Here we are two adults and I feel like we have to sneak around like children."

"We are definitely not children." She grinned and grabbed his hand, her earlier nerves and fears gone. The door to Manel's cottage was unlocked. Inside the light revealed the table, the one chair, and the sleeping area in the corner, all freshly cleaned since Luc's impromptu departure had left it in a shambles.

"That bed's almost as small as the one in my cell," Víctor said looking at the cot against the wall.

"It's better than inside a rock," Rosa said, turning off the light and lighting the candle on the table. "I want to be able to see you." She reached for him and pulled him down to sit beside her on the bed. She stroked his hair, which was so short it pricked her fingers. She felt his cheek and his recently shaved jaw line. Slowly she kissed one soft eyelid and then another. She put her cheek against his and felt its softness caressing her own. His palms cupped her chin and as his moist lips touched hers, his hand stroked her neck, her collarbone and reached inside her blouse. She felt his hot hands grip her breast and the thumb stroke her nipple. Víctor gasped. "Rosa, I can't stand it," he said and pulled her to him almost in panic. She felt his body melt against hers as they slid back onto the bed. His excitement was throbbing against her hip and he moaned deep within his throat, clinging to her and hardly breathing. After a few moments, he whispered into her neck. "Can we just lie here together for a while? I'm afraid I'll finish things before we've even started."

She stroked his hair and pulled his face away so that he was looking down at her. "Of course. We have all the time in the world." She held his cheeks. "We are free now."

After spending the whole night in Manel's bed and sleeping for just an hour before the sun urged their eyes open, Rosa and Víctor pulled themselves out of each other's arms and began to dress.

"They're going to notice we're missing," Víctor said.

"Let them notice. It's time everyone realized that things in this country are changing."

"Because people like you are changing them." Víctor stroked her cheek and she scrambled and found her camera, the one he had given her years ago, with the pile of her clothes on the floor. She held up a hand.

"Stay like that. Don't move."

Víctor was leaning on the bed, supporting his weight on his elbow. The morning sun was turning the white sheet draping his hips a honey yellow. Rosa adjusted the objective and clicked. It was an image that she wanted to keep forever, though she knew that her mind would remember it more clearly than any camera.

"I wish you could come with me," she said as she covered the lens.

"You don't have to go yet." Víctor swung his legs over the bed and sat up.

"Yes, today. But I'll try to come back for the All Saints long weekend. We'll have to convince my mother to make her usual dinner for the *castanyada*." Rosa bit her lip. "Unless you come with me to the city."

Víctor was resting his elbows on his knees and he looked at the floor and shook his head. "You can't ask me to do that. Not right now."

"Haven't we waited long enough?"

"We've waited far too long. You know I can't do that to Àngels."

Rosa swallowed and nodded.

"I can't reappear and disappear again in practically the same day. I'm going to stay for a while. I have to find out what happened with Manel and bring him back to her. Once she's taken care of, I will come to you. I promise." His eyes held hers.

Rosa nodded and put her arms around his shoulders. "Do what you can and do it fast. But I'll tell you now, Manel is not the solution."

***

The next day, when Víctor was settled in Àngels' cottage, Àngels sat across the table staring at him. It was like she still could not believe he was here. He looked sleepy but content, as if something was newly bursting inside him. She reached across the table toward him.

"You are such a wonderful sight for my weary eyes. You couldn't have come back at a better time."

"Are you going to tell me what happened with Manel?" Víctor took her hand. "Maybe you can pretend like he never existed, but he's the closest I've had to a father."

Àngels let go of his hand and looked at her fingers. "I know. I'm sorry to take him away from you, but you have to believe that I have a good reason."

"I think I have a right to know what it is."

"Did you know that Manel used to be a *Franquista*?" She smiled weakly at him. "I'd always thought he'd changed and maybe he did, but he can never change enough to make up for some of the things he did. Maybe someday Manel will tell you. I would like some explanations myself."

"So would I. Who is Carles Puig? Is he of the Puig family from here in town?" Víctor asked and Àngels' smile faded.

"Yes." She frowned. He was the last person she expected Víctor to mention, unless... "Why would you bring up his name right now? Has Manel already talked to you?"

"No. They told me this Carles had me released. Why would he do that?"

"Because I asked him to. Let's say he owed me." Àngels stroked Víctor's hair. "It took him long enough."

"Does Rosa know?"

Àngels shook her head. "It may as well have been her. Víctor, she didn't let up for a moment. Not really."

"I know. Even if she didn't get me out, I wouldn't be here if it weren't for her."

Àngels looked at the pale fright on his face and realized that she had been wrong in her thinking. Víctor's experience had been nothing like her own and, in fact, she had no idea was it was exactly. She had no idea what he had been through. Now she felt a surging regret for not going to visit him and being there to help him. Maybe Rosa wasn't always enough.

A knock on the door pulled Àngels from her thoughts. When she opened it the postman handed her a telegram. "For me? From someone who doesn't know that I now have a telephone." She opened it and was silent for a moment.

"What does it say? Who is it from?" Víctor came along beside her.

"*Returning to Pujaforta. Stop. Get ready for a surprise. Stop. Manel. Stop.*"

"He sent it from Madrid."

Àngels turned it over in her hands as if trying to find more information. "Why would he dare come back?"

"Maybe he has a good explanation."

"He may have an explanation, but it will never be good enough," Àngels said and Víctor rubbed her back.

A few days later when Manel returned, the surprise was in the passenger seat. He parked his little rental car in front of Àngels' house and ran around to open the car's side door. Àngels was watching at the window and felt repulsion at the sight of Manel, a symbol of the past that she would rather have forgotten. He looked thinner, and he had grown a moustache like many men of late. She looked again and gripped the ledge to steady herself. Manel was walking toward her with a woman with very curly hair and a large cowlick at the crown of her head. Àngels' knees buckled and she landed on the floor. She held her hair in her hands and shook her head. It couldn't be. It was impossible. She'd given up the idea so many years ago. She felt herself being lifted to her feet and a garbled voice was talking in her ear. Shaking her head, she focused and saw Víctor's face in front of hers.

"What's the matter? Come lie down. I'll fetch Dr. Sort." There was a confident knock on the door. "Maybe that's him."

"I don't need Baltasar."

When Víctor went for the door, Àngels said, "No, it's for me."

Before she could open it, Manel was standing in the backlit doorway with the silhouette of a woman.

"Àngels, please forgive me," Manel said. "There's someone," he began.

"Joana," Àngels said and reached trembling hands toward this woman. She searched her face, her freckles, her brown curly hair, her gray startled eyes. Àngels felt her legs wobble underneath her and Manel and Víctor supported her on either side. "This can't be." She was shaking her head. She tilted her head and looked at Joana again. "Do you know who I am?"

"They told me that you're my mother," she said without moving. "Although I already have one."

Àngels nodded slightly. She felt her world spinning around her once again as they gently sat her in a chair. She brought her hand to her forehead.

"Is it true?" Joana asked. She was fanning herself with an intricately painted fan and the frills on her blouse were shaking.

Àngels felt a chill, nodded slightly and said, "I would know you anywhere." Joana sat across from her and Àngels watched her in silence. Despite the wide skirt and the blouse buttoned to her chin, Àngels could see that they also had the same solid build. She also had gray eyes, a straight nose, and a sallow complexion as if she needed some sun. Joana continued to fan herself, although the mountain air was cool.

"You look just like I did at your age," Àngels said and the shock seemed to choke her and she covered her face with her hands. "This is impossible." She looked up at Manel who was embracing Víctor so tightly his arms were shaking.

"That's what I thought, too," Joana said. "When I found out that I was adopted, my parents told me you were dead." Her look was slightly accusing.

Àngels sniffed and nodded. She reached out for Joana's hand and held it in hers until Joana pulled it away. She was looking over Àngels' shoulder.

"Who's he?" she asked.

Víctor gently pulled away from Manel and lightly slapped his cheek. Àngels reached toward him. "This lovely man is Víctor, my son. He's a few months older than you are, actually."

"What? How?" Joana said, sitting straight up in her chair. Then she nodded as if it had all become clearer. "*Rojos.*"

Àngels brushed aside the comment. "Víctor is actually the son of a very close friend of mine, may she rest in peace. You were both born around the same time."

Joana nodded and observed Víctor, who approached and shook her hand. "It's wonderful to finally see you again," he said also looking at Manel. "I hope you'll be staying for a while." He pulled Joana to her feet. "Let me show you the view of the mountains from the back garden before the family swallows you up."

Àngels found herself alone with Manel. She could feel his presence in the room as if he was sitting on her chest asphyxiating her. But he was across the room looking out the window, his back turned towards her and his shoulders sloping. As she glanced toward him and the window overlooking the back garden a million questions temporarily replaced her anger.

"I see that you put some flowers on our shrine while I was away," Manel said before she could ask them.

Àngels nodded and slowly approached. "Manel, I'm telling you now that I will never forgive you, but I will let you explain. First, tell me about Joana."

"I hoped that bringing her here would help me make it up to you," Manel said quietly. "I don't blame you if you still hate me. Just know that everything that I've ever done has been so that I can be near you. When you rejected me all those years ago, it hurt me more than you can know. The only good aspect of my life has been you and your family. We've become so close yet I was afraid you would change your mind about the wedding." He shrugged and looked from her face to the floor. "I thought that having more money would help."

"If you knew me like you say you do, you'd know I'm not interested in money."

He looked back up at her and his eyes bored into hers. "That's what your brother told me. I wanted to have enough money for the wedding. It took you so long to accept." He looked away. "I couldn't bring myself to believe that it was just because you didn't love me."

"No." Àngels shook her head and pointed. "The answer is right outside that door. But I didn't realize it until I was looking at her face. I hardly knew her when they told me she died. Before I saw her I didn't want her. She was like a tumor growing inside me, a reminder of that prison, the pain, the filth I felt. But when she arrived she was pure and perfect. I didn't know that I could love anything so much until she was gone. It was like anything of my flesh, my daughter, my twin brother, died and left me with gaping wounds. And then there was Carme. I couldn't let myself love anyone, not like that, not even Víctor and not even you."

"But I didn't fall in love with you on purpose. I couldn't help it. It's not mind over matter."

Àngels sighed. "So are you going to tell me how you found her?" She had an even more horrific thought. "Or did you know that she was alive all this time?"

He held up his hands and looked shocked by the question. "No. I had no idea. They told me she'd died of pneumonia. I could never keep anything like that from you." He reached toward her and she stepped back. "When you sent me away, I lost all my bearings. It was like you'd severed my roots and I was floating. I wandered for a while and then I started thinking." He looked toward the door. "I thought about Carles' visit. He seemed so smug, like he had all the answers. He also said he had a surprise for you." He looked from Àngels' hands to her face. "Then I thought about something Rosa said one day when you weren't there. Her magazine was working on a story about newborns taken from their mothers and given to *Franquista* families. Some of those children are now adults and they're looking for their birth mothers." He shook his head. "I remembered how scheming Carles Puig was and it was like suddenly the two pieces clicked together in my mind. I started asking some questions and digging, like I was digging for my life, trying to regain your roots and mine. I was right. When I finally tracked down Joana in Madrid, Carles was there. He was with her. She knows who her father is, but she was curious about her mother. Carles had promised her he would take her to you. He was going to play the hero and bring her here."

"And you decided to do it instead." Àngels was pacing and shaking her head. "But something doesn't make sense. We were taking Joana to hospital when they arrested Baltasar and they took Joana away with him. When they released him, he was the one who told me how she died. That her lungs closed and she stopped breathing. I had insisted on seeing her, but he assured me that she was at peace, that he himself had seen her. Why would he have lied like that?"

"I imagine that they tricked him. He could hardly have known what she looked like."

Àngels sighed and sank into a chair. She looked up. "Where has Joana lived all these years? Who were her parents? What has Carles got to do with them? She's thirty-seven years old. She has a whole life behind her."

"I'll answer all your questions as long as you answer mine," Joana said from the doorway. She stood backlit in the foyer, the light filtering through her curls, turning them auburn, like an aura of fire.

Àngels stood slowly and waved her inside. "Come, make yourself comfortable then." She gestured to Manel. "Manel, you and I will talk later."

Manel and Víctor excused themselves while Àngels led Joana to a chair at the table. Àngels looked at the stranger beside her and thought she felt so familiar. It was the determined expression on her face, the way she moved, trying to keep her shoulders straight without slouching. Àngels had an urge to hug her and touch her, but she felt Joana stiffen each time she moved toward her.

"Would you like something? A coffee?" Àngels jumped from her seat. "I'm going to have one."

"I'd prefer tea," Joana said as she fanned herself.

"I'll see if I can find some." Àngels began searching in the cupboards. "This has all been quite a shock."

"Yes, it has. I think we will both need some time. We may supposedly be related but we don't even know each other," Joana said and scrunched her curls. "At least now I know who is to blame for this hair."

Àngels chuckled. "It is a bit of a curse. However, at one time I was very glad to have it grow back. Here's some." She shook a small jar of tea at Joana.

When they were sitting at the table sipping their drinks, Àngels asked her to start filling in the long years of blanks. Joana gripped her teacup and told her how her parents were a very respectable couple in Madrid. Her father ran one of the official tobacconists in the Salamanca neighborhood while her mother handled all the official forms the shop distributed. They loved her and cared for her well, at least until their own son was born when Joana was ten. She felt treated differently then, but she always assumed that it was because she was a girl. Every so often her uncle Carles would come to visit and always to see only her. He would take her out to the museums or for a stroll in the Parque del Retiro.

"I didn't know who he was," Joana said. "He spoke to me in a different language from my parents but I understood him. He gave me so many presents over the years. Like this." She opened and closed the fan with a snap. "Carles arranged for me to go to secretarial school and then he started introducing me to officers." She wrinkled her nose. "He knew I wasn't interested because Sergio had always been my boyfriend. He was the son of a customer at the tobacco shop." Joana sipped. "Sergio and his family always hated the *Rojos*. So did my parents. They said how they were responsible for the attacks, for killing innocent people."

Àngels cleared her throat. "And what about Franco?"

"That's what Carles helped me see. Everyone's hands are dirty. Especially his, he told me."

"He said that?" Àngels put down her coffee cup and bit her lip. "Did he tell you why?"

"Not precisely. He told me he was my real father. That was why he was looking out for me. He said that was why he wanted me to leave Sergio and study instead." Joana tapped her thigh with her closed fan. "He got what he wanted. Sergio married another girl in the neighborhood and I am a legal secretary."

Àngels reached out and squeezed Joana's hand and this time she didn't pull it away. "You have an education. You're independent. That makes me feel proud. Joana, you must know that we don't need men to take care of us."

"My name is actually Maria Juana. Carles is the only one who calls me Joana."

Àngels sighed into her fingertips. "I didn't even think of that. I don't even know your name."

"Maria Juana García Sánchez, but Carles says my real name is Joana Puig i Balaguer."

Àngels swallowed. "I'm Àngels Balaguer i Hereu. Carles named you as if we'd been married."

"But you weren't, were you?"

"No, we were not. I promise I will tell you the whole story some time. I think that's enough for today."

Joana nodded. "So you've never been married then?"

"No, I haven't. And I never plan to be," Àngels said and whisked their cups from the table.

Later that afternoon Àngels took Joana to meet the family. Dolors had dough up to her elbows as she was experimenting with a new batch of *ensaïmades*, trying to make them lighter and smoother than even the Mallorcans could make them. Josep and Baltasar were sitting at the table watching the television news, though with each interjection, neither of them heard a word. Each had his opinions of the prime minister persuaded to resign by the king, but both were equally dubious about the new one to replace him. As far as they were concerned they were all *Franquistes* by another name, like cava and *xampany*, but less delicious and inebriating. Both sat on the edge of their seat as if for a champion football match, when it was the country's political future at play. The sight of an adult Joana looking much like Àngels had at her age calmed them in an instant. No introductions were necessary, at least for them. Baltasar appeared particularly dumbfounded and when Joana was busy talking to the rest of the family he pulled Àngels aside.

"Are you absolutely sure that it's her? What proof do you have?" he asked her.

"I'm sure. Just look at her. She's like me and Carles Puig combined." She shuddered. They both turned to observe Joana, whose stance and hand movements as she talked were as much like Àngels as her curly hair. Plus she had the Puig cowlick and bushy eyebrows.

"You're right. As strange as it may seem. She is." Baltasar looked at Àngels. "But she can't be."

"How do you explain it?" Àngels begged.

Baltasar shook his head. "Àngels, I saw her. I listened to her chest. She wasn't breathing. I tried to find her little heartbeat. Not only was there not one, she was cold. Stone cold."

"Are you sure it was my daughter?"

"Yes, they brought me out of my cell. They said that they wanted me to identify her and confirm that she was dead." He looked at her with eyes of shock and covered his mouth.

"And then you would tell me. They knew I would want to see the body and they knew that you would convince me."

"Àngels," Baltasar said and took her hands. "I know that it's ridiculous to ask you for forgiveness for such a thing. In any case, I'll never forgive myself."

"They tricked you." She squeezed his fingers. "They tricked us. It's them I can never forgive. They knew you'd hardly even seen Joana and that you wouldn't be able to tell the difference." Àngels' eyes welled with tears as she imagined Joana taking her first couple of steps, putting on her school uniform, going to her first town festival. All the moments stolen from them.

They looked at Joana who was standing in front of Víctor holding her fan as if it was a shield. Then she dropped it and laughed at something Víctor said.

"Those two look nothing alike, yet they might actually get along," Baltasar said.

"Like Carme and me, perhaps. It's going to take a long time. Joana was brought up to hate the likes of us. And we won't be very open to her way of thinking. I hope we can all be civil." She watched Joana talking to Dolors. "We'll see how Rosa accepts her, and Montse and Pau, whenever they come back." Àngels sighed. "I really wish my mother were here."

"I heard she's gone to see Pau dance. Write to her or call her and tell her what's happened. She'll come back."

She nodded. "I think I might do that."

When Àngels turned back toward the group, Manel was tilting his head looking at her. His hair was slightly longer over the ears and it was now more gray than not. He came toward her but she stayed stiff in her spot. Reaching towards her, he said, "You don't know how good it feels to see you look so happy."

She avoided his hands. "Maybe this is a good time for us to talk. Outside." She led him into the garden until they were standing between his refurbished shack and the open mountain. The crisp autumn air lifted Àngels curls, even though they were bound at the nape of her neck.

"She reminds me so much of you," Manel said motioning inside. "Physically at least."

"Politically she has more in common with you." She turned her back to him.

Manel kicked the ground with his heel. "No she doesn't. How can you say that after all these years together? You know I left all that behind me."

"I can't put it behind me."

He threw his hands in the air. "You and your excuses."

"Manel, you know that this is far more than an excuse. You know what that prison did to me. Carles came here and he brought it all back. I could see you again in that ridiculous uniform. You with your muscatel and *flam*, with that debonair Sr. Peix ready to swindle an illiterate woman out of her life's work. And that's just my mother. Carles is not only responsible for Joana existing, he stole her from me. I can't begin to tell you what all that did to me."

"What about what it all did to me? Those days destroyed me as well. I lost my whole family. I lost my town. Yours is the only family I have." He stepped closer. "Of course, I had no idea what Carles was up to when he wanted you in the prison. I was trying to protect you."

"You did a very poor job." She felt it all fresh again as if decades had not passed between her and these events. "So you admit to helping him."

Manel looked at the ground and as he looked up a tear ran down the crease of his nose. "I did, but I didn't know. I didn't know what he had planned. I thought he wanted to help you. He introduced me to that Sr. Peix. I believed him because I cared so much about you, even way back then." He tried to take her hands but she backed away, remembering Manel trying to kiss her all those years ago right in front of her house. Right before she was arrested. Manel's hands fell to his sides. "But we're getting married. That's all I've ever wanted, to spend my life with you."

"How do you expect me to trust you with my future when you ruined the better part of my life?" Àngels' breath was heaving. She was trying to stop the angry tears from choking her.

"If you won't marry me, tell me that you'll at least forgive me. I can't live otherwise."

"You'll have to learn to. And you'll have to leave." She swallowed. "Out of respect for my family and because you brought me Joana, I will let you spend a day or two with them here, but then you have to go."

"Where do you expect me to go?" Manel was turning in circles with his arms spread to the open mountain, but Àngels was walking away.

The next day was the eve of All Saints' Day and Dolors had announced that rather than commemorate their dead, she would make the traditional *panellets* and sweet potatoes to celebrate the arrival of Joana and Manel. Evidently it would also serve to distract her from the sudden departure of her two children. Àngels, however, had yet to tell her that it would also mark Manel's last supper with the Balaguers. She suspected that Dolors would be almost equally heartbroken that the engagement was off.

When Àngels awoke that morning she felt that her life had taken a sudden unforeseen tack. A daughter she hadn't known existed was sleeping in the loft and Manel, with whom she had expected to share this bed, would soon be long gone. She had already spent so long mourning for him and tried to concentrate on the new aspects of her life. She had also managed to speak to her mother, who was on tour with Pau in Vienna. Núria was flabbergasted by the news about Joana and said she would come home as soon as she could. Gaspard had been easier to reach in France and Àngels informed him that he now had another cousin to get to know. He readily agreed to come meet her and partake in his first *Castanyada*, the Catalan chestnut-eating tradition.

Àngels and Joana spent most of the day chatting at the table. Joana had warmed to her slightly, despite the constant use of her fan. Àngels soon suspected that it was more due to a nervous twitch than to body temperature. Since Joana had given her a brief summary of her life, Àngels told her about her mother's co-op, about Josep's travels and his return, and Eduard's continued exile.

Joana turned squarely towards Àngels. "My father said that you would blame all of that, all of your troubles, on his family."

Àngels shrugged. "I do, but it was also the events of the day, the impossible situations we found ourselves in."

"Carles says that his options were limited then. He believed strongly in The Caudillo and then he was left alone. His father died, and before his brother died he caused him a lot of pain. He regarded his stay in Madrid as an exile of sorts. He said that he couldn't stay in Pujaforta."

"I'm glad he didn't, but he certainly could have stayed. There were plenty of families on his side and the rest of us had no choice. Besides, I suspect that he wanted to be near you, from what you've told me."

Joana smiled. "He's wonderful. Did you know he's joined the Alianza Popular with all the important people from The Caudillo's government? I'm so proud of him. He'll be great for the country. He gives such fitting advice. I could have married Sergio and it would very likely have been a disaster. He wouldn't let me do anything." She looked up. "Carles did tell me that he didn't treat you well, but I am the result of the two of you. I need to understand why you hate him so much."

"For taking you away from me, for one. He's denied us a whole life together." Àngels smiled gently as she clenched her teeth. "Are you sure you're ready to hear it?"

Joana nodded.

Àngels took a breath. "Right after the war, when my brothers were gone and it was just my mother and I, the regime put me in prison."

Joana began to fan.

"They held me there against my will, for a number of weeks," Àngels continued. "Carles was one of the guards. And he did other things against my will."

Joana's arm fell to her lap and her face was white. "Are you saying?"

Àngels looked her straight in the eye and nodded.

"But why were you in prison? What did you do?" Joana's face was red and her mouth was pursed.

Àngels tried to blink. She shook her head and tried to breathe. She knew that it would take time. It was all far too sudden, but maybe the years had molded them differently. Maybe they could not take another shape.

"I did nothing."

"That's hard to believe, isn't it?"

"I hope that one day you will see that it is."

In the early evening, when Àngels was getting ready for dinner, a small Renault chugged to a stop in front of her house. She saw Rosa get out of the passenger seat. She wore a long scarf around her neck and it fluttered behind her as she ran purposefully to the door. Àngels dropped her potato peeler and kissed and hugged her niece.

"You did come," Àngels said. "I thought you might not make it this weekend. We have a huge surprise, which I imagine Gaspard has already told you." She looked over Rosa's shoulder and saw her nephew running towards her with a bouquet of flowers in his hands.

"Yes, look who I found along the way, or more accurately who found me. He told me all about your news," Rosa said. "You have a daughter? Does Víctor know?"

"Yes, of course. It's all such a long story." Àngels took the flowers from Gaspard and kissed his cheeks. "Gaspard, I didn't expect you to come all this way. But I'm very glad that you did." She covered her face with her hands and tried to hold in the tears that were filling her eyes. "Sorry, these last few days have been rather emotional." She gasped and looked toward the car. "Is Eduard here? Are you hiding him somewhere to play a trick on me?"

Gaspard squeezed her hand. "No, but I wish I was. He couldn't get away this time."

Rosa stroked Àngels' arm. "I hear that Manel has come back. So have you changed your mind about him?"

"No, I have not. Today we will be welcoming Joana but saying goodbye to Manel. At least I will be. Can you warn the family? I just can't do it." She covered her face again, but Rosa grabbed her hands.

"Are you entirely sure? Manel's part of the family. Where will he go?"

Àngels shrugged. "He'll find somewhere. I know that all this is a shock, but I do have a good reason." She stroked Rosa's cheek. "By the way, Rosa, I have to ask you to be patient with Joana. She doesn't quite see things the way we do, if you know what I mean."

Rosa stepped back. "She's a *Fatxa*?"

"A little. Well, quite a bit. I'm hoping to bring her around. She's waiting with Víctor at your parents' house. You can go on. I'll be right there."

"Víctor is with her? I can't wait to surprise him."

***

Rosa led Gaspard to her family home and opened the door to find Víctor and Joana sitting alone at the table. The air in the room felt closed in and stale. They appeared lost in conversation and didn't look up until Rosa said, "*Bona tarda*, Víctor."

Víctor jumped up, rushed to Rosa and kissed her and hugged her. She breathed in the soapy smell of Víctor and felt its calming effect. He stroked her back and said, "They did give you the long weekend. I'm so pleased. If we'd known we would have sent someone to pick you up."

"Someone did." Rosa pulled away and pointed to Gaspard who was standing on the threshold, still wearing his gabardine and carrying a beaten leather briefcase. He ducked his head and entered the kitchen and came shoulder-to-shoulder with Víctor. Rosa took his elbow. "Víctor, this is my cousin Gaspard. He's Uncle Eduard's son."

Víctor raised his head. "Really? It is a pleasure to finally meet you." He shook his hand energetically. "I missed your other visits. I was a little held up."

Gaspard nodded. "So you're Víctor. I'm glad to see that you've been released. Rosa told me all about it when I drove her to France last time. In fact, that's all she talked about." He grinned and slapped Víctor's back.

Rosa cleared her throat and looked at Joana sitting very straight backed at the table. She was holding her blouse at her chest where the frills met her neck and the ends of the curls of her hair. Víctor gasped and pulled her from her chair without releasing Rosa's hand. "This is Joana. In fact, the three of you are cousins."

"Yes, we've heard the good news." Rosa approached and took Joana's hands in hers and kissed her on either cheek. "Looking at you, there's no doubt whose daughter you are."

"It was just as much of a surprise to me," Joana said, smoothing her hair. "Not only did I learn that I have another mother, I have her entire family."

"Yes, there's us and my brother and sister, who are both traveling, as you probably know."

"Yes, it does sound like you are all more Bohemian than I'm used to."

311

"I wouldn't call us that, though we've been called worse," Josep said as he shuffled into the room holding his back.

Rosa ran towards him. "*Pare*, don't tell me you've done your back in again."

He shook his head and winced. "It's all your mother's fault."

"Isn't it always?"

"She made me go mushroom hunting. I found a good basketful, but, no, that wasn't enough for Manel. So she sent me out again. Then finally she came with me and now she can hardly walk either. She'll be glad to see that you're here to give her a hand. And, just so you know, Montse is safe. She's in Montreal. But that's all she told us." Josep looked towards the door and suddenly straightened up. Then he grasped his back and moaned. "Gaspard, I didn't know you were here. Is Eduard with you?" He reached for his hand while his eyes searched behind him and toward the door.

"No, I'm afraid he isn't. Not this time."

Josep shook his head and muttered. "Or any other time."

"About Manel," Rosa said. "There's something you should know. Àngels has asked him to leave for good. This will be his last meal with us."

"Really?" Josep said, sinking into a chair. "I thought she'd forgiven him for that smuggling."

"I think there's a lot more to it than that."

Josep shook his head. "Would you go in there and break the news to your mother? I'll have to go fetch Baltasar."

"She's really sending him away now?" Víctor asked.

Rosa nodded slowly.

***

When they were all gathered at the table that evening, the whole family looked up to see Àngels enter alone, smile, and take a seat between Joana and Víctor. When Manel entered they all looked up as if they had seen a ghost, but Àngels didn't raise her head. Víctor jumped from his seat and held out a chair for him, which he quietly sat in. The table was carefully set with all the best dishes, used only at the most important occasions, like Christmas or the *Castanyada*. Josep quickly set about serving some *vermut* as loudly as he could. As he filled Manel's glass he squeezed his shoulder.

"Let the celebration begin." Dolors called as she limped towards them carrying plates of *truita de bolets*. "The mushrooms are very fresh. We picked them for you, Manel, though Josep needs a little more practice choosing the right ones," she said. "I've also baked plenty of sweet potatoes and chestnuts for later so leave some room. After all the work cooking by myself, I won't let them go to waste."

Josep raised his glass. "To the cook. And welcome to you, Joana. We hope you enjoy our All Saints' traditions."

They all raised their glasses and drank quietly, not meeting each other's eyes.

"Eating sweet potatoes is an odd tradition, isn't it? I heard that the Catalans were a bit different," Joana said and sipped daintily. "Aren't we supposed to go to mass?"

"My mother did ask me to put some flowers out for Albert. I wish she was here to meet you," Àngels said. "Other people go to mass."

"We do not," Rosa said and emptied her glass.

"Are you what they call *comunistas*? Everyone mentioned you were dissidents." She looked shocked. "Is that why you were in prison, Víctor?"

Víctor cleared his throat. "No, that is not why."

"And we are not Communists," Dolors said. "I run a perfectly respectable business."

"So, Joana," Rosa said taking some toasted bread and rubbing garlic on it. "If you live in Madrid, why do you speak Catalan?"

"My father is Catalan."

Rosa raised an eyebrow but before she could say anything Víctor squeezed her leg in warning. As if to head off any untoward exchanges, everyone reverted to silence, which was soon filled with the clanking of silverware.

Finally, Víctor turned to Gaspard. "What do you do in France?"

Gaspard wiped his mouth with a serviette and swallowed. "I'm a professor."

"At the university?" Rosa asked, leaning around Manel towards him. "Professor of what?"

"Literature. Mostly French classics, but some Spanish."

"Why didn't you tell me that before?" Rosa asked.

Gaspard appeared to kiss the air as he hesitated. "The only opportunity was in the car and you were talking most of the time. About Víctor." He winked.

Rosa winced. "I'm so sorry. I suppose I was stuck on one subject." She glanced at Víctor and his eyes held hers as he ran a hand up her thigh under the table.

As everyone's plates began to empty, Dolors brought out platters of sweet potatoes, chestnuts, and *panellets*, marzipan balls rolled in pine nuts and glazed to perfection, though she kept sighing and groaning about having to do all the baking without Montse's help. Josep meanwhile poured some muscatel. Víctor put an arm around the back of Rosa's chair so that he was hugging her along one side.

"When do you have to leave?" he whispered.

"Tomorrow." Rosa poked him in the leg. "When are you going to come to the city? You know I have a new place that's big enough for the two of us."

"I'm working on it. You know I can't leave Àngels right now. I'm hoping that Joana will come and spend more time with her."

"In that case I will try to bite my tongue."

"Can I meet you in Manel's house tonight?" he whispered in her ear.

She nodded but raised an eyebrow. "I don't suppose Manel will be needing it."

The sparkle in Víctor's eyes dimmed. Rosa squeezed his leg under the table as he shifted his chair backwards and leaned around Rosa towards Manel. "How are you holding up? I want you to know I'm sorry, Manel."

"So am I."

"I tried to talk to her but she's a very stubborn woman." Víctor shrugged.

"She is and she's right. I did some horrible things and it's time I paid for them. Lord knows you've already paid far more than your share."

Víctor swallowed. "I wouldn't wish that on anyone. So, what are you going to do?"

"I'm going to stay in my workshop. It's mine. I figure it is far enough out of Àngels' way." He looked at his hands folded in his lap before looking up at Víctor. "I also hope some of you might come to visit me. If Àngels doesn't mind. Will you come?"

"Of course I will, whether Àngels minds or not. You're going to get sick of seeing me." Víctor raised his glass and clanked it with Manel's. "Does that mean that you'll be sleeping down there tonight?"

"Yes, I've already cleared out my house. In fact, here." He reached into his pocket and took out a key. "It's never locked, but you can take care of it for me."

Rosa was leaning on Víctor's shoulder and he grinned and waved the key at her.

Manel cleared his throat and as he stood up, everyone fell silent. He looked slowly around the table. "I'd like to propose a toast to all of you, you who have been my unofficial family for years. I'm sure that you are all aware that I will be leaving. I ask you not to blame Àngels, since it is entirely my own doing. I ask you all for your understanding. Each and every one of you," he held his glass toward each of them individually and lingered at Àngels, "has a very dear place in my heart. Frankly, I don't know what I'm going to do without you." He cleared his throat again and held up his head. "Please enjoy your celebration. Víctor will know where to find me." He sat down and Víctor put a hand on his shoulder, Rosa stroked his cheek, and Josep came up behind him and slapped his back. All the others, even Àngels, raised their glasses toward Manel.

"To you, Manel," Dolors said.

"*Chin, chin,*" they all echoed after her.

Àngels stood and pointed her glass towards Joana. "Manel, thank you for bringing me Joana. This is the best gift I could ever have." Àngels kissed her fingers and touched Joana's cheek. Joana smiled and looked at the table and put her fingers to her face.

Joana looked up. "I hardly know any of you, and this is all overwhelming," she said. "I've just met Manel and now he's leaving. Anyway, thank you for being so kind and accepting of me. I've had a very interesting weekend. I'm sorry that it has to end."

Àngels turned to Joana. "End? What do you mean?"

"I've just come for the long weekend," Joana said. "I have to go back to my home and to my work."

"No you don't," Àngels almost shouted. Víctor put a calming hand on her shoulder and eased her back into her seat. "When are you leaving?"

"We can talk about this later. We're having such a good time," Joana said.

"But when? I need to know."

"Tomorrow afternoon." Joana fanned herself.

Víctor whispered in Àngels' ear. "Don't worry. I'm working on it. She just needs time. Probably you do, too."

Gaspard cleared his throat and stood. "May I say something? I was waiting for the right moment and it seems like the perfect time for some good news." He reached inside his jacket pocket and took out a piece of paper which he unfolded. "My father, Eduard, had wanted to come today but couldn't. He asked me to read this to you." Gaspard cleared his throat again and everyone leaned forward in their chair. "Àngels, my dear little sister," Gaspard said and looked at Àngels. "I am so very glad to hear that you have been reunited with your daughter. I remember what a tragedy that was so many years ago. I hope that you can make up for lost time. That is what I would like to try to do. Since it appears to be time for reunions, I have an announcement for you: you can expect me, your brother Eduard, in Pujaforta this coming 22nd of November for a birthday celebration. I look forward to seeing you and my brother and everyone else, and meeting your daughter, on that day. *Una abraçada molt forta*, Eduard." Gaspard looked up from the paper. Àngels was covering her mouth with her hands and Josep was shaking his head.

"Is it true?" Àngels said.

Josep was standing. "Do you really think he means it? We've heard this before. I would hate for everyone to get their hopes up. Especially me."

Gaspard nodded. "This time he means it."

CHAPTER TWENTY-ONE

IN THE WEEKS leading up to Eduard's visit any observer would have thought the Balaguers were preparing for a papal visit, especially Josep, who wanted Eduard to feel as proud as he did of what they had accomplished, despite the circumstances. With no coaxing from Dolors, Josep varnished the weathered tables on the terrace, daringly climbed onto the roof and replaced old shingles, and weeded the garden even though by the time Eduard arrived it could be beneath the snow.

Dolors had been in a spin about how she would handle it all without Montse's help and was so enthused about Josep's fixing spree that she baked him his favorite bread and acquired the highest quality blood sausages for his breakfast. Josep, however, had noticed that his love handles had expanded and sagged. He needed to get back out to the mountain as in his days of smuggling. While the activity hadn't been good for his nerves, it had been good for his physique. When he refused Dolors' blood sausage and suggested she do the same, she put a fist to her long-gone hips.

"I am happy with my figure. Women have shape," she said, shifting her weight onto one foot. "Wait a minute. Why are you so concerned about your looks all of a sudden?" She scowled. "Geneviève is back, isn't she?" Her look brightened for a moment. "Maybe she's brought back my Pau."

"No, there is no Geneviève or anyone," Josep said, hardly even hearing his wife. "I've got to go for a walk." He headed for the door.

"Gather mushrooms, the good ones, and pine nuts while you're out there," she called after him.

Soon after the house, the bakery, and Josep himself were in improved physical shape, the family began to gather in preparation for Eduard's visit. Josep spent much time pacing, his slightly deflated stomach churning with nerves. What if Eduard didn't like the house, or worse, didn't like him?

What if he didn't even come? This would not be the first time Eduard did not materialize.

He could hardly believe that almost a year had passed since their last birthday, when the thought of Eduard not coming had almost killed him. It was also almost a year since Franco's death had officially removed him from office. Since then The Transition had not been very transitory, but there was hope. The *Franquistes* in Madrid had been squabbling over the future, under the guidance of King Juan Carlos' more democratic hand. Now it would seem they were making some progress: they had just passed a new law for political reform declaring the country a parliamentary monarchy. So the Republic was dead, and the monarchy was alive and offering what Baltasar deemed some quite encouraging advice. By passing the new law many, but not all, of the *Franquistes* were committing political suicide. Josep grinned, walking in circles around the garden, imagining being able to vote for the first time in his long life, when Baltasar arrived at a run with his doctor's bag in hand.

"Shouldn't you be in bed?" Baltasar said.

Josep looked up from the patch he was wearing in the dirt and said, "Why would I be?" He pointed to the house. "Did Dolors call you here?"

Baltasar put down his bag and flattened his tufts of hair. "Yes. She told me that you were dying again."

"That woman exaggerates. I hope she didn't pull you away from a real patient." Josep was relieved that all of Dolors' doting on Baltasar had not changed a thing between him and his good friend. He held his stomach and belched slightly. "Now that you are here, I think I have something seriously wrong. I would swear it's a tumor. It's all this politics. And the waiting."

"I hear you. Let's go inside." Baltasar slapped Josep's back. "I'm sure it's as much of a tumor as it was last time. You really shouldn't get so worked up."

They both stopped mid-stride as Dolors came running toward them. Her much wider stomach made her legs appear even shorter. "Baltasar," she said hanging on his arm. "It's so wonderful of you to come. You are so reliable. Josep keeps murmuring about a tumor, but I'm sure that you can fix him."

Indeed, Josep's stomach ache subsided with a couple of Baltasar's pills, a swig of milk, and a glass of *ratafia* in the company of his good friend, so much so that he was feeling entirely recovered when a taxi pulled up in front. A woman jumped out of the passenger seat while the driver unloaded bag after bag from the trunk. From his spot on the terrace, Josep saw a stylish lady walking confidently towards them. He was about to ask Baltasar if he knew the woman when he did a double-take.

"Josep, *fill*. Don't you recognize your own mother?" Núria laughed and pulled Josep into her arms. He let her squeeze him until he could hardly breathe before pulling back, taking in her new short hairstyle, permed stylishly into place. She looked years younger than when she had left.

"*Mare*, you look so different," he said. "It's no wonder. You've been gone so long."

"I am so thankful that Àngels talked me into going. Life is too short and I've seen so much." She grasped Josep and Baltasar's elbows. She blinked at them repeatedly. "These spectacles have made a world of difference," she said, lightly touching the round tortoiseshell glasses perched on her nose.

"I told you years ago that you needed proper glasses," Baltasar said.

Núria patted his cheek and looked toward the family cottage. "How is my dear Àngels? I tried to get back sooner but there have been horrible strikes in France. Those people really know how to put up a fuss. I called as often as I could. Did she really send Manel away?"

Josep and Baltasar nodded simultaneously as a voice came from behind.

"*Mare*, is that you?"

"Àngels!" Núria ran towards her daughter and the two hugged and held each other cheek to cheek, rocking back and forth. Finally Núria pulled away. "Let me take a look at my daughter who is once again a mother herself." Then she leaned in and whispered. "Is she here?"

Àngels nodded and pulled her mother by the hand. Joana stepped forward with her shoulders almost at her ears. Núria approached her and gently took her hands. "You are Joana. Àngels and I have talked about you on the telephone a number of times, but I feel like I already know you." She reached out and scrunched Joana's curls and Joana cringed slightly. "The resemblance is uncanny. And the situation must be very overwhelming for everyone. Especially you. All this family coming out of the woodwork to smother you."

Joana smiled as Àngels put an arm softly around her shoulders and said, "We're all adjusting slowly and it will take some time. Víctor has adapted incredibly well. He arranged this visit, didn't he, Joana?"

"Yes, he said he would come all the way to Madrid to fetch me, but I said I could take the bus. This Uncle Eduard must be someone very special."

"Yes, he's finally coming." Núria shook her fists in victory. "I spent the whole time I was at his house trying to convince him to come. I'm glad it eventually worked. Darling, Àngels, I'm so happy you talked me into going. I haven't regretted it for a moment."

"I have," Àngels began, but Dolors had stepped in front of her.

"Núria, I'm so thrilled you're here." Dolors hugged Núria and kissed her on either cheek. "Since two of my children have abandoned me." She hardly took a breath or let Núria take one. "So tell me, have you really seen Pau?"

Núria gave a definitive nod. "He's fabulous. I have seen him dance all over. His troupe has performed in many major European cities, but none in Spain so far. It may be too soon yet, for a number of reasons."

"Does he miss us?" Dolors clenched her hands to her chest. The others gathered around expectantly.

"Of course he does, dear," Núria said. "Although he doesn't have much time. But I think he has managed to dance that monkey right off his back. He's also met someone. You'd be so proud of him."

"I am, really." Dolors clasped Núria's shoulders. "So my boy is both healthy and attached?"

"I'll tell you all about Pau later. He's quite the budding star. I even have pictures." Núria looked around them. "And Rosa?"

"She and Víctor will be with us shortly." Dolors sighed. "We have received another letter from Montse and it doesn't sound like she's missing us much either." She scowled at Josep clearly to remind him that he was at fault. "She chased after that Luc fellow for a while, but she was moving on to—," she looked at Josep.

"Walamagou," Josep said.

"Lord knows why," Dolors said and leaned in. "She says that Josep owes some major explanations." She nudged Josep. "And I agree."

"I'm glad that nothing has changed around here." Núria grasped Dolors' hands, touched Joana's cheek, and put an arm around Àngels. "Dolors, you know I've had the finest croissants in Paris, the most delicious strudel in Vienna, but what I want is some of your pine nut *coca*. It feels so good to be home."

When they were all finally gathered around the table, Rosa came in from the cold with Víctor. The chill had not seemed to affect them; on the contrary, they were both glowing. Rosa dashed to her grandmother's side as Núria jumped out of her chair.

"*Iaia*, you're back." Rosa put her rosy cheek against Núria's. "I can't wait to hear all about it. I was afraid that the strike might keep you away."

"Nothing would keep me away from my family on such a grand occasion." Núria reached toward Víctor. "I am so happy to see you, my boy, though you're not a boy at all, are you? Àngels told me you were back. Rosa is a real fighter, as you must also be."

Víctor put a hand on Rosa's shoulder. "Indeed, we are. Rosa's still working on changing things from Barcelona, and all the protests keep her in the city too much. For the time being we've been working on Manel's shack, haven't we, Rosa?"

Rosa looked over her shoulder at him. "Yes, but I think we have a little more to do."

"Yes, we have to keep at it," he said, and looked from Rosa to the family. "The rest of the place is looking fabulous, Josep. So when exactly is Eduard arriving anyway?"

"Tomorrow," everyone said at once.

"If he shows up," Josep said, putting a hand on the table to steady himself and the other on his stomach. "Baltasar, I don't know if I'm going to make it."

***

Josep hardly slept all night. By the time the sun was peeking in his shutters, he had played out Eduard's entire visit in his head. Now he was convinced that he wouldn't come and as he pulled himself out of bed, Josep felt the lightness of relief. This way they wouldn't have to discuss all their troubles and misunderstandings. Some things were better left unaddressed, particularly if Eduard still had bouts of paranoia and a general lack of reason. There would be no point in reliving the past with someone with a warped view of it.

His conviction that Eduard would not show up grew during his birthday breakfast. The rest of the family ate in uncommon silence, almost swallowing the nerves in the air with their breakfast. Josep cut into an oversize blood sausage and as he chewed, his brow filled with disappointment and anger. He rested his fork and told his family he was going back up to bed where he shouldn't be disturbed. But as his chair scraped the floor they all heard a car backfire and Josep jumped as if it was a cannon.

Outside, the little Renault was parked at the curb. Everyone ran out in time to see Gaspard emerge from the driver's seat and Francine unfold from the passenger's side. She was just a fist shorter than her son but the width of their foreheads was the same. The whole family, except for Josep, surged towards them.

"And Eduard?" Josep stepped forward swinging his arms nervously. "He hasn't come, has he."

"Indeed I have," a voice said from the backseat. Gaspard lowered the front seat as if pushing aside a curtain and Eduard emerged from the car. He straightened up, stretching his back and pushing his very compact stomach toward them. "I feel like a sardine," he said to no one in particular. Then he looked up as many gray eyes just like his were staring at him. "Good morning, family," he said looking at them as if he had just seen them yesterday. He then stopped as the reality struck him. His face collapsed and he buried it in his hands. Deep sobs wracked his chest. Then he dropped his hands from his face, the emotion leaving him as quickly as it had seized him and he breathed deeply and smiled. The family stood frozen watching, and when Eduard reached toward them they rushed to his arms.

Soon everyone was gathered around Eduard, kissing his cheeks, touching his sparse hair, squeezing his one hand. Àngels was stroking his cheek and Núria was gripping his arm. Josep hung back and waited. When finally the group parted he walked toward his brother with an outstretched hand.

Josep took a hesitant step forward and said, "Good morning, brother." Their gray eyes locked.

Eduard took his hand and pulled Josep toward him until their chests were touching. He slapped him on the back. "Josep, Josep," he said. "What fools."

Josep felt the years of sadness and their foolishness rise in his chest and sobbed. His anger flowed out in his tears until he breathed in and it was gone. He kissed his brother on the cheek. "There's no fool like an old fool, as *Pare* would have said."

Eduard slapped Josep's back once more and pulled away. He looked over Josep's shoulder toward the house, the garden, and Àngels' cottage. He reached out for Àngels and Núria, who both grasped his elbows.

"Uncle Eusebi's house. It's so fancy," Eduard said. "And our house is looking so charming. Do you still plant corn?"

Josep shook his head and looked at his sister. "But Àngels and I did replant the rose bushes. You'll have to come back in summer to see them."

"You've done a splendid job for now, particularly with the weather," Eduard said, waving a hand toward the bright sunshine reflecting off the thin layer of snow.

"Consider it my present to you. Happy birthday, brother." Josep slapped his shoulder, hoping that their conversation would not be so mundane as to discuss the weather. Then again, maybe they would find that was all they had to talk about. "Now come inside. You'll have to see what Dolors has done in there. I can't take the credit. Then I imagine you'll want to rest, after the long car ride."

"And waste another moment?" Eduard held Josep's arm in the crook of his and took Àngels' hand.

"Papa, why don't you relax a bit? No need to overdo it," Gaspard said.

Eduard shook his head. "Children. We raise them so that later they can judge us and tell us what's best for us."

"Papa." Gaspard shook his head.

"He's looking quite well, isn't he?" Àngels said while Eduard, Francine, and Gaspard were getting settled.

"And he seems quite healthy up here," Josep tapped his temple. "A little emotional, but aren't we all? He's like my old Eduard."

"Of course he is," Núria said, putting plates on the table. "What did you expect? When I visited him in France he was just like the boy I knew. Josep, you'd filled my head with all these ideas about him. Then he seemed perfectly normal."

The whole family looked at Josep accusingly. "Did he tell you about his hand? Did you ask him how that happened?"

"He told me all about the past, his days in that horrific camp, his time in the Resistance. He even talked about his attachment to Manel's brother, that Artur fellow, and that now he realizes it was overblown. He was reluctant to talk about his hand, perhaps because it brings back unpleasant memories."

"I am more than sure that it does," Josep said.

There was a footstep on the stairs and everyone turned as Eduard approached them. He was shuffling slightly and kept his good hand on his abdomen. The whole family jumped up to help him.

"Speak of the devil," Eduard said. "I know you were all talking about me. Don't worry, I'm used to it."

Gaspard and Francine appeared behind him and they all took a seat at the table, which was overflowing with food. Dolors had made a special *escudella*, the traditional soup, and endless *truites*, tomato bread, *croquetes*, *botifarra* sausages—all the food that would be sure to awaken Eduard's childhood taste buds. It appeared to do so, and everyone else's as well. Once all of her fare had been consumed, Dolors brought out her trays of *coca* and said, "It's a special birthday *coca*, and I've made a special *flam* for Josep since it's the only sweet of mine he'll touch."

"I will touch this," Josep said opening a bottle of cava with a resonating pop and rescuing some foam with a glass. "You said no to the wine, but you won't be able to say no to cava, unless now you only drink French champagne." Josep tilted the bottle over Eduard's glass but Eduard waved his hand.

"Maybe later," Eduard said.

"There's plenty for now and later," Josep said.

Eduard shook his head.

Josep shrugged and raised his glass in the air. "Here's to families reunited. And to long years of better understanding ahead of us."

"Here, here, *chin chin*," everyone repeated.

"*Per molts anys*," Baltasar said and raised his glass. "To many more healthy, happy years to the two of you."

"And to everyone," Eduard said.

Núria stood. "I was afraid I would never see my three living children together here with me." She stretched her glass toward each of them. "My prayers have been answered. Eduard, I hope that this visit does for you what my visit to your house did for me. I realized if I was going to see and do anything in this life I had to do it now. Let's make the most of every moment together. And that means no talk of politics."

Eduard smirked and raised his water glass. "To slowing down time."

At that point, Àngels placed identical boxes in front of Eduard and Josep. They were wrapped in paper with wild colors and print and sealed with gold stickers from a shop in Barcelona.

"What's this?" Eduard said, looking up.

"It's so that you can keep track of each other."

The two brothers shrugged. Josep tore the paper off his while Eduard slowly peeled his away with his good hand, refusing any help. Inside were matching boxes containing identical wristwatches. As each struggled to fasten it to his own wrist, Eduard held out his arm and let Àngels adjust the strap for him. He kissed her on both cheeks. Josep stood up to join him. After both brothers kissed everyone in the family, they stopped in front of each other and kissed on the left cheek, then the right. Both were wet with tears.

Later the rest of the family discreetly disappeared and left Josep and Eduard alone, sitting across from each other at the cleared table. Josep felt a wave of nerves and was even more uneasy than during his most treacherous smuggling missions. It was only Eduard sitting across from him, not a Guardia Civil or the mayor, yet he felt he would be more adept at reading them. At that moment, it came to him that he didn't even know his own brother. Josep stroked the wisps of hair above his ears and in an attempt to gain some time he offered Eduard a cigarette, which he declined.

"Funny how your hair is like mine," Josep said finally, observing that while the years had formed layers on his brother, he still looked almost the same as always.

"What's left of it," Eduard said, and smiled timidly. "But yours isn't all gray yet."

"And you're about as thin as you were in Argelès. And we were starving." Josep thought of their months in the French camp, of the two of them in their dugout, and in his memory they all seemed like different people.

"Maybe I'd be heavier if my wife were a baker." Eduard looked at the floor. "With Francine working at the post office, I do most of the cooking."

Josep shifted in his seat, trying to get more comfortable with this conversation. "I don't go near the kitchen. So I heard you were working in a bar?"

"Not any more," Eduard said, offering no other information.

"Incidentally, how about that drink?" Josep stood, feeling anxious again. "*Ratafia*? Or do you still prefer Ricard?"

"Josep, I don't drink. I don't gamble. I don't handle any money. I don't work."

Josep sat down. "I see."

"And my life is so much better."

"I must say you seem like the calm after the storm, compared to the last time I saw you." Josep thought of the little house hidden in the woods and the loud argument that made him leave.

Eduard winced and pushed himself forward in his chair. Reaching into his shirt pocket, he withdrew the *caganer* figurine of the squatting man and pushed it toward Josep. "You know, I took that from the church for you on the day of the battle. It was meant to be a joke. I didn't reckon it would take this long to be able to tell it. I know that it's far too late now, but I was young and far too impressionable. I can never forgive myself. But I want to ask you for your forgiveness."

"Nonsense, there's nothing to forgive," Josep said without hesitation, surprising himself. He stared at the figurine looking at him from the table, the one that appeared every time they abandoned each other. The man with his trousers at his knees seemed to drive home the ridiculousness of it all. "There's no point in digging up all that. Let's not waste time with that nonsense. Even our families are reminding us." He lifted his wrist and showed his watch. "As today would indicate, we're not getting any younger."

"So we can bury the hatchet?"

"As *Pare* would have said." Josep didn't even have to think about it. He had been thinking about it all for far too long. He reached out for Eduard's hand, which felt slightly limp in his. He leaned forward and hugged his brother. It was like all the years of bottled resentment were expulsed from his body and he held onto Eduard to anchor himself to the earth. It was as if once again they were chasing each other through Uncle Eusebi's garden, then fighting Franco's army side by side and stashing their weapons together in the woods. And he once again felt complete.

As Josep pulled away, Eduard said, "Before we entirely close the subject, I do have something I want to do."

"In Pujaforta?"

"In Catalonia," Eduard said. "I want to go back to Barcelona. I want to walk up today's Passeig de Gràcia, not a deserted night-time version. I want to see where that prison camp was."

Josep winced as he felt dragged back toward the same overtraveled road. "Don't you think it's better left in your memory?"

"I have been thinking about my life and where it went astray. I've managed to trace it back to that time. That place. Now I think that if I could see it all again, I could tie it all together, lock that part away."

"It probably looks entirely different now."

"That's what Gaspard says." Eduard sighed. "But I feel it almost like a physical need. I can't go back to Adiol to see Artur's town since it is now under water."

"You know." Josep leaned back and looked at the ceiling. He thought it would be better to change the subject from Artur, since it had always been a perilous topic of conversation. "I wonder whatever became of that fellow Jaime, the one who took us in at the camp in Argelès, the one who carved all the time. I wonder if he ever met up with his family back in Murcia."

"He didn't," Eduard said. "At least he hadn't when I saw him."

Josep practically jumped in his seat. "You saw him? Where?"

"He came into the bar where I was working and recognized me. When he smiled at me with his missing teeth it was like we were back on that beach again. We had some drinks together, too many drinks. With all the talk of the camp I drank myself sightless. I only remember waking up in a jail cell. After all my years of hiding, I couldn't believe I'd allowed myself to let down my guard. That's when I began to take stock of things, but it took me a long time."

"But it looks like you managed," Josep said trying to lighten Eduard's darkening mood. "With much willpower, no doubt." He lifted the glass in his hand. "I have little of that where food and liquor are concerned, and particularly women."

"Gaspard did mention that you knew his dance teacher." Eduard shook his head. "That was so long ago. I can't picture him dancing now. But he is good before crowds. When you see him in the lecture hall he has so much presence. He's the one who saved my mind."

"In the classroom?"

"At the university. I just sit in. That's what helped me, and all the reading. It is the most fabulous way to escape without going anywhere. Not that I want to escape my life, mind you, but it does bring me peace. I've read all the classics, French, Spanish, English, German, Russian, you name it."

"Sounds like Rosa, my daughter. She read all the books when I smuggled them over the border. Behind my back, of course."

"But you never read any?"

"No, I was busy with other things."

"The dance teacher." Eduard nodded.

"And fighting the regime, in my own way. Geneviève brought me news of you, you know."

"I know. Gaspard mentioned that as well." Eduard nodded. "Do you know one thing I regret?"

"Not having an affair?" Josep winked.

"No." Eduard waggled his finger. "I could never cheat on my Francine. I regret never writing about my life."

"You could do it now."

Eduard shook his head. "Who would want to read it? Besides, it's too late now. Every year it seems like my last birthday was just weeks ago. And here it is again."

"But this time we are finally together." Josep put his hand on top of Eduard's, wanting to hold it there for good.

"I've just had the most peaceful sleep in years," Josep said when he came into the kitchen the next morning. "Good book?" he asked Gaspard who was sitting at the table in a square of morning sunlight reading a book written in Russian.

"Excellent analysis of the human mind and what it's capable of doing to itself. Dostoyevsky."

"Do you think that reading this makes you understand your father better?"

"His reading it has helped him understand himself, or at least help him not to worry so much." Gaspard closed the book. "It's a form of distraction."

"It seems to have worked." Josep reached out and took the book in his hand, feeling the ribbed texture of the cover. "If this is what I think it is, I once held a Spanish copy in my hands. Maybe I should have read it."

"It's never too late."

"Not according to your father. He seems to have turned the page on a few of his dreams."

"He told you that?" Gaspard leaned on the table. Outside some birds cawed, bidding stragglers to join their migration southward. Gaspard paused. "Did he tell you why?"

"Are you going to tell me? The man is only a year younger than me and I feel years away from being ready to pack it in. We have to make up for all the time we lost."

"You're going to have to do it fast." Gaspard lowered his head but then looked Josep in the eye. "You'll have a few months, maybe, depending on his treatments. But they're practically worse than the disease itself. Every time he takes longer to recover."

Josep nodded, trying to absorb this information. "It's those intestinal troubles, isn't it?"

"That's what we originally thought. But it's his stomach. Papa said it's taking its revenge for starving it for so many years, that it's eating him from the inside instead." Gaspard shook his head. "He's always been a bit of an exaggerator and a cynic."

"So, does he know?"

"Certainly, we couldn't keep it from him. It's his life. He needs to be able to deal with its ending."

Gaspard's final words seemed to hit Josep front on. Josep felt his own stomach twist and the air block in his lungs. When he released it, it was an inhuman sounding sob. He once again felt their hands touching just hours before, the same hands that had touched before they parted in the church square all those years ago. Now the hand was being dragged away, a blur sweeping from the past to the present and vanishing over the lip of the mountain, another Balaguer man lost. He covered his face and shook his head. "They can't take him away from me now. Not now." After a few moments he felt Gaspard's warm grip on his shoulder and Josep wiped his face and loudly blew his nose in his handkerchief.

"That's why you need to use every moment. He will need to think about other things, about life, and not spend his last days dwelling on the past or the disease. Can you do that for him?"

Josep looked at his crumpled handkerchief and nodded slightly. "I can and I will," he said, and handed Gaspard his book.

Later in the day the family gathered again over another marathon lunch. This time Josep didn't offer Eduard any alcohol and he observed that he ate only small bites of food, which he seemed to chew endlessly. Eduard appeared to be taking in all the conversation as if memorizing it all for later. When the women were washing up in the kitchen and the men were sitting around the table digesting, Eduard pointed across the table and said, "Where is that Manel fellow?"

Josep looked over his shoulder toward Àngels, whose ears appeared to prick up at the name. "He's gone." Josep whispered.

"*Mecachis*. I wanted to ask him some things about his brother, Artur."

Josep put a hand on Eduard's shoulder. "I thought we said we weren't going to talk about the past."

Eduard's face flushed and his forehead appeared clammy with perspiration. "I know," he said. "But this is another topic on my list. There are some things I need to know."

"I'll tell you if I can," Àngels said standing over them and wiping her hands on a towel. "But you were the one who was with him most of those years."

"Yes, I know. But I never saw the letter about his death. Did Manel believe it?"

"Yes, he definitely did. Artur died in that camp in Austria."

"Mauthausen. I was there." Eduard tapped the table with the tip of his finger. "I asked all over about him. The Americans, the British, no one had any word of him or even of his existence. I've had this hovering feeling ever since." He motioned as if to a halo over his head. "No one has ever received any word from him since?"

"No, no one has." Àngels put a hand on Eduard's shoulder. "Perhaps you would like to see something. It's not as definitive as a grave, but it helped Manel and it has helped me tremendously over the years." She stroked his back. "You should bundle up."

As they all moved towards the door Josep whispered to Gaspard, "This Artur business could drive him back over that edge."

Gaspard shook his head. "I don't think so. This new turn in his life has made him incredibly strong." Then he whispered, "She's not going to show him anything horrendous, is she?"

Josep shook his head and followed them all out to the tree at the edge of Àngels' garden. Víctor brushed the snow off the rock underneath it and the patch of earth around it. "This is where Manel used to come almost every day to talk to him," Àngels said, keeping her arm around Eduard. "Artur's Republican flag is in here and a few other objects Manel found in their house. We buried some of his belongings with Carme's so we would have a place to visit them."

Eduard stood silently looking back and forth between Àngels and the stone. Then he nodded.

Àngels rubbed his back. "Maybe you'd like a moment alone?"

"I would," Eduard said.

Josep put a hand on his shoulder. "Are you sure?"

He motioned for them to leave him. "I am. This is just what I need."

Eduard returned to the house a while later looking cold but peaceful. Only Josep was waiting for him in the sitting room, where the aroma of their copious lunch still lingered. Josep had asked the family for another private moment with Eduard and he pulled out a chair for him and sat down across from him. Eduard still wore his jacket and blew into his hands. Josep reached out and patted the good one.

"You're sure you're well?" Josep asked.

"As well as I can be, mentally. I'm not going to lose control and get arrested again if that's what you're worried about." Then he sighed. "Gaspard told you, didn't he?"

Josep looked to the side and back again. "He wasn't supposed to?"

"It's not a secret, but it's out of the question for you to look at me like you are now."

"How's that?"

"With pity in your eyes."

"It's not pity. The pity is for myself. After all this time, here we are and now I'm going to lose you again. I'm the pitiful person who gets left behind."

"I'd swap places with you."

Josep sighed. "I'm sorry, I'm not belittling the fact that you are the one who has to die. In fact, I would swap places with you. What have I got to live for now anyway?"

"Am I hearing this? Your family. Your children. Your wife. Your friends. Yourself."

"None of my children live here anymore and my wife can't stand the sight of me."

"Sure she can. I see how she looks at you."

"In disgust and disappointment."

"It's up to you to change that." Eduard shifted in his seat. "You know, Josep, maybe you can use this predicament of mine to put your life in order. Perhaps you'll learn something from me."

"You do seem accepting of it all. I don't know that I would be. I think I would rather just be hit by a truck, or even fall suddenly off a cliff. All this time to ruminate can't be good."

"At first it wasn't. I was angry, so angry. All that did was make it worse for Francine and Gaspard. Once I figured that out it was better for everyone. And now here I am with you. I might not be otherwise."

"So I should be thankful for this disease that has brought you to me but then will be taking you away? And just when it finally seems safe for you to come back."

"No one said life was fair," Eduard said. "Incidentally, I'll have to be leaving tomorrow."

Josep grasped Eduard's hand. "But you've just arrived. What about our trip to Barcelona?"

Eduard sighed. "They have to try to calm the beast within me. Tame it with their drugs."

"I'll go with you. I can take care of you. Do you need money?"

"That's all covered now." Eduard shook his head. "It takes everything out of me. Gaspard will be there for me. So will Francine. I'd rather you remember me as I am now. Can you do that for me?"

Josep was silent, thinking that in most of his memories Eduard was in his twenties. On top of it, now he would have to erase the images that had been forming in his mind of all the brotherly things they were going to do together. He looked into Eduard's eyes and swallowed. "I can try."

As Eduard, Francine, and Gaspard gathered outside the next day to say goodbye, the Balaguer family mood was at its lowest. Àngels and Núria tried to save themselves by clinging to Eduard, who rocked them and assured them that he would see them soon. None of them dared acknowledge the lie. Josep gently urged them apart and hugged Eduard, feeling his stubble clinging to his own and fearing his bones may crumble in his very arms. As Eduard's family climbed back into their car ready to head back to France, Josep refused to say goodbye. Once they were gone, Josep felt that the house, the table, and his life were empty.

A few weeks after their departure, when the Balaguers had hardly recovered from the visit, they were called to the urns to vote in the referendum on the new law about the political future of the country. Although they went in celebration as a family, Josep felt that some of the joy had been taken out of his first experience of putting the ballot in the box. When he saw the overwhelming result in favor of the law, he knew that one more vote from his brother would have made no difference, but it made a difference to him. Nonetheless, he and Baltasar celebrated with a glass of cava while watching the television news.

Right when he thought that life would return to normal, another car pulled to a stop in front of the house and Josep almost collapsed. Luc was walking purposefully through the knee-deep snow toward their door. Josep searched desperately behind him for Montse and called to Dolors in the kitchen just as the bakery doorbell chimed.

"Luc, what are you doing here? Where's Montse?" Josep said opening the door, searching for his daughter, but not really wanting to know what could have brought him back. Luc stomped his boots on the mat, then looked up at Josep, but his golden eyes gave no hints.

"Sorry for the surprise. I was afraid that if I wrote to warn you, you might not be here when I arrived."

"Where's my daughter?" Dolors' voice came from behind them.

Luc cleared his throat and shuffled his feet. "Montse? That's one of the reasons I've come." He looked up at Josep and whispered. "We need to talk." Then he called out to Dolors. "She's as fine as can be, although she didn't come with me. We have sort of lost touch."

"What do you mean you lost touch? You took a young woman all the way to Canada and you lost her?" Dolors scrambled closer, her face red and her voice trembling.

"That's what I've come to talk to you about. I'm on a break for Christmas. I had an exhibition relatively nearby, in Paris, and then a meeting in Toulouse." He pointed over the mountain. "Will you invite me in? It's been a very long trip. I've hardly slept and I haven't eaten all day."

Josep and Dolors looked at each other. Josep shrugged and Dolors scowled before waving Luc inside. "You may as well come in then, but just if you're going to tell us about our daughter."

"I'd be much better able to do so on a full stomach," Luc said, holding his middle and looking up.

Dolors sighed and shook her head. "You North Americans are very direct, aren't you? Luckily we are very hospitable, though you don't deserve it." She headed for the kitchen and Josep grabbed Luc's sleeve.

"So where is Montse?" Josep asked.

"In Montreal. She was also up in Walamagou with Marie-Claude. When things were clearly not working out between the two of us, I talked her into doing some traveling. I didn't want to give her the wrong impression about my feelings."

Josep shook his head at him. "She chased you all the way over there. What about her feelings?"

"I was gentle. Besides, it's all worked out for the better, believe me."

"Isn't that lucky for you. Is that all you're going to tell me? It's an awfully long way to come."

"It's Marie-Claude who wanted me to visit. She wanted me to see how you are." Luc gazed down at him. "I'd say you're looking pretty well for someone who must feel as guilty as you do."

Josep grabbed his sleeve again and swore they were not going start the same conversation over again. "I've had it with guilt. That's all I've ever felt and I'm not giving into it anymore. I've learned some things since you left. And I learned them from my brother, in case you want to throw that in my face again."

Luc nodded, obviously impressed. "So you've finally met up. Is he here?"

"No, he had to go home. He has commitments there."

"Speaking of reunions with long lost family, I also wanted to tell you something, something concerning you." Luc's eyebrows drew together. "I did meet with my father and I've figured out the whole story without your help. The story you thought I already knew. Well, I didn't, and now Montse knows as well."

Josep's gut sank. "She knows? How?" Now he was sure that Montse would never come home. He reached for Luc and clutched his shoulders. "Was it you who told her?"

Luc stepped back pulling Josep with him. "I've done nothing but try to help her."

"Help her with what?" A voice came from behind them. Dolors was standing in the doorway with a steaming omelet on a plate perched on her palm. "Josep, what's going on now?"

Josep released Luc's shoulders and stroked them, stepping back and looking at his shoes. "Luc's been helping Montse get settled, isn't that right, Luc? Now where did you say that was?"

"In Montreal. And she's working in a bakery, a Jewish bakery."

"What?" Dolors said. "Why would she bake all the way over there when she could be doing that here. And with me?"

"She may never come back," Josep said, shaking his head. "So, Luc, if that's all you have to tell us, I really can't understand why you would come this far out of your way."

"Because it's just one of my reasons for coming. The other is to see Rosa. I have the perfect opportunity for her personally and professionally," Luc said and looked around the room. "Is she here?"

"She is not," Dolors said and slammed the plate of *truita* on the counter. "And if I have anything to say about it, you will not see her. Is taking one of my daughters not enough?"

***

When Rosa returned to Pujaforta for Christmas she seemed surprised at the sight of Luc standing alone beside a pine tree inside the house. He had cut it down himself to break the ice when he had learned that the Balaguers had never had a Christmas tree, although many families did have them. He said that afterwards he would use it to sculpt a giant baguette for the entrance to the bakery. Nonetheless, despite Manel's uninhabited shack and all the empty rooms in the house, he was still staying at the hotel in Adiol La Nova.

"So you have imported your tradition, have you?" Rosa said. "Have you brought my sister back with you too?"

"No," Luc said and stepped toward her. "Just the tree. I am very glad to see you, though. I think you'll be pleased to hear what I have to tell you."

She looked into his amber eyes and once again took in his darker skin and his lighter hair and sensed danger in his aura. The skin on her cheeks tingled and instead of backing away she took a minute step forward. Conflict had always been like a magnetic field for her. "First tell me where my sister is."

"She's safe in Quebec, no doubt with snow over her head."

"And her trip there with you was also over her head, I gather."

"You were the one meant to come with me." Luc stepped closer.

Rosa turned her back. "Things have changed since you were last here. You ran off with my sister for one."

"And you're very snug with Víctor no doubt, now that he's a free man."

"He is and he means more to me than anyone ever could."

Luc looked around them. "Where is he now?"

"He'll be back any moment. He went to Madrid to bring back my cousin, Àngels' daughter. It's a long story, but she required some persuading to come for Christmas."

"You don't mind him traveling alone with another woman?"

"I trust him entirely. His going is all part of the plan for our future."

"I hope to be able to be part of that plan. I have the venue arranged." His eyes glowed at her and the giant tree hovered behind him, its needles too long and branches too sparse for a story-book Christmas tree. "You remember the sculpture of my mother I made while I was here? It's was a hit and now it's even on show in Paris. That's why I could come here."

"I'm really pleased for you," Rosa said, and she was. "The piece was lovely and full of feeling."

"That's what I was told. In the process I've been able to talk to people, some important people about your work. A gallery in Ottawa, right near the Parliament buildings, is interested in an exhibition." He leaned toward her. "They're almost as thrilled about it as I am."

Rosa felt the spark of excitement pass between them. She took it for a flow of inspiration between artists, and for a moment she could see all her pictures on display, something which was far too soon to happen in Spain. Things were slowly changing, but she knew that as long as the official "Pact of Forgetting" existed, it would be ages before she could show anyone her pictures. She bit her lip. "I do appreciate it, Luc, but my photos and I have to stay here. It's where we belong."

Once Víctor and Joana had returned, they accompanied Rosa to meet Luc in the town bar for a pre-Christmas lunch *vermut*. Rosa found that her parents seemed increasingly annoyed at Luc's presence. They said he'd supposedly told them all he knew about Montse, and so why was he still at their house? Rosa became convinced that once Luc saw her with Víctor he would leave for good. When they stepped into the bar and stomped their boots in the puddle inside the door, Rosa felt the warmth from all the people and the fire roaring in the fireplace. Luc was sitting alone against the wall at a table for four and looking very at ease. He was looking up, making an attempt to chat with the bar woman and when he saw them, he jumped up and came out to greet them. As they approached, taking off their coats, Rosa noticed that Luc's hair looked even more golden in the firelight. He stepped toward her and held her by the shoulders before kissing her cheeks very slowly.

Víctor stuck his hand between them and said, "*Je m'appelle* Víctor. You may remember me. Shall we sit down?" He gestured towards Joana. "This is our cousin Joana from Madrid. She understands some French but doesn't speak it, so we should probably make this short since she's come a long way."

"As have I," Luc said sitting down and pulling Rosa into the chair next to him. Víctor frowned as he and Joana sat across from them. Rosa felt Víctor's dark eyes drilling into hers as Luc put his arm across the back of her chair.

"I'm pleased to meet you," Joana said and shrugged. "I've always been fascinated by the French. By the culture, the language, and their very strong central government."

"Luc here is not French," Víctor said. "So, tell me something, Luc. I saw Montse leave with you. What exactly happened with her?" Víctor tapped the table with all four fingers.

"Last I saw her, she was looking very happy and fulfilled," Luc said. "Trust me, she is better off than you could imagine. She's been spending a lot of time with my family."

"So she's not alone at least," Víctor said and gestured to the bar woman for four glasses of local vermouth. "She went back there with you and you are here. How did she handle that?"

"She was a little upset at first, but when I introduced her to people in Montreal, she easily forgot about me." Luc offered them a cigarette and lit his own. "Fortunately, because she wasn't really my type." He put his arm back on Rosa's chair.

"What do you mean by that?" Rosa asked shifting away from him.

"I need someone I can take to my shows. Someone I can connect with on an artistic level." He looked toward Víctor and Joana. "Rosa here has done wonders for my art. I had a block that I couldn't break. I thought Rosa's father could help me, but Rosa was the one. I suppose Montse isn't worldly enough for me."

"And you're worldly?" Víctor said.

"I've been around. I've been to France and I've been here."

"Not exactly world traveling," Víctor said, and Rosa tilted her head at him hoping that they could leave the conversation there, but everyone was acting very prickly this Christmas morning.

"And where have you been, Víctor?" Luc asked leaning closer to Rosa. "Other than behind bars."

Rosa balked at him while Víctor slammed down his glass. "Here things were different," he said. "If we'd been free to do what we wanted, I would have gone places. Whatever you might think, I did meet some fascinating people in prison. People from all over and I was even able to help a number of them. That is more useful and gratifying than turning logs into statues."

Luc clicked his tongue, evidently not even listening. "What I don't understand is why you didn't just overthrow Franco? I couldn't have sat back and done nothing. Now I've found Rosa the perfect opportunity to show everyone what it was all about."

"Though it's clearly something you can never understand." Víctor stood and leaned over the table. "What I'll never understand, Rosa, is what you are doing with him."

Rosa pushed her chair back. "I'm not doing anything with him. He came here to see my father."

"No, I didn't," Luc said. "I came here to see you."

"I rest my case," Víctor said. "Joana, shall we go home?"

Joana nodded, followed Víctor and said, "Doesn't he know how many people respected The Caudillo?"

335

Rosa watched him turn away and slapped Luc on the arm. "You're certainly not scoring any points with me." She grabbed her coat and followed them out the door.

***

Josep was in the bakery kitchen stealing a freshly made Christmas bun when Joana, Víctor, and Rosa came in the door. Rosa was pulling on Víctor's elbow and Josep didn't know what all the fuss was about, but he was able to imagine.

"Víctor, stop being so ridiculous," Rosa was saying. "I'm not the slightest bit interested in Luc."

"Is that Quebecker stirring things up again?" Josep asked, heading toward the table. "He seems to like that." He raised his eyebrows at Àngels and Baltasar who were sitting across from each other. "So where is he? Is he coming for lunch?"

"He'll ruin my appetite," Víctor said, sitting down heavily as Joana went to the other side of the table, kissed Àngels on the cheek, and sat beside her. "I'd like to know what he's doing here anyway," he added.

"I wouldn't. In fact, I'm still dreading finding out why he's here," Josep said.

"Let's not talk about him." Rosa took a seat beside Víctor and put her arm around him. "We're here to have a good time together. Joana will never want to stay if there is some sort of drama every time she comes, will you, Joana?"

She shrugged and smiled. "Everyone always told me that the Reds were rather hot under the collar. It's all new and exciting to me. I'm glad Víctor talked me into coming." She looked at Àngels and smiled. "I was afraid my family would be upset."

"I told you earlier how I understand, and I am very pleased that you're here." Àngels stroked Joana's hand and looked at Víctor. "Thank you, Víctor."

"Now you're going to learn about a real Catalan Christmas," Josep said. "*Mare* and Dolors are about to bring out the *carn d'olla*. You can tell them about it in Madrid. We don't want them forgetting about us." Dolors had been busy making enormous meatballs and the hearty broth they were boiled in. The smell was tantalizing even in the far reaches of the house.

Víctor seemed to relax and rubbed his hands together. "You'd better love it, or at least say you do."

"Of course she will love it," Dolors said, as she put an enormous pot in the middle of the table. "And wait till you try the special marzipan and *torrons* I've made for dessert."

336

"Hold it there. Let me take a picture," Rosa said, posing her camera as Dolors filled the first ladle with *sopa de galets*. The camera clicked, the telephone rang, and Dolors splattered soup on the table.

"Who has the nerve to call now?" Dolors said, as Núria ran to answer it.

Everyone watched her as she nodded into the receiver and said, "*Sí, sí, sí*," before slowly hanging up. She straightened her glasses on her nose and announced, "It's Eduard. If we're going to go, we have to go now." Her voice broke.

"Now?" Dolors said, and dropped the ladle into the pot.

"And fast," Núria said. "God help us. Let us get there in time." She looked at the ceiling and put her hands to her head.

With Baltasar at the wheel of his car, Josep, Dolors, Àngels, and Núria sped across the mountain to Eduard's house in Fontsec. As they pulled up in front, Josep saw that the paint was peeling off the shutters. The faded gray house looked like Josep felt. It had definitely seen better days. Inside the door, Gaspard was anxiously awaiting them in the same foyer where Eduard had greeted him years before. It was still dim and smelled of mildew and medicine. Gaspard ushered them all in kissing and hugging them. He grasped Josep's elbows and said, "It's so good you've come. It means the world to him."

"It means everything to me and to all of us," Josep said, stepping into the dark foyer of Eduard's home and breathing in the closed up air. "Where is he?"

"In his room."

"Why isn't he hospitalized?" Baltasar asked.

"He's beyond that. It's his choice. He wanted to die here."

"But he can't die," Núria said, and pushed her way in. "Not my son, not while I'm alive. Let me through. He just needs to see his mother."

"Please come in," Gaspard said. He stood at the bottom of the stairs blocking their way. "Listen, he's very weak. I think you should see him one or two at a time."

"Yes, that is definitely advisable," Baltasar said. "Do you mind if I see him first to check his general state?"

"Certainly," Gaspard said, and the others nodded. "But I'm sure there's not much you can do." He led them upstairs until they were all standing in the carpeted hallway in front of a shut door. Light streamed in one window at the end of the hall and suspended the family in its beam. Knocking lightly, Gaspard opened the door and disappeared as if into a cave. When he reappeared, Francine was squinting beside him. Everything about her seemed to have shrunk, except for the circles under her eyes. She whispered to them and squeezed their hands, "Thank you for coming. This means more than you can know."

Baltasar then disappeared behind the door.

"So what have the doctors said?" Josep asked, trying to focus on the practical.

Francine closed her eyes. "It's out of their hands now. He has morphine for the pain, but it doesn't appear to be working. He keeps waking up in a panic trying to take a knife out of his stomach."

Núria covered her mouth. "My poor boy. Tell Baltasar to hurry. I've got to see him."

As they opened the door, Baltasar emerged with his face as ashen as his hair. When he looked at Núria he smiled slightly. "He's not that bad."

"I'll be the judge of that," Núria said, and pushed past him, insisting on seeing him alone.

"It is that bad, isn't it?" Josep grasped Baltasar's forearm. "There's no need to lie to us." He looked at Dolors and Àngels, who were gripping each other.

"It's very bad," Baltasar said. "He's quite lucid, but don't raise your hopes for a meaningful last visit."

"He told me he didn't want us to remember him like this," Josep said.

"People tend to change their mind. They would rather see the faces of their family than the face of the dark unknown."

"That's awfully morbid for a physician," Àngels said, looking at Josep and gripping his forearm. "Maybe we can see him together? I can't handle this alone." He nodded and took her hand.

"I wouldn't linger," Baltasar said. "Give everyone a chance to see him."

Francine covered her face. "Please hurry."

A few moments later Núria flew out of the room and straight down the stairs. They all stared after her. Josep put an arm around Àngels' shoulder and reached for the door. He felt the cold of the doorknob in his hand and the heat of the room as he entered it. The air was heavy with the smell of exhaled medicine and slept-in sheets, all contained by closed windows and dark drapes. By the light of a single lamp he could see the shape of Eduard under the covers, which were rising and falling with the slightness of his breath. Josep took a step closer and hesitated. Perhaps this was not the last image he wanted of his brother. He reached out for Àngels' hand, which seemed to burn in his palm.

"Come closer. I can't see you," a voice whispered from the bed and Josep pulled his sister toward it.

"Eduard, it's me, Josep. I'm with Àngels. Do you need anything?"

"A healthy body, or a sip of water."

Josep laughed at his humor, but the raspiness of Eduard's voice suggested it might be a last attempt. Taking a glass from the bedside table, Josep put a straw to his brother's cracked lips. Àngels smoothed back his wisps of hair. His face seemed to have yellowed since they last saw him.

Eduard drank and rested his head back on the pillow. "After all those drinks I took, if only I'd known that in the end I would only have water."

"If I'd known I would have come so many years earlier," Josep said, and took Eduard's hand. "We can never get it back." Josep felt the regret fill his chest and feared it would trap the last words he had for his brother.

"I think we've all learned something," Eduard whispered. "For me it's too late to put it to practice. But for you it's not."

"It won't save you or bring you back."

"No it won't. But you can save yourself. From yourself. Both of you can. Josep, you have your family and Àngels, you have your daughter. Don't let politics get in the way of either."

Àngels gripped his hand and put it to her lips. "You're right. I've bitten my tongue all these years and I can do it again."

"Maybe she'll come around," Eduard said weakly. "Ask Gaspard or even Josep here to recommend some books for her to read. They can have an extraordinary influence."

Josep released his sob and put his head on Eduard's chest. "How did my younger brother become so wise?"

"Life can do that."

"But you weren't meant to do it without me." Josep could feel Eduard's faint breath on his face and Àngels' hand on his back. He breathed in the air coming from Eduard's mouth, from Eduard's lungs, air that Eduard's living body had emptied of oxygen and he held it inside his own. Eduard coughed, shaking Josep's head to the reality of the dark room. Lifting his head from Eduard's chest, Josep rested his hand there instead. "You have always meant so much to me, even when you didn't think so. Both of you." He looked at both Eduard and Àngels.

"I know," Eduard said as Josep stood. "And I'm sorry."

"So am I," Àngels said.

Eduard cringed and winced. "Please ask Gaspard and Francine to come in."

Josep nodded. "Of course, we'll do whatever you ask." He watched as Àngels softly kissed Eduard's cheek and stroked his forehead. He then bent down and put his lips on Eduard's strangely cold forehead. Gripping his hand, Josep closed the squatting figurine in Eduard's fingers and whispered. "Everything is forgiven."

When he and Àngels exited into the light beyond the door, rather than feeling a shadow of death, Josep had a sensation of rebirth. Dolors put her arms around his waist and he held her there and felt her soft chest against his stomach. He kept his other arm around Àngels as they all stared at the closed door, both trying to see through it but not wanting to witness what was beyond it. Finally, well after the sun had set, Francine and Gaspard came out. Francine's head was bent and when she raised it to look at them she nodded. "It's over." Both pain and relief blended in her voice. Her words reached Josep as if filtered through thick sand. When their meaning registered in his head and in his heart, he embraced Dolors and Àngels and the family folded into a circle.

After a brief and intimate funeral for Eduard, his body was cremated and handed to Francine in an opaque urn.

"To think a man is reduced to this." Francine held the urn to her chest before handing it to Josep. "He wants to go with you. To fly off the cliff behind the house."

Josep swallowed and took the urn from Francine and it actually felt heavier than he expected. "He said that?"

"Those were his last wishes," Gaspard said.

Àngels wiped her cheek and put her hand to her chest. "He had another last wish, a wish that he expressed to me, Gaspard, when you were hardly a year old." She withdrew a small key dangling from a chain. "Your father told me recently that you would know what it was for. The address he gave me is the address of this very house."

As she pressed the key into Gaspard's palm, he frowned at it. "Yes, I know what it opens. He kept asking me if I knew where his old travel chest was kept. Not long ago he gave me his key." He closed his hand around it. "The chest is in the attic. Josep, will you help me bring it down?"

Together they climbed up into the space that was like climbing into the past, with years of dust protecting it. In a far corner Gaspard squatted down beside a chest and rubbed the dust from it with his forearm. The leather looked cracked and worn. They slid it out towards the entrance and down the stairs until it was resting in the center of the living room. They formed a circle around it and observed it as if expecting it to move or speak. Then Gaspard took a step toward it and put the key in the padlock. He turned it and it clicked open. "Are you ready?" he asked. The whole family nodded emphatically. When he raised the lid and they looked inside, a blanket covered the contents. Gaspard withdrew the dark blanket that was so old and dusty it almost disintegrated in his hands.

"What is this?" Gaspard held it with two fingers and dropped it on the floor.

"His blanket." Josep reached down and touched the frayed wool. "He wouldn't let it out of his sight. It may seem ridiculous today," he said looking around the fully furnished room. "But that blanket saved his life. He gave it back to Artur, but Artur must have left it with him."

"I suspect that he wasn't that well of mind when he saved this for me," Gaspard said. "What will I do with it?" He reached in again and pulled out a carving of a bird in crooked flight, a discolored pachisi board, a Canadian passport bearing someone else's name and picture, a fraying boat ticket. Josep grabbed the items from his hands.

"I can't believe he saved all this stuff." Josep sat back on his heels and stared at it.

With two fingers Gaspard then pulled out another piece of gray, moth-eaten fabric and when he shook it to unfold it they all coughed. The thing smelled like an animal had curled up and died in it decades before. Josep opened his stinging eyes and jumped on it. "It's my jacket." He took it carefully in his hands and slowly examined it. It no longer resembled his ancient corduroy jacket. It was thin, discolored, and disfigured, and Josep wished with all his heart that it could speak. It had followed Eduard throughout his life instead of him. It had kept him warm and protected him. Josep ignored the smell and hugged it.

"You can keep that if you like. It looks like these are yours, too," Gaspard said, withdrawing a small stack of letters sealed in a plastic bag and wrapped in rubber bands. He handed them to Josep, "They're from you."

Holding the jacket under his arm, Josep took them and turned them over in his hand. They were the letters that he had sent to Eduard from Canada. He frowned at the package and withdrew the envelopes, which had all been opened and arranged in chronological order. Gaspard handed him another envelope. He looked inside and saw a stack of Canadian money.

"What is it doing in here?" Josep shook it at Francine. "This must be the money I gave you on my first visit here."

Francine took it from him and ran her finger across the banknotes. "When Eduard saw me with it he took it away. I never knew what he did with it."

Dolors took it from Francine and frowned at it. "I was also always wondering what had happened to it. I don't reckon it's worth anything now."

"It's worth something to me," Gaspard said. "He was looking out for me. Looking out for my future, despite himself. Just like you were looking out for his." He reached to the base of the trunk and pulled out stack upon stack of envelopes. Each contained a letter addressed to Gaspard, one for every month of Eduard's adult life.

CHAPTER TWENTY-TWO

IN PUJAFORTA, ON the edge of the precipice, the family formed a circle around the dust of Eduard Balaguer. It was the final day of the year and the cold wind on their backs threatened to push them from the cliff into the snow-padded valley below. Above, hovering clouds beckoned. Josep was glad to be wearing his old, newly recovered jacket despite Dolors' threats to burn it. He wouldn't even let her wash it. When he had first put it on, feeling the worn fabric tight across his shoulders, he thought of his brother's thinner shoulders inside it. With a burst of urgency, he stuck his hands in the pockets, searching for any message left there. His fingers went straight through; the pockets were now gaping holes. It was later when he had arrived back home that he felt the weight in the left breast pocket. He reached inside and pulled out a handful of sand. Cupping it in his palm, he stared into it and smirked, seeing their blanket-covered dugout. Gently he poured it back in the pocket and patted it into place.

The urn in Josep's hands was icy cold. Despite the warning of Eduard's illness and the car ride home with his remains, it all felt far too sudden. All his hopes of becoming friends with his brother had turned to ashes in this urn. He gently shook it, as if trying to send a message to each and every bit, trying to make his brother whole again. As Josep stood tall in his jacket and stepped to the very edge of the cliff, his family bowed their heads for their own private prayers. Josep's mind remained silent, since he'd already made all the pleas he could. Josep lifted the lid and sprinkled most of the ashes into the breeze so that they soared skyward, almost forming wings before dispersing into the air. Josep watched as the dust seemed to migrate towards France before scattering into the valley that had broken their father's fall so many years before. Josep held the almost empty urn to his chest and dried his cheeks. Brushing a few wayward specks from his front and rubbing them tenderly between his fingers, he turned to address his family.

"So we've done as Eduard wished." He shrugged his drooping shoulders. "His other wish was for no tears or long faces, so let's wipe them away and celebrate in his honor," he said, and watched as Àngels smeared away her tears, Núria let hers run freely, and Baltasar blew his nose.

Josep gave the urn to Àngels, who they all slowly followed to the tree-side shrine, where a freshly dug hole was waiting. She scooped the ashes in a gloved hand and slowly released them, letting them flow inside it. She sobbed and covered the small mound with earth and put her fingers to her lips. Holding her handkerchief in one hand, Núria bent down and touched the blend of frozen earth and ashes. Each of them did the same before rubbing their dirty hands against the cold. Although Josep felt the irony of celebrating a life that he knew so little about, he knew he had nothing else but to commemorate his recent memories of his brother. He had received Eduard's message, almost his last words to him. They had inspired Josep to make a major decision: to cure his long diseased relationship with his wife and to bare his guilty soul to his family. He hoped that one did not preclude the other.

***

When they had all had their moment, Àngels told the family to go back inside without her. She needed a minute alone with all the phantoms of her past. Bowing her head over the fresh patch of earth, she thought of the Eduard of late and how all her worries had been realized. Then she saw the garden behind her and rather than dusted in snow, it was leafy green with rows of corn. She spotted movement as the stalks parted in a flourish. Eduard, with a laugh on his lips, was giving chase up a row towards her, the tall leaves whipping his shoulders. Diving forward he caught his prey by the ankles, ankles as thin as Àngels' had been at that age. It was then that she heard the voices, the laughing, the giggling of her brothers. Eduard and Pau. Her two dead brothers. She gasped and stepped away, halting the motion in her mind and seeing a patch of snow-circled dirt at her feet. Jumping back, she felt something against her back. Two hands held her shoulders and she looked up. She had been wrong, not all her worries were realized; in this case her hopes had come true.

"Víctor, you startled me." She gasped and turned toward him.

"Are you all right?" He put his arm around her. "I couldn't leave you here to face this on your own."

She smiled and patted his cheek. "I've pretty much always been on my own. That must be how I like it. But I do wish I could be with my brother."

"Of course, you do. You do have one left, you know." Víctor hugged her and kissed the top of her head. "And if I have anything to say about it, at least you'll be able to be with your daughter."

"She's a grown woman, with her own ideas and a job in the city. I hardly know her."

"You just need time together." Víctor gestured toward the earth under the tree. "Do you still think of her, my mother, I mean?"

"Of course, I do. I think about Carme every day." Àngels smiled slightly. "I think about how to her life was almost a game, a constant battle that she had to win. She was very unique, and I see that in you, you know. You're my little piece of her."

Víctor sighed. "I wish I could remember her, recognize her in myself." He took Àngels' hands. "In prison I thought a lot about something. Did she ever tell you about my father? I know practically nothing about him. I don't even know his name."

"I know, dear, and frankly I don't think Carme knew it either." She looked up at him. "After everything you've been through, I don't need to tell you how those were different times. We had nothing, no food. Nothing. The only thing Carme told me about her time in that camp was that she was starving and that the man who was your father got her food. So maybe in a way he saved her, from starvation or who knows. It also put her in a situation that brought her back here to me, and brought you and me together. We can be thankful for that."

Víctor nodded and stroked her hand. "I hadn't thought about it that way. For a long time I have been thinking that I'd like to learn more about his country, to know where part of me is from."

"That's a wonderful idea, but I doubt there is much information about Senegal in Pujaforta." Àngels gripped his arm. "Rosa could help. She's good at digging up information."

"She has offered. And in fact she's offered more." He looked at the patch of earth and took a breath. "I know this isn't the time, but one day relatively soon I want to go to Barcelona to be with her." He held her hands looking hopeful. "Would you approve?"

Àngels felt her earlier sadness dissipate and she smiled brightly. "Of course, that's fantastic news. What are you waiting for?"

"Really? I thought you would be upset that I was leaving you here."

"I can manage," Àngels said, feeling very strong. "I can survive perfectly well knowing that you're in the city with Rosa and not locked in jail somewhere. But you'll have to come visit. Often." She squeezed his hand. "So does this mean you're going to get married? Dolors might be traumatized if you don't."

"Let her be. By now she knows that her daughter is not one for convention." Víctor smiled. "I don't need a contract. I know that Rosa's dedicated to me. I chased that Luc fellow out of here. I don't think he'll be back."

"Josep will be quite happy about that, though Lord knows what he's hiding now. I am far beyond worrying about what Josep is up to."

***

Once time had passed, emotions had calmed, and Eduard's ashes had settled, Josep asked the question that had been nagging at him ever since they had returned from France.

"So what happened with Luc, then? He was gone by the time we got back," Josep asked Rosa one day. He knew that Luc sometimes talked out of turn and he was afraid that during his absence, he had talked too much about other subjects as well.

"He left," Rosa said. "Finally he realized that he's not going to get what he wants from you or from me."

Víctor leaned in. "I don't think he'll be back. I made sure of it."

"Really?" Josep said. "So you think you scared him away for good? What did he tell you?"

"He wanted me to go back with him and I, of course, am not interested," Rosa enunciated clearly looking at Víctor. "He hardly had the chance to finish the last word and Víctor was chasing him out of here."

"So he didn't say anything about me? I had wanted to talk to him," Josep said, thinking that it was time he told them all the truth anyway. Then again, if Luc was gone and wouldn't be coming back, he saw little point in further tarnishing his reputation.

"Yes, actually, he did mention you. He said that he had found out some things about you and that Montse knows about them, too. *Pare*, what was he talking about?"

Josep said nothing. The emotional extremes of the last few days were too much for his stomach and he felt it turn. Now if Montse knew, even so far away, it was just a matter of time. Plus he knew he had no hope against Rosa's curiosity. He heard his brother's voice in his ear, stronger than it had ever been in life. This was his chance to make things right. "Can you get your mother? And Àngels? And maybe Baltasar, too? I won't speak a word until they are all here. Then I'll tell you the truth but I only plan to say this once."

When they had all come running in, panting and taking a seat before Josep and looking at him with concerned eyes, he reached for Dolors' hand and took a deep breath. He had to find his courage somewhere.

"I have something to tell you all. It doesn't really affect you, but it affects me and the way I see myself. I've been holding this guilt inside ever since I came back from Canada. Luc has been hounding me about it, but I haven't discussed the matter with him. I want to come clean with you. You know that I am anything but perfect." He looked at Dolors and she nodded. "But you are all I have. And you are a lot."

"Well, what happened?" Rosa was sitting with her camera and notebook.

"You know that Luc came here asking about his mother. Well, there was an incident, an accident."

They all looked at him and nodded.

"And it was my fault."

None of them appeared surprised.

"Well, who was she?" Dolors finally asked.

"She was a fine friend and lonely woman with a bad hand in life. She had a boy and an estranged husband with a violent temper. In those days, pretty much the only profession for a woman alone was the oldest one around."

"So she was a prostitute." Rosa nodded, chewing her pencil.

"In a clandestine brothel. She was unique looking, an intriguing mix, and she loved boiled sweets."

"What has that got to do with anything?" Àngels asked.

"It has everything to do with it. You see, I visited them often."

"I'll bet you did," Dolors said.

"It wasn't like that. I did pay her for her time, but it was mostly just to talk and to play with her son, Luc. She told me some incredibly insightful things about myself. She tried to help me understand what happened between me and Eduard at the time. But it's only recently that I've actually heard her." Josep breathed in. "I would visit her most Sundays and bring them sweets. They devoured them every time. Then when I had everything arranged to leave town and return here, I paid one last visit, with one last tin of sweets. I sat down beside her on the bed and she begged me to take Luc to safety. She was afraid of his father." Josep raised a finger. "That gave me an idea and I suggested they go to Montreal with me. I meant for them to stay with a friend after I'd left, but Esmeralda took it another way."

"You and your women." Dolors swatted him with her handkerchief.

"When she realized the truth, that she would stay and I would leave, she gasped and one of the sweets lodged in her windpipe." Josep pointed to his throat and looked into his empty hands, feeling her once again in his arms and hearing the staccato sounds of her choking. "I tried everything but I couldn't make her breathe again. Then I looked down and there were two hands around my ankles. Luc's little hands. So I pulled him out from under the bed and took him away from there. I was trying to protect him, but I was also protecting myself. If the police had found out, they would have shut me away. I would never have been able to come back here." He looked at them and blinked, just then realizing the implications. "Some of you would not exist."

The family sat squinting at him, chewing on this news. Àngels shook her head. "That's all horrible, Josep, but why are you telling us this now?"

"Because we've had enough secrets. I can't hold any more. I need to know that I will die in peace."

"You're not ill, are you?" Dolors said.

He shook his head. "I'm perfectly healthy and hoping to make the most of every second we have left," he said, smiling at her.

"Just one thing," Rosa said, and pointed her pencil at him. "Why did Luc say that Montse might be in danger?"

"What?" Dolors said.

Josep cleared his throat and swallowed. "I'm not certain, but it may be because his father, the violent one, spent many years in prison for something he didn't do. And now he knows that I did it. The question is whether or not he knows that Montse is my daughter. Luc swore to me that he was trying to protect her."

Dolors sucked in her breath and covered her face.

Rosa rubbed her back. "*Mare*, don't worry. I'll write to her and make sure that she's fine."

Josep held up his hands. "If she was in danger, wouldn't I be the one crawling the walls? Montse will be in Montreal far away or with Marie-Claude, my friend who took in Luc when I left. Marie-Claude will keep her safe."

"Marie-Claude." Dolors huffed.

"I hope you won't hold all this against me. I just want to make peace with myself." He turned to Dolors. "And particularly with you, my dear."

"You have a strange way of doing it," Dolors said.

Despite Josep's recent revelations, Dolors seemed like the happiest person of all when he pushed his favorite armchair across the hall and into her bedroom. Nor did she protest when he began to transfer his clothes and other belongings. On his first night with Dolors, when Josep climbed under the sheets and felt her warm body next to his, he reached for her and held her against him. He could smell the baked bread in her hair, taste the sugary coating on her forehead, which she burrowed deeper into his chest hair. After spending a good while listening to each other's hearts, Josep began to rub Dolors' back and felt his heartbeat accelerate. She hugged him more tightly and whispered into his chest, "Let's not rush things." Josep nodded against the top of her head.

After the first peaceful moment, the remainder of the night was restless, due to their lack of recent experience in sharing a bed and to each other's deafening snores. Josep lay on his side and watched Dolors' sleeping face. Her round cheeks pulled taught most of the lines on her face. She grinned at something in her sleep and moments later her mouth fell open like a trap door. Josep gently pushed her chin up until her teeth clanked, and he stroked her cheek. He was quick to grow used to her shape beside him, to her warmth, to her snorts and strange outbursts in the night.

Josep wondered why he had trekked across the mountain for comfort when it was just across the hallway. The years had masked their reasons and both had silently agreed to leave them where they lay, until Dolors broke their personal pact of forgetting. She had a particularly fitful sleep, thrashing her head from side to side and whimpering like a netted animal. Josep put a hand on the crown of her head and her breathing stilled. With a shake of her head she awoke. Josep was looking down at her and brushed a sweat-soaked lock of hair from her forehead.

"You had a nightmare."

"I know. I've been having the same nightmare for years and I have to make it stop. I have to tell you something." She sat up in bed as her sleepy eyes slowly focused on Josep. "You made your confession. Now I need to make mine."

"What?" Josep pushed himself up in bed.

"It's horrible." She cringed behind her hands. "I'm a horrible person."

"After everything I told you about Canada," Josep said. "Mind you, we weren't married then."

"I know. You have plenty to be ashamed of. This also happened before we were married, long before." She uncovered her face and winced. "Remember your father's rose bushes?"

Josep nodded, not saying a thing, although he knew well what she was going to say. He was happy not to be the only wrong-doer for once.

"Remember when they were cut to pieces?" she whispered.

"Yes, they basically made my father fall off the cliff. I never forgave your father for that."

She covered her face again. "Could you forgive me?" She peeked between her fingers.

"So you are saying that you destroyed them?"

She nodded.

"I might forgive you if you tell me why you did it."

She sighed heavily. "I was angry. I was jealous. I was alone with my father, who everyone hated, and there you all were. A full, complete family living just outside my window. Every time I looked out, there you were. You all seemed so happy."

Josep took her hand and looked at the ceiling. "We were, but the problem was that we didn't know it. We were all too busy hating your father and our situation."

"My father wasn't as bad as he seemed. He was just angry. He never forgave my mother for dying on us." She held Josep's hand to her lips. "I hope you'll forgive me for what I did to your father."

349

"It was an accident. A horrible accident. Of course, I forgive you for destroying the flowers," he said not daring to reveal that he had already known and was thankful to have had time to come to grips with it.

Tears ran over Dolors' cheeks and she sobbed. "I should have told you so long ago. I would have saved myself so much suffering. I thought you would be so angry that you would have left."

"I'm a reasonable man," Josep said. "Listen, there's something I don't understand. Why then did you agree to call our daughter Rosa to commemorate my father?"

"Because it was important to you and it reminded me of what I did. Every time I look at her I have that reminder. Then ironically you two have always got along so well." Dolors tilted her head. "So do you forgive me?"

"Of course. I'm the last person to judge. We've both had our share of accidents and guilt."

"Let's wipe the slate clean." She sat up in bed and crossed her arm. "Let's do something together to mark the new life in our marriage, something we've never done before."

"What did you have in mind?" he asked gently kissing her neck.

Josep and Dolors decided to begin their newfound marital bliss with a trip to the coast. After the hour-long bus ride, Dolors ran directly for the beach dragging Josep by his free hand. When they were standing on the edge of the sand he put down their suitcase and watched the elation flood his wife's face. They looked across all the sunbathers toward the Mediterranean Sea, which was turquoise and calmly lapping the shore. He saw Dolors' face turn from thrill to shock as she noticed the bodies lying between them and the water.

"They're practically naked," she said. "All those tits in the air. It's indecent." She stared at all the exposed skin as she freed her feet from her espadrilles.

"It's not so bad," Josep said with an appraising nod. But Dolors was already dodging all the people, spraying them with sand in her rush to get to the water. She was running and taking off her cardigan at the same time. Josep followed behind carrying their suitcase. At the water's edge he kicked off his shoes and joined Dolors, who was looking at her wiggling toes through the translucent water. As he put the blue-white of his bare feet beside hers, he felt the coolness of the wet sand hug the soles of his feet.

"And all you did was complain about that beach in France. This is paradise." She swept her arm across the turquoise water reaching from one rock cliff to another.

"It was not like this." Josep felt the peace of the sea and the comfort of Dolors on his arm.

"Let's find our hostal." Dolors looked at him suggestively. "I'm going to put on my new swimsuit. We can come back to the beach and then go for a paella. Maybe after that we can have a *migdiada*. Imagine, a nap." She raised her eyebrows and kissed him on the ear. "I love the coast already."

When they returned back to Pujaforta with the coast still glowing on their skin, the whole family welcomed them and expected a detailed report. Josep and Dolors stood inside the door with their suitcase at their newly bronzed feet.

"So how was your first glimpse of the sea?" Baltasar asked Dolors. "Worth the wait? You two look like a couple of honeymooners." He chuckled and nudged Josep.

"Yes, it was." Dolors smiled, and stood as tall as her short stature would allow. "I think I could become used to this concept of holidays." She took Josep's arm and glowed at him.

"So how was the seaside?" Àngels asked. "What does it look like?"

"Isn't it splendid?" Núria said. "I particularly like what they've done at L'Estartit."

Josep shrugged. "The seaside itself is lovely. There are so many coves and hidden beaches and little fishing villages. But frankly, most of it is chockablock with apartment buildings. I'd heard what Franco's tourism plan had done, but it was something to see it."

"That is true. And there are Germans everywhere," Núria said. "You'd swear that it was another Occupation."

"Plus the English, Swedes, and French," Dolors said.

"But somebody sold them the land, didn't they?" Rosa said. "And they do make for cultural variety." Everyone turned to look at her. Núria and Àngels hugged her from either side.

"Always so political and reasonable, aren't you, *maca*?" Núria said. "I think the coast is lovely. So when are the two of you going back?"

"As soon as we can," Dolors said, and stomped her foot. As it turned out, every summer for years to come, Josep and Dolors returned to the same beach and the same hostal to inject some new life into their marriage.

When Josep wasn't with Dolors or helping her in the bakery he was reading the endless stream of letters they had found in Eduard's trunk. Every time he read them, he would first put on the old smelly jacket (recently let to air in the mountain breeze), inhale deeply and sit with a pile of Eduard's letters on his lap. Josep read them eagerly for mention of his name, which did not appear until almost the final batch. When it did appear, his name became the subject of most of the letters to come. Eduard was clearly trying to work through some of his own struggles.

The first letters were accusing, the next were more accepting, until finally the letters at the bottom of the last box were apologetic. Most of all, they expressed Eduard's gratitude to Gaspard for making him understand the reality: Josep had sacrificed so much early on to save him. He even said that he had begun to doubt Artur's role in having him released from that camp, but he had refused to give Josep the credit, as he blamed him for being imprisoned there in the first place. Years would pass before he could start to accept it.

Josep felt as if each stack of letters helped fill the gap between Eduard's early life and his final moments. It made his brother a true, living being with fears and needs and joyous moments. Having read Eduard's account of it, Josep felt more included not just in his death but in his life.

Some time after Josep had carefully folded the last letter and put it back in the box, another of his dreams came true and he was once again able to exercise his democratic right to vote. He, Baltasar, and Àngels made a day of it. They went to the Casal and put their ballots in the box, before sitting around Dolors' television set together, with a bottle of cava on ice beside them waiting for the results that would make their unionist father proud: the socialists won by a landslide, and their new prime minister came from Republican and unionist stock. Red had once again become a color of acceptable vocabulary. While time would tell what this could mean for Catalonia or even Pujaforta, Josep now felt that if death came after him, he could welcome it peacefully.

CHAPTER TWENTY-THREE

NOT LONG AFTER the cava was consumed and the post-election celebrations had abated, Josep heard the bakery door jingle much more shrilly than usual. Then he heard his wife squeal. When he entered the bakery he saw that yet another dream had come true. Montse was standing inside the door with a suitcase beside her and Dolors' arms wrapped around her middle. Dolors pulled away and he could see his eldest child looking very much like a woman in command. She held her head high and smiled brightly at them. She appeared different yet the same: she had clearly gained back any weight she had shed.

"Montse!" Josep ran towards her and held her shoulders in his hands. "Finally, you've come home. Are you well?" He looked into her shining eyes and shook her shoulders. "Why would you do this to us? We've missed you so much."

"I told you all about that in my letters," Montse said.

"All five of them," Dolors said and tapped her foot. Then she looked at her daughter, squeezed her cheek, and hugged her all over again.

Once Montse broke free she seemed to dance on the spot. "I've come to tell you something, although it should be obvious."

"What?" Josep and Dolors said simultaneously.

"I'm going to have a baby."

"A baby?" Dolors said, and grabbed her daughter's hand and felt her forehead before touching her rather bulky middle. "Come take a seat." She led her to the table and looked towards the door. "Where is your husband?"

"Who is your husband?" Josep said and sat down beside her.

"He's not my husband yet," Montse said. "That's why I've come. We're going to get married here."

Dolors clasped her hands together. "A baby and a wedding? One of my children is finally getting married." She hugged Montse and jumped to her feet. "When is it? It must be soon. What will people say?" She touched Montse's abdomen. "There's so much for us to get caught up on. All this time and you come and drop this on us."

"Where is your husband to be?" Josep said. "When can we meet him?"

"He'll be here in a week."

"A week?" Dolors said. "But there's so much to do."

Montse pulled Dolors into a chair and held her there. "*Mare*, we don't want a fancy affair. Just close family, if they can come."

Dolors jumped to her feet. "We'd better start contacting people. Àngels and Víctor are here. So is *Iaia* Núria. We'll have to tell Rosa. And we'll have to book the church. We'll buy you a nice little flat here in town, won't we, Josep?" She began to pace and didn't even look up.

"We're having a civil wedding now that we can. No church. Rosa already knows. She's helping me with the paperwork."

"Rosa knows and she didn't tell us?" Dolors frowned.

Josep reached for Dolors' hand. "You can start planning the menu, then. Mushrooms are still in season. And we'll have to order lots of cava." Josep turned to Montse. "So when will I be a *iaio*?"

"In three months."

"Three months?" Dolors said. "I'll get your room ready. We'll tell Dr. Sort."

Montse shook her head. "I'm just getting married here. I'm going to have the baby in Quebec. Besides, they're expecting me back at the bakery where I work."

Dolors swooned and Josep caught her and held her in her chair.

"So you mean to say that we won't even know our own grandchild?" Josep asked.

Dolors held her head. "But we can get you a flat right here in town. You can't come back and then leave again."

"We'll visit every year. You can come to see us," Montse said.

"I think I need to lie down," Dolors said as Josep helped her towards the stairs. He looked back over his shoulder toward Montse.

"Tell us that the father is not Luc," he said.

"It is not Luc," Montse said, and smiled.

Upstairs, Josep helped Dolors into bed, but as soon as her head touched the pillow she bolted upright. "Josep, there's so much to do. I can't just lie here."

"Yes, you can. You're not going to work yourself into a state like you always do. We're all going to help. You rest and I'll start contacting everyone. We need to use this time to get caught up with Montse, not making wedding arrangements."

Dolors moaned. "But she's left us no time. How can she hold this baby under our nose and then snatch it away? Has she come here to humiliate us? When the town finds out her state before her wedding, everyone will talk."

Josep eased her back in bed. "Dolors, calm down. Times have changed. Besides, did you notice she was pregnant?"

"No. I thought she was just, you know, heavy again."

"See. No one has to know," Josep said. "But I would like to know who will be our son-in-law."

Over the following days, Dolors was in the kitchen, Josep was mushroom picking, and Àngels was taking charge of the planning until Rosa could arrive from the city. Josep was disappointed to learn that he and Dolors had been the last to know about their daughter's impending marriage and motherhood. Rosa had kept it from them, and just when he thought they no longer had any secrets. Rosa had already contacted the whole family and warned them to be at the ready. At Montse's request she had arranged all the paperwork and reckoned she may as well organize the rest.

Josep tried to get Montse to tell him about her days in Montreal and Walamagou, but all she said was that she was in charge of pastries at a bakery in Montreal, and that Dolors' *coca* recipe was quite a success in the neighborhood. At first it had been slow to catch on, but now she was able to experiment with more original varieties without her mother looking over her shoulder. Up in Walamagou, where she had spent a number of months, she said there were no more horse carts, and electric refrigerators had replaced the ice deliveries. Where Josep and Marie-Claude's father had cut ice blocks from the lake, young boys now played hockey. The unofficial brothel had been officially closed down. The school had moved to a much bigger building and Marie-Claude was the principal.

When he discreetly asked Montse if she had had any contact with Luc's father, she said that while she had never met him, she had heard all about him. Although she didn't like what she heard, she was most concerned about the stories about her own father. She had put a hand on his, saying that both she and her fiancé understood. After what happened, they would have left town as well. And they both admired him for taking charge of Luc. Josep found that that was the extent of her revelation about her husband-to-be. Secrets and surprises seemed to be the order of the hour.

The day before the wedding, when the whole family was expected and all the food was almost prepared, Montse entered the bakery with a tall man gliding in behind her. Josep and Dolors jumped up from the table where they had been busy filling tiny bags with candied almonds. They stood and

355

stared at this man, whose smile left creases running from the corners of his eyes to the corners of his mouth. His teeth were as white as milk and his salt and pepper hair was more on the salty side. He emitted such an air of calm it was as if a cloud of oxygen had flowed in after him. Montse was holding his hand and smiling up at him.

"*Mare, Pare*," she said and added in French, "It's time you met Thomas, my fiancé, the doctor."

Josep stepped forward to shake Thomas' hand, which was long and elegant and stretched toward him, but Dolors pushed between them. She grasped his hands in both of hers. "A doctor? We'll have a doctor in the family?"

"Yes." Thomas kept his hands in hers and bowed slightly. "I'm an oncologist."

Dolors looked at him blankly.

"A cancer doctor," Montse said. "Thomas works at a special hospital for children in Montreal."

"If only you had been here before, when Eduard was ill, God bless his soul," Dolors said and nudged her husband. "Come to think of it, Josep, how is your tumor?"

Josep shook his head. "It's fine." He looked into Thomas' green eyes and noticed the specks of yellow dancing around the pupils.

"*C'est un plaisir*," Thomas said to Josep in the Quebec accent that had been so familiar to him long ago. "I'm so thrilled to finally meet you after everything Montse and my mother have told me about you." He put a comforting hand on Josep's shoulder. "You're not ill, are you?"

"No, I'm strong as can be," Josep said, closing one eye to examine this man. "Your mother?"

"You knew both my mother and my father. My name is Lefèvre. Thomas Lefèvre."

Josep stood back and regarded him with both eyes wide open. Thomas' look was familiar, but he was so much older than Josep had expected. "You're Marie-Claude's son. It's as plain as day." Josep laughed and slapped the man on the back.

"Marie-Claude?" Dolors blanched.

"*Pare* lived and worked with her family in Quebec," Montse said.

"I know who she is." Dolors threw her hands in the air. "There were the letters and then that Luc came all the way here and talked about her, just before he took you away." Her hands were now planted squarely on her hips.

"I got over him very easily," Montse said. "I needed to get away and Luc was a means to an end. We are still on friendly terms. It's a good thing since he and Marie-Claude are resting at the hotel in Adiol la Nova right now."

"Marie-Claude is here?" Josep asked.

"At the hotel?" Dolors said.

"Luc said you would understand why he was staying there," Montse said. "Thomas will stay here with me." She took his hand, interlocking her fingers with his.

Josep stepped closer examining Thomas' features, his easy stance, his build. "What year were you born, son?"

"In 1942," Thomas said. "I hope you don't think I'm too old for your daughter."

"That's ridiculous," Montse said, pulling Thomas towards her protectively. "There are only a few years between us. Shall we get you settled, darling?" she said and led a nodding Thomas towards the stairs.

"In your room?" Dolors said looking slightly horrified, then she sighed. "I suppose the damage is done, isn't it."

"How can we let her get married like this? We hardly know anything about this man," Josep said when Montse and Thomas were upstairs.

"But they have to get married. Look at her. Besides, he's a doctor. You know I've always admired that profession," Dolors said as she stacked bottles of cava in the refrigerator. "And you know much more about him than I do. You know his family."

"Yes, I do," Josep said, thinking how close he had come to bringing the man's mother away with him. They had had so much in common, although Marie-Claude was even more politically inclined than he was. The chemistry between them had also been very potent and he feared it might now explode in his face. He started pacing the kitchen. "I'd like to talk to Marie-Claude about this whole business."

"What could possibly be wrong?" Dolors said. "We can't stop it now anyway. Montse's going to have a baby."

"And they're going to take the baby away. We'll never see it." Josep turned toward the stairs and yelled. "Montse, come down. I need a word."

Montse came running as fast as she could down the stairs considering her condition. "What is it?" Her eyes were wide and her cheeks were flushed. "Has something happened?"

"Now that we know who your husband is, I want you to tell us more about him," Josep said gruffly, thinking it was better to have everything out in the open than to have regrets later.

"What's the matter? I thought you would like him, especially *Mare*," Montse said looking at Dolors, who nodded her agreement.

"I didn't say that I didn't like him," Josep said. "I don't know him. Tell me something. Does Marie-Claude approve of this?"

"Entirely."

Dolors pulled out a chair and put Montse in it. "Tell us all about him then."

Montse smiled with her shoulders at her ears as she hugged her rather full middle. "He's wonderful. He's both intelligent and funny. He hates politics. He paints incredible landscapes for a scientist. He loves the city and he loves the outdoors. And he loves me." She grinned. "He adores children and can't wait for this one to be born. He's impatient to be a father again."

"Again?" both Dolors and Josep said.

"His other children are older now and they will be such a great help with the baby. They're as excited as we are."

"How many children does the man have?" Dolors asked.

"Just two so far."

"How many wives has he got?" Josep asked.

"None at the moment. Thomas is divorced. They allow that sort of thing in Canada."

"Divorced?" Dolors said and squinted.

"They are working on putting that through here, too," Josep said. "We are getting up to speed."

"And are you looking for a fast way out then?" Dolors nudged him roughly.

"I am absolutely not." Josep stroked Dolors' cheek and turned to Montse. "So you say that Marie-Claude is in favor of this and that he loves you. I take it that you also love him."

"As much as this baby I am carrying."

"Then we are very happy for you both," Josep said, and both he and Dolors squeezed Montse's hands.

Montse pulled away. "I think I'd better warn you about Luc. He said that since his last trip here didn't go well, he really wanted to make it up to you. He told me the whole story and he wants to be forgiven."

"For what?" Dolors asked. "I thought everything was Josep's fault."

"He said he should have been more understanding, particularly with Víctor. I think that more than anything he wants to make it up to Rosa," Montse said.

"Good luck to him," Josep said.

A few hours later, the house filled with people. Rosa had arrived from the city and was standing near Víctor, who had just come in from fetching Joana. Joana had been slightly reluctant to come, since every time she visited, the events seemed to combust and she hoped that she wasn't the active ingredient. Àngels assured her that drama ran in the Balaguer family, which she was now a part of. Over these years, Joana had seemed to lower her political guard and to gradually warm to Àngels and the rest of the family.

Víctor had been spending most of his time in the city to be with Rosa and he had planned an official move. At the same time, Rosa had found herself back in Pujaforta at regular intervals to arrange Montse's wedding, a legal tradition which she swore to Víctor she would never partake in. As they curled up in Manel's narrow bed, she vowed that no bureaucracy was needed to bind them together. Life had already done that.

Not long after everyone had gathered in the house, the door opened and Pau leaped through it. He was dressed entirely in black and his normally fair hair was dyed to match. His smoky eyes flashed at them through dark eyeliner. If it weren't for his sleek gracefulness no one might have recognized him. In his shadow came a delicate woman with the straightest spine and a head held so tall that a stack of Rosa's books could have balanced on it. The only thing that would have stopped them was the brush of hair standing on end across the top of it. At the sight of Pau everyone gasped. Dolors squealed and ran to him holding his head against her breast and rocking him back and forth.

"I can't believe this," she said, suddenly out of breath and wheezing. She put a hand over her heart as the others guided her into a chair. "This is the happiest day of my life. You have all come home."

"*Mare*, I meant to surprise you, not shock you to death," Pau said, reaching behind him and taking the hand of the young woman. "This is Ita, the greatest experimental dancer you will ever see."

"You are likely the only one we will ever see." Josep stepped forward and kissed the young woman on either cheek while noticing that she had safety pins in her earlobes. He put his arms around Pau and slapped his back as all the others crowded around him. "I assume that you're my son under that outfit. I do hope to see you dance someday, despite what you all may think of me. I am not really that ogre you thought I was."

"Yes, you are," Rosa said and pinched his cheek.

"I can tell you he is the most splendid dancer," Núria said. "Maybe he can dance a little for everyone at the wedding." She turned to Montse who was looking at the floor. "Wouldn't that be wonderful, Montse?"

"Perhaps. Isn't anyone going to ask me how I am?" she said softly.

"You're elated," Rosa said. "You're about to get married." Everyone hugged Montse in turn and all the others continued to flock around Pau and his friend, and when practically not a word could be heard for the raucous, the door opened again.

They all went silent as Luc and Marie-Claude came through it. Josep stepped back and took in this vision that had been warped by time. While Luc had aged slightly, Marie-Claude had done so significantly. Josep looked down at his belly and put a hand to his thin hair and realized that the same could be said of him. While Marie-Claude stood shyly in the bakery door, Luc shook hands with all the men, except Víctor, who stood like a rock and looked ready to throw Luc out for good. Luc, with a few silver chest hairs visible at the V of his shirt, came to stand in front of Rosa.

"I'm very glad to see you again, after everything that happened," he said. Rosa raised an eyebrow, ignored his outstretched hand, and didn't answer. "This is Marie-Claude," Luc added and before anyone could greet her, Josep was holding her hands in his. He looked into her older face and saw the same eyes as always looking back at him. Her hair was short and streaked widely with gray, and her thin body had puffed slightly. She appeared to be taking an inventory of his face and puffiness as well.

"It's been so long. You look the same," he said for the sake of politeness.

"So do you, more or less," she said, squinting at him. "Who would have thought that after all these years we would finally become family?"

Josep frowned. "Yes, we will be grandparents together." He took a step closer searching her green eyes for any sign of a secret. "Does that not concern you?"

She looked him squarely and shook her head. "Not in the slightest. I only wish that Thomas' father were alive. Montse is a wonderful, strong woman, and an excellent baker."

"Just like her mother, Dolors," Josep said, and put an arm around Dolors, in an attempt to contain her.

Marie-Claude stepped forward first. "Dolors, hello. Josep and I were friends long ago. He may have mentioned me before." She kissed Dolors on either stiff cheek.

"Funny, he never did," Dolors said and looked at Josep. "And you seem like such a lovely woman."

"It was a long time ago and we have only exchanged a few letters," Marie-Claude said.

"Letters? Really? Josep must have kept those to himself. You'll have to tell me all about yourself since we are going to be family. Montse says you're a high school principal and a communist."

"I'm more of the former than the latter nowadays," Marie-Claude said. "We used to have some quite heated encounters, didn't we, Josep?"

"Speaking of heat," Dolors said, "I have to go put my head in the oven. To check on my baking, that is." She whispered to Josep. "You won't get rid of me that easily."

The next morning Montse arrived at the town hall dressed in a flouncing white dress that emphasized her diminishing waistline. Josep, in a contrasting dark suit, helped her keep her heels steady on the cobblestone. When he led her into the building to sit before the same desk where both he and Àngels had sat for numerous interrogations by the Puig family, he tried to shake off any feeling of foreboding. It disappeared when he saw his daughter's beaming face against the background of those of his family. Among them were Luc and Marie-Claude, and for a moment he wondered if this intertwining of his past and present lives might unravel.

Once the legal contract had been signed, family and friends went to the house for a day-long feast. Dolors had planned a lingering *aperitiu* with drinks and various *truita* squares on toothpicks, cured ham cut as fine as parchment, and a variety of *coques*, both sweet and savory. Later they would have a sit-down meal with courses of fish and meat. She insisted that she had to show the Quebeckers a Catalan feast, as such an occasion warranted, and she would not trust the task to any restaurant.

The mountain air and sun floated in the windows as the rising chatter in the living room soared out over the trees. Àngels was wearing a new dress that Núria had made for her out of the finest blue fabric she could find. Núria's skirt was matching. Joana was standing between the two of them casually holding a champagne glass in one hand and Àngels' elbow with the other. Víctor's efforts to persuade her seemed to be working. He was looking particularly dashing in a gray and white striped suit that set off his dark complexion and whitening hair. Rosa held onto his arm, like a shadow dressed in black at his side. The gold scarf around her shoulders added a little glitter and reflected off of Pau's powdered face. He had an arm around Ita, whose vertical hairdo made her two fingers taller than he was.

"So I hear that you are rather famous," Rosa said to Pau.

"Not really. *Iaia* was always one to exaggerate," Pau said. "We do travel quite a bit, but always to small theatres. People may not be ready for us yet. Soon we'll be performing in Barcelona. You'll come, won't you? Ita's family will also be there."

"You couldn't keep me away," Rosa said and pinched her chin. "I'll tell you what. I'll take some photos and I'll even talk to the culture editor at the magazine. Maybe we can publish something on it." Rosa put an arm around her brother. "Tell me something. When you left here, you ran off to that Geneviève woman. Do you still see her?"

Pau clicked his tongue. "No. I haven't seen her in a number of years. She sank into a deep depression after her husband was caught with those drugs. I was glad to be free of all of them. Ita has been incredible in helping me. She may look alternative, but she's actually rather conservative."

Rosa looked at Ita's stiff hair and the spiked collar around her neck and nodded. "If you say so. Will you dance for us later?"

"If they let us."

After popping the corks on a handful of cava bottles, Josep put his hands on his hips and breathed in the compound smells around him: sweet cakes, crispy pork and fish, perfume and hair cologne. The odors were almost as varied as the crowd and the languages they were speaking. Out of the bodies before him he saw Luc heading straight for him, backing him into a corner.

"Luc, you must be quite at home here to make this trip all over again," Josep said. "Surely you could have given us some warning about Montse and Thomas."

"I was sworn to secrecy and I was on a reconnaissance mission," Luc said. "Marie-Claude insisted I come. She had no idea what had become of you and she didn't want her son to marry just anyone. He already had one failed marriage."

"So she didn't trust me to bring up my children properly? Is that what you're saying?"

"I suppose. You did such a fine job with me." Luc put his hand against the wall. "To tell you the truth, I think it was an excuse. I think she still thinks about you, if you know what I mean."

"She surely can't think about me like that. It's been decades. She was married to Thomas for most of them."

Luc shrugged. "Think what you like. In any case, you know I had my own reasons for coming here. And I want you to know that I forgive you for what happened to my mother."

"So, you remember it was all an accident," Josep said calmly, feeling absolutely nothing. He was now free of all his guilt.

"I don't remember, but I don't care any more. There's no use harping on the past."

"Precisely. I'm trying to see things that way." He looked around the room at all the people with whom he had shared the better part of his life. "In fact, I have now come to realize that my life is more past than future."

At that moment, Núria clapped her hands and held them in the air to silence everyone. She looked at them all clearly through her thick spectacles and motioned for them to move to the edges of the room. Once everyone had backed away and was looking at her in puzzlement, she swung her arm towards the door, "Everybody, my grandson, Pau Balaguer, the dancer. And his friend, Ita."

Pau, dressed in a red leotard from neck to ankle that left no muscle concealed, leaped into the room. Everyone stepped back. After a series of jumps and pirouettes and gyrating movements, Ita dived towards him in a black body suit covering just the right half of her body. The other half was flesh colored and rather transparent. She landed at his feet and curled around them, her body in spasms. Pau fell backward with his jet-black hair flying outward and collapsed to the floor, where his red body intertwined with her blackness. They rolled until they were at the bride's satin shoes, and Montse looked at them in fright. Pau pulled himself to his knees and wrapped his arms around Montse's thighs, forming a red stain against her white dress. Ita lay as if crucified in the middle of the floor. When neither one moved for a long moment, slowly everyone began to clap. Pau and Ita bowed and leapt out the door as Gaspard appeared in their place. He was dressed in a dark suit and held a package with a giant bow. He looked as confused as everyone else.

Josep dashed towards him and replaced the present with a glass of cava. "You were able to come. I'm so thrilled. You've just missed an intriguing performance." He shook Gaspard's free hand energetically.

"Sorry I'm late. I had a lecture that I couldn't get away from, but here I am."

The others circled around him. Montse smiled at her cousin and introduced him to her new husband. Àngels held Gaspard's hands and admired his suit, while Rosa pulled a worn book out of her bag and gave it to Gaspard. Before too many people could monopolize his time, Josep negotiated him into the corner.

"I'm glad you're here. Over the years I've been rereading that letter, the final one about your father's life."

"Again." Gaspard sipped his *cava* and raised an eyebrow. "You didn't expect him to mention you so much."

"I expected him to mention me much earlier. Then his reflections in his final years surprised me. At least he appeared to have a change of heart. I quote: 'I must thank you, my son, for helping me realize how important family is. With every passing year I spent in France, I managed to put my other family to the back of my mind, and you to the front, of course. Yet there was always room for all of you. You don't know how many times I've wished I could go back to the day of the battle and just shoot Ivan Puig. It would have changed everything. I lost my mind. I lost my family. But I would not want to change having you. And then you brought them back to me, even my dear brother.' It's such a relief. I don't think I could have handled reading it all if I thought he always hated me, rightly or wrongly. Plus he explained why he took my money in Montreal all those years ago."

"He didn't intend to desert you. He really believed that you would join him, which is the main reason why I gave it to you to read. But I didn't expect you to memorize it or to keep it, for that matter." Gaspard winked and reached over Josep's shoulder to let Baltasar fill his glass.

"So what did you tell him?" Josep asked, wondering what changed Eduard's mind after all that time when nothing he had done seemed to matter. "Why did he suddenly want to spend time with me?"

"I told him the truth."

"How do you even know what the truth is?"

"I told him that you really did do a deal with that *Franquista* to get him out of prison. And you had to leave because of it." Gaspard leaned in and whispered, "Remember my dance teacher? I told my father everything that

Geneviève told me. Over the years I gave her information, but she also told me about you." When Josep gave him a disbelieving look, he added, "And Àngels also wrote to me and told me everything. She also told my father. It took a long time for him to accept it."

"I've never understood what there was to accept." Josep stepped back, shaking his head. "I was his brother. I did everything I could for him. Why would he not believe me?"

"It wasn't that. It was how his failure to believe you ended up changing him. That and the prison."

"Yes, and Balaguer pride." Josep shook his head. "At least eventually we did seem to understand each other. I am grateful for that," Josep said, once again seeing Eduard in his home, sitting across from him at the table, with the sunlight streaming in the window beside them, brightening his face and turning his gray eyes a celestial shade of blue.

"I'm sorry it was a little too late."

"It's never too late." Josep stepped back and let Gaspard past him. "We are all finally together, those of us who are still able."

At that moment, Josep saw Àngels and Joana approaching them. Àngels' arm was linked through Joana's and her face appeared peaceful. The inverted peak of lines between her eyes had softened and her forehead appeared smooth and worry-free.

"So that's one down," Àngels said gesturing towards Montse. "Though I suspect we may never see the others take that step."

"Nor will we see you." Josep smiled softly at her. "How did I end up with such an unconventional family?"

"Rebels at heart, just like their father."

"And their aunt."

She raised a finger. "And their unionist grandfather, who they were never able to meet. I suppose it does run in the family."

"I think conflict is in our blood. I certainly have a nose for it." Josep looked toward Gaspard and Joana who had begun chatting between them in their only common language, strongly accented Catalan. "You are looking splendid, Àngels. Joana was just what you needed."

"Yes, she was. And I'm hoping that she'll come up this way more often." Àngels smiled. "I must say I am pleased to see that this blissful stage between you and Dolors appears to be lasting. I never thought I'd see the day."

"Nor did I, actually." Josep raised an eyebrow and looked across the room at his wife, who was making sure everyone's glass never went blow half-full. "But for me, it's always been Dolors, since way back when. There's no one quite like her."

"I know." Àngels kissed his cheek. "There certainly isn't."

Josep moved toward Dolors, who was looking both frazzled and radiant in a green satin dress. She took a momentary break to stand beside him and admire the guests enjoying themselves. Together they watched their daughter as her white frills shook with her laughter. Montse had barely let go of the arm of her new husband, whose eyes had hardly left her face. Rosa was on the other side of the room with Víctor and Gaspard examining Pau's calloused feet. Àngels and Joana were opposite them and appeared to be carrying out a similar observation of the family.

"I'm happy that Joana was able to come," Dolors said. "I thought she might be reluctant."

"She has her own life and her own history," Josep said. "But she and Àngels seem to have found some middle ground. I'm so pleased that Àngels now has her. And I have you."

"Lucky for that because they're all going to be gone." Panic flitted in Dolors' eyes. "Montse will be in Quebec with her husband and her baby. Pau will be off dancing somewhere, and Rosa will be with Víctor down in the city."

"At least the city is not that far away." Josep looked down at her and smiled. "We should go and visit."

Delight replaced all panic on Dolors' face. "Do you mean it? Finally? It will have changed so much since I was there. That was just after the war and I loved it. I hear there are lots of little cafés and bakeries, practically one on every street. Imagine the competition." She grasped Josep's arm and hugged him to her. "I am so happy that we now have each other. We were so silly."

Josep kissed the top of her head and for once he really agreed with her. He looked up to see Marie-Claude approaching. Her lined face was free of makeup and she smiled at Josep and winked. "It's nice to see you looking so happy after all these years of marriage. What is your secret?"

Josep and Dolors looked at each other and smirked. "It's an old family recipe," Josep said.

"I've been watching you, Josep, and you really haven't changed that much. I think you still have your charm." Marie-Claude tilted her head at him and Josep felt Dolors stiffen at his side.

"It's natural perhaps. I do try to keep fit." He wiggled his trousers around his hips. It had been a while since he'd had such a compliment, particularly from a woman.

Dolors stepped closer. "What a terrible hostess I am. Some cava?" She looked around for a bottle. "Just wait till you see the meal I've prepared. Have you tried my famous *truites* or *coques*?" Dolors ran to the kitchen and returned carrying a plate in each hand.

"This is really Dolors' specialty," Josep said, and pointed to the round omelet jabbed with toothpicks. Marie-Claude licked her lips and picked up a cube as Josep did the same. "They're filled with wild mushrooms. I picked them myself." He raised his toothpick as if to toast and both of them took a bite. Marie-Claude nodded and before she could eat it, Dolors put the plate of pine nut *coca* between them.

"This is my other specialty," she said. "It's slightly sweet, but I think you'll find it blends perfectly with our local champagne."

Marie-Claude took a small piece and nibbled. "This is very nice. Very tasty. Montse told me about hers, but I'd never tried it. It reminds me a lot of a pastry we have back in Quebec. It's very similar."

"It can't be that similar. This is unique. It's a special Catalan pastry and my own recipe." Dolors thrust out her chest.

"And it is one of a kind." Josep put a hand on her shoulder and felt her muscles relax for a moment. He took some more omelet instead.

"How would you know? You've hardly even tried it," Dolors said.

"You know I don't like sweets," Josep said but took a square from the plate that Dolors was jabbing into his belly. He bit it and noticed how the light pastry flaked on his tongue and the flavor of toasted pine nuts spread across the roof of his mouth. Nodding, he bit and chewed some more before taking a larger piece from the plate. "This is much better than I remember. It's delicious." He turned to Dolors. "We could have made a fortune from this."

Dolors nodded emphatically and tapped her foot.

Josep took another bite and another. Swallowing loudly, he put a hand on Dolors' shoulder and drank back some cava. Marie-Claude and Dolors were smiling at him. He felt his skin tingle strangely and rubbed his face. He coughed and lightly tapped his sternum. Then he saw their smiles fade and they were tilting their heads at him. As he took another drink, the air in his lungs compressed. It was if the oxygen was being filtered through a fine-holed sieve. Josep tried to swallow and loosened his shirt collar. His view of Dolors was now awash before him.

"I'm feeling a bit dizzy."

Behind Dolors he saw the crowd: Montse in a flash of white, Pau in a streak of red. Then he reached out toward his Rosa, but she disappeared in a streak of black and gold as he slumped to the floor. Dolors screamed and silence hit the room. But Josep hardly heard any of it. Instead his mind was flying over oceans and mountains with vast trees closing in before him until he saw beaches packed first with women in bikinis, then with men and women dressed in layers of dirt. Out of a hole he saw Eduard's face looking at him like life was one big question. The sand turned to ashes, formed wings and soared away. Josep was no longer in the room and his ears could no longer hear the panicked voices of his family.

"Stand back," Baltasar shouted and separated Dolors and Marie-Claude from Josep's side while all the others looked on. "He's probably had a bit too much to drink with all the excitement," Baltasar said over his shoulder as he loosened Josep's tie. He undid the buttons on his shirt. "Josep," Baltasar said slapping Josep's cheek and his chest, but Josep's face and neck were turning violet. Thomas, the groom, also tried to revive him. Dolors stood over them covering her mouth with her hands. Her plate of *coca* was on the floor beside them.

"What happened?" Rosa said holding her ears with her hands. "Did he fall?"

Dolors was shaking her head.

Àngels stood over them, her eyes filling with tears. "Is it his heart?"

Dolors' lower lip trembled. "If it isn't his, it is mine."

Later in the day, when the ambulance had come and gone, the living room bore the signs of a party stopped short: half-full glasses of cava, entire plates of *truita* with the toothpicks untouched, endless platters of *coca*. In the kitchen, trays of raw sea bass shone silver beside the oven, and inside it five suckling pigs had turned to charcoal. Most of the wedding party was in the kitchen sitting in silence. Only Dolors rocked back and forth in her armchair and sobbed into her handkerchief. Everyone else was still in shock.

Baltasar was staring at his open palms and was the first to break the long silence. "If only I'd known. I would have had a shot ready. He just needed a shot."

"You couldn't have known," Àngels said, wiping her nose. "He'd never had that *coca* before. He'd never wanted to eat it."

Dolors' whole body shuddered with her sobs. "It's all my fault." She shook her head. "I made him eat it. And all because I was jealous. I was always jealous."

"You once had reason to be," Montse said. "But not of Marie-Claude. *Pare* could have married her years ago, but he didn't. He came back and he married you."

"What a sad wedding day you've had," Rosa said, and put an arm around Montse's shoulder.

"If I hadn't come back here to get married, none of this would have happened," Montse said as more tears ran into her smeared mascara.

"No one should blame anyone," Baltasar said. "You could all easily blame me for not saving him."

"I don't think anyone could have saved him," Thomas said, the tie of his wedding suit hanging loosely around his neck. "I'm no allergist, but I don't think it was a reaction to the pine nut *coca*."

Everyone turned to him with lifted eyebrows.

"Not entirely anyway. He also ate some mushroom omelet, didn't he? I believe it was either an interaction between the pine nuts and the mushrooms or a reaction to the mushroom itself. Who picked them?"

"Josep did," Dolors said, slumping in her chair. "And then he insisted on cleaning them and doing it all himself." She shook her head. Everyone looked at the floor and once again there was silence.

Víctor cleared his throat. "I know that we are all still trying to come to terms with this, but we have to talk about the practicalities."

"He'll be buried in the family niche," Núria said. "With his father and Pau."

"He wouldn't want that," Rosa said. "Besides, isn't that where you want to go, Iaia?"

"Yes, but I've got a few more years left in me, surely," Núria said.

"That's what Josep thought, too," Àngels said and wiped her cheek. "He would want to be with Eduard."

Dolors sighed. "He would."

"So would I," Àngels said. "In case there is any doubt when it's my turn."

Núria shook her head and covered her mouth. "Don't even say that. I can't lose you too. Let me go first."

"I would want to be with all of you," Víctor said, looking at Àngels and Rosa.

"Well, so would I," Núria said, looking very worried through her tear-stained eyeglasses. "But you can't all abandon the plot to be thrown off a cliff."

"I can," Rosa said.

"So can I," Víctor said.

"I'm with all of you," Baltasar said.

"Just one thing," Montse said. "Don't you think part of Pare would want to be on the mountain? He loved it up there."

"Yes," Dolors said. "And he did love our seaside holidays."

"And we mustn't forget our little shrine under the tree," Rosa said. "We need one fixed place where we can talk to him."

Dolors threw back her head and sobbed. "Why can't he just be here with us?"

"He'll be everywhere, just like he would have wanted," Àngels said.

So it was that the ashes of Josep Balaguer sailed off the cliff in Eduard's wake, dusted the top of the mountain and inside Turtle Rock, floated around the calves of seaside bathers, and blended with the earth and Eduard's ashes under the tree in the back garden.

The ritual of scattering Josep's ashes helped the family come to terms with the sudden emptiness in the house and around the table. Àngels, however, was having difficulty adjusting. First thing every morning she saw to the rose bushes she had planted with Josep near the plot under the tree. She knew too many people under there. Every day she talked to her brother, much more than she ever had when he lived next door. She told him how she missed his escapades, how they had brightened up her dull, stunted life, despite what she had told him. She also asked him to forgive her for the times that she had wished he would disappear and Eduard would appear in his place. She hadn't wanted any of her brothers to disappear. But she had never really had what she wanted. She dreaded the quiet; she feared herself and what her mind could do to her. Carme had been a warning sign. When they had been scattering Josep's ashes, she had sensed someone behind them, silent, and recognized the sad stance of Manel. Víctor must have told him. As soon as Josep's ashes were gone, so was Manel and she did not regret it. Slowly, Àngels returned to the house and put on the old corduroy jacket, thinking of her brothers who were gone. Then she began to think of those who were still here: Joana, Víctor and Rosa, even Dolors, Montse and her new family, who would be leaving at any moment. She took off the jacket, folded it over itself and went to the Balaguer house to say goodbye.

Inside the bakery, Montse stood, looking less the radiant bride and more the expectant mother as she prepared to leave on the arm of her new husband and her new mother-in-law. They reached out and pulled Àngels towards them.

"Where have you been?" Rosa asked. "We were worried that you would miss this big event."

"I would never miss it," Àngels said. "I just wish it wasn't a goodbye."

"It doesn't have to be," Rosa said, taking hold of Montse's hands and looking into her eyes. "Take care of yourself and let us know as soon as you have any news." She poked the ball of Montse's stomach. "I've always wanted to go to Canada, so you can count on *Tieta* Rosa. Besides, your child is going to want to meet his cousin."

Montse dropped her hands and stepped back. "You're not!" she exclaimed and when Rosa nodded, Montse hugged her and spun around. Rosa reached for Víctor, for her mother and Àngels, the latter two appearing equally shocked.

"I'm going to be a *iaia*," Dolors cried and joined them. "I can't believe I'm going to be a grandmother. Twice." Then she stepped back and looked at the floor. "Josep would have made a wonderful *iaio*. I wish he'd known before, you know." She looked to the ceiling.

Rosa broke free from the others and held her mother's cheeks. "I only found out after Montse's wedding. I think of it as a new beginning. What do you say we all do that?"

Dolors nodded and they all put their arms around her.

"Well, we need to go," Montse said, pointing to her wide middle. "I don't want any beginnings starting here. Promise me you'll come to visit us."

"You know I will," Rosa said.

"Only a baby could get me on one of those airplanes," Dolors said. "But I hope that you will be back. You children are all I have." She put an arm around Montse, Rosa, and Pau.

"You have me," Àngels said, and put her arm around them.

"And what about me," Núria said.

"And me," Baltasar said.

"Don't worry, I will be back," Montse said and hugged them all. "As soon as everyone in Quebec is sick of *coca*, I will be back."

"But that will never happen," Dolors moaned, as Rosa broke away to get her camera. They all laughed as they were blinded by the flash that knotted them together forever.

EPILOGUE
Summer 2000

Once Núria was sitting comfortably in the car's back seat, with the seatbelt holding all her fragile bones in place, and her wheelchair was shut into the trunk, Àngels climbed carefully in beside her. The upholstery was hot under her thighs and she tried to straighten her skirt to keep it from creasing. They had, at least for her, a long journey ahead of them. She tried to concentrate on her thrill rather than on her apprehension about venturing far from Pujaforta. Dolors winced and grunted as she folded her round body into the seat next to her. Àngels could feel Dolors' ample hips squishing against hers. She shifted away, sure that they would bake inside this car before they even got to the city. The car door slammed.

"All ready to go?" Montse asked from the driver's seat, where she was gripping the steering wheel confidently. She looked beside her. "Baltasar, you can put the map away. I can get us as far as Barcelona."

"If you think so," Baltasar said, looking over the top of his glasses and scratching his sunspotted forehead before examining once again the map on his lap. "In fact, I could even drive. That is one thing I haven't forgotten."

"But you've forgotten pretty much everything else," Dolors said, and Àngels nudged her. "Anything recent, anyway," Dolors rectified. The car revved and began to float smoothly down the road out of Pujaforta, hugging the narrow curves in the mountain road and causing the women to sway into each other. Àngels braced herself against the front seat for this journey they had always vowed to make but had never found the courage to see through. This time Rosa had left them no option. If their lives were to be on display to the public, the least they could do was bear witness.

"So, Montse, how long did you say you're back for?" Baltasar tilted his head, which in addition to more vital functions, had long since lost its two tufts of hair.

"Baltasar, I've told you. I'm back for good."

"You remember, Baltasar," Dolors said, sighing. "Montse is running the bakery. And she's doing a fine job. Some of the pastries are a bit odd and foreign, but I promised to keep my mouth shut." Dolors had managed to stay quiet for the last two years while Montse had taken exclusive control of the bakery. Her *coca* lined with the darkest chocolate, plus her muffins and maple tarts, recipes learned during her time overseas, brought people mostly from near and some from afar to the family terrace, which was now sealed in by glass in winter and open to the mountain air in the hotter summer months like now.

"And where is your husband?" Baltasar asked. "Or have you already told me that?"

"Yes, I have told you that my ex-husband is in Montreal. I'm here and our son, Josep Jr., is studying in Barcelona."

"Right." Baltasar nodded, squeezing his eyes tightly as if to hold in the information. "When I retired it's too bad he didn't take my practice in Pujaforta. I do clearly remember that he was a doctor."

Dolors stuck her head between them. "That would have been a splendid idea. He could have advised everyone to eat more bread, and Montse, you wouldn't have to live all alone at the Palau mansion."

"It's good for her to have some space," Àngels said pulling Dolors back. They had all spent these last years trying to avoid spats and to accept each other for who they were. Some had been more successful than others.

"Perhaps," Dolors continued. "But I'll never understand how she could have divorced an oncologist, a cancer doctor." She looked at the rest of them for support. "But then again, what can you expect from a man who had been married and divorced before?"

"Precisely," Montse said. "The man spent all his time with sick children and not with his healthy son. But I am the heartless one for not supporting him." Montse's round cheek reddened as she glanced toward the back seat. They were now leaving the steep mountain road and entering the highway southward. "How are you doing back there, *Iaia?*"

"I'm all ears," Núria's trembling voice said. "And bones. We must be getting closer to the coast. I can feel the humidity." She gently patted her tight curls. "I hope my hair will hold out." She stared straight into the back of the seat in front of her. Her eyes were now filmy and unseeing. Though it made little sense for an ancient woman whose bones threatened to disintegrate, and who had seen nothing but a blur of light for over a decade, to attend a photography exhibition, she insisted that she would not be left behind. It was her life, her family. Without her there would be nothing on display.

"How Josep would have loved this," Dolors said, looking out the window over the hills. Her thinning hair, sprayed into perfect waves away from her face, was flattening in the wind and she put up her window. "You know how we'd always meant to come down here. But he was always busy with much more important things. Josep was such a hard worker, daring the hills and the patrols to get me my flour. Such an incredible man. He would be so proud of our Rosa." She sighed. "If only he were here."

"I'd say we are all very lucky to still be here," Àngels said. "Especially *Mare*."

"I'm grateful," Núria said. "I just wish I was able to appreciate the view or all the pictures we're about to see, and my grandchildren."

"I think it's the strong-hearted Balaguer i Hereus. I have a theory," Dolors said, and wiggled in her seat. "Baltasar might agree, if he could remember. A heart needs to be shared to make it strong." She nudged Àngels slightly.

"I share my heart with many people," Àngels said, this time choosing not to ignore Dolors. "I just don't share my bed or my house, except with *Mare*, of course. And I'm all the happier for it. I've even put up with you all these years."

Montse cleared her throat loudly at the wheel.

"I'm only ever trying to help. Look how happy Josep and I were," Dolors said.

"I beg to differ on your theory." Baltasar raised a pointy finger. "Many women have tempted my heart, but not one has managed to tame it. And I'm still here."

"In body but not in mind," Dolors said faintly. "And your legs were always too fast for any woman."

"But one always managed to get away," Baltasar said, as Àngels looked at her lap.

Núria hissed and waved her hand up and down. "If you're going to dig up ancient history, I would quite like to listen to the rest of the ride in silence."

After a long while with nothing but the sound of the tires on the pavement and other cars whipping by, the traffic became more congested when they reached the first traffic light into the city. Brake lights filled the view in front of them, horns honked, and exhaust-stained façades rose up on either side.

Baltasar was still gripping the map on his lap. "Montse, do you know where you're going? I've never seen so many cars." He looked from the windshield to the map, which he turned every which way to examine. He quickly pulled his elbow in the window as a city bus tore by, practically brushing the side of the car.

"That's the big city for you. I've memorized the route. And I used to drive in Montreal all the time," Montse said, but her knuckles were white against the steering wheel. As they slowly advanced into the core of Barcelona to drive up its spine, Passeig de Gràcia, dividing the city into left and right, Àngels and Dolors sucked in their breaths. Àngels now felt only excitement, as if a secret door had opened before her.

"What is it?" Núria asked, her eyes and ears widening.

"It's fabulous," Àngels said, leaning forward trying to get a view of the majestic buildings lining the street. Most were about ten-stories high, with narrow balconies jutting over the pavement. "*Mare*, I wish you could see this building on our right. The front is all wavy like the sea. And I've never seen so many people anywhere."

"People wearing hardly any clothing," Dolors said, wrinkling her nose. "This looks nothing like when I was here after the war. They've fixed it all. Look at all the tourists. You'd think they could cover themselves."

"I don't think they're all tourists," Àngels said knowingly, since she regularly read the newspaper and its weekend supplements about modern life and trends. Rosa made sure they always had a subscription. "Locals can suffer equally in this heat." She shifted and her legs stuck to the seat. "The next car we get will have to have air conditioning."

They continued up the avenue until they were in the neighborhood of Gràcia, where the car entered the narrow streets and stopped at the entrance to a long square circled by benches and bars with terraces full of people. Children were kicking a football up the center, almost hitting the people that were flowing from underground into the square. Àngels took it all in, the activity and excitement, but felt reluctant to leave the quiet of the car. There were so many elegant-looking people, bright fancy signs, so much noise, she wondered if she'd waited too long. Perhaps her old, frumpy body would not handle such vibrancy. Ever so slowly they piled out of the car, unfolding Núria and her wheelchair and putting her in it. It hardly fit along the narrow pavement and they pushed it into the wider square. They all looked at the short buildings around them, with the dark and dirty fronts and wrought-iron balconies, the little cafés and bars, with trees casting shade on the tables underneath.

Dolors put her hands on her hips and looked around, grunting in glee. "Montse, look at all these terraces. This should give you plenty of ideas. I don't think people are ready for all those foreign cakes you make."

"I think they are. Don't worry, I have plenty of ideas. Besides, if I get fed up in Pujaforta, which I just might, I can always come and open a café in the city." Montse folded her arms across her bosom. Before Dolors could respond, a man's voice called toward them from across the square.

They all looked and Àngels recognized Víctor still standing taller than most. He wore a bright smile that matched his very short white hair. First he held Àngels by the shoulders and she could feel that his hands were still strong, and as he kissed her she felt his smooth cheeks on hers. Though they saw each other in Pujaforta almost monthly, every time she saw him again it felt like it had been too long. Víctor greeted everyone, kissing them and squeezing their hands. He began to push Núria's wheelchair towards a narrow door, too narrow for her chair. Then he bent over and pulled Núria into his arms.

"I hope you don't mind," he said. "But it will be much easier this way."

Núria gasped and then giggled. "This is rather fun," she said. "Just don't squeeze too hard. I'm rather fragile."

As Víctor entered cradling Núria, the others followed him, leaving the daylight behind them and squinting in the dimly lit bar with its black-painted walls. Àngels saw the miniature lights lining the pictures on display and felt like she was entering a tunnel into her past. Rosa was standing in the center of the room wearing a black dress. Her short curls were died black and carefully uncombed. She seemed to be rocking on the balls of her feet and bounded towards them. Behind her was Pau, looking sleek and elegant and strangely exotic for a local. As they both dashed forward, the whole family kissed and hugged and swirled around each other. Everyone was talking at once, making a general raucous.

"I'm so happy that you actually came," Rosa said to each of them as she reached out to touch them.

"Of course we did," Núria said from her lower vantage point. "This is an occasion. The Balaguer family for all eyes to see."

"I know, though I don't know if many people will come," Rosa said. "I'm a bit ahead of my time. A lot of people aren't ready for this yet. But I'm sick of waiting."

"So am I," Núria said, clasping her hand between hers. "Better to do it now than never. In fact, I wish you had done it when I could still see."

"Who wants some cava?" Víctor removed his arm from around Rosa's shoulders and picked up some already-filled glasses. As he handed them out, shadows appeared in the doorway. Montse had arrived from parking the car and behind her came a young man and woman who looked nothing alike except for their smoky eyes.

"*Iaia*, your great-grandchildren are here," Rosa said to Núria before putting an arm around her daughter. "Àfrica, you're just in time." The girl with slightly toasty skin and long hair wound into one thick dreadlock hugged Rosa's side. She glanced at the walls around her with her darker version of the Balaguer eyes, like a storm cloud against her darker complexion.

"See, *Mare*, you had nothing to worry about. It all looks brilliant," Àfrica said nodding at Rosa.

"The city looks good on you," Àngels said and stroked her tangle of hair, wondering how and if she washed it. "How are the studies going?"

"I'll never understand it." Dolors' belly arrived between them. "Why would anyone want to study history. You're young. Why dwell on the past?"

"It's all about then and now, *Tieta*," Àfrica said and gently squeezed Dolors' cheeks. "Besides, I'm studying African history."

"But why?" Dolors asked. "Obviously there is your name and your father, but what history is there to study?"

"Plenty." Àfrica stomped her sandled foot and reached for Víctor's hand. "The immigrants my father's organization has been helping have taught me more about life and survival than any course ever could. But I want to understand more about what would make someone spend days in a flimsy boat to come here."

"Yes, they show it constantly on TV." Dolors turned up her nose. "All those filthy people arriving on our beaches."

Àngels raised an eyebrow at Dolors. "You don't like the news to interrupt your soap operas. And you like to forget what beaches our family had to camp on."

Dolors ignored her and looked at her grown son beside her. "Pau, are you going to let your *Tieta* speak to me like that? I'm so happy you're back in the country."

"It's good to be back. Some things never change," Pau said, raising a finely sculpted gray eyebrow.

Àngels touched his arm and pulled him away from Dolors. "So, Pau, how are the shows going? I saw an ad for the Fura dels Baus and I was so proud of you."

Pau smiled and stood taller. "It's going very well. We're doing a futuristic adaptation of Quijote." He ran a folded handkerchief over the shine of his head. "All the traveling does get tiring. Everyone wants to see us for some reason."

"Search me, with all the blood, fire, and naked people," Víctor said. "I just saw one show and it made its mark on me, I must say."

"This show will be less bloody, but everyone will be hanging from the ceiling, everyone except me," Pau said and grinned. "I'm just an artistic consultant."

"And a fantastic one, I'd bet," Núria said, reaching a shaky hand toward him. "I always told you that your moment would come. So where are your lady friends?"

"I'll be meeting one later. This one's an artist."

"Like father, like son," Àngels said, and Dolors huffed and looked upward. Montse's son, Josep Jr., had joined them and was two heads taller than most of them. His body looked like it was struggling to catch up with his height. Montse held his thin waist like the protective mother she was. He had the Balaguer eyes and in one quick move he hid the male Balaguer hairline under a baseball cap.

"And how is your cooking school?" Dolors asked, looking skeptically at her grandson. "I've never understood why anyone would need classes on how to cook."

"I learn about cuisine from some of the world's finest chefs," Josep Jr. said, straightening his shoulders. His Catalan still had a slightly French-Canadian accent, which he was rather reluctant to shake. He shoved his hands further into the pockets of his jeans. "You think Uncle Pau's work is experimental. We can do some incredible things in the kitchen."

"I don't think a restaurant of that kind is really what Pujaforta needs," Dolors said.

"I never said I would move back to Pujaforta," the young man said. "In fact, I might take what I learn back to Montreal."

Montse held him closer. "Let's not get ahead of ourselves. You've just started the course. Remember how cold and snowy it gets in Montreal."

"And in Pujaforta," Josep Jr. added.

"Speaking of Pujaforta," Rosa said. "Has anyone had a look at my pictures?" She motioned to the black walls lined with photographs, each one under an individual spotlight. There were now a number of people lined up observing the display. They had been slowly filtering in, many stopping for a word with Rosa or Víctor first.

Rosa nodded at them and cleared her throat. "I'd like to thank you all for coming," she said as the voices quieted and family and friends gathered around her. "These pictures are from my own private collection, some of which I took myself and others that I borrowed. As you all know, when I took these, times were very different. I was also very naïve and took a number of pictures I shouldn't have. Or I should have been better at hiding them." She grinned at Montse. "When they were discovered and my father and others close to us could have been arrested because of it, I already knew far too well what prison meant." She reached out and squeezed Víctor's hand. "For many of you, these pictures will just be people. For each of us, each one is a story and a chance to remember friends and family who unfortunately are no longer with us. My father, Josep, my Uncle Eduard, Víctor's mother, Carme, and many others we have lost along the way. Time has passed, times have changed, but some will remain young forever on film and in our memories." Rosa put an arm around Víctor, who raised his glass.

"I'd like to propose a toast to the photographer," he said smiling down at Rosa. "She's the most stubborn, perseverant woman I know. She always gets her picture or whatever she's after. Lucky for me. She is why I am with you here today and I wouldn't want to be anywhere else." He raised his glass and the others did the same. "To Rosa."

"To Rosa," they all said. "*Chin, chin.*" Glasses clanked around them.

"*Salut. Salud. Santé.* Cheers," Rosa said. "Now go and enjoy the pictures."

The family went silently and everyone looked at the photographs. Àngels drifted away from the family, drawn to a picture in front of her that she had been trying to decipher from afar. It was just as she had expected. It was Manel's original shack glowing in the summer light and Manel was standing beside it leaning onto a wooden post and nonchalantly grinning at the camera. Àngels put her hand to her mouth. He looked so young and happy. Squinting, she recognized the post in his hand, the beginning of birds flying upward, the same birds she still looked at on her bed every day but had ceased to see. She lowered her head and stepped back, feeling an arm around her shoulder.

"It seems strange to see him like this, doesn't it?" Víctor said.

"Yes, it does. It brings a lot back, the good and the bad. I thought it was all buried away."

"With Manel," Víctor said, examining her face with concern. Àngels couldn't help but think of how horrific his last moments must have been.

"None of us could have done anything to prevent it," Víctor said.

"I know. But despite everything, he didn't deserve it. I'd always warned him to keep all the cabinet doors open when he was working. I can't help but think that if I had still been working with him, I would have been there to save him."

"You had already saved him long ago." He hugged her against him. "You don't know how much I wish I had found him earlier." He swallowed and shook his head and, as if to quickly change the subject, pointed to the next picture on the wall. "Here's one of you. Have you seen it?"

"But," she said, blinking repeatedly. "I'm with Carme." Àngels looked more closely at the grainy photo that had been reproduced and enlarged. "And you." She pointed to a small boy standing between them hugging a leg of each of them, his face hidden in her skirt. She tapped the edge of the frame. "I remember when this was taken. It wasn't long after my mother married Sr. Palau. I look so shy, but no wonder, I was in a rather bad state at that time. Carme looks her usual daring self. Look at her standing with her hands in her trouser pockets. Those trousers weren't very common at the time, but they were practical for her outings in the woods." She looked up at Víctor and smiled. "Where did Rosa get this photo?"

"I found it among your old things."

"You're a sneak," Àngels said, and slapped him playfully. "So what do the kids think of all this?"

"Basically that they're just a bunch of old pictures. But Àfrica does appreciate them."

"One day, when we're all gone, she really will."

Together they walked on past the other pictures. Àngels saw another one of herself, this time with Dolors and Montse, on the day that Franco died. Dolors was wiping her red eyes, Montse was brushing flour from her cheek into her hair, and Àngels felt strange to see her own smile. Another was of Víctor as a young man, sprawled in an almost yellow light, with the folds of a sheet draped over his hip. Àngels felt a hand on her back and looked up to see Rosa standing between them. Her darkened lips were smiling and her cheeks were rosy.

"That is my very favorite," she said, putting an arm around Víctor and kissing his cheek.

Àngels nodded. "I see why."

"Have you seen these others?" Rosa asked, leading them by the hand past one of Pau in a red leotard with Geneviève supporting his arm, and another of jewels on the palm of a dark glove. Another was a string of skiers holding a rope tow, like beads on a necklace. Leading them across the room she swept her arm toward the whole wall. "This side is for him. For *Pare.*"

Àngels stepped closer and saw that indeed, Josep appeared in almost every picture. There was one of him seen from behind wearing a giant pack stuffed with bread and sausages. In another he had a book open on his palm, a cigarette smoking between his other fingers, and he was striking an intellectual pose. On closer inspection, she saw wrinkled pesetas protruding from between the pages, a dirty wad of a book mark. Other pictures were family shots, with all the Balaguers and Baltasar lined up outside the house or leaning around a table with Dolors serving great platters of food. They were all there, Víctor, Joana, and even Luc, admiring plates of Dolors' *truita* and *coca* in a square of sunlight. At one of the final pictures, Àngels paused and looked at Rosa. She stepped closer. It was a shot taken indoors beside a window, with the light streaming inward outlining two silhouettes in profile, their matching noses almost touching. The faces still showed enough contrast to make out the detail, the lined cheeks of Josep and Eduard.

"It's beautiful," Àngels said. "You couldn't have captured them better." She crossed her arms across her chest and admired it, thinking of all the years of anger and stubborn misunderstanding, and not only between he brothers.

"I had to seize the moment," Rosa said. "Rare as it was. Àngels, I v you to have it. I thought you might also like the blowup of the one Carme."

Àngels gasped. "But Rosa, they're yours."

"I have copies and negatives. I want you to have them."

Àngels kissed Rosa's cheeks and squeezed her hands before moving on to the next picture. She tilted her head. It was Eduard alone. He was sitting at a table that Àngels recognized from his kitchen in France. He looked almost like he had when he came for his final Pujaforta visit. His hands were folded wisely before him and a small bundle of letters was in the shadow beside them. Àngels shook her head. "When did you have the chance to take this? I didn't know that you went to see him there."

"She did, back when she was working from France," a man's voice said from behind them and Àngels saw Gaspard standing over her. He kissed her cheeks with his full gray beard scratching her cheeks. His face was wet and clammy with sweat, and he loosened his tie. "I was there, I saw her." He patted Rosa's shoulder. "She helped convince my father to go to Pujaforta before it was too late."

Rosa shook her head, clearly not comfortable taking the credit. "But, Gaspard, you're the one who really convinced Eduard in the end."

"I think we all did, didn't we?" He also looked at Àngels. "But he really convinced himself." He reached for Rosa's hand. "Sorry I'm late, but since we're in the neighborhood I wanted to see the place where my father was in prison all those years ago."

"And?" Àngels said.

"Blocks of flats, like it had never existed. He wouldn't have been very impressed. We weren't."

Àngels searched behind him. "So she did come with you?"

"Of course," Gaspard said, and reached across the room taking a woman's hand. "Joana, your mother is asking for you."

Joana came between them. Àngels held her hands and kissed her cheeks slowly, stroking her shoulder as she did so. Joana straightened her hair, which was dyed dark blond, before fanning her face with a brightly colored fan. "Hello, Àngels. I'm so happy that you made it. If you weren't here, Gaspard and I would have stopped by on the way home. Rosa, I'm sorry we're late. We had the side tour, plus it's a longer trip from France."

"It can't be that much longer," Dolors said. "Pujaforta is practically on the border."

"It's a good thing," Àngels said taking her arm. "You can visit more often."

"You should all visit more often," a weak voice fluttered below them. Núria was sitting in her wheelchair with her ears at their waist level. "I like to hear my family around me. All of you together. What a joy and what an occasion. I can't imagine I'll be here for another one."

"Don't be silly, Núria," Dolors said. "You say that every year and you'll probably outlive us all. I know I've practically had my fill of this life. All these pictures show me just how much that has been. Plenty."

"But, *Mare*, things are different now," Rosa said, shaking her head. "That's the whole point of this. Can't you see how far we've come?"

"If you don't mind me saying so," Àfrica said, waving toward the photographs. "I understand what you were saying before, about all the risk and danger, but when I look at them, I just see people. Times may have changed, but surely people are still the same. We laugh, we fight, we reconcile, or we don't. I need you to tell me the stories."

"You're awfully wise for someone so young," Rosa said, and stroked her daughter's cheek before pulling Àngels, Dolors, and Núria closer. "With some help, I will tell you every last tale so that these pictures come to life."

"If only we could bring back everyone who's gone," Dolors said looking at the pictures and back at them. "Because soon it will be our turn."

Núria patted her hand as Baltasar stuck his bald head in. "Our turn for what?" he asked with a particularly blank look on his face. "By the way, who are all those people in the pictures?" He put his frail arms around the women as silence fell over them. Suppressing a smile, he gently shook their shoulders and said, "I might not know how I got here today, but I certainly remember all of my friends, my family. Though I do recall a few things I might rather forget."

"Yes, I can think of a number as well," Dolors said. From their huddle they all looked from each other's faces to those of their friends and family on the wall. Josep's smoky eyes were staring confidently back at them in both color and black and white. One picture was particularly striking, a close-up with Josep's face turned toward the camera, a shadow falling over one side of his head like a *boina* hat. He looked as if he was listening to something in the distance. He would have been in his mid-forties; he still had most of his hair and traces of the years were just beginning to show at the corners of his eyes, eyes that held the gaze of all the admirers and seemed to follow them everywhere.

Rosa put her arm around Dolors. "*Mare*, this one is for you. I know of the perfect place for it in the bakery."

"For me?" Dolors' face brightened. "So do I, *filla*. I have never found the right picture for that spot. Wouldn't Josep love to replace The Caudillo?"

"And he will be able to oversee everything," Rosa said.

"And we will never be able to forget him," Àngels said.

"Why would anyone want to?" Dolors asked.

ACKNOWLEDGMENTS

The story of the Balaguer family is a work of fiction, although it is set during some real historical events. Numerous books and individuals have provided helpful information. For the early years in *Steep Climb to Elsewhere. The Fall*, three books were particularly useful: Solé i Barjau Q. *A les presons de Franco*; Aixalà E, Gabancho P. *La història amagada. El segle XX a través de les àvies*; and Rafaneau-Boj M.C. *Odyssée pour la liberté – les camps de prisonniers Espagnols, 1939-1945*.

The poem that Manel reads to Dolors is a translation and adaptation of *Mester d'amor* by the Catalan poet Joan Salvat-Papasseit.

For their encouragement throughout this eight-year endeavor and for their insight on initial drafts of the manuscript, I would like to thank Sarah Wateridge, Uxua Yanci, and Nancy Chatham. I am also thankful for the keen eyes and support of Lisa McManus in the final editing process. Many others are also to thank and know who they are, but any errors are, of course, my own.

ABOUT THE AUTHOR

L.P. Fairley obtained her journalism degree in Canada, and after extensive traveling, she moved to Barcelona in 1993. She now lives in the hills along the coast and has become a "new Catalan", absorbing the culture, food and language of her adoptive land. Her work is in journalism and communications and the *Steep Climb to Elsewhere* series is her first work of fiction.

Printed in Great Britain
by Amazon

26968241R00219